NIGHT SHINE

ALSO BY TESSA GRATTON

The Blood Journals Duology

Blood Magic

The Blood Keeper

The Gods of New Asgard Series

The Lost Sun

The Strange Maid

The Apple Throne

The Weight of Stars

Strange Grace

NIGHT SHINE

TESSA GRATTON

Margaret K. McElderry Books

NEW YORK   LONDON   TORONTO   SYDNEY   NEW DELHI

MARGARET K. McELDERRY BOOKS

An imprint of Simon & Schuster Children's Publishing Division

1230 Avenue of the Americas, New York, New York 10020

MARGARET K. McELDERRY BOOKS is a trademark of Simon & Schuster, Inc.

For information about special discounts for bulk purchases, please contact Simon & Schuster Special Sales at 1-866-506-1949 or business@simonandschuster.com.

The Simon & Schuster Speakers Bureau can bring authors to your live event. For more information or to book an event, contact the Simon & Schuster Speakers Bureau at 1-866-248-3049 or visit our website at www.simonspeakers.com.

Interior design by Hilary Zarycky

The text for this book was set in Bembo.

Manufactured in the United States of America

First Edition

2 4 6 8 10 9 7 5 3 1

Library of Congress Cataloging-in-Publication Data

Names: Gratton, Tessa, author.

Title: Night shine / Tessa Gratton.

Description: First edition. | New York : Margaret K. McElderry Books, an imprint of Simon & Schuster Children's Publishing Division, 2020. | Audience: Ages 14 up. | Audience: Grades 10-12. | Summary: An orphan girl undertakes a dangerous journey to rescue her friend the prince from a powerful sorceress

Identifiers: LCCN 2020009412 (print) | ISBN 9781534460775 (hardcover) | ISBN 9781534460799 (eBook)

Subjects: LCSH: Wizards—Juvenile fiction. | Magic—Juvenile fiction. | Kidnapping—Juvenile fiction. | Identity (Psychology)—Juvenile fiction. | Quests (Expeditions)—Juvenile fiction. | Secrecy—Juvenile fiction. | Fantasy. | CYAC: Wizards—Fiction. | Magic—Fiction. | Kidnapping—Fiction. | Identity—Fiction. | Secrets—Fiction. | Fantasy. | LCGFT: Fantasy fiction.

Classification: LCC PZ7.G77215 Ni 2020 (print) | DDC 813.6 [Fic]—dc23

LC record available at https://lccn.loc.gov/2020009412

For the genderfluid teens, enbies, and transgender kids who, like me, want to be the dark, wicked love interest more than we want to kiss them.

THE SORCERESS WHO EATS GIRLS

A T THE FORK OF the Selegan River, a full morning's walk from the Fifth Mountain, a girl knelt against the damp bank, carefully holding the end of a fishing thread between her thumb and forefinger.

She was alone, wrapped in a robe embroidered with spring leaves and crocus blossoms. At any moment she could fling it off to leap naked into the water and grasp the tail of a rainbow eel caught by one of her shiny lures. Her fishing thread stretched across this narrow channel of the Selegan, tied at the opposite bank to a strongly rooted maple with leaves as wide as dinner plates.

For a little while, the girl thought she was being watched. But when she looked over her shoulder at the line of moss-covered alders and spearing-tall hemlock trees, nobody was there.

As it flowed, the river rippled, catching sunlight in flashes and white-hot winks like the scales of the river's inhabiting spirit. She reached her free hand to stroke the surface as if stroking a friend, for the Selegan was as friendly a river spirit as they come. Her bargain for fishing in its waters was that in return she always left a coil of delicate hibiscus incense burning against the nearest bed of ferns. The smoke collected in the curling fronds and lingered for the spirit's pleasure.

Water splashed up for her attention, licking her cheek. She brushed it away.

"Hello," said a cool voice behind her.

The girl squeaked and dropped her fishing lure. She scrambled to the edge of the water, one hand diving beneath the surface before fear caught up with her and she let the lure go to turn and face the stranger.

Standing under the dappled shadows at the edge of the rain forest was an elegant lady in a draping silk gown. Strings of dark pearls twisted through her black hair, and thin obsidian rings circled her bare toes. By the soft beauty of her features and fine clothing, and her sudden appearance so far from a road, the girl suspected this was a spirit of some kind.

"Hello," she said, for she ought to be polite whether this was spirit or human, ghost or demon.

The lady stepped carefully against the moss, leaving narrow footprints. Not a ghost, then. Her voluminous skirts were gathered in one arm, but still a gilded hem trailed behind. None of the creeping ferns she brushed against withered and died—not a demon, either. The lady carefully chose a place to kneel and arrange her gown around her on the bending grass. Surely a spirit's skirts would've arranged themselves.

Nearer, the girl could see the lady's eyes were a deep brown, streaked with gray and rust red, like the lava fields around the Fifth Mountain. The lady seemed only a few years older than the girl, and her skin was powdered a perfect moon-white, with a pink like peonies upon her lips.

"How may I help you?" the girl asked, shifting the folds of her robe to hide her dirty knees. She knew she must smell like fish and mud, and her hair had fallen out of its topknot, black wisps itching down her neck. Compared to the lady, she was grubby and inelegant.

"I saw the glitter of water and thought to seek relief in a drink." The lady tilted her head so the dancing shadows slid over her face like a caress. "Then I spied you, and a sparkle of rainbow in your lure. I thought to myself, the Queens of Heaven have brought me here."

Breathless, the girl blinked a few times to clear her heart of its fluttering distraction. "The river will share a drink with you if you ask. And perhaps drop it a pearl."

"A pearl?" The lady laughed sweetly and touched her hands flat together in delight. Her nails were lacquered a shocking black.

Both offended to be laughed at and tingling at the lovely laughter itself, the girl asked, "Would a pearl not be a wonderful gift?"

"I have heard the Selegan River needs nothing so rich, but prefers more intimate bargains. An eel or two in return for pleasant smoke? That is personal, at least. Nothing like a pearl, which anyone might have."

"I have no pearls," the girl whispered, dropping her gaze to her hands, confused how this stranger knew her bargain with the river spirit. Her own nails were even, and mostly clean, but the skin of her knuckles was roughened and dried out from so often being dipped in water.

One lovely white hand touched hers, pleasant and gentle as a

3

blanket warmed by the fire. "What would you give me for one of my pearls?"

The girl turned her hand over so the lady's palm fell against her own, and heat collected there. Beneath her robe, the girl's skin prickled with a yearning she recognized but had never felt at the touch of a woman before. When she glanced up, the lady had leaned nearer.

Those pink lips parted, revealing a small sliver of blackness. Beyond that pretty entrance, mystery and breath mingled.

"Oh," said the girl. "A kiss. A pearl for a kiss."

"That seems a fair bargain," murmured the elegant lady. She lifted a hand to pluck free one of the combs holding her hair behind her left ear. Two round gray pearls shimmering with ocean reflections were set into the edge. "Or two kisses for two pearls?"

The girl giggled and touched her finger to a pearl. It, too, was warm.

Then the lady took her chin in hand and put their mouths together in a sweet, tender kiss.

It ended before the girl even realized it had begun, and as her eyes fluttered open, she was very glad the bargain had been for two.

But the lady's eyes, so near, had changed: no longer rich as lava flow, one had sprung pure green; the other faded death white. Both pupils stretched long and narrow as a snake's and were as red as blood.

Before the girl could cry out, the lady took her second kiss.

ONE

OTHING KILLED THE PRINCE.

TWO

KIRIN DARK-SMILE WAS EIGHT years old when Nothing met him playing in the wide Fire Garden in the third circle of the palace. Smaller, slighter, two years younger than the prince, Nothing stared at him from between willowy fronds of imported elephant grass and a dying orange tree that housed a skinny demon sticking its tongue out for her attention. She paid it no heed, perfectly intent upon the prince. Seven other children played in the garden, different ages and shapes but with mostly the same light-copper to shell-white skin, with black or brown hair and round faces. Nothing stared because Kirin was extremely deliberate in a way few children were: it came from being the heir to the Empire Between Five Mountains and knowing, even at a young age, how to pretend he knew who he was and what was his place. Nothing had no place, being Nothing, and her own deliberation was the result of taking great care never to offend or especially entreat. She recognized their similarity and was so pleased, she stared and stared until Kirin Dark-Smile walked around the star-shaped field of gilded impatiens and put his face in hers. He said, "A heart has many petals," and stared right back until they were friends. They'd seen into each other's spirits, after all.

That was why Nothing knew, eleven years later, she had to kill him.

THREE

S HE PREPARED VERY CAREFULLY, for any mistake might ruin her chance to destroy him and escape unscathed.

It would have to be done before the investiture ritual began, in the presence of many witnesses, in case Kirin vanished into the wind or crumbled into crossroads dirt. Nothing would greatly have preferred taking this risk privately, to kill him alone and never be noticed.

She entered the hall between two black pillars, dressed simply in black and mint green, her face unpowdered and set with determination. In one deep sleeve she carried a long, keen-edged dagger, its hilt beside her wrist. She would draw it when she reached Kirin, slicing free of her sleeve and into his neck before anyone suspected.

Nothing stepped lightly, slippers threadbare and silent. Her blood raced, giving too much color to her cheeks, and she struggled to walk at an even pace, to keep her eyes lowered as usual. She was terrified. Even though she knew she was right.

The Court of the Seven Circles was a perfectly symmetrical

fan-shaped room, from the black-and-red lacquered floor to the vaulting red-and-white ceiling, the number of pillars and their black spiraling tiles. The Empress with the Moon in Her Mouth ruled from the heart of the court, near the tip, enthroned upon a dais with six points. Her headdress lifted in five spires for the five mountains, and a thousand threads of silk and silver fell from the spires, veiling her in shimmering rain.

Courtiers filled the room like chains of pearls and clusters of songbirds, in elaborate robes and gowns of contrasting color. Black and white was the mode of the empress's family, and so most courtiers chose from the other bold colors: red and purple, pink and orange, or all six at once if necessary. Priests mingled in their dreadful pastels and palace witches moved in pairs, shaved heads painted with the sigils of their familiars and cloaks a blur of messy gray scale. Nothing saw Lord All-in-the-Water, commander of the navy, and his brother, the Lord of Narrow, and a scatter of Warriors of the Last Means in dour blood-brown lacquered armor. Only servants with their peacock face paint noticed Nothing, for they were trained to notice her. Notice, and ignore the prince's creature. They might wonder why she'd come, but they would not ask. Nothing belonged in Kirin's vicinity.

Everyone necessary was present but for the First Consort. Once Kirin's father arrived, the investiture ritual could begin. Nothing had to act now.

She spied the prince a few paces from his mother, chatting with a lady of the empress's personal retinue.

Kirin Dark-Smile was willowy and tall, with white skin still slightly tanned from his summer quest but powdered pale

9

to better contrast with his straight black hair, which was long enough to wrap a rope of it twice around his neck. He wore a sleek black-and-white robe that accentuated the same bold contrast in his natural features. Black paint colored his lips and lashes, and cloudy-white crystals were beaded into his hair. One flash of bloodred clung to his ear as always—a fire ruby, warm and glowing, which made his golden-brown eyes light up from within. Exactly as they should.

Nothing slipped between two gentlemen and stood beside Kirin's elbow. "Kirin," she said, breathless with fear.

He glanced at her, pleased. "Hello, Nothing!"

It was his face, his friendly and teasing voice. His shape and tone, his long fingers and bony wrists, the lean of his body upon one hip so it seemed he lounged more than stood. That mole along the hairline at his temple belonged there, and the slight knot in his nose.

But how could anyone mistake the left tilt of his dark smile when her Kirin always tilted to the right?

He'd been gone for three months this summer, returned only yesterday, and everyone in the palace decided, it seemed, that such slight changes were but the result of maturation and adventure on the open roads.

In her heart—in her stomach—Nothing knew this was not her prince.

"Come with me," he said. "Let me tuck your hand against my arm. I have missed you."

For the first time since she was six years old, she did not want to do as he bade.

Nothing drew her long knife and stabbed it into his throat.

It cut too easily through his flesh, up to the hilt, and Nothing let go, stumbling back. Her slippers skidded across the floor.

Kirin Dark-Smile, Heir to the Moon, fell, his eyes already cold.

Sudden silence fell with him.

Nothing bit her lip, staring at the corpse of the prince, and nearly giggled her horror: the prince was killed by Nothing. How would they sing such a thing in the villages tomorrow? She caught her breath, eager to flee, but the court tightened around her. Silk robes whispered frantically, and she heard the clatter of lacquered armor closing in.

Then the Second Consort screamed, and like a burst dumpling, the entire court bellowed in panic.

Nothing backed away slowly. If she made no noise, attracted no more attention, they might ignore her another moment, and then another. Focus on the prince's body. It couldn't have been Nothing, could it, she begged them to say to one another. They'd missed the perpetrator—it was a knife that appeared out of nowhere. Search for demons!

But Lord All-in-the-Water said her name with the weight of an anchor:

"Nothing."

She froze.

Her name whispered again and again, then rang out in cries of shock and wonder. They all said it. Ladies and lords, the musicians who circled the edges of court, servants, dancers, priests, and even from behind her silken rain, the Empress with the Moon in Her Mouth said it: "Nothing!"

"But look," said Kirin's bodyguard, Sky, as he shoved past

a pair of witches whose raven familiars shrieked through the aether—Nothing could hear them, but few others could.

Sky said again, "Look at him."

The empress's doctor and the pastel-robed priest who bent over the body fell back because they saw already what the bodyguard would show the court.

There was no blood at Kirin's neck, and his skin flaked away like the ashes of a banked hearth. It was an imposter.

Nothing sank to her knees in a wash of complete relief.

FOUR

T HE PRINCE'S BODYGUARD WAS named The Day
the Sky Opened, and it was he who lifted Nothing
back to her feet. He caught her gaze with his demon-
kissed eyes and cuffed her gently on the chin. This was his only
way of communicating to her his shame for not seeing the truth
and his appreciation that she had. He'd never been one to speak
volumes, especially to Nothing.

"How did you know?" the priest beside the crumbling
imposter demanded.

Everyone stared at her. Sky shifted out of the way but
remained at her side, looming.

The Empress with the Moon in Her Mouth had stood
from her throne, and though she did not speak, she moved
one hand, demanding an answer. Her veil of silver tinkled
softly.

Nothing knew not to say that to her it was obvious the thing
wearing Kirin's dark smile was not their beloved heir. She knew
not to act angry or upset, but to answer in the least memorable
way. It was how she'd survived all these years.

She said, "Because I am Nothing, the monster did not know to hide so well from me."

It worked. The empress sank gracefully into her throne again, and most courtiers turned away from her to speculate and worry and demand action, comfortable with thinking of Nothing as little as possible.

Lord All-in-the-Water called for a great party of warriors to set out to scour the country for the heir, and the empress touched the red pearl at her right shoulder to approve it. While the Second Consort fled in a cluster of her ladies and the First Consort was sent for, the witches and priests danced around one another to study the remains of the imposter. Nothing listened to their conference, to the *there was no demon residue* and *my raven did not shriek at any aether-marks* and *only a sorcerer with a great spirit—or a great demon—could make so neat a simulacrum.* Then: *Not a great demon—only the Sorceress Who Eats Girls keeps a great demon, and why would she touch our prince? Did the great demon of the palace know? How did Nothing know?*

As they argued, Nothing darted her eyes everywhere for a path through the colorful labyrinth of people. If she could slip behind one of the screens, from there she could climb into the smoke ways in the ceiling and disappear. She needed to be alone before she began to tremble.

But there *were* eyes upon her. Eyes painted fuchsia and eyes painted peacock green and blue, the bright paint of the palace servers who usually avoided Nothing, or otherwise pretended to cough when she darted past. They would see her vanish and spread the tale that Nothing was a coward. She couldn't have that. Coward or hero: either came with too much attention. Kirin—

the real Kirin—had told her once, "If you do not wish to be taken from me, you can't remind people you're with me at all."

She leaned her shoulder into Sky's chest, and the warrior stiffened but did not remove her. It was the closest he'd allowed her to be since she fell down from the rafters upon him and Kirin alone together last year. (It wouldn't have mattered that they were alone but for how they'd been occupying themselves. Sky had suggested they kill her to keep their secret, and Kirin had laughed, promising he trusted Nothing's discretion even more than he trusted Sky's. That perhaps hadn't been the wisest way to put it, but Kirin disliked allowing wisdom to hold him back from what he wanted.)

Too late it occurred to Nothing that taking comfort from Sky's present strength was the wrong move. They surely were the two people most in danger at that moment. She for stabbing the prince, even though it'd been an imposter, and Sky because he'd been with Kirin on his summer journey and was therefore the only person who might've witnessed the change from true heir to imposter. If Nothing correctly read the frequent glances of Lord All-in-the-Water and his brother, Lord of Narrow, they'd be coming for Sky soon, to demand answers. And she'd be in their way, reminding the world again that she existed.

She pulled slowly away from Sky, eager to slip behind him, when someone hidden within the crowd called out wondering if Sky, too, was an imposter.

Nothing shook her head, believing Sky was Sky, though only one of the frightening witches seemed to acknowledge the gesture. As the First Consort swept in ahead of his retinue, Sky stepped forward and plucked up Nothing's fallen knife.

He turned his back to the empress and scoured the room with his hard demon-kissed gaze.

Sky put the knife blade to the copper skin at the back of his wrist and sliced deep enough for bright-purple blood to spill immediately over, splatting vividly against the polished red-and-black floor.

A wave of shocked cries rippled through the court at the offense of bleeding before the empress, but they swiftly transformed into sighs of relief, and the First Consort called majestically, "Bring them to our rooms."

Nothing chose to misinterpret, as was her frequent habit, and pretended "them" could not include "Nothing." As the palace guard herded Sky, avoiding the drops of his blood, she slipped between a lady in harsh pink and two painted servants, into the corridor, and scrambled up a lattice into the ceiling. Between the ceiling plaster and the steep slant of the roof were tiny pocket-rooms all over the palace compound. Fans run by water wheels circulated the air, sucking smoke away from the lacquered walls and decorative ceilings of the palace through many small shafts and peepholes.

Once perched on a crossbeam in the dark palace cavity, Nothing closed her eyes and felt the panic and terror she'd not allowed herself before plunging the dagger into the imposter.

With trembling hands she unwound the volume of her hair until it hung around her shoulders in ragged layers. Only Kirin had touched her hair in four years, since she'd sliced it all off. She grabbed fistfuls of it, pressing it into her eyelids, against her mouth, while her very bones shook. Kirin was gone, but where? He lived. He had to live—she felt it in her heart and stomach just as she'd felt the imposter—but what could be done? What could she do? Her breath stuttered in tiny little gasps. For her entire life she'd truly cared about only one thing, and she'd lost him.

Smoke tinged with spicy perfume swirled around her, soaking into her hair and the robe she wore. To calm down, she tried to think of regular things: that she needed a bath, but would wait until late in the night to slide into the Second Consort's bathhouse and avail herself of the cold water. If she traded a chit of information about one lady's new lover to the imperial steward of the second circle, she might win an hour in the steam room, too. The heat would relax her, and she could interrogate the little flashy fire spirits about what might have done this to Kirin. Once she was composed, she could ask the great demon of the palace, too. It was supposed to protect the scions of the empire but had not noticed a simulacrum within its own walls!

Nothing reminded herself to be fierce. She stood and balanced along the rafter to the corner of the cavity and tucked her slippered feet down into the wall. She lowered herself smoothly and walked sideways along the narrow corridor, making little enough noise anyone passing would say, "It's only a mouse in the wall; nothing to be worried about."

Nothing at all.

Sometimes she played a game with herself guessing which of the palace residents knew the truth of what they said. "Remember that you may be nothing to them but are everything to me," Kirin had whispered to her when she was twelve and he fourteen.

This afternoon there was little chance of her whispered footsteps being detected, for the corridor on the other side of the thin wall rushed with servants. Once she heard the telltale clatter of armor moving opposite her, and she was glad not to be heading in that direction.

Nothing slipped out of the wall behind a narrow banner painted with rainy skies, just outside the gate to the Lily Garden.

A croaking cry erupted beside her, and Nothing squeaked, darting back. Straight into the hands of Aya the witch.

"Hello, little Nothing," the witch said as Nothing twisted free.

Aya's sister-witch, Leaf, boxed Nothing in.

It had been years since she'd had to worry about being ambushed by witches.

They were twice her age, with tan skin and shaved heads, their scalps marked with aether-sigils. Gray robes hung from their bony shoulders and each carried a staff of King-Tree wood hooked at the top into a perch for their raven spirit familiars. The ravens stared at Nothing just as their mistresses did: both birds had one black eye and one eye of glowing aether-blue. A sacrifice from their binding, when they'd agreed to become familiars.

Nothing avoided them harder than she avoided witches.

Aya spoke again. "We traced you through the aether, little Nothing. You cannot hide from us."

"Not unless we allow it," Leaf added.

That was not true: the great demon of the palace sometimes hid Nothing from their aether-eyes. But Nothing pressed her lips tightly closed.

"How did you know?" Leaf asked. Her raven croaked again, a low, bizarre sound like a summons.

"I don't have to tell you anything," Nothing said.

Both witches pressed nearer. "The prince—as you so fero-ciously proved—is not here to command us away from you."

"But you are not released from his previous commands," Nothing said, desperate to remain calm. Her voice was too tight; they had to know she was afraid.

"No," Aya said conversationally. "We cannot compel you, but what harm is there in telling us what you know? In helping us?"

Nothing stared between them. The hairs on her neck tingled, and she shivered down her spine. Witches made her nervous because their sigils and familiars connected them to the aether, the windy layers of magic surrounding the world. They could hear the warnings of spirits and the laughter of demons—and Nothing could too. She'd worked to hide her sensitivities because Kirin had told her she must if she did not wish to be forced into a witch's life. The priests of the palace left her alone, being concerned with philosophy, gods, and the occa-sional ghost, but the witches: they suspected she was more than she seemed.

"I have not a single thing to say," Nothing said. She tilted her chin up, imagining Kirin's easy arrogance. "It is not my fault you did not see what was obvious to me."

Aya narrowed her eyes; Leaf laughed.

"We see you," Leaf said, "even when the rest of the court has forgotten you are anything but a slip of a girl the prince has taken for a pet."

"Nobody will forget you after today," Aya said softly, relishing the words.

Nothing pushed past them. She hated that they were right.

The aether-eyes of the raven familiars remained on her back

as she walked silently away. Nothing felt their cold gazes tickling at the base of her skull.

The Lily Garden bubbled off the inner wall of the fifth circle of the palace. This was a small garden, as palace gardens went, shaped like an eye: it curved in a teardrop against the wall, the round head home to an equally round pond, the tail narrowing gently in a path trellised by hanging sunset lilies. Concentric beds of various types of lily circled the pond, creamy and white and the fairest blushing pink. Climbing star lilies graced the red-washed walls. Though the garden was rarely empty at this time of day, the uproar in the palace had cleared it for her now. Nothing headed straight to the pond, tucking herself against the short lip between two red-glazed pots of cluster lilies. She sighed and closed her eyes, breathing deep of the comforting air this near to the ground. Still water, moss, cloying floral perfume, and the sweet, persistent smell of rot.

It was into this garden that Nothing had been born.

Oh, not literally, but here she'd been discovered as a baby, the week of the spring turn, swaddled in light-green silk embroidered with a flower none could name. The same flower shape was burned into her tiny sand-white chest like a brand.

Sometimes the scar ached, and she put cold water against it; other times it throbbed and the only relief to be found was bringing it nearer to heat.

That was a detail she'd never told anyone but Kirin. He said she was a Queen of Heaven reborn, with a fire spirit for a heart, though such things were impossible. Spirits had no flesh—they were shards of aether. Demons were dead spirits and could only possess and steal energy from their houses.

Though no woman claimed to have borne her, and none could be discovered, Nothing had been raised with the babes of the court until she was old enough to slip into the walls and smoke ways. Then she'd met Kirin, and being his friend was enough to ground her here, despite uncertainty, despite having an impossible name and no other place.

The great demon of the palace, that one time Nothing had asked who she was, shrugged deeply enough to crack plaster off the walls in the empress's bathhouse and said, *I don't mind you are here.*

Which was hardly an answer, but the best it would give.

"Where are you, Kirin?" she whispered.

A splash in the pond answered her. Nothing blinked and did not move. The splash was followed by the swish of water as a small tail waved across its surface and a dragon-lily spirit drifted toward her side of the pond.

Dragon lilies were elegant and occasionally grotesque if not sculpted by a master gardener. From their heart-shaped leaf pads, their stalks rose in a curve like the sinuous shape of a dragon, and their white flower faces spread like whiskers, with one heavy petal dropped open like a gaping dragon's maw to reveal blister-pink stamen. This dragon-lily spirit's head mirrored the shape of its flower, with eyes just as blister-pink as the stamen that flickered with simple thought, and of course it was a flower spirit, not a dragon, but every time a gardener mentioned its name, the spirit latched on to the power in the word for dragon and puffed a slight bit larger, a slight bit brighter, until it had chased the other species of lily spirits from the garden. It did not mind Nothing hiding here, naturally, because Nothing was no competition.

"You smell like tears," it said.

Nothing tilted her face to show the round curve of her cheek, and the spirit licked her tearstains with a tongue softer than petals.

This spirit was one of Nothing's only friends. She had a few because once Kirin had told her it was safe to make them, so long as she never loved any more than she loved him. So she didn't.

The Day the Sky Opened was not Nothing's friend, though they knew each other better than most.

Her nonhuman friends included this dragon-lily spirit, the great demon of the palace who liked the tickle of Nothing's fingers and toes as she climbed and slipped through the smoke ways, and three dawn sprites who hovered in the window of the Second Consort's changing room. Nothing fed them tiny crystals of honey the color of Kirin's eyes on every Peaceday.

Beyond that, Nothing considered only Whisper, the youngest tailor in the palace, to be her friend. A small list, but a dear one.

So small that it might never recover should she lose Kirin forever.

Another tear slid down her cheek as Nothing contemplated a life without him. It made her feel empty. As if she did not know what to be without Kirin telling her. She'd only managed this summer by knowing he would return. Without that certainty, she worried she'd fade away. A bad state of affairs, she knew, but it was simply the way of her heart.

"Other side?" asked the dragon-lily spirit, and Nothing lifted her chin so it could slither across her collar to her other shoulder and lick her left cheek. It curled there, a skinny white-and-green wisp of light, nuzzling her, quite hidden by the fall of her loose hair.

Nothing was a pretty girl, neither beautiful nor remarkably otherwise, with cool sand-white skin too dull in tone to be considered a bold contrast to anything, half-moon brown eyes with short lashes, round cheeks, and a mouth that might've been charming if it did not rest in a flat line most of the time. Her hair was thick, unevenly black-brown, and haphazardly wavy—she could have straightened it with little effort and dyed it for vivid contrast, but she preferred to remain unremarkable. She cut it herself, and the ends were ragged as a result. She did not maintain proper bangs as had been in fashion for girls this past year. Nothing was considered helplessly unfashionable by the consorts, when they considered her at all, but Kirin had always defended her fundamentally blurry nature by telling his father that a perfect prince such as himself could only truly find contrast with an accessory like Nothing. The First Consort had replied that Kirin was appallingly rude sometimes, even for a prince, and Nothing only sank lower in her bow. Kirin had saved her from explaining to his father the truth about why she'd ruined her hair: Someone told her when she was very small that her mother must have touched the black fringe around her baby face, and so Nothing believed the ends of her hair were all of her mother that remained. She'd refused to cut it and worn it in plain looping braids with the ends trailing against her jaw so when she moved, they brushed her in a soft maternal caress. At thirteen, in fury at some fault she could not remember, though likely Kirin did, Nothing braided it all into a thick rope and hacked it off. A weight had lifted from her. With the ends, she'd made two bracelets: one for herself and one for Kirin Dark-Smile. The imposter had not been wearing it.

She stretched her hand farther out of the torn sleeve of her robe to study the old thing. Its weave had loosened over time, some hairs snapping so they stuck out of the bracelet messily. "Do you think you could become my familiar and lend me power to find him?" she murmured to the dragon-lily spirit.

But the dragon-lily spirit hissed and huddled against her neck. It pinched her earlobe for balance as she turned toward the tail of the garden, having heard the sound of careful, deliberate footsteps.

"Nothing?"

It was Sky.

Nothing hugged her knees to her chest and waited.

"I know this is your place of refuge, Nothing, but I must speak with you."

"Speak, then," she said, still hiding.

Sky sat upon the rim of the lily pond, putting the potted cluster lilies between them. He gripped the stone in his strong hands, flexing muscles up his bare arms. He'd been dressed in formal black today, for the investiture ritual, and new black lacquered armor. But the armor was gone, and only the black finery remained, edged in vivid blue silk the same color that streaked his hair, for Sky was one of the demon-kissed, born to those families cursed generations ago by the Queens of Heaven. All such children had the demon-blue in their hair or eyes or underlying their skin tone and all received some additional gift: perfect pitch or night sight or an inability to lie. Sky's gift was physical strength. He was rather huge. Once Kirin dared him to toss Nothing over a palace wall with only his forefinger. Sky had declined, as he'd not needed to prove anything.

"They won't find him," the prince's bodyguard rumbled. More than hear it, Nothing seemed to feel it reverberate through the stone rim of the pond and into her spine, which pressed there. "They sent the Warriors of the Last Means in only four directions."

Surprised, Nothing leaned forward, peering around the cluster lilies. The spirit grasped her hair. "Four is a balanced number," she said. "And only a Mountain Sorcerer could have made such a convincing imposter. Of course they sent to the Four Living Mountains."

Sky closed his eyes. "But the sorcerers of the Four Mountains do not have him, and the warriors will not hunt for him where he is to be found. Kirin was taken by the Fifth Mountain and the Sorceress Who Eats Girls. You must go with me to steal him back."

FIVE

NOTHING THREW HERSELF TO her feet, and the dragon-lily spirit hissed its fear as it clung to her hair. She said, "You are lying! The sorceress would not take Kirin! She only takes girls."

Twenty-three girls in the past seventeen years.

Sky stared at her, eyes dark, haunted, and said, "You must not speak of this to anyone."

"Speak of what?"

Nothing's heart pounded as she clenched her fists and shoved them onto her hips, trying to appear stronger than she felt. Suspicion arrived in a burst of images and memories, tiny shards of Kirin's life thrusting themselves suddenly into clarity: side glances and swallowed words, almost-confessions and very soft sorrow when he glanced at certain things.

The demon-kissed bodyguard forged ahead. "Kirin trusted you over all others."

"Even you," she said, lashing out in her fear.

His eyes slid to her shoulder and the spirit dangling there.

"Will this flower spirit tell? If so, I must strangle it into a demon and plant it in salted earth."

Nothing bit her lip and raised a hand to cradle the flailing claws of the dragon-lily spirit. "Tell what, Sky? Tell what?"

The large young man knelt before her and tilted his face up in a pleading, penitent angle. "When I traveled the long roads this summer with Kirin Dark-Smile, I traveled with a wife."

"Oh no," she whispered.

Sky held her gaze. "Kirin said, 'Sky, go with me for this three-month journey as if you go with an adventuring daughter, not a son. I will put on gowns and braid my hair with flowers. I will walk and speak as a woman might, and you will be like my husband, not my dearest friend. This is my only chance to live as I wish to live, Sky, with you. Do not make me beg. Do not deny me.' And so what was I to do, Nothing, but agree? What would you have done?"

His copper cheeks flushed with his deep-purple blood. "What would you have done, Nothing?" he demanded again, low and rough.

Nothing had not guessed he had such depth of emotion in that hard body of his. Though she was afraid, she stepped close to him and put a hand on his shoulder. "I always give Kirin everything he asks, even if I shouldn't."

"Will you give me what I ask and go with me to the Fifth Mountain?"

The Fifth Mountain, far to the north of the empire, was a dead mountain: its heart had erupted more than a century ago, its spirit transformed into a great demon. At the time, the

27

Emperor with the Moon in His Mouth had bargained with the demon, sending it tributes in return for peace. But since the Sorceress Who Eats Girls had come, there had been no peace: she took girls from across the empire and turned emissaries away at her gates. The sorcerers of the Four Living Mountains would not attack a great demon so long as it held the border, and the great demon of the palace refused to rally itself.

Nothing said, "Why do you think I can help, Sky?"

"They say nothing can penetrate the Fifth Mountain."

She pursed her lips in a frown. A trick of words did not a rescue make.

Sky added, "You knew what it was. You knew it was not Kirin and . . ." He ducked his head in shame. "I was not brave enough to admit the truth and act. You are fearless."

The dragon-lily spirit snorted and leaned down, one claw tugging on her hair.

"You are friendly with the great demon of the palace and so maybe can be friendly with the great demon of the Fifth Mountain. And while the sorceress will not be interested in me, not enough to open her doors, you are a girl with a heart she can eat."

Nothing imagined an elegant lady cracking open her chest to lick the bloody mass of her heart, and she held her tongue.

Sky said, "I will do whatever I must to save the Heir to the Moon, Nothing. Will you?"

"I want to go too," the dragon-lily spirit said, and its blister-pink eyes sparked with determination.

"You must remain with your house," she said absently. She felt light-headed and wondered if this decision had been made the moment she stabbed her knife into the imposter's neck.

"Meet me at the gates of the seventh circle in two hours," Sky said. "I will have some food and supplies. You need only bring sturdy shoes and layered robes. Do you have one in wool, or leather? As we go higher, it will grow colder and damp."

Nothing said, "I will manage."

The demon-kissed bodyguard stood stiffly and departed.

SIX

NOTHING SLIPPED INTO THE elaborate corridors of the Second Consort's tailoring suite to find Whisper. The young woman's stitches were so tiny it was said she did not sew seams but murmured pretty songs to convince the silks and threads to join together of their own accord. Her nature of tender tolerance had made her ideal for befriending Nothing, and she'd done it with glances and the occasional touch that never was followed by a demand or a need. Whisper had simply made it known to Nothing that she was available, and interested. To most, Nothing was an oddity or no better than an exotic pet, or a trick to be suspicious of. It was a relief to be welcomed into Whisper's space like a ray of quiet sunshine.

Many people might notice when Nothing vanished, but only Whisper would miss her.

At first Nothing went between the walls and through smoke ways, but eventually she had to step into the open corridor alongside the bright embroidery hall, her slippers silent on the wooden floor, her robe a hiss against the painted screen door. Latticed windows composed the entirety of the southern wall, open to the air and sun now, though they could be closed with thin fibrous screens or heavy wooden shutters. Whisper sat at the end of a row of six tailors, each of them working on a different elaborate flower along the same hemline. This wide train would be for the empress herself, it seemed, a silk so black it swallowed light, with white and fire-pink rhododendron along the hem and black starbursts nearly invisible. The spread was so beautiful Nothing paused to stare, wondering what such glory would feel like draped over her shoulders, sweeping behind her in a way none could ignore or miss.

A tailor gasped, his mouth open and staring straight back at Nothing. Vivid green colored his lips and streaked up in swirls like clouds to cup his dark-brown eyes. "Nothing!"

Another tailor squeaked and put her finger in her mouth to lick away blood.

A third said, "We might rename you, for the action you have taken today."

Nothing exaggerated a grimace, as if her face were a mask.

"Little Hero," suggested the first, and "Prince Killer," another, then "Brave but Extremely Strange and Quiet."

How terrible it was to be noticed.

Whisper kept quiet, but she set down her embroidery and put a bare arm around Nothing. Most tailors wore sleeveless robes wrapped tight to their bodies to keep low any chance of entanglement. She led Nothing to a low table in the resting corner set with cool tea and sweet cheese soft enough to eat with a spoon. "Are you well?" Whisper asked, kneeling upon a flat pillow the crystal color of a noontime sky. It clashed perfectly with Whisper's rust-red robe.

31

Nothing knelt. "Yes," she said quietly, "but I am leaving the palace, and you may not see me for some time."

Whisper handed Nothing a small cup of tea and Nothing sipped it, though she did not much like this mix unless it was steaming hot. She let Whisper sprinkle fennel seed onto a spoonful of cheese and feed it to her, then herself.

"Why?" Whisper asked, folding her hands in her lap.

Nothing resisted a glance over her shoulder to see that the tailors continued their work and did not strain to hear every word. "I am going to find Kirin."

"Alone?"

"With The Day the Sky Opened." She held her face blank, not wanting to accidentally express something she was unsure of: she did not know how to feel, except anxious, but she knew she wanted to say goodbye without creating a burden of worry for her friend.

"I am sure he will be a fine companion," Whisper said softly.

For a few sips of tea, they remained silent.

Whisper said, "Do you know where he is?"

"Sky believes he does." Nothing said no more, because she could not hint at the truth. The truth would ruin Kirin. It was not that Sky loved the prince or that the prince loved him in return; such was to be expected. But they were not allowed to touch before Kirin's investiture. As the Heir to the Moon he was required to remain pure—he could not have anything inside him before the Moon was inside him. Not finger nor tongue nor unblessed spoon. Kirin and Sky had certainly broken that purity—Nothing had seen so with her own eyes—and if any priests suspected the truth of their relationship, the entire line of inheritance would be destroyed.

Worse, by taking up the identity of a woman, Kirin had slipped into an unhallowed space: just as there was night and day, left and right, up and down, there was man and woman, and anything in between was the realm of spirits, demons, and the Queens of Heaven. That was what made dawn and dusk the holiest of times, made blending colors and shape-shifting the space of sorcerers, not humans. Decent people had to be one or the other. Anything else was too frightening.

Kirin had risked everything to spend his summer with Sky, to live as he wished. And he hadn't told Nothing his intentions.

She'd have argued ferociously against endangering himself. Kirin always told her to avoid attention if she wished to be safe, but he'd not taken even a sliver of his own advice. Now the Sorceress Who Eats Girls had him. Nothing felt he was alive, but for how long? And how could they keep this a secret? Everyone would want to know why he'd been taken by the sorceress.

But Whisper asked no more. It was part of why they were friends. Nothing said, "I will not return without our prince. You may say that if you are asked."

"I will." Whisper took the tea from Nothing and clasped her hand. "You ought to adopt a facade to venture out into the world. At least some face paint to be The Day the Sky Opened's servant."

Nothing leaned in and kissed Whisper. Then she quickly rose and left, sparing no glance for the other tailors. Her chest felt tight as she walked down the corridor and out of the second circle of the palace. She made her way back to the fifth circle, clambered up into a stale smoke way, then down into the old abandoned bath she used as her secret home. The tiles burst red and white, blood purple and orange, in elaborate star patterns. The plumbing had failed several years ago, and the great demon kept it broken for her, but the heating mechanisms worked, warming her when she slept tucked among scavenged old pillows and threadbare blankets. She'd strung threads between thin pillars from which to hang curtains in a variety of sheer colors, giving the bathhouse a rainbow blur of light at different times of the day.

Inside a wicker basket full of broken pottery, tiles, and toys, Nothing kept the pale-green silk cloth embroidered with the many-petaled flower she'd been swaddled in as a baby, and she withdrew it to wrap around her throat like a scarf. She stuffed her feet, still slippered, into walking boots and hooked them closed around her ankles, then put her hands on her hips, wondering what to wear. Layers, Sky had said. She had nothing weatherproof at all.

Twisting her lips in dissatisfaction, Nothing removed her robe and undergarments, then tied on a new loincloth and baggy trousers that laced just over her boots. She put on a long shirt and purple tunic, then a threadbare red wool jacket. Around it all she tied a wide sash of eye-piercing green. She clubbed her hair high at the back of her head, wrapping that, too, with scraps of silk ribbons, until she looked more like an actor than like Nothing. The vivid colors very likely washed out her face into a wan mask, but Nothing did not even own paint. She'd have to rely on whatever Sky carried.

Before she departed, Nothing pressed herself against the wall, hands flat until her palms tingled against the red-wash, her cheek brushing it too, so that when she closed her eyes and whispered, "I am leaving, great demon," it would hear her. Having once been spirits, living pieces of aether, demons craved life and magic and possessed to survive, draining powerful life from people, animals, and places until they were dead too. There was debate among the priests as to what made a demon great— either it was as simple as a great spirit dying, becoming a great demon quickly enough to maintain connections to the aether, or a demon managed to find a permanent home, somehow rooting itself deeply enough to reconnect with aether, so that it could again be its own source of power.

This great demon of the palace was one of only two known in the world. The other lived in the Fifth Mountain. It *was* the Fifth Mountain, some said.

Nothing had never cared much for the details of why or how the great demon of the palace existed. She liked the comforting rumble of its presence as it took little strands of life and power from everything, so subtly nobody much noticed except for her. Besides, the great demon gave trickles of power back, too, as if the empress and her court were all its masters.

"Did you hear me?" she whispered again. "I must leave."

A sigh trembled through the foundations, gentle enough only someone similarly pressed would notice.

why? have I not warmed you little one?

"Oh very much, great demon. I need to find another friend. The prince is missing—Kirin Dark-Smile."

My prince he has not returned from his investiture summer when he returns he will be Mine forever.

Nothing frowned. She did not understand the connection

35

between the investiture ritual and the great demon. "We thought Kirin *had* returned, great demon. Did you not hear the celebrations these two days? We gathered for the investiture, but I—it was not him. It was an imposter."

The wall beneath her palms shivered with a growl so deep it could not be heard.

"I am going to find our Kirin," Nothing said. "I swear."

bring him to Me.

The command rumbled loudly, and Nothing closed her eyes. Everyone must have heard it.

She brushed her hands against the plaster. "Shh, shh. I promise, great demon," she murmured.

It purred, liking her touch, as always. Nothing kept up her soothing and felt the tingle of other prayers as priests knelt at shrines throughout the palace, making promises too, to calm it down.

your leaving will change My walls, the demon grumbled eventually.

"You will miss me," she said, pleased.

who will tickle Me in the afternoons with her little feet? who will scratch at the itchy crack in the fourth circle roof?

Nothing kissed the rough red-wash. "When I return, for my reward I will ask the prince to have the itch repaired."

Its answer was a satisfied sigh.

With that, Nothing left the only home she'd ever known. She crawled and snuck through the smoke ways, still—especially dressed in these bright colors—concerned about being stopped. All the way to the lowest seventh circle she went before emerging to walk across a sand garden striped in red and black, with pink granite and sparkling white marble boulders disrupting the pattern. Her boots sank into the sand unexpectedly, and Nothing paused, startled. How odd it would be to leave marks wherever she passed.

Nothing had never been outside the seven circles of the palace. She rarely thought beyond its borders, as if she were a spirit or demon herself and this palace her house to inhabit. Demons never leave their house.

She had to remind herself that she was a human, and humans are their own house—if a human died badly they did not become a demon, but a ghost, lost and homeless and angry, and only a priest could bind it with a naming amulet and send it to the Queens of Heaven.

Nothing was a human. She carried her house with her.

Shivering, though it was the end of summer and quite warm, Nothing dashed across the remaining garden and into the shadows of the gatehouse where Sky waited.

Gardeners lifted their heads as she passed, and she ducked between warriors serving as gatehouse guards, ignoring their gossip and questions. Sky stood with a bag over his wide shoulder and another dangling from a strong hand. He wore his sword sheathed at his hip. He'd clubbed his hair back too, and put a streak of blue paint over his eyes. His clothing was black and sapphire blue. It did not contrast, but rather matched. *I do not care if I am beautiful*, it said.

"Nothing," he murmured.

"I don't know how to paint myself for the outside world," she said.

Sky smeared his thumb across the wide band of blue paint on

his cheek. He pressed it to her forehead and drew an arc there. It was like claiming her, for she was not demon-kissed. "That will do," he said.

"I'm too young to be a wife," she muttered.

For once the bodyguard smiled. "It will be a good excuse for traveling quickly and without fanfare, if we've gone to elope."

"You would make Kirin your First Consort and me your Second?" she snapped. He was the only person in the world who made her sharp.

"Better than you his First."

With that Sky started off, moving as if he belonged, as if he'd been commanded to go. Nothing scurried to catch up, stepping purposefully upon the edges of his shadow cast by the setting sun.

SEVEN

DEEP IN THE HEART of the Fifth Mountain, a sorceress walked along a black corridor. Her silk slippers shredded against the rough pumice floor, and she dragged her fingernails along the walls, sharpening them into claws. Above her head tiny blue lights bobbed, as if pieces of the afternoon sky had been torn free and tethered to her crown of delicate bat-wing bones.

She hummed to herself as she went, a hollow melody intended to fill the space before her, which had been empty since the mountain itself had stopped breathing. The sorceress was beautiful, and monstrous, for she was both woman and spirit, and her flesh shaped into smooth pale-copper limbs draped with layers of black and white and heart-pink silk. Her hair looped in a layered cascade, pinned with crystal forks and cloisonné combs that dripped with seed pearls and amethyst unicorn tears. She smiled with ruby-red lips, and her cheeks spread prettily, but her teeth were as sharp and jagged as a shark's, her eyes evergreen and death white, bisected each by a long red snake pupil. Perhaps her fingers were too long, which made the claws tipping them seem just right; perhaps her silken slippers hid the cloven hooves of a unicorn or the gripping talons of an eagle balled into a fist the better to walk upon. Perhaps her feet were perfect, delicate woman's feet. Her pace was smooth as a snake, and her voice whispered like a lovely moon sprite's cry as she sang a gentle dirge.

Her shadow drifted behind her reluctantly, bound in the shape of flared wings. The darkness drew in her wake like caressing hands, pulling sound with her, until every echo was swallowed up and stitched with magic into the trailing hems of her robes.

The sorceress turned a curve in the deep corridor, into a low-hung cavern that dripped with glittering diamond and ruby veins and thick black obsidian eyes that once had glowed with the presence of the Fifth Mountain's great demon.

Far in the corner the sorceress had bade rocks heat and flow into the shape of teeth from both the floor and the ceiling, until they joined into thin bars. It had become the grinning, sharp mouth of a prison cell. Within: an oil lamp, dimly lit; a gilt-edged ceramic bowl too pretty for the use to which it had been put; a nest of woolen quilts; a maiden in a tattered gown.

"O Prince Who Is Also a Maiden," said the sorceress, "good afternoon."

Kirin raised his face, and a beautiful face it was, despite soot-streaked tears and chewed away lipstick, despite the tangle of impossibly black hair framing his ashy-white cheeks, spilling in knots still half-braided with silver threads and sky-blue threads, despite the necklace of white and green pearls looped again and again around his long neck, despite the torn peacock-green

40

gown and black-gold-red embroidered flowers. Despite the blood at his fingers from scraping against the bars of his cage.

He did not reply, only studied her with eyes the chipped-brown color of ancient amber.

The sorceress knelt, skirts and robes pooling perfectly about her, and the winged shadows wrapped up the dim lamplight until only her shards of sky-blue crown tossed away deep darkness. "Are you hungry? Would you eat today?"

Still the prince said nothing.

"There is water," she said, and a narrow pitcher appeared beside his bare foot. "Flavored with mint and rose petals, just how you like it."

The prince reached and dipped a single finger over the rim, touching a ripple to the surface of the water.

"Prince, will they discover my secret? Will they notice the thing I sent back to them? Maiden, will they come for you?"

Kirin smiled then—a soft, dark smile. "Nothing will come for me," he said.

EIGHT

For the first several days, Nothing and The Day the Sky Opened traveled easily along the Way of King-Trees. The Way was broad and filled with travelers and merchants heading north into the rain forest. Because of the crowd, Nothing and Sky were ignored entirely. At first the road was paved with bricks and long flagstones, the edges marked by massive pillars of redwood gilded at the top to glow like the sun, with tiny shrines cut into their bases. These pillars were meant to invite the spirits of the King-Trees lining the road farther north to venture south sometimes, protecting the entire Way. Every traveler paused occasionally at one of the small shrines to drip wine or leave the last of their breakfast bun, a flower, or a tiny seed.

To the west of the Way, the land dipped into the floodplains surrounding this royal branch of the Selegan River. Many of the crops had been harvested already, except for redpop and the occasional lines of brilliant green where new beans sprouted for a second harvest. To the east spread wide swaths of grazing fields dotted with cattle and goats. Small towns and farming communities appeared every hour or so as they walked; at the turnoffs and crossroads children sold fresh well water and mint tea, hard cheeses and bread. Spirit shrines climbed over one another in such places, like tiny spirit villages.

Nothing stared at everything like a suspicious puppy, eager to investigate, awed, yet shy of direct contact with strangers. They sometimes stepped off the road to allow a cart to pass that was pulled by flat-horned buffalo or drifted in the wake of a large crowd of pilgrims with their fanned hats. When royal messengers charged by on galloping horses or a company of warriors passed, she and Sky casually hid either among a crowd or off the road. Nothing's eyes remained wide as she tromped at Sky's side. If not for the dire circumstances, she might've enjoyed the newness and adventure.

They slept at first in crossroads shelters, free to all on foot, so long as each person thanked the fire spirits or the spirits of the foundation. Such shelters were tended to and kept up by servants of the Empress with the Moon in Her Mouth as a gift to her people.

Neither Nothing nor Sky was especially talkative, and so time passed in silence but for Sky's occasional instruction or quiet explanation of a crossroads custom. Nothing's mouth turned dry as linen and she had to remember to take drinks of water. The sun burned crisply in the blue skies every morning, and most afternoons rain clouds drifted in to bless them with bright mist and diamond drops before parting in time for a rainbow sunset. Nothing's wool jacket came in handy for pulling over her head like a hood. She was glad of the sturdy boots that survived all manner of mud. Even with the decent roads and Sky's knowledge, it was hard walking all day every day. Nothing slept deeply, like a snuffed candle, and woke up sore.

Though they were disinclined to talk on the road, the constant presence of others added to the need for silence. It wouldn't be right to speak of Kirin or the Sorceress Who Eats Girls where any traveler or trader could overhear. Sometimes Sky took Nothing's hand without warning or set his arm around her shoulders as they walked, and if she protested, he directed her attention to a fellow traveler darting glances at them. She sighed and leaned into him, or offered a sugary smile as if they were sweethearts. Nothing never noticed such attention before Sky did. She was bad at reading people.

One afternoon at a crossroads shrine Nothing crouched to crumble the last of her cheese into the offering bowl, and a spirit slipped out of the jolly old woman statue tucked in the dark corner. "Hello," it said.

Nothing blinked, surprised at the forward manner. Spirits seemed shy, but it was just that most people couldn't hear or see them. The spirits in the palace had been disinclined to talk until Nothing had convinced them she was friendly. Except for the dawn sprites always clamoring for light and attention. Demons were more talkative. The better to persuade you out of your life, she supposed. "Hello," Nothing whispered back.

The spirit was a scrap of mist shaped exactly like the jolly statue, with cherry-pink cheeks and hair curled into diaphanous clouds. "Do you have something sweet?" it asked.

"You don't like cheese?"

"Everyone leaves cheese."

Smiling at the dry tone, Nothing leaned down further. "How about a kiss?"

The spirit eyed her suspiciously. "Keep your teeth away from me."

Nothing kissed her finger and held it out for the spirit, who opened its mouth in delight and put Nothing's finger into its mouth up to the first knuckle. The swallowing kiss tickled her, and Nothing wiggled.

"Nothing," Sky said like a grunt. He grabbed the collar of her outer robe and hauled her up. "Don't converse with spirits. That will mark you as different faster than a chain of royal moon pearls."

She scowled and said, "Blessings for your house," to the spirit as it melted off her finger and pooled back into the lap of its statue.

Then she stormed off, and Sky had to take a few longer strides to catch up. "Tell me what else I should not do, The Day the Sky Opened," she demanded hotly. "And never drag me around like a child."

Sky slid her an unperturbed look. "Act like a person, not a goblin."

But he glanced over his shoulder, and Nothing realized he could see the spirit as easily as she did.

By the sixth day the first of the living King-Trees appeared. Massive trees as wide around as a house, their rough red trunks pointed straight to Heaven, and when a wind blew, small green needles scattered from hundreds of feet up. This was the start of the rain forest, and the Selegan River narrowed, curving west away from the road until it vanished into the misty green forest.

There were fewer villages in the rain forest, and those there were no longer pressed up to the road but were set a ways off. Travelers branched out at crossroads until Sky and Nothing were alone more hours than they were not. Even at midday the sun barely penetrated the thick canopy, making daylight gentle and shade green. Wisps of light and seeds and aether fragments floated in the air, birds chirped and yelled across the huge empty spaces here where the King-Trees dominated, and sometimes the ferns shivered with the passing of small creatures.

Nothing said, "It's like walking inside an emerald."

And Sky studied her for a long moment before he nodded in solemn agreement.

They'd been traveling for eight days when it happened that they reached no way station nor traveler's lodging at sunset and Sky had to make a camp for them. Locating a decent clearing was easy, as folk camped frequently. There were even stumps and logs in rings around fire pits built of stone and permanent stakes for tying up an oilcloth shelter against the damp. Sky had such a cloth rolled tightly at the bottom of his bag, and he showed Nothing how to secure it with hemp rope. They gathered armfuls of soft needles from the smaller fir trees that nestled among the King-Trees and made nests of them. Sky quietly taught Nothing to dig for onions and edible bulbs they could roast in a fire, and how and where to cover her waste. He soaked a handful of fallen nuts in a shallow bowl of water gathered from the stream and said in the morning they'd have fresh salmon for breakfast.

Nothing surprised him by making a fire herself with a handful of dry needles and sticks. She knelt and coaxed the tricky fire spirits out of the earth to dance.

It was their first night alone.

A long twilight gave over into night, and beyond the ring of their fire the rain forest was complete darkness. The moon was too thin to penetrate the canopy. Besides the crackle of flames, Nothing listened to the light tapping of water as it trickled and dripped from high branches and the low call of an owl.

She sat very near to Sky, their shoulders brushing in an effort to share warmth. Though it was the end of summer and the days were warm, the damp crept into their clothes and hair, chilling skin and sinking all the way into their bones. Part of Nothing liked it, for she imagined moss growing on her bones, her teeth shining like pearls, and her hair tangled as those ragged vines. It made her feel like she belonged in the rain forest. Like she could be at home here.

In the dark, Sky's brown eyes gleamed bluish like a demon's. It was a very comforting light; he was as dangerous as anything in the rain forest, Nothing thought. Even more than grizzled bears or a spirit of a King-Tree. Now, if any King-Tree had died and become a demon itself, perhaps Sky would be no match for it. But Nothing supposed she could make friends with such a demon.

"Did you come exactly this way with Kirin?" she asked. It was the first full sentence she'd spoken in two days.

"No."

Nothing expected he'd say no more, because Sky stared at the fire's vivid blue core hard enough to burn his eyes. But then he said, "We came this direction, though not directly. Kirin liked to wander at crossroads or venture into villages to speak with people. We waited until we were at least three days from the palace, but then he wanted to be anonymous and we ate at wayfarer inns and bargained rooms for labor at farms."

"Kirin knows how to be a farmer?" Nothing asked incredulously.

"He was my wife, and so sent me to shoulder bales of wheat and muck stables while he learned to tuck cherry dumplings and steam a perfect tea in the kitchen. Or"—Sky's eyes crinkled in amusement—"once or twice I found him with his gown tucked between his legs, chasing babies through the garden."

It was difficult to imagine, but Nothing liked it.

"I think he was happy," Sky said quietly. "As happy as he's capable of being."

"You don't think he can be happy?"

"He thinks too much."

Nothing huffed. "What name did you call him?"

Sky snorted. "He told me to call him sweetheart, because he didn't want to hear anything from my mouth but his real name."

"That's . . . romantic."

"The first time we stayed with a farming family, I introduced him as Too Pretty for Her Own Good."

"Was he angry?" Nothing shook her head. She never so directly disobeyed Kirin.

"He liked it," Sky muttered.

"Was it difficult to refer to him as . . . her? As your wife?"

"No. That's what he was." Something in Sky's posture shifted, closing, and Nothing fell silent.

In the morning they did have fresh salmon, caught in the stream. They ate it plain on the bone, and it was so soft and flaking Nothing forgot to be cranky, and skipped ahead to search for a good spot to make a tiny shrine to the stream's spirit. She spread the delicate bones into wings against a flat boulder, giving the fish flight, and murmured a prayer to the forest and earth.

They were alone all day again, and though Nothing had thought of the most important subject they should cover, she could not bring herself to speak while the sun was up and the rain forest glittered and glowed happy green. She whistled to the birds and tickled the curling fern fronds; she patted her palm to the soft red bark of the King-Trees and waved at the heavy pink flowers dripping from vines on spreading maple and skinny hemlock trees.

She knew better than to be happy, because Kirin was in danger, and they were only passing through. But it was hard. Maybe she felt free out here because Kirin had been free too.

In the evening, once she'd coaxed two fire spirits into snapping their tails together for a spark and once Sky had baked tubers, she said, "What do you know of the Sorceress Who Eats Girls?"

"Probably the same as you."

"Tell me anyway, for you've traveled and have different friends. I know only whispers, hints, and demon secrets."

Sky snorted. "Demons might know better than anyone what the sorceress is."

Nothing drew her knees to her chest and hugged them.

After a moment Sky said, "A sorcerer is made when a witch or a priest somehow reaches so far into the aether they are able to forge a connection to it that they then bring back into the living world with them. It is nearly impossible, and every sorcerer manages it differently. They exist between things, able to call on powers of life and death that only spirits and demons and the Queens of Heaven can touch. In order not to be consumed by their power, they must find a house, like a demon, and anchor themselves there, or bond with a great spirit. The Four Living Mountains each have a sorcerer: they are named Skybreaker, Still Wind, A Dance of Stars, and The Scale. Each is powerful, each as benevolent as he is isolated, unless one takes something of his or denies him a thing he—or one of his familiars—desires.

"A hundred and fifty years ago, the Fifth Mountain erupted, killing its spirit—or the other way around. The newborn great demon spat fire and bled lava for weeks, until the Emperor with the Moon in His Mouth sent an emissary to bargain. He offered a tribute to the demon, on recommendation of the great demon of his palace. This bought the emperor and his descendants peace with the Fifth Mountain. Then, eighty years ago, a massive storm broke around the Fifth Mountain, roiling the veins of lava deep within, arguing so loudly and long that our great demon leagues and leagues away turned over in discomfort, and a single wall cracked on each of the palace's seven circles. When the storm dissipated, the Fifth Mountain housed a sorcerer."

Sky paused, and Nothing's eyes, which had sunk closed, flashed open. His low voice had lulled her nearly into leaning her head upon his shoulder. She swallowed and poked at the fire, then turned her face to press her cheek against a knee and stare at Sky.

He was scowling at the fire. His dark eyebrows drew low over his eyes, his mouth turned down, and his handsome jaw clenched in a perfect square. His breath did not shift his shoulders, but his back and stomach instead, for he'd been trained to control his body's rhythms and breathe from his core.

Then suddenly Sky continued. "A sorcerer capable of bonding with—mastering—a great demon must be vastly powerful and vastly dangerous. The empress, Kirin's great-grandmother, sent emissaries, but they were turned away again and again. The new sorcerer did not care for any bargain, it seemed. Everyone speculated, wondered, and moved on, waiting for some word or act to point us in a direction of action. Nothing. Nothing happened."

Nothing smiled to herself. She hadn't been born yet, at the time.

"More recently, just after Kirin was born, the sorcerers of the Four Living Mountains reported that great magic rumbled in the Fifth Mountain, and storms assailed the whole northwest of the empire, but the sorcerers were turned away when they inquired. Then a girl disappeared from a village at the foot of the Fifth Mountain. Another, several months later, who'd been fishing eels in the Selegan. Girls disappeared again and again, at first all from that area, soon from across the empire. But the Fifth Mountain allowed no access to its sorcerer or its secrets. Then, eleven years ago, a unicorn walked into the palace and directly up through the circles until it stood in the court and spoke to the Empress with the Moon in Her Mouth. I was not there, nor were you, but Kirin was. He remembers the trilling voice and the smell of the sea, the pearlescent, twisted horn curving like a young moon off its forehead and long nose. He remembers the pretty clicks of its delicate cloven hooves and the threads of starlight woven into its mane and the casual flick of its tail."

"What did the unicorn say?" Nothing asked, knowing when to urge on a story, like any who'd grown up surrounded by them.

Sky nodded slightly at her knowing question. "It said, 'The Sorceress of the Fifth Mountain requires the most beautiful maiden in the empire. Do you know where she might find such a girl?' Lord All-in-the-Water said, 'We will not feed her our children; it's monstrous.' The unicorn said, 'That is no concern of mine, only the message I bring. She will not stop until she finds the one she needs.' And in a rare display of public opinion, the empress herself parted her veil of silver to ask the unicorn, 'Why does she hunt beautiful girls?' and the unicorn said, 'I understand they taste good.'

"The uproar at that answer caused chaos enough the unicorn was able to vanish. The story spread, and girls learned to fear the Sorceress Who Eats Girls."

Nothing waited for Sky to deliver the final piece of the story, about the empress sending warriors to the mountain, asking the Living Mountains to attack, but he did not. As the silence stretched, invaded slowly by the snapping fire spirits and the soft hum of the wind through the midnight canopy, she lifted her head to peer at him.

The demon-blue gleam of his eyes glistened, and Nothing realized Sky gritted his teeth against tears. Furious tears. His lips parted, and she could see his bared teeth as he hissed a sigh.

"You're afraid she's eaten him," Nothing cried, leaping to her feet.

Sky covered his face, scouring it roughly with his hands. Nothing hit his shoulder, which was immobile as a boulder.

He caught her wrist. "You have never seen a more beautiful maiden than Kirin Dark-Smile."

Nothing did not tug free, or try to. She stared down at him. His up-tilted face was a mask of forced optimism. His grip was warm around her wrist, and he applied just enough pressure to pull her down beside him again.

"He's not dead."

"No," Sky said.

"I would know, just as I knew the imposter! She didn't eat Kirin because he's not a girl."

Sky pressed his mouth into a line of disagreement.

"Sky! What even makes a girl?"

"She took him, so she decided whatever the answer is, Kirin qualifies. And I—I agree with her. When he wants to be a girl, he is."

Nothing took her turn clenching her jaw. She seethed for a moment, then carefully opened her mouth. "I don't know anything else about the sorceress. That is the same story I know. I cannot think of more details, though I wish I'd asked the great demon of the palace."

"You could ask at the crossroads shrines. If you're careful and no one is watching." His voice rumbled in his big chest. He still held on to Nothing's wrist.

She turned her hand around to put their palms together. "He's not dead," she said again.

When Sky remained silent, she pressed, "If she ate him, why send the imposter? She's keeping him alive for something."

Sky looked directly at her then, and his terrible expression curdled the slight food in her belly. After a long, long time, he said, "Even if he is dead, we need to know that, too."

NINE

IMMEDIATELY AFTER THEY LEFT the Way of King-Trees, onto a road marked as the Cedar Pilgrimage, it rained so hard they were forced to stop and shelter in the hollow of a King-Tree snag for two entire days.

The hollow's peaked entrance was covered in tattered pilgrim flags pinned to the bark and prayer ribbons twisting in rainbow ropes. Strings of tiny bells made a pretty shimmering song in the heavy wind, and the rain splattered onto the gray boulders and ruffled the ferns, darkening slips of moss and trailing in streams down the deep furrows of the snag. The sky was so dark it seemed like night outside, and occasionally rain spat down onto their fire from the high boles rotted out into round windows. The floor of the hollow was dry, but Sky covered the back section with his oiled cloth and they huddled near their fire, pressed together under extra robes. Wind could not shake the ancient old tree, but its bones creaked as if the King-Tree still lived.

A crossroads demon had led them here when they stopped to give offering and Nothing inquired about the Sorceress Who Eats Girls. "Ask the snag demon," it said, flicking claws toward the west. It possessed a striped raccoon, furry and emaciated, with tiny hands to climb its shrine and pluck blessing ribbons or pull apart redpop cakes, which rotted in its tiny claws. Dark-blue demon-eyes gleamed even in the daylight.

"What is a snag?" Nothing asked.

Sky said, "A dead tree. Lightning struck or taken by disease."

"Right, brother," said the raccoon demon, showing all its teeny-tiny teeth.

Sky turned his back, and Nothing fed the demon a drop of blood soaked into a crumb of cheese—the last of their stores. From here they'd be subsisting on what they could gather and hunt and bargain for from the spirits of the rain forest. The demon said, "Find the snag demon less than a day along that road; turn off when you hear the rattle."

The rain began midafternoon, and she and Sky hurried, but there was only so much Nothing could do to make herself faster. Sky offered to carry her. She hissed at him just like the raccoon demon.

Even with her jacket drawn over her head like a hood, Nothing got wet. She scowled and trudged on, listening for a rattle.

But the whole forest rattled when the wind shook the canopy and thin, cold breezes cut down to rush through ferns and dying leaves. Or so she thought, until she heard it: a huge, low sound like a bear's snore, which filled her head. Even Sky stopped. He twisted around to stare at her, and they darted off the path, following the sound.

The dead King-Tree itself caused it, when the wind blew through its ancient branches and slithered into the boles and the massive hollow.

Nothing knelt in the wide swath of barren earth surrounding the tree. Had the demon been a spirit until the tree was struck, killing them both, or had it found this home after? She put her hand to the cracking bark, exploring splatters of white and blue lichen. "Hello, beautiful old tree. We would like to sleep in the shelter of your hollow, with your permission, friend."

"Friend?" rattled the voice of the demon. It echoed in the dark hollow.

"I am friend to the great demon of the royal palace, and would be yours."

Sky passed her a small knife, even as rain plastered his hair to his cheeks.

Nothing cut the meat of her thumb and touched her hand to the bark. "Here is a sign of my honesty, and a gift for you. While we stay here, we will feed you."

"I like it," drawled the demon. Branches rattled overhead, shaking more rain upon them.

"And mine," said Sky, cutting his hand too and gifting the dark-purple blood.

"Ah!" said the demon. "You may remain."

Sky moved inside with all their goods, ruffling the pilgrim flags. Nothing said, "Snag demon? Do you know the Sorceress Who Eats Girls?"

"No." The demon's voice had turned petulant.

"Do you know of her?" Nothing wondered what this demon looked like. Had it taken the shape of its tree house, or something more like a worm or an owl or a badger?

"Whispers . . . ," it hissed, for effect, Nothing suspected. She smiled a little.

"What sort of whispers?"

"She hunts when she leaves her mountain. Hunts and hunts and takes and takes."

"What is she hunting for?"

"If I knew I would find it for her and bargain to be hers."

Nothing stroked the wet bark. Rain trickled down her spine beneath her robes. "You think it would be better to be her demon than to have this magnificent old tree?"

"Flattery," the demon scoffed, pleased. The air seemed to warm slightly.

The rain did not abate. Sky ventured out to find food, returning with nuts to soak and roast and stringy sura hearts that tasted like apples about to spoil. He was drenched, and Nothing took over cooking while he spread his quilted robe and shirt out to dry, stripping down to his skin.

Nothing tossed him her bright-green sash to use to towel at his hair and then he sat near the fire on the oilcloth, holding his underwear up like a chicken ready to roast, hoping it would dry quickly.

His copper muscles were outlined in blue shadows and red-orange firelight, and his dark hair clung in thick waves to his neck, the ends lifting as they dried into soft blue wisps. Tiny dark-blue hairs scattered against his chest, lightly down his belly, and along his forearms. With her eyes she could trace layers of muscle from his wide shoulders and down his back, along the dip of his spine and bottom. A few scars nicked and gouged him, all a mottled purplish color, lovely stories written against his skin. Nothing felt vulnerable when she was naked, but Sky seemed stronger with nothing to hide his demon-line.

The demon-kissed were said to have the blood of demons in them, which was impossible because demons had no blood and could not reproduce even with other demons. The priests taught that an offended Queen of Heaven had taken a demon and shattered its essence into such tiny pieces that it could be infused into living blood like tea into water.

"You're rude," Sky said.

It was true: she was staring. Nothing sniffed. "I've seen it before."

Sky wrinkled his nose mightily, but she suspected he acted gruff to hide embarrassment. Nobody was supposed to witness that moment between him and Kirin, and Nothing had been watching because she'd come to ask Kirin a question, then been stunned into complete stillness, entranced by the way Kirin had seemed to worship Sky with his mouth and tongue, like Sky was a god. Until Nothing distractedly put her hand in the wrong place and fell through the ceiling. She'd hit the woven mat hard enough to knock the breath from her body and bruise her whole skeleton. When she'd blinked through the pain, Kirin, who'd been kneeling before Sky, was kneeling beside her instead, and laughing.

That was when Sky had decided she was dangerous and she'd decided Sky was selfish. If she'd caught them, anyone could. It would have ruined Kirin.

Nothing checked the progress of the sura heart. Nearly soft enough to pull apart and eat. She plopped down next to Sky and without looking at him said, "Kirin kissed me once."

Sky went still. "He didn't tell me that."

"We both thought it shouldn't happen again. I think he wanted to see if he was wrong."

"Wrong about what?"

"You?" Nothing shrugged a little. "If he liked kissing me as much as he liked kissing you, maybe you were only his friend, too."

"That's not how that works." Sky's hands holding his underwear out curled into fists.

"It worked for him. He kissed me, then laughed a little, but in a sad way. 'Did you like that, Nothing?' he asked. I told him it was fine, and he laughed harder, not sad anymore."

Sky slowly relaxed his hands.

She didn't tell Sky that Kirin had calmed down and asked if Nothing would let him do it again if he asked. She'd said of course, but he hadn't. Instead, she said, "He'll ask you to be his Second Consort."

Not the First. The First Consort had to be capable of making heirs for the Moon.

"I know."

"You'll hate it."

"I know." Sky sighed. "I am a better bodyguard, but if I remain so I can never be family. If I become his Second Consort, I will be his family, with my own household, my own bodyguards. It should be obvious."

"But you could never leave the palace."

Sky nodded. "Would you? Be one of his consorts?"

"I do anything Kirin asks me to do," she said easily.

There was little else to say. Sky put on his underwear and helped her peel and pull out the meat of the sura hearts, using the roasted skins for bowls. They ate the hot mash with their fingers and, when they'd finished, wrapped the nuts that had been soaking and stuffed them into the embers of the fire.

Outside the snag, wind and rain blew; lightning flickered.

Scrabbling overhead told them some smaller forest creatures used the upper hollow for shelter too. They must have been desperate, if willing to tempt a demon to suck their marrow. Or perhaps they had their own bargains. Nothing gave in and leaned against Sky. He was cool, but not cold, and he wrapped his quilted robe around them, for it was marginally dry.

Nothing closed her eyes. She felt relaxed and more comfortable than she thought she ought when resting in the hollow of a snag demon's house. For some reason, she couldn't be afraid of the demon. She trusted it. There was definitely something wrong with her. When she listened, she could hear its very soft, creaking fizzles of power. Not quite breath, but more like tiny connections through the aether, drawing at the life at the edges of the snag tree's roots, at the kinetic rain, at the scrape of wind.

Sky shifted to get more comfortable with her head on his shoulder. She wondered if he felt the demon's fizzles. And she wondered if she should ask about his family or for a story his grandmother told him. Anything to pass the time and share between just the two of them. They'd always been separated by Kirin in the middle, and she didn't know how to speak of anything but their prince.

And maybe if they spoke of him, kept him alive in their minds and hearts, he would stay alive in his own mind and heart.

Sky must've been thinking the same, for he said, "I was afraid to admit to myself that it wasn't him. The summer changes someone—it's supposed to, preparing the heir for the investiture—and I felt changed, so why shouldn't he be?"

Nothing remained quiet. There was a difference between changed and imposter. But Sky knew that.

"I think I lost a few days. Nothing—at the time I didn't realize it. But I must have." His voice took on the hushed tone of a confession. "How could she take him and replace him with such a detailed, skilled imposter in mere moments? No, she had us for days. Then made me forget."

"You met her?"

"We encountered a dragon." At her tiny gasp, Sky glanced at her and nodded confirmation. "Sinuous, with scales like liquid sliver and eyes brighter than the noontime sky. It was a ribbon of light, and Kirin argued with it. Can you—of course you can believe that."

Nothing closed her eyes again, pressing her head into his shoulder.

"And the dragon vanished in the middle of their argument but brought her back with it. She was just as beautiful, a lovely woman in silk and pearls, until she smiled. Her mouth was full of shark's teeth, and she had one eye like summer leaves, the other white as bone. I remember trying to protect him, trying to throw myself between them. I remember pain, and Kirin's voice, and then we were alone on the banks of the Selegan. I'd thought she was a spirit. Or one of the Queens of Heaven, or a ghost, or even a witch without familiars or aether-tattoos. I never thought she was the Sorceress Who Eats Girls until you killed him."

"And you just got up and came home?"

"Kirin—the imposter Kirin—said he was exhausted and it was time to be back at the palace. The encounter had been enough excitement for me, too, so I didn't question the decision."

"Did you kiss him?"

"Nothing . . ." Sky leaned away abruptly enough she staggered heavily against him. He shook her off.

She scowled. "Did you?"

"Yes."

She spread her hands to ask for more.

"It was different. But not . . . I didn't know what to think."

Nothing curled her knees up and hugged them. She always knew what to think. Just not what to do.

"You knew right away," Sky accused softly.

"Kirin looked into my spirit long ago, and I into his. When you returned, I looked at him and my whole body rejected him, like instinct."

"I need more instinct, and you less of it."

Nothing snorted. "How many more days to the place where you lost him?"

Sky didn't answer at first, probably irritated at how she'd phrased the question. Then, "Three weeks, without more delays like this. The roads meander through the rain forests along the best paths for trading between villages. If we could go overland, faster. But there are too many spirits and demons, not to mention wolves and eagles and bears. I'm not skilled enough to always find my way without the sun or a map."

"I've never left the palace before," she whispered.

After a pause, he said, "You're doing all right."

Nothing drifted into sleep soon after that and dreamed of rain, of Kirin's tilted smile, and of dragons with one green eye and one bone-white.

TEN

THOUGH IT WAS DIFFICULT to know with certainty, when the sun finally broke through the rain, it was morning, and Sky guessed they'd been in the snag's hollow for two nights.

The long delay should have weighed heavily on Nothing, but the sunlight gleamed warm and bright on dripping leaves and brilliant green ferns, sparkling in the air as if the whole world was clean and freshly ready for mischief.

As she emerged, she paused to smear a little blood for the demon, in thanks that it had left them alone, then walked toward the sounds of a stream. Her eyes ached from the light, but she lifted them toward the blue sky peeking through gently swaying branches of the rain-forest canopy. Everything smelled thickly of water and fertility. How had she never ventured out into the world? What had she been afraid of? No, she'd not been afraid; it simply never occurred to her to leave. Kirin had been in the palace, and so was she.

Nothing ducked her head and knelt at the stream. The clear waters trickled and danced around smooth stones flinty gray and bright marble white. Veins of glittering silver winked, and Nothing touched the rippled surface. She whispered, "Hello," and thoughtlessly plucked a hair from her head and dropped it in. The long black hair fell gracefully to the water, contorting like an eel or Peaceday kite against the gentle flow.

Farther down the stream, a bubble emerged, the size of a human head, and two huge eyes blinked at her. The eyes popped atop the head, like a frog's, and were grayish green. It rose slightly higher and opened a mouth that gaped toothlessly. But its gullet and tongue were vibrant red. The strand of Nothing's hair slipped into its mouth and down its throat. The spirit snapped shut its mouth and blinked at her, then sank down into the stream again.

"Well," said Nothing. "I hope, little stream, you like the taste of nothing."

"Who are you talking to?" Sky asked, hunching down against the bank beside her.

Nothing cupped water in her palm and splashed him.

He cried out and batted her away. "I only just got dry!"

With a wicked smile, Nothing leapt at him, flinging her arms around his neck and laughing in his ear.

Sky roared, dropping the bags and water gourd. He stood effortlessly and reached up to grab her, still growling like a bear. Instead of dragging her off him and flinging her away, he dug his fingers into her ribs and tickled her.

Nothing's mouth and eyes flew open and she kicked wildly, shrieking.

He did not let up, pinning her to his shoulder with one huge arm, tickling her side and stomach until she gasped for air, choking on her laughter. "Please . . . !" she managed, and Sky stopped. It was only then, as he cradled her more gently, that she realized he was laughing almost as hard as she'd been, and had fallen to one knee.

Bent over his shoulder, she patted the small of his back, and he patted her bottom in return, then pulled her around to perch her upon his thigh. It was secure as a bench and just as stony. She blinked a few times, focusing, and felt the heat in her cheeks. She murmured, for it was all she could manage, "I fed a hair off my head to the spirit of this stream. I think it liked it, so we can fill our cups."

Sky nodded. His glee had sunk into a quiet smile. This close the demon-blue in his eyes was dark enough to be called black, and the flecks of human-brown were few.

"I didn't know you could laugh," Nothing teased.

"Babies have always made me laugh," he teased back.

With a huff, she pushed to her feet, but a smile tugged at her mouth all morning.

ELEVEN

THEY WERE JOINED THAT day by a trio of pilgrims with fanned hats and long green sleeves, their white faces painted with black stripes. Each wore spirit rings on all their fingers and thumbs, meant to charge with every step they took on their journey.

Nothing did not speak, letting Sky give their pretense of elopement. The two young men and one young woman laughed and offered to share their fire so long as everyone traveled the same road. They'd joined the Cedar Pilgrimage trail from the southwesterly Road of Seeds, and would walk north two days with Nothing and Sky until the Crossroads of Heaven, where the Green Way branched deeper into the rain forest. They'd climb higher as they walked northeast, up into the steep foothills of the Third Mountain, to the zigzagging Canopy Trail that led to the Shrine of All Gods.

The pilgrims sang and told stories as they walked, clearly glad of an audience to practice their favorite tales. They went before Sky and Nothing, like an honor guard. Gali, one of the men, kindly teased Nothing for being shy, and Sky told a distracting story about a mischievous dog spirit that made a bargain for teeth too big for its head. Then he said, "Heia might sing for you when the sun sets, if you ask kindly."

It took Nothing a moment to realize Sky meant she was Heia. She ducked her head and nodded. Nothing was hardly a name to share. Especially if rumors about the imposter prince had reached ahead of them on the road thanks to witches sending news through the aether or army scouts.

The rain forest, by now, had changed: King-Trees no longer towered over everything, and the canopy had lowered, thickened, with delicious-smelling cedar and spruce trees whose red limbs spread like perfect umbrellas. Clinging balls of sura decorated the lower branches, their heavy hearts dragging their vines into nests of flowers with beautiful pink petals. River birches marked the streams that tucked into the rocky ground, and the moss was striped in every variation of green and blue. Ferns as tall as Nothing unfurled beside the trail; yellow and vivid green birds darted between the moss-patched alders. The woman pilgrim, Sits in Sunlight, pointed out a deer path and the tiny grooves their hooves made in the moss.

While Nothing remained silent, she listened and watched, guessing that Sunlight and Gali were sister and brother, having the same almond-shaped eyes and light-copper skin, and the second young man, Ginger, sand white like Nothing, was courting one of them. Or trying to. Perhaps, she thought, the pilgrimage to the Shrine of All Gods was a quest to determine which sibling would have him.

That night they made camp in a mossy clearing of alders, surrounded by several large boulders streaked with golden veins.

They shared food, and Nothing made a quick fire with crisp fallen alder branches, their gray bark a glorious contrast to the vibrant red wood. She pretended to strike flint as she whispered to the spirits, for the pilgrims' sakes—and Sky's peace of mind. After they'd settled and eaten, Gali brought out a ceramic flask and passed it around. His sister and their friend sipped, then breathed heavily out over their tongue as if to give a taste of the vapors to the forest spirits. Sky thanked Ginger as the flask was handed over, then did the same. He turned to Nothing. "It's a smooth liquor, with bite."

"Dreams of Wheatseeds," Gali said, "distilled from the golden wheat we grow down in the south."

Nothing saluted with the flask and carefully sipped. It tasted of nothing, and that made her smile a little. But her gasping breath turned more to a cough, and tears sprang to her eyes. After she hurriedly passed it to Gali, Sky rubbed her back in circles.

"Will you sing?" Sits in Sunlight asked.

Nervously, Nothing glanced at Sky and nodded. She swallowed once or twice, until her throat felt recovered, then sang a serenade the Second Consort often crooned to herself. Its rhythm and dialect were old, with odd stop-starts lending it a melancholic quality. And it suited Nothing's soft, high voice.

When the song faded, the three pilgrims brushed their hands together in appreciation.

Nothing slept curled beside Sky that night, her back against his side and his arm as a pillow. In the morning, for the first time in a while, Sky smeared blue paint over his eyes and dotted it in an arc on Nothing's forehead. The pilgrims reapplied their black stripes, and Nothing, for the sake of friendliness, quietly offered to rebraid Ginger's straggling hair. He accepted gratefully, and she made quick work of the thick, dark-brown waves, pinning it atop his head in a knot. She plucked a flower from a root cluster to tie against the base of his fanned hat so that its stem bent over his head and the petals caressed his forehead and temple like gentle kisses as he walked. It was charming, and she hoped whichever sibling he favored liked it too.

They parted ways with the pilgrims two hours before sunset, when they reached the Crossroads of Heaven.

These crossroads were marked with four shrines shaped like the Four Living Mountains, and Nothing felt a bite of annoyance that the Fifth Mountain would be so ignored just because it had a demon instead of a spirit. She scowled as the rest paid their respects and knelt in the center of the crossed dirt roads. She dug a shallow hole and spat into it, whispered, "I have not forgotten the Fifth Mountain," then quickly patted the earth back into place.

All four of her companions were staring at her, though they could not have heard what she said.

"Heia," Sky said, hauling her up.

Sits in Sunlight said, wide-eyed, "Best luck, both of you," reaching to take the sleeves of her brother and friend.

Ginger blew Nothing a kiss, shaking his head in amused worry, and Gali nodded to Sky before going off east.

Sky didn't release her for several long moments, until she jerked free. "What?"

"I told you. Normal people don't spit into the center of crossroads, especially when surrounded by four perfectly good shrines."

"They were leaving. We don't have to worry about them anymore."

"You're still a nuisance," he grumbled.

Nothing crossed her arms over her chest and stomped angrily down the Cedar Pilgrimage trail. The day was warm, the sun pressing against the back of her neck. She wanted to stop already to camp and be just herself—Nothing! Not Heia the girl running off to be some demon-kissed's consort against her family's wishes!

Sky strode behind her and stopped at her side, keeping to her pace. They didn't speak until the sun had dipped below the canopy and Sky chose a bent tree to mark their shelter. The sky was clear, purple with emerging stars, and they spread the oilcloth over the ground. "I'll hunt again in the morning," Sky said. "We need fresh meat."

"We need to *get there*."

"If you have wings you haven't told me about, Nothing, we can get there faster."

She glanced sharply at him.

He was not smiling but scowling as he handed her a piece of hard cookie he'd traded for with the pilgrims. As she munched on a corner, enjoying the slight sweetness, she tried to relax. It didn't work, and she sighed, then started to sing again.

This time she chose a hopeful maiden's chant, filled with rhymes for silk and descriptions of suitors. She forgot a few of the words, and Sky murmured them for her. It was good to sing, even something that never would describe her life. When the song ended, Sky sang a low working song. His forefingers tapped in the off-rhythm, and she wondered if it was because he'd learned the song with a weapon in hand.

The stars gleamed in the sky, along the narrow strip of it visible exactly over the road, like a seam in the rain-forest canopy.

Just then Nothing heard a shuffle of leaves, a loud *shush* of ferns that could not be ascribed to the wind. She stood slowly, peering into the dark rain forest. Shadows played across the waist-high sea of curling ferns, and the gray-moon-pale trunks of alders were like thin spirits.

"Oh," said Sky, resigned. Nothing glanced to see him turned toward the north approach of the road. Down it lumbered a huge creature.

But Sky seemed unafraid, so Nothing quashed the thrill of panic, despite the creature's size: it was bigger than a grizzled bear! Bigger than a small family's barn.

Nothing smoothed her hands down her hips, wishing she had armor instead of tunic and trousers. Sky did not stand, and he reached over to tug at the hem of Nothing's jacket. "Sit. Be welcoming. This is no threat to us."

"What is it?" Nothing whispered, reluctantly allowing herself to be pulled down into a crouch.

"It's a great alder spirit."

"A great spirit of this forest!" Nothing whispered, glad to finally meet one. Greater spirits were stronger from linking their power with smaller spirits, or becoming the focal spirit for a large community of spirits. They held not only their own connection to the aether, but those of their flock as well.

The spirit walked slowly, having no need to be nimble or quick. It was bulbous with fat and muscle, its skin gray-white and patched with vivid white lichen and moss in spirals and teardrop shapes. Huge red catkins dangled from its belly and down its wide thighs, while smaller upright catkins grew like tiny cones off its shoulders. Green oval leaves fell like hair down its head and neck, and its eyes were gashes of red wood, its mouth the same. "Hello, The Day the Sky Opened," it said in a creaking, windy voice. "I thought I recognized your singing."

"Alder spirit," Sky replied firmly. "Join us, if you like."

"I like!" The alder spirit stretched its gash-mouth wide in what Nothing supposed was a smile. Then it bent its knees and sank down to its haunches across the fire.

"Hello," Nothing whispered, eyes wide. She offered it a tentative smile.

"Ah! Sky, my friend! Your wife looks ill tonight—lost a bit of vitality, has she?"

Nothing gasped.

Before she could answer, Sky put his hand on her shoulder. "I travel with a different woman now, alder spirit."

The spirit clapped a mossy hand on its knee. "Another consort so soon? I have seven, but gathered over a hundred years or more. And two of mine have two of their own."

"I am not anyone's consort," Nothing said. "How powerful are you, alder spirit? Can you bend the rain forest to your will or whisper in the language of the wind? Can you hear the Queens of Heaven making love in their cloud castles?"

Sky frowned at her, but she ignored him. This spirit had no name, and Nothing was full of ideas.

It puffed its lichen-covered cheeks. "Quite powerful! I can bring all the alder catkins to seed at once and wake up butterflies before their season!"

"Hmm." Nothing shrugged.

"I can talk to thunder!" it argued.

72

"I see. If you're so powerful, it must be that you're very stupid, to mistake me for a prince."

For a moment silence engulfed them.

Sky snapped his teeth shut hard enough Nothing heard it, and the alder spirit threw itself to its feet. "What?" it demanded, thrusting the word into the nighttime like a roar.

Nothing held her ground, despite the tremble of her stomach. "I said, you must be stupid to mistake me for the Heir to the Moon."

"By what power do you say such things, little girl?"

"My own power."

"Alder spirit," Sky said, moving to put himself between Nothing and it. "My friend is—"

Nothing interrupted. "Can you answer a riddle, then, if you are smart?"

The alder spirit stomped once, then said, "If I answer your riddle, you will give me a piece of your flesh."

"And if you do not, you will guide The Day the Sky Opened and myself safely through the rain forest to the foot of the Fifth Mountain."

Sky grabbed her wrist. She did not shake him off, but held her gaze on the spirit.

It hesitated, all its catkins and leaves shivering in the night wind. "The Fifth Mountain."

"Yes." Nothing nodded encouragingly. "And I will give you a name."

"Bah! You are wild!" the alder spirit cried, throwing up its huge arms. The gesture released a damp mossy smell that wafted around their fire. "Nothing can give a spirit a name but a wife or a sorcerer or a unicorn or a Queen of Heaven!"

Nothing allowed her triumph to gleam in her smile. Sky's grip loosened, and he let out a soft sigh of surprise. She said, "Do you accept the bargain?"

"What is your riddle?" it asked, resigned. And perhaps desperately curious, for its red-gashed eyes blinked and narrowed eagerly.

"Your name is Moss Tear on Red Alder. Now it is yours. Here is my riddle: Why could I give it to you?"

The spirit fell still and slowly sank back onto its haunches. "My name is Moss Tear on Red Alder," it murmured, testing the sounds and taste of it. "Yes. It is. You . . ."

"Why could I give it to you? Tell me, or take us through the rain forest to the Fifth Mountain."

Moss Tear on Red Alder chewed on a lace of moss that fell over the top of its mouth like half a mustache. "You are—you are not a Queen of Heaven. I can smell unicorns. And you are not his wife, so perhaps pledged to be mine?"

"That would be a good life," Nothing answered, "but no. I am Nothing, and by your own word, nothing can give a spirit a name."

"Nothing is not a name!"

"It is what I am," she said, and shrugged again. "Are you hungry, Moss Tear? We have a small bit of hard cookie to share."

When she sat again, her hands shook.

Sky gave the great alder spirit a cookie and crouched beside Nothing. "You're a nuisance," he said, "but you're going to get me into that mountain."

TWELVE

———

FROM THEN ON, NOTHING and Sky traveled fast, passed through the rain forest from spirit to spirit.

Their friend Moss Tear on Red Alder took them directly north into the dense forest. Ferns and small trees shifted out of their way, not quite enough to shape a path, but only for the two to pass easily. Within the wildest parts of the rain forest, Nothing's boots left tracks on the moss and she touched everything she could: shelf lichen that climbed spirals around the trunks of cedars; fallen trees half-rotted to become magnificent damp cities for brilliant moss, blue beetles, and ground squirrels with bushy red-gray tails; vines with heart-shaped leaves and furry cones that spilled off branches like curtains. She saw orange foxes sunning on rocky outcrops and ravens with wings that gleamed blue and green and silver.

The alder spirit handed them to a trio of spotted owl spirits next, who insisted on traveling at night. The light of their wings drew the light of the moon, and Nothing could see well by the glow. The rain forest at night shone with blinking diamond flies, floating pink spores, and certain iridescent moss. Nothing went too slowly from gazing around at the dreamlike beauty. The owl spirits flew silently, and by the time dawn arrived, Sky said he believed they'd been given wings at their backs themselves and done the work of three days' walking just by a single arc of the moon.

From the owls, they met an eagle spirit named Sleek Eye who walked like a woman in a dress made of light-brown feathers. Its fingers curled like talons and were just as sharp. Together the eagle spirit and Sky caught a half-dozen fish. Nothing ate one, Sky two, and the spirit the remaining three: it tore into the flesh and crunched the bones, swallowing every scale. Then it picked Nothing and Sky up, growing huge, and took off into the air. They burst out of the canopy, and Nothing's surprise and fear melted into wonder at the glorious rolling green landscape of leaves and occasional spearing evergreen. Flocks of birds joined them, wheeling all around like living clouds.

They curved northwest over the rain forest. Nothing, secure in the eagle spirit's arm, reached for Sky and touched his cheek. When their eyes met, she smiled, and he let himself return it.

In the far distance, hazy with clouds, they could see the outlines of the mountains.

Though exhausted by the time they landed, Sky and Nothing did not sleep that night, for the eagle spirit brought them to a stagnant pool inhabited by a water demon. It slicked out of the still water, dripping with pond scum and rotten grass, and smiled.

Nothing bowed low and gave it a hair from her head, explaining they'd been granted passage through the rain forest to the foot of the Fifth Mountain by a powerful red alder spirit. The demon said, "I will grant you passage through my trees on behalf of the red alder, but if you want to stay alive for such passing, give me bone and blood."

Sky took a small bag out of his pack and withdrew a tiny, sharp fishbone. He cut his hand with it, and while bleeding removed more salmon bones, then tossed them all into the pond.

"Tasty purple blood," the demon said, dragging filthy surface water as it climbed out of the pond. The scum lifted away with it like a cape. "This way," it said.

They had to walk far behind the demon, because of the smell, and still Nothing picked around dead fish and rotten roots and rivulets of stinking water. She wanted to ask this demon about the Sorceress Who Eats Girls but sensed that it would extract a further price that she could not spare. Still, she was tempted. So very tempted. Her throat went dry imagining the bargain, imagining what it might be like to face the demon head-on.

It was a rough day, and yet again the hours seemed to fold and the rain forest contract so that by the time the demon left them, it said, "Only another two days to the great lava break, where the Selegan was crushed when the Fifth Mountain died."

Nothing and Sky collapsed and slept against each other. This mode of travel drained them as if they'd sprinted the whole time, with boulders on their backs.

A roar woke them.

Nothing scrambled away from the noise while Sky got to his feet and brandished his sword.

It was a bear spirit with two heads. As large as a grizzled bear, its fur was black as night and strewn with stars. "Come," it said, mouths both open but neither moving to form the words.

"Thank you, bear spirit," Nothing said, and Sky sheathed his sword.

The spirit sighed and touched each of them. They no longer were hungry or sleepy. And all day they walked fast, never lagging.

When they stopped at sunset, the bear spirit patted Nothing on the head and said, "Blessings on you and your master."

"I'm not—" Sky said, perturbed.

Nothing smiled, knowing the spirit meant Kirin.

"Go," the spirit said, pointing with both hairy paws along a narrow deer path directly west. "Tomorrow afternoon you will arrive at the lava field and the Selegan. There is the end of our rain-forest territory, and the beginning of hers."

"The Sorceress Who Eats Girls," Nothing said.

"So," the spirit confirmed.

Nothing began to ask more, but the spirit dissipated into the twilight, becoming stars and shadows.

Sky sighed. "We should rest and take up the path at dawn."

Nothing agreed. Best to be fresh when they reached the riverside.

In the morning they ate and packed up and walked under no power but their own. The sky rolled with friendly clouds, and the wind kissed their cheeks and shuffled the canopy enough that sunlight flashed constantly. The air was thinner in Nothing's chest, and she worked harder to breathe the cold. Finally she was grateful for every layer of bright clothing Sky had made her bring.

The rain forest fell back, trees fewer and farther between, and ferns gave way to moss and low grasses. For several days their way had sloped up, occasionally climbed a rough incline of rocky roots and clinging trees, but now the ground leveled again.

When they stepped fully out of the rain forest, a shining green field spread before them. The surface rippled and bubbled like liquid, only it was stiff and still as stones. This was the old lava field. Once it had swirled, bulbous with molten earth, and slowly cooled, blackened, and been covered by moss, lichen, and hearty grasses. It was the greenest green Nothing had ever laid eyes on, with tiny white flowers in creases and the occasional trickle of pure, crystal-clear water in the miniature valleys. The field sloped gently up toward the north, toward foothills and sudden jagged bare stone, and there—rising black and silver to consume the whole north of the sky: the Fifth Mountain.

Nothing stared at it.

A few splotches of pale green suggested low trees or shelves of scrub bushes, but the sharp cliffs and rough teeth of the peaks were bare of life. It lifted so tall, so daunting, with no suggestion of doorways or gates or turrets for humans.

It was only a mountain, barren and desolate. It was also the home of a vicious sorceress, and Kirin's prison. Nothing felt her heartbeat quicken.

"This way," Sky said quietly, moving on over the slick moss. He held his hand back for her and Nothing took it.

They made their way across the beautiful lava field. The climb was difficult for the ground was uneven, with no trees or shelter to steady them against the cold wind. But it smelled delicately of earth and sweet plants: good smells. Sweat prickled down Nothing's spine despite the chill in the air, and by the time Sky paused, Nothing was breathless.

He'd stopped to gaze out at the wide expanse of the Selegan River.

The river cut through the lava field—or rather, it seemed the lava had been thrown back away from the water, almost like a wave of stone and moss. The river ran and rippled, reflecting the blue of the sky and silver light off the clouds. It seemed happy and healthy, and across its expanse the opposite bank was only a strip of mossy lava field before a tree line rose, of alder and juniper and other smallish trees, and the ground cover was livid with flowers! Pastel blue and purple, pinks and white and the occasional poppy red like drops of blood for contrast.

Wind tore at Nothing's hair, pulling some of it across her eyes as if to block her from the beauty.

There was something about the clash of desolation and delighted color, the ribbon of perfect water, the undulating green earth and wild, free wind that filled her with joy.

Nothing loved this place.

She sighed happily, despite the looming presence of the Fifth Mountain, and let herself smile. She'd grown to love the palace and the Lily Garden, the between spaces that belonged to none but her and the great demon. She'd grown to love much about the palace, the place itself. But Nothing could recall no incidents of falling immediately in love with a thing or a place. Not like this, not until now. It was a heady feeling, lighthearted and rooted at the same time, as if she could be both deeply invested in the earth, while flying overhead. The intimate details of moss fibers, the veins within the soft pink petals, the gentle lapping at the riverbank were as important as the entire landscape and how massive pieces of it fit together: lava field and river and forest line and sky and clouds all reflecting beauty again and again and again.

Nothing gasped at the tears that suddenly blurred her sight. She was not used to such strong emotions.

"Nothing?"

"I'm all right," she said, wiping her eyes. "We're here."

"We're here." Sky squeezed her hand and led her toward the river. "It's very near to where Kirin and I were."

It was difficult suddenly, remembering Kirin had been taken here, that it had begun here, his imprisonment, his torture, whatever he suffered. A dark thread of fear reminded Nothing it could have been his end. Kirin Dark-Smile might be dead.

But the river glittered with silver-gold waves, and the blue sky gleamed, and fields of wildflowers bowed in the wind. It was too beautiful for death.

Nothing shook her head at her fanciful thoughts. She knew death could be anything, especially beautiful.

And Kirin lived. She knew it as well as she herself lived.

They came to the riverbank. The lava field had eroded into chunks of black rock, lumpy and pocked, and fine black grains that were not quite sand but rough pebbles that crunched and turned to powder under her boots. The bank slipped into the water, visible for several paces because the water was clear and cold. Nothing saw thin slips of fish, silver and flashing green, and a few bright-green grasses clumped in the riverbed that waved thin tendril leaves. It was such welcoming water, clean and tasty looking, and everything smelled so very alive.

"Hello, Selegan River," Sky said. He untied the sash holding his bags to his back and let them hit the black beach.

Nothing knelt at the edge of the water with her knees just at the waterline. She placed her palms flat to the surface. "Hello, Selegan River," she repeated. "We have come to the foot of the Fifth Mountain to bargain with the Sorceress Who Eats Girls. Will you let us go alongside you? Cross your wide waters and sip from your waves?"

They waited a moment as the thin fish darted away and the eddies of water swirled against Nothing's fingers. It was cold but refreshing.

Then the water was an undulating body, sinuous and scaled. The dragon rose from the river long enough to twine around the top tower of the palace. It had scales like silver and sunlight-on-water, massive blue eyes, and its lipless mouth parted to show Nothing a pink tongue and sickle-sharp teeth. Wide, silver-feathered wings rose in twinned arcs, blotting out the bright sky. It had three slithering tails, four legs that ended in claws gouging the sand and air, and hard white-capped ridges down its back like rolling waves of water. Feathers flared off its eyes and along its neck, continuing down its silver-white stomach in the kind of rainbows that appeared around the sun or in a drop of oil. It hissed and said, "I am Selegan, and I know you."

Assuming it remembered Sky, Nothing bowed deeply and kept silent for her companion to speak.

But Sky cried in shock and said, "You are the dragon that stole Kirin from me!"

The great blue eyes blinked slowly, and the dragon rippled its scales. Nothing got the distinct impression that was its version of a shrug.

"I thought you were her demon or familiar, not a river

spirit! How can you ally with such a creature?" Sky drew his sword.

The dragon reared back on its hindquarters, dipping its nose like a disapproving tutor. "She saved me," it said. Though its size lent a depth and noise to its voice, Nothing thought it spoke softly. Gently, even. "When my waters slowed, cut off from my long bed by the cold lava. I was a trickle, a new, ugly, sucking lake, and soon would have become a demon. But she saved me."

Nothing glanced at the place where it seemed the lava field had been shoved back in a frozen, solid wave.

"And so you deliver princes into her clutches?" Sky demanded. "Do you collect maidens for her, too, hearts ready to be devoured?"

"Sky," Nothing murmured, but the bodyguard gripped his sword in both hands and lifted it so that the wide blade caught sunlight. It flared.

"This human desires to fight me," the dragon said. "You can never have your prince back."

"Why?" Nothing asked.

"I will have him back!" Sky yelled as he charged.

His feet splashed heavily in the river, sending up spray that flashed in the sun like his sword, like the dragon's scales. Nothing shaded her eyes even as she cried his name.

The dragon reached to pluck him up, but Sky turned, slashing his sword against the dragon's paw. The blade screeched against the scales, then penetrated: silver-blue blood dripped into the river.

Sky did not let up, but drove toward the dragon's feathered belly.

The dragon leapt into the air, twisting over Sky. It swung a tail and batted Sky downriver; the bodyguard stumbled but dug in his feet and did not go down. Water gushed against his waist, slowing Sky as he yelled wildly at the flying dragon.

Nothing watched, horrified, but did not think she should stop either of them. It was Sky's choice, Sky's burden—though if he died, Kirin would never forgive her.

Sky fought on, slashing at the dragon, who dipped and darted as much as a creature that size could. Soon it bled from several gashes, and Sky's shoulder bled too, vivid purple blood that soaked his shirt, vanishing below the quilted outer robe. Sky panted; the dragon's color flushed silver-gold and mottled blue. Several scales flaked off and dropped into the river, where they became dark water.

Demon-kissed strength gave Sky more endurance than any regular human, and he caught the dragon's feather beard in one hand, hauling himself up with a furious cry. He dug his sword into the dragon's neck. With all his strength he shoved it into the hilt, and the dragon bellowed in surprise, whipping its head.

Sky was thrown against the shore. He hit hard, grunting, and then gasped openmouthed for air. Nothing flung herself to her knees beside him, crying his name. Blood made his teeth purple as he grimaced.

The sword remained lodged in the dragon's neck. It crouched on the opposite bank and pulled the sword carefully out. Then it tossed the sword into the river. It seethed through its teeth, dripping silver-blue blood. Tendrils of hot breath curled around its fangs and lifted like spirits into the air.

Sky coughed and cried in pain. "Nothing, something is—is broken inside me."

"Be still. Be still and let me bargain," she said, trying not to sound desperate. "It is my turn."

"If he's—if Kirin is—"

"Stop," she hissed, touching his mouth.

Sky closed his eyes and a tear fell down his temple. Just a tear, clear as water, though a part of Nothing expected it to be as purple as his blood.

"Do better than I did," he said.

Nothing stood and looked across the river to the dragon.

It stared back at her—no, not at her, at Sky.

Suddenly the dragon was smaller, and it dove into the water, flicking all three tails for momentum, and it crawled out, encircling them both.

"Do not try to eat him or kill him," Nothing commanded.

The dragon said, "He is becoming water."

Nothing swallowed fear. She took a deep breath. "Selegan, I don't want him to die. What can I bargain for his life?"

But the dragon leaned nearer to Sky. Now its head was the size of a plains horse's head, long and broad, and its mane of feathers and scales glimmered like oil rainbows.

Sky turned his face to it, grimacing in pain, and said, "I will not curse you for my death, but if Kirin is dead, I will haunt you for all time, dragon."

"He is not dead," the dragon replied. Its crystalline-blue eyes stared at Sky's cheek. "May I have a taste of your water?"

When Sky frowned, Nothing thought of her tiny dragon-lily spirit and its fondness for her tears.

"If he allows it, will you heal him?" she asked.

"If he allows it, I will forgive his trespass into my waters and the wounds to my flesh."

Sky managed to whisper, "There will be plenty more of my tears to come, I think."

The dragon flicked its tongue, bright pink and skinny as a garden snake. It touched Sky's face, licking his temple and cheek, and the dragon shivered. The sound vibrating from it was like the purr of a very large cat.

Nothing crouched, lifting her hand to touch the silver-gold scales that rippled against the dragon's long neck.

But the dragon said, "Mistress," and the sky turned black.

Turning, Nothing saw tendrils of perfect darkness spreading like a cold wind, bright eyes—one green, one white—and a smile that curved crimson over sharp, jagged teeth. She saw lava fields coursing in hot rivers, crystals cut into knives, and she heard a single heartbeat so loud it cracked her skull.

And Nothing fell asleep.

THIRTEEN

I N THE HEART OF the Fifth Mountain, the Sorceress
Who Eats Girls smiled down at the sleeping body of the
most beautiful maiden in the empire. He curled upon a
grass-woven pallet in the remnants of his lovely silk dress, rather
like a pile of expensive rags. His ribs lifted slowly, calmly, and in
sleep his black lashes were ink stains against his pallid face. Even
his lips were colorless. Kirin Dark-Smile was drained to stark,
sick whiteness, a dreary reflection of the moon against the hard
black of his hair and all those bold rainbow silk tatters. The sorceress wondered if his mother and her court would approve of
this dramatic contrast brought on by Kirin's weakness.

"Kirin," she said.

His breathing paused, his lashes twitched, and he opened his
eyes, looking directly at her. He did not move.

"You told me the truth," the sorceress continued.

That got him up. He trembled as he drew himself onto his
knees. "Nothing."

The sorceress smiled and knelt before him, the long teeth of
his obsidian cage striping between them. Her dresses billowed

out like perfect petals, arranging in waves of crimson and teal, luscious pink edging, and silver embroidery. As she faced him, her skin dripped off its delicate copper color until it matched his exactly, except she glowed with health, a warm pearl instead of a watery moon. Her terrible eyes—one green and one white, slit-pupiled—shaped themselves into his: vivid honey-gold flecks emerging in her irises like clovers pushing up in the springtime.

Then the sorceress was the prince's mirror: a study in contrast, beautiful, elegant, and girlish.

Kirin huffed, annoyed. He wiped under his eyes, though his makeup was weeks gone.

She smiled, and it was half-cocked, dark, and a good imitation of what his had been once. "Do you think she will do well?"

"Do well to what?" Kirin asked, voice rough. He was thirsty, hungry, frustrated with imprisonment.

The sorceress removed a flask from the folds of her outer dress and passed it through the obsidian bars to set it upon the ground before him. "Wine. Selegan will be down with a meal soon, the same that will be served to your Nothing."

Kirin drank, though the wine was sharp and soured in his empty stomach. "Do well to what?"

"She did not come alone."

Silence.

The sorceress shrugged. "But the warrior picked a fight with the Selegan and may not survive."

The prince set the flask of wine onto the stone with a *click*. He remained silent.

"I see. You don't care. Then I suppose I shall let him die."

Kirin surged to his feet, and she lifted her chin to peer calmly up at him. He gripped the bars, looming over her, jaw clenched.

"Yes?" She did not smile now, pretending a lack of concern.

"Save him."

Kirin's words were soft, hovering between command and plea.

The sorceress slithered to her feet. She was exactly as tall as him now, looking into his eyes like looking into a mirror. "What will you bargain for his life?"

He tightened his hands around the warm obsidian bars. "What do I have left?"

Silence again as they stared at each other. The still air of the cavern whispered into her ear, news from higher in the mountain brought by the voices of dawn sprites. She needed to wrap this up, and so the sorceress said, "You bargained well for your own life. Can you not do as well for your lover?"

Kirin swallowed a surge of panic that tasted like acid and sour wine. "Save him."

"Your heart beats so vividly," the sorceress murmured.

"I will do anything."

She grinned then, and her teeth had become rows of jagged shark's teeth.

FOURTEEN

NOTHING WOKE SLOWLY.

She shifted a little, rustling silky sheets, and drew a breath as loud as a gust of wind. It was the only sound. When she opened her eyes, she saw a gleaming obsidian ceiling. Its peaks were sharp, its valleys curved like a moon, and lines of black on black rippled in bluish light.

A chandelier dripped from the ceiling, made with a hundred tiny silver-black bones. Blue flames burned from its thin black candles, casting the eerie light.

As she stared, the light brightened to illuminate the entire chamber. It was carved of solid obsidian and the walls hung with dozens of mirrors in every shape and size. The door was stained black with red and pink lacquered flowers. A set of trunks with similar red and pink flowers waited across from her, their tops open and spilling vividly dyed robes and embroidered gowns, slippers, veils, strings of pearls, and crystal beads. There was an armchair carved with feathers and scales, and a narrow red desk set with pots of paint and powder. Beside it a tall round table stood on legs of ivory, holding a shallow bowl of water.

"Hello?" Nothing called, sitting up among frilly pillows and sheets. The bed swayed as if it floated in the air, and Nothing clutched at the smooth wooden edge. It was like a nest made of a giant walnut shell.

Carefully she climbed free and walked across the cold stone floor to the water bowl, wondering if she should risk drinking it. She touched the surface, setting off little ripples that obscured the painted flowers in the bottom of the bowl.

Oh well, she thought, and lifted the bowl to sip at the water: it tasted bright with minerals and clean as rain. She drank until she had to breathe.

Refreshed, Nothing turned a full circle. She was hungry and needed to relieve her bladder, but most important, she needed to find Sky. She made for the door. Its knob was a carved flower: like a rose with pointed petals. She brushed her fingers against it, finding it familiar, and then the knob turned and the red-and-pink door swung open. Nothing leapt back, hands in fists, but the opening revealed a girl her own age, brown eyes wide, with sweet pink flowers woven into her black hair.

"Oh," the girl said. She smiled prettily. "You're awake."

Narrowing her eyes, Nothing remained quiet.

The girl held a tray with steaming pot and tea bowls, dark bread, and another bowl covered with a cloth. The ceramic of the teapot and bowls was delicate and thin, painted with tiny people farming. One little orange cow stared off into a distance of rolling hills. The cow blinked, and Nothing's eyes flew back to the girl.

"I'm Spring," the girl said, stepping into the room though it crowded Nothing. As she entered, the light brightened from this wintery, watery blue into sunnier candlelight. Spring set the tray upon the red desk and poured pale-green liquid into the bowls. With both in hand, she turned back and offered one.

Nothing glared. "Where is the warrior with whom I arrived? Where is Kirin Dark-Smile? Who are you?"

"In that order?" Spring smiled prettily. "The warrior is sleeping under a spell, the prince below us, and I told you, I am Spring."

"Below us? In the mountain? Is he alive? Will Sky live?"

"These are questions for the sorceress."

"Then bring me to her!"

"She would like to have dinner with you tonight," Spring said, again offering the tea.

"What will this do to me?" Nothing took the bowl. She covered the little orange cow with her thumb.

"Warm you?" Spring sipped her own, then plucked the bowl from Nothing's cold fingers and traded.

Nothing responded with a long-suffering sigh to cover her anxiety. She drank the hot tea in a single swallow. It tasted of grass and a richer, soothing darkness. Something familiar she could not trace. Like the flower on the knob. "What sort of spell has she put upon Sky?"

"She holds him asleep while he heals."

"Why is she helping him?"

"The river asked her to."

Giving back the empty tea bowl, Nothing studied this girl. She was slightly taller than Nothing, with white skin and softly waving black hair loosely braided with trailing pink flowers. They seemed like miniature orchids. Spring's up-tilted eyes were the color of honey and sunlight and seemed quietly content to hold Nothing's gaze, as if with no secrets to hide.

A strange breathlessness caught Nothing, and she parted her lips to gasp a little air. Spring's pretty eyes dropped to Nothing's mouth and so Nothing glanced at the other girl's too. Those lips were pink and soft-looking as the tongues of the orchids in her hair.

Nothing swallowed and stepped away.

"Does the Sorceress Who Eats Girls always do what the river asks?" she demanded.

Spring shrugged and moved to the trunks across the room. Her slippers were pale-pink silk and silent against the obsidian floor. "You've been bathed. Would you like to dress?"

Startled, Nothing glanced down at herself. She hadn't thought about how she'd become clean, only vaguely realized she felt so. Her hair slid around her face as she looked, gleaming and trimmed. A creamy linen shift softer than anything she'd worn before covered her to the knees. Its hem was embroidered in such detail it should have belonged to a queen. "I need to pee," she said with a surge of anger.

Where had anger come from?

Nothing clenched her jaw. She was unused to fluctuations of emotion. She was not supposed to attract attention.

Spring pointed to the curve of obsidian wall behind the nest. A lidded stone bowl settled in a short tiled stand. "There is cloth in the basket beside, and everything will be taken care of for you."

Huffing, Nothing went to the chamber pot and used it. The other girl widened her eyes as if surprised at Nothing's lack of modesty.

"Now my mouth? My teeth are furry."

Spring pointed again, and Nothing, flushed with an unfamiliar mingling of anger and triumph, cleaned her teeth, too.

When she finished, Spring glanced at her over her shoulder, holding a beautiful expanse of red silk across herself as if she'd been measuring the size. "Ready?"

Nothing took an angry breath and nodded. She strode to Spring, trying to seem larger and more powerful than she was. The other girl watched her, admiration in her honey gaze. Nothing liked and disliked the expression: she both wanted this girl to admire her and wanted this girl to fear her. Or dismiss her. "I want to see Sky, and Kirin."

"I will take you to the warrior," Spring said, holding the red cloth up to Nothing's face, eyes all for fashion. "But not to the prince."

"Why?"

"Ask the sorceress at dinner."

Nothing pursed her lips. "Red is too harsh for me."

Spring laughed. "You think you need pastels?"

"I don't care," Nothing amended. "Put me in something and take me to Sky."

The other girl smiled in amusement and dropped the red silk at Nothing's feet. She returned to the trunks and pulled out a light-blue robe and a deep-purple long vest with curved black-horn clasps. The robe wrapped tight to Nothing's waist, looser as it fell to her calves. Spring's hands worked quickly and with certainty, nudging Nothing's hip, then batting her hand away to tie the robe. She helped Nothing into the vest, buttoning it swiftly. She stood so near that Nothing found herself holding her breath.

Spring's lashes were long and a brighter brown than the rich black of her hair. They barely curled at all. Nothing wished to touch them. To feel them against her cheek.

Nothing frowned. What was wrong with her? This strangely intense focus on details, on Spring, the surge of anger, and breathlessness. "What are you?" she whispered.

Spring lifted her eyes. She was so very near. Nothing could see individual flecks and swirls in her honey-brown eyes. They seemed familiar too. Nothing shuddered, fighting the urge to back away. Why was everything here familiar?

"What are you?" she asked again.

"A girl," Spring said. "Like you."

"Did she take your heart? Why are you here?"

"I like it here." Spring touched the overlapping collar of her beautiful silk robe. She pulled it down, revealing smooth white skin, the slight swell of breasts, and a thin, almost invisible scar between them. It was jagged, dark pink, not very old.

Nothing thrust away.

Spring smiled sadly and remained silent.

Covering her face, Nothing tried not to think. She tried not to listen or feel. She was nothing. She was Nothing. Nothing could escape the Fifth Mountain. Nothing could rescue Kirin. It would be all right. She threw her hands down and glared. "Take me to Sky."

"Slippers are—"

"No, take me."

Spring turned and gestured for Nothing to follow. She did, barefoot on the cold, smooth obsidian.

The red-and-pink flower door opened out into a maze of

narrow corridors carved into the mountain. Nothing reached to trail her fingers against the wall. They'd left obsidian behind and walked through glimmering granite. When she noticed the glimmer, she wondered how she could see: no lanterns nor candles gave light; no tunnels to the surface nor alcoves held natural sunlight. It was as if the air itself simply was light. Nothing wondered how deep within the mountain they were. It felt comforting, as if she belonged here. When she realized that, Nothing was a little bit afraid.

She kept track of their turns and the distance they went, passing forks and offshoots of the corridor, doors carved of dark wood, some painted merrily like hers, others blending into the walls. Nothing was good at internal maps, having spent her life in the pocket-rooms and smoke ways of the palace. They climbed a staircase, and soon Spring opened a door carved in waves and painted blue. Brilliant light fell out as if they'd come into a happy afternoon.

Nothing hurried in: it was a chamber with a vaulted ceiling that glittered with hundreds of crystals pointed down like frozen rain. In the center a slab of crystal rose like an altar, and upon it was Sky.

She grasped his hand. It was folded with the other over his chest. A long blue cloth covered him from waist down, spilling off the foot of the altar and to either side. His head rested on a thin pillow. Nothing waited, staring, until she saw the slow rise of his stomach.

Relief closed her eyes, and she leaned over to rest her cheek against their layered hands. "Sky," she said.

Standing again, she moved to his head, skimming her fingers

over his shoulder and jaw to cup his face. "Sky," she said again, soft and cajoling. He did not twitch. His copper skin seemed healthy, the blue-violet tinge of his hair and streaks of vivid blue normal. No blood remained dried to his skin, but there were cloudy bruises dark as ink on his left forearm and just peeking up from the blanket along his right ribs. "Is he all right?"

She turned, but she was alone. Spring was gone.

Nothing huffed to herself. "Hello?" she called.

Her voice echoed dully. She glanced up at the winking crystal ceiling. She hadn't even had a chance to ask Spring more questions. What was she supposed to do now?

Nothing leaned over Sky and kissed his cheek. "Get better. I'm going to find him," she said.

With that, Nothing left the crystal room.

She'd come from the left, so she turned right. "Hello?" she called again. Her voice flowed before her as if drawn by the dark stone walls.

For a while Nothing walked. She touched the wall, noticing as the type of rock changed, rippling into obsidian at times, or rough as granite, coined into huge crystals in others, and there were sometimes steps of octagonal basalt. Pink quartz speared out of the ceiling sometimes, glowing softly, and in other places threads of gold sliced through the granite. When Nothing came to a door, she opened it. None were locked: some swung into empty, dusty rooms. Sometimes she found a nest like the one in which she'd awoken, unused, or a single desk, or shelves covered in glittering crystal dust. She found a library, she found a room with only candles and mirrors, and she found a long oval room with a rain forest carved into the walls and clouds in the ceiling.

She found a room filled with crumbling carcasses of dead dawn sprites.

She did not find Kirin.

There was no sign of Spring, nor spirits nor demons.

Nothing stopped along the bed of a granite corridor and put her hands flat to the cool stone. "Demon," she whispered, in the same tone she used to speak with the great demon of the palace. "Demon, I know you are here. You are the Fifth Mountain. I am Nothing, and a friend to demons."

Quieting herself, Nothing listened. She evened her breath, went still. "Demon," she whispered.

There came no response. No word, no vibration of a snore or laughter. It did not wish to speak with her.

Curling her hands into fists, she pushed back and then with all her might screamed, "Sorceress!"

The cry cut away, and then the mountain shivered.

Nothing heard a huge heartbeat; it knocked her off her feet. She landed on her knees.

Then all was silent again.

She panted, and in between her frantic breathing, she heard something come into focus, as if she'd removed a stoppage from her ears: that heartbeat pulse, soft and slow.

Nothing stretched out on the ground, palms flat, cheek and breasts and belly and thighs pressing down, her knees, too, and the tops of her feet. She listened to the heartbeat. It was too slow to be human. Too slow to even align her breath with easily.

It couldn't be the demon. Demons had no life, and thus no heart. But what if it was Spring's heart? What if the sorceress took the hearts of maidens and set them somehow into her mountain to fuel . . . what? Her power? Was it her bargain with the demon? A greater demon shouldn't need such a thing, but perhaps a demon and a sorceress together liked to augment their strength.

If the demon wouldn't talk to her, how could she convince it to help her?

Frustrated, Nothing squeezed her eyes shut.

"Where is Kirin?" she whispered.

She had no idea what to do.

For much of her life, she'd been idle. With no daily work other than entertaining the prince or suffering at his side as his tutor attempted to teach, or learning the smoke ways or gathering gossip to trade, or tickling the great demon of the palace. When she hadn't known what to do, on the rare occasion she needed to do anything, Kirin told her.

All her life, Nothing had known the rules.

In the Fifth Mountain, she didn't know where the smoke ways could be found or what gossip was worth. She didn't know where to go, what was safe. She didn't know much at all.

Turning over, Nothing stared at the arched ceiling. These walls were narrow and low, shot through with quartz. But where she'd sprawled, several corridors came together and their crossing place climbed into a dome. At the peak of the dome was a carving like the one on her doorknob: a many-petaled flower, like a chrysanthemum or a rose with pointed oval petals.

Suddenly Nothing recognized it.

It was the same flower as on the silk she'd been wrapped in as a baby. The same as the burn scarred into her flesh.

Nothing's hands flew to her chest, fingers finding the point

99

even through layers of clothing. She pressed on her scar. It didn't hurt. But as she stared up, her entire body warmed.

She'd not recognized the carved version of the flower. The colorless lines of its dimensions, bent around a knob. But there, at the height of the dome, it was shaped flat.

Nothing stared, feeling like her whole heart gasped. What did it mean?

Was she from here? From the Fifth Mountain?

Flinging to her feet, Nothing ran back down the corridor the way she'd come, saying, "I want my room," again and again.

She found it much too soon for magic to not be involved: the door carved with red and pink flowers and its knob the many-petaled flower.

Nothing opened it, dashing in.

Snoring on the chair behind the desk was an extremely old woman.

Nothing stopped abruptly and made a little noise of surprise. "Hello?" she said. "Sorceress?"

With a snort, the old woman opened her eyes. They were pink from exhaustion, and teary, but the color was dark brown. The eyes were like tiny black beetles in the wrinkled white landscape of her face. Her steel-gray and black hair was twisted into three topknots pinned in place with long-toothed crystal combs, and she wore thick, quilted robes in bright brown and bloodred. They were embroidered thickly in black and silver in patterns Nothing had never seen before. It all coordinated. No contrast: she might've been made of earth and wood but for those silver flashes of starlight embroidery. "Hardly," the old woman grumbled.

"Um," Nothing said. "Are you the great demon of the Fifth Mountain?"

"Pour me some tea, girl."

Reacting to the crotchety command, Nothing hopped to action, unsurprised to find the teapot Spring had left some time ago still hot and still full. Nothing poured both bowls and brought one to the old woman. She handed it over wordlessly, then waited for the old woman to drink first.

She did, closing her eyes. Her thin lips were possibly more wrinkled than the rest of her. When she finished, she put the bowl down and stared at Nothing until Nothing hurriedly finished her own bowl.

"Now, girl, are you ready to dress for dinner?"

"But who are you?"

The old woman got up from the chair, moving with ease despite her appearance. She was a little fat, though it hung from her bones with dragging age, and her back bent like a grand-mother's grandmother. "You may call me Insistent Tide. What color shall we use as your base? Do you have perfume?"

"Um. I don't care. And—no. I don't need perfume." Nothing trailed behind the old woman, shocked because she recognized the name, and when the old woman pushed up the lid of the largest trunk, Nothing reached out and touched her shoulder. "Do you mean Queen-Before Insistent Tide?"

"Yes, yes, I was part of the tribute sent by the Emperor with the Moon in His Mouth to the great demon of the Fifth Moun-tain after the mountain died."

"But that was more than a hundred years ago!"

But Insistent Tide was humming to herself, spotty and off-key, as she pulled through dresses and robes and underthings, sashes and veils and clothing Nothing had no idea what to call.

"Insistent Tide," Nothing said urgently, and the old woman turned. Nothing bowed her head politely. "You're still alive."

"This is a sorceress's mountain."

"But—"

Insistent Tide made an impatient face. "What else do you want to know?"

Nothing opened her mouth, still shocked.

The old woman said, "Yes, I volunteered for this, you know, as I hadn't left the palace in decades. I wanted adventure, and here I am, losing track of the aches and pains and what to call my own age."

"Do you—do you know Kirin?"

"Is that the maiden with the heart she wants?"

"Maybe," Nothing whispered. She could not imagine the sorceress wanting a heart and not getting it. "Why hasn't she taken it yet?"

"Why does she do anything?" Insistent Tide grumbled. "Now, orange or blue?"

"Um, orange?"

The old woman eyed Nothing. "Blue."

Nothing crossed her arms, annoyed at being asked then dismissed. "Is Kirin well?"

Insistent Tide shrugged and began undressing her, with none of the gentleness of Spring's hands. She stripped Nothing, put her in a new shift and underclothes, knotted her hair out of the way with a wide sash, then began layering a thin, spider-silk delicate gown onto Nothing.

Without doubt, it was the most beautiful thing she'd ever worn, and Nothing could not even see her full reflection in any of the small mirrors. It shifted against her with whispers like a winter breeze, slipping along her slender body, hiding her lack of curves in a way that made Nothing want to touch her hips, her belly, her breasts to make certain they were there. Instead, she touched her tongue to the back of her teeth, wondering if that was the point. She was being dressed for temptation. For the sorceress.

Maybe she could trade her heart for Kirin.

Insistent Tide pressed her down onto the stool before the table with all the makeup, and the old woman began to fuss with her hair. Nothing stared in the spotty mirror. The collar of the gown rose to her neck, pulling straight along her shoulders to fall down her back, and her throat was a touch too dark or not dark enough to contrast perfectly with the pale silk. Nothing shivered at the touch of Insistent Tide's hands in her hair. She clenched her jaw against the urge to tear free: only Kirin had touched her hair in years. Ever.

It didn't take long for Insistent Tide to realize Nothing's hair was too many layers to braid without wisps or choppy pieces falling free, and too fine to take pins or combs well. With a disgusted scoff, Insistent Tide pinned only a little back from her temples and clipped in a vine of sweet-smelling white flowers with light-orange centers. They were real, Nothing discovered when she touched their petals.

Insistent Tide picked up a pot of moon-white powder, but Nothing said, "No."

"No?"

"I can do my own."

The old woman frowned her obvious disbelief but backed away with her hands up. She hobbled over to the chair in which she'd slept when Nothing entered and collapsed back into it. Her dark eyes held on to Nothing, already judgmental.

If this was what it meant to have a grandmother, Nothing thought with a scowl, perhaps she was better off.

Nothing looked at herself in the small oval mirror. She was pretty, but not as pretty as the dress itself. Lightening her skin with the powder would be a better contrast with her hair, and vivid blue on her lips would pull at the dress. That is what a lady of the empress's court would do.

Taking quick inventory of the available pots of color, the brushes and palettes, Nothing had an idea that made her smile.

She used her fingers and a single dark-blue pencil, slapping green and red in thick streaks against her cheeks and forehead, around her lips, giving herself the appearance of a monster. A goblin with green cheeks and swirling red eyes, a red mouth, and horns pulling away from her brow into her hair. The pencil she used to color her lips a blue darker than the dress. When she finished, it was as if a demon, not a girl, had dressed up in a diaphanous blue dress and put on twilight-blue lips, to have dinner with a sorceress.

Nothing grinned, showing herself her little white teeth, top and bottom rows, and her brown eyes glittered against the makeup, almost red.

Insistent Tide snored in the corner.

"I'm finished," she declared, standing. The long gown swept around her legs, and Nothing remembered she wore no shoes. She'd keep it that way!

104

"By the Queens of Heaven!" The old woman groaned. "You're a disaster."

"I'm a demon, and you'll take me to my dinner."

Insistent Tide cocked her head and peered closely at Nothing, then laughed in a way that was almost a snarl.

It seemed to Nothing that she approved.

Warmth spread in Nothing's chest, and she let her grimace fade into a smile.

FIFTEEN

T HE DINING ROOM WITHIN the Fifth Mountain
was a massive amethyst geode, glittering from every
angle with facets of livid purple. The bottom had
been covered with a crystal floor, translucent and laid against
the spearing amethysts to give the illusion of walking across
their sharp heads. The table was low, surrounded by gold-thread
kneeling cushions.

Nothing entered alone, having been nudged inside by Insistent
Tide before the old woman shut the door and it vanished into
the crystal.

Immediately, Nothing lost track of the seams and was trapped.

She sighed and looked around.

Each slice of the geode sphere was as lovely and dangerous
and purple as the next, like being imprisoned inside some kind
of violet star.

Nothing loved it. Just as she'd loved the meadow of flowers
and hard black ripples of ancient lava married together in the
valley below the mountain.

At the wooden table, Nothing knelt, sniffing at the smell of pine resin and the rich, fatty aroma of whatever broth steamed from the bowls already set. A flask of wine waited too, beside two cut-glass cups in the shape of fish.

"Hello," the sorceress said.

Nothing spun to face her, mouth open in surprise.

For a moment the sorceress's mouth dropped open in similar surprise.

Before Nothing could think of why she'd surprised a sorceress, she was captivated by her: a young woman with the appearance of a twenty-year-old: smooth, light-copper skin; black-brown-red-streaked hair pulling straight back from her face to pour down her back like a velvet veil; a gown of sunset pink and crimson, edged in delicate sea green. And her eyes. Oh, her eyes were inhuman. One the brilliant green of summer leaves, the other bone white, and both with vertical red-slit pupils. A monster's eyes in a perfect face.

Her mouth was unpainted, soft-looking lips ever so slightly darker copper than her round cheeks and elegant jaw. The sorceress smiled to reveal jagged, triangle teeth crowding her mouth.

Nothing gasped. Just like this geode, just like the lava-and-flowers valley, the sorceress was more beautiful because of the threat.

"I thought you were Nothing, but you know otherwise," the sorceress said, studying Nothing's face.

"I am Nothing," Nothing replied in a whisper. She swallowed and said in a stronger voice, "Where is Kirin Dark-Smile?"

The sorceress glided toward one end of the oval table and knelt. Her skirts billowed around her like a pool of blood. "Join me?" When she gestured, the flask of wine rose from the table and poured thin red wine into both fish glasses. As if an invisible hand served them.

"Is that the great demon of the Fifth Mountain?" Nothing asked, unmoving.

"No."

"Where is it?"

"At home," the sorceress said with a secretive smile. Her unmatched eyes flicked to Nothing and her shark-tooth smile widened.

Nothing's stomach fluttered nervously, and she knelt on the firm golden pillow at her end of the table. Out of reach of the sorceress. She took the cup of wine. The glass was cool, its scales pressing sharply into Nothing's fingers. She drank, a little too much.

The sorceress laughed prettily. Those eyes stared at Nothing, and her lips parted with hunger.

Fear thrilled in Nothing and she cast the cup away with a little cry. The wine arced against the crystal floor; the glass cracked in two perfect pieces. One drop of red splashed the sea-green hem of the sorceress's gown. Nothing stared at it, panting. "Was it so easy?" she cried. "To take my heart?"

"I don't take hearts."

Nothing bared her teeth, suddenly remembering the demon's face she'd painted upon herself.

The sorceress leaned forward. "I accept hearts."

"What does that mean?" Nothing put both her hands flat over her chest, but she could not feel her racing pulse through dress and skin and bone.

"I have not poisoned you, nor drugged you in any way." To prove it, the sorceress took her own fish glass and drank half of the wine, just more than Nothing had swallowed.

The sorceress let go of her glass and it floated toward Nothing. She said, "Drink."

Nothing plucked it from the air and put it to her lips, breathing the heady fumes. Her sip was barely there, barely a taste.

"The soup is my favorite," the sorceress said. She lifted her bowl in a slight salute before setting it down and taking a lovely crystal spoon.

Nothing stared at the reddish-brown broth. It smelled like beef and peppers. Not what she expected from the table of a sorceress who could have anything, presumably. There ought to have been songbird eggs and fluffy pastries, thinly sliced fish laid out in a rainbow, jellies and towers of fruit Nothing had never seen before.

"Eat," the sorceress commanded gently.

Nothing did not lift her spoon.

"Kirin will eat what you eat."

"What?" She lifted her gaze to the sorceress.

"I have told the prince that he will be served what you eat. So feed him."

Nothing ate. It was good, spicy, and surely better for a starving prince than any of the magical, strange food she'd imagined. Halfway through the deep bowl, she slowed down. The sorceress had been eating too, and when Nothing paused, the sorceress patted her lips with a napkin.

"Why do you have him?" Nothing asked.

"I thought I needed his heart."

"But you don't."

"I need what his heart will bring me."

"What?"

The sorceress blinked, and her eyes were more human seeming, without the long red pupil, though still one was bright green and the other dull white. They could be, under certain circumstances, those of a very strange woman. It shifted the sorceress's face to less magnificently beautiful and more approachable. "An answer. That is what I look for in the hearts of all maidens."

"An answer to what?"

"A curse, of course."

Nothing froze. "You're cursed?"

"Yes."

"What is your curse?"

The sorceress smiled wryly.

"You can't say," Nothing grumbled.

"I can tell you a story. Eat."

Somehow the sorceress had acquired a new glass of wine, though Nothing's broken glass remained where it had fallen.

Nothing put another spoonful into her mouth.

"Once a girl climbed into the core of the Fifth Mountain asking to speak with the demon. She wanted to be a sorcerer and bargained with the demon to teach her magic in return for a wife."

"You're the wife of the Fifth Mountain!" Nothing interrupted.

The sorceress's eyelashes fluttered: Nothing hadn't noticed how long and curving they were before. Like the line of a soaring raven's wing. "The demon agreed, and they married, and she learned so much it could not be told in words. The sorceress and her consort were happy, and powerful, for many years, and so the sorceress decided what many sorcerers do: she would find a way to give her demon life again—a form of its own. But demons are not meant for such things. Spirits live; demons exist. They make new homes in the houses of others. They devour. They take. To live is to give, to create, and so it is a trap to think it possible to give life again to a demon. But the sorceress asked herself, is love not giving too? Is it not creation? If a demon can love, can it not live?"

The sorceress paused. Nothing stared at her. Despite having eaten so much, she felt empty. "Was she certain demons can love?" Nothing whispered.

"She believed it, which is better than knowing," the sorceress said. She drank more wine before continuing. "The sorceress began her attempt, gathering power she could barely contain, to make a living form for her demon. Storms racked the Fifth Mountain, and its core burst and burned, and when the sorceress finished, instead of embracing her from a cradle of new life, the great demon of the Fifth Mountain was simply gone."

"You said the demon was home!"

"It is. Now."

Nothing scowled.

"When the demon vanished, the sorceress searched high and low, across the empire, but could not find it. She asked dragons; she begged the wind to take her pleas to the Queens of Heaven and demanded answers of the rain-forest gods. She even sent messengers to the Four Living Mountains, though their sorcerers hated her. None knew. Finally, the sorceress succeeded in summoning a unicorn, and it offered her a single piece of wisdom: *You will find your answer in the heart of the most beautiful maiden."*

The sorceress paused to sip her wine again, and Nothing was breathless.

"It was a very unicorn answer, for they are drawn too well to beauty themselves. Nevertheless, the sorceress hunted for years. She hunted beautiful maidens and asked for their hearts."

"Asked?" Nothing nearly spat the word.

"Asked," the sorceress continued. "Bargained. Seduced."

"How can anyone give their heart? Their actual heart? Don't they die?" Nothing stopped, thinking of Spring.

"That is a different story," the sorceress said gently. "Shall I tell it instead?"

Nothing was torn, wanting to hear about hearts, too, about seduction. But she shook her head, no. Kirin mattered more.

The sorceress said, "The hearts she was given fueled the Fifth Mountain and kept the sorceress's magic bright. But none held her answer. None pointed to what had happened to her demon consort. Until the height of this summer, when she found the most beautiful maiden she'd ever seen."

"You. You found."

The sorceress leveled her uneven gaze on to Nothing. "I found," she said silkily. "And this maiden, this beautiful maiden, said she was a prince, not a maiden. I said, 'Both, then, maiden and prince.' But the prince replied, 'Not quite one or the other, but I am the Heir to the Moon. I want to be—must be—*he* to the world no matter what else, and so call me such. Remind me what the world expects of me.'"

Nothing glanced down at her soup, hurt that he'd never said such things to her. Had he thought she wouldn't understand?

With a soft sigh, the sorceress continued. "The prince's sadness reminded me of my own, and so I brought him here to my mountain, thinking at last I had found the right heart. The heart of a maiden that was not the heart of a maiden, in a prince between both. We spoke of men and women, night and day, life, death, good and bad, and I reminded him that power lies in change, in shifting, in more than two possibilities. The empress and her court—humans—force contrast, force two-sided thinking, as if the world could possibly conform to such a thing! What is twilight? I asked him. What is a shadow? What is a tree with both flower and seed? I asked him if perhaps he was not a prince, but a sorcerer like me, and perhaps his heart was where my demon hides? He was the right age, after all. To have been born when my demon vanished."

Nothing believed it.

For a moment she absolutely believed it: Kirin was a demon reborn.

He was power and beauty, and trouble. Mischief and wickedness, wildness and passion—and stuck, too, in between. And he took and took and took. She felt her own heart stutter and set down her spoon; she could not possibly eat.

The sorceress continued to stare at Nothing with her life-and-death eyes. "I told him I could split him open and look into his heart for my consort, my lost demon. If Kirin did not remember who he was, maybe I could free my demon from that uncertain house and begin again. But Kirin pointed to a carving in the wall and said, 'I have seen that many-petaled flower before.' And so I did not split open his chest. He said, 'Do what you will. Nothing will come for me.'"

Warm gladness burst in Nothing. "He trusted me," she whispered at the sorceress.

"He gave you up," the sorceress replied. "You came, just as he promised you would. Nothing, indeed."

"I'm here. Let him go."

"That is not in my nature."

Nothing crossed her arms over her chest. "That is an excuse."

"Bargain with me," the sorceress murmured. She skimmed a finger along the rim of her glass while her eyes held Nothing's.

"Let Kirin go, and I will stay."

"Stay and what? You're not as beautiful as he is. I am looking for my answer in the heart of the most beautiful maiden. I have that. What better could you offer? Your heart?"

Angry suddenly, Nothing said, "That was a terrible story! I still don't know your curse."

"That isn't the end of the story."

"What is?"

"Have *you* seen the many-petaled flower before?"

Nothing stopped. She had. She knew.

A lifetime of spying, collecting hints and gossip, of living in the walls, served her now, and she knew. She touched her cheeks, dragging her hands down the paint, smearing the green and red demon makeup. She realized why the sorceress had been surprised to see her like this. "You think I'm your demon! Not Kirin. I'm the—you think I'm the great demon of the Fifth Mountain!"

That heavy heartbeat roared in her ears.

The sorceress stood and knelt just beside Nothing, putting her hands palm up against her silk-covered lap. Nothing stared in abject astonishment. The sorceress's pupils turned red again, elongating. She said, "Marry me, my love. Before it is too late."

Nothing leapt to her feet. "No!" she cried. She flung herself away, turning for the missing door. "Let me out!"

A small arched doorway appeared, and Nothing ran through it.

SIXTEEN

NOTHING QUICKLY FOUND HER room with its red-and-pink carved door. She touched the many-petaled knob and hissed, letting go as if burned. But it opened and she stormed inside, throwing herself down before one of the many mirrors leaning, nailed, hanging from the obsidian walls. Her makeup was a raw, rotting wound on her face, melting between girl and monster.

With paint-stained fingers, she pulled at her clothing to bare the scar. It was tiny, pink, wrinkled like a fresh burn. A dried-out cluster of petals pressed between the pages of a book. A peony lipstick mark from a kiss to the heart.

Just like the many-petaled flower carved all over this mountain.

"I'm Nothing," she whispered.

Jerking to her feet, she tore through the room, digging through the trunks and among the sheets of the hanging nest until she found it: the green silk baby blanket with its delicately embroidered flower.

Nothing pressed it to her face, breathing in: it smelled like *nothing* at all. Or the slightest hint of shrine incense.

Curling up her knees, she clutched it to her chest and felt—nothing.

SEVENTEEN

MAYBE NOTHING SLEPT: SHE felt restless and scattered, her mind spinning in choppy circles, her pulse erratic, her legs sore as if she needed to move them. She tried to think through her entire existence, for evidence she was a normal girl, or at least a slightly strange one. Not a demon. It was impossible! Demons were dead; she was alive. The sorceress couldn't have succeeded. The witches in the palace would have noticed, or the priests, or at least the great demon of the palace.

Unless that was why it liked her. Because she was a demon reborn. Maybe it was true: the great demon had known but not said anything. Demons kept their own counsel.

What else explained her brand? The matching many-petaled flower here in the mountain? That she'd appeared from nowhere, without a mother or name?

No, Nothing thought. There could be countless other explanations.

She closed her eyes, but as she traced her memories, she found herself awash in random moments with Kirin. Kirin tying the bracelet of her hair reverently around her wrist, and allowing her to do the same to him; his gentle thumb brushing a tear from her cheek the first time she escaped from the witches; that same day, eleven-year-old Kirin's fury as he demanded the witches be banned from Nothing's presence; racing across the patterned sand of the Garden of Moons; shooting her an approving dark smile when he noticed her crawling above the First Consort's library, perfectly balanced on the ceiling beam; kneeling together at a shrine to the great demon of the palace and tapping coded messages against each other's knuckles while the priests recited prayers. And his arms tight around her when they said their farewells at the beginning of this summer. "I'll see you soon, and then after the investiture, we'll never be separated again," he'd murmured, and Nothing had whispered into his ear, "I want to go with you." "I don't think you truly do, and this is my only time with Sky." And Nothing had realized suddenly that he was correct: she hadn't wanted to leave the safety of her palace house. It was too frightening. Kirin knew her better than she knew herself, sometimes.

Every part of her life was anchored somehow to Kirin, since that day in the garden when he'd stared her down.

No matter what else, she had to find him. Somehow he would know who or what she was.

Nothing got up. She still wore the fine undergarments from the night before and stripped them off. With a bit of fresh water from the ceramic bowl on the stand, she rubbed as much of the demon paint away as she could, on the hem of the very lovely blue dress. It smeared on the silk like an old wound.

Nothing didn't feel like a demon. She felt like . . . nothing. Like herself. What was she supposed to feel?

Standing, Nothing glowered at herself in one of the little mirrors, then went to the trunks to pull out something to wear.

Once dressed in a short black tunic over a wrap skirt, her hair finger-combed, Nothing marched to the door.

It opened before she could touch it.

Spring stood with a tray of food balanced against her hip. "Oh," the girl said.

"Spring." Nothing blocked the way.

"I brought you breakfast."

Nothing bit her lip, thinking of what the sorceress had said: Kirin would eat what Nothing ate. With a firm nod, she backed out of Spring's way so the other girl could set the food down upon the makeup table.

"You have green under your ear," Spring said. Her pink orchids bobbed gently against her braids as she lowered her chin shyly.

"Huh," Nothing said around a bite of warm bread, rubbing absently at her ear.

"No, ah . . ." Spring reached for Nothing's other ear, but paused just before touching her.

Nothing stopped chewing and stared at Spring, wide-eyed. She dropped the bread back onto the tray and used the sleeve of her robe to rub where the girl indicated. It was satisfying to ruin another piece of the sorceress's gifts.

"I want to see Kirin," Nothing said.

"The sorceress will bring him to dinner."

"Really?" Nothing leaned forward to stare into Spring's honey-colored eyes.

"That is what she said," Spring murmured.

With renewed energy, Nothing tore back into the bread, adding a strip of bacon to her quick meal. She ate it all while Spring watched. Bread, bacon, sliced pear, and a little bit of peppery cheese. It was too much, and Nothing felt a resulting huge rock in her stomach.

She thought of Kirin, full. She supposed this promise was the only thing that would have gotten her to agree to have dinner with the sorceress again, and the sorceress had guessed as much.

Annoyed to be so easily manipulated, Nothing said, "Are you alive?"

"Yes."

"How can you live without your heart?"

"Magic."

Nothing scoffed. "Will you get it back?"

"Only if it's given back, only if . . ." Spring looked away, toward the door.

"If what?" Nothing tried to sound gentle, though she felt anything but. Where had this aggression come from? In the palace she'd never made demands, nor spoken up for herself. But if this was what she had to do to help Kirin, she would.

Spring met her gaze and finished. "Only if the demon comes back before the mountain kills my heart."

Guilt choked Nothing, for no good reason. Her throat closed with it, though Nothing pretended it was nausea from eating too much. She managed to ask, "Is your heart somewhere I could find it and restore it to you?"

"It's in the mountain," Spring murmured. "But if you take it, everything else will die."

"The mountain is already dead; that's why it had a demon, not a spirit."

"Not the mountain."

"The sorceress! If I take it, she'll die." Nothing wanted to throw something.

Spring nodded. Nothing touched the lowest of the pink orchids, bobbing beside Spring's jaw: just the tip of her finger to the tip of one of its long petals. She thought of the sorceress's mouth when she did, and Spring's matching pink lips.

"I don't care if the sorceress dies," Nothing said quietly. She knew it was a lie.

"I appreciate you asking about my heart," Spring replied just as quietly.

Nothing swallowed and stepped away. "What am I supposed to do today, while I wait for dinner with Kirin? May I see Sky again?"

"You may go wherever you like."

"I would like to see Kirin."

"If you can find him, you can see him."

"Ugh!"

Spring smiled slightly. "It is not my rule."

"The sorceress," Nothing said again.

"The sorceress."

It was so simply said that Nothing found herself touching Spring's hand in sympathy.

Spring brushed her knuckles to Nothing's palm, collected the empty tray, and left.

Nothing sighed heavily, thinking surely it would be more difficult to find Kirin than anything else. She put her fists on her hips. She supposed she should look for an exit. Once she had Kirin and managed to wake Sky, she'd need to lead them out of this mountain.

She left the chamber, skimming her hand along the corridor as she walked to the right. If the sorceress planned to bring Kirin to dinner, he would survive a few more hours.

"I need sunlight," Nothing said aloud. "A stairway up, perhaps, a little mountain lake would be nice."

If she had been the demon of this mountain, surely she could find what she needed.

Then again, if she was the demon, she had been yesterday, too, and that hadn't helped her find Kirin.

With no other direction, Nothing walked and searched, opening doors just as she had previously. She found the library again and wished to examine it, but could think of no good it would do either herself or her friends. She found dusty guest rooms and finally a staircase. It twisted both up and down, and she paused, smelling the cool air, wondering if there were a trick to it.

She went up.

The stairs were cut perfectly into the stone of the mountain, and the granite glittered with flecks of quartz that glowed enough for her to see. She wished she'd picked shorter skirts, but found a rhythm kicking the hem out as she climbed. It was almost fun, though it left her winded.

She emerged into a cavern cut with tiny alcoves, each home to a shrine or a statue. Every god whose name she knew was represented, from the Queens of Heaven to the gods of rain, and there were rain-forest spirit shrines too, and demon houses made of tiny bones. The center of the floor was carved with the many-petaled flower. Nothing skimmed her bare toe against the clean line of one petal. If she lay down and spread her arms, she might just touch either edge of the carving. Unlike most of the similar carvings she'd seen, here there was no inlaid gold or mother-of-pearl, no colored glass, no paint. It was simply a carving, as if it needed nothing else.

"It's a beautiful flower," she said.

Across from the stairwell entrance was a wide arch, and she went to it. The darkness beyond was a tunnel; at the end was a gentle light.

The air turned cold and smelled of grass and dirt.

Nothing walked faster, watching the growing light. It was another arch, leading toward brilliant green and blue.

She stepped out of the mountain and into a small tucked valley surrounded by grim black peaks. But scraggly grasses and tough spruce grew down toward exactly what she'd sought: a small lake the color of the sky.

And there were tiny pink and white flowers blossoming around the mirror lake in a pretty explosion. The breeze was as cold as snow, but in the light she could feel the thin warmth of the sun.

Nothing dashed toward the lake. Her bare feet numbed against the cold flowers and earth, pricked by sharp pebbles, but she liked the tickle of flowers and leaves and the wind pulling at her hair.

At the lakeside, dawn sprites hovered just above the water, dipping their feet in and buzzing over the surface in games of tag. Nothing had never seen anything more idyllic.

The sprites looked like tiny naked human children with orange and bright-yellow bodies and translucent wings sparkling in every shade from deep violet to red to vivid orange. Like the dawn sky.

"Hello," Nothing said. "May I swim in this lake, or drink of it?"

Three of the ten sprites zipped to her, wings abuzz, and studied her with the black eyes of bumblebees. "Ask Esrithalan," they said in unison.

"Who is Esrithalan?" she asked, wondering what powerful spirit had such a name. It occurred to her in a flash that it might be the sorceress's name, and what a boon that information could be, but the thought was dashed when the sprites sang, "The unicorn!"

A stunned Nothing looked around. There, within a copse of thin, trembling alders with golden leaves and gray whorls in their bark, a small creature knelt watching her.

Nothing walked carefully around the edge of the lake toward the unicorn.

It was delicate and gray-white, like clouds and ocean waves, or rain streaming down glass. The horn was impossible to miss, curving gently off its brow and full of so many colors it seemed almost a dull steel. Cute as a goat, proud as a pony, it had purplish eyes, solid as pearls, and its nose was a soft-looking pink. Its fur seemed downy, and Nothing wanted to touch it, pet her hand down its back to the small, sleek tail.

"Hello, Esrithalan," she said, breathless. "May I join you?"

"Yes," it said prettily.

Nothing knelt near enough to touch the unicorn but without

crowding it. "I'm Nothing," she said. It smelled of salt and brine.

The unicorn snorted. "Hardly," it replied.

"It's my name."

"Is it?"

Frowning, Nothing said, "Yes. It is."

"Is that what you are?"

She supposed she ought to have expected as much from the unicorn. They were avatars of the gods, according to priests: neither spirit nor living creature, not quite a god. Made of god-stuff, not aether nor matter. Nothing remembered Kirin liking the definition when they'd been taught it, and the phrase *god-stuff*. Because it was both generic and specific.

Nothing said, "The sorceress thinks I'm her demon."

"Are you?"

"I'm just a girl."

"What is just a girl?"

Nothing opened her mouth, then glanced down at her body, unsure what to say. She touched her lips, then her chest, and slid her hand down over a breast and let it fall into her lap. Everyone had assumed Kirin was a boy because of his body. Was she making the same mistake? Assuming she was a girl because of her body?

The unicorn closed its long-lashed eyes. It spoke as though it had overheard her thought: "If a body was all it took to be something, there would be no demons."

Nothing paused to understand. Demons were dead spirits and needed a new house, a new body, to exist. "Demons possess new bodies all the time," she murmured. "I don't feel like I'm possessed."

"I wonder what that feels like," the unicorn said.

"You aren't a very helpful unicorn," Nothing said.

The unicorn made a huffing sound she suspected was laughter.

Sunlight glinted off the lake, and Nothing sighed. Flowers bent and danced in the breeze and that breeze chased their ripples straight across the lake, marring the reflected sky with tiny wavelets. Nothing loved it here, too. There was so much she loved about the Fifth Mountain and its foothills and lava fields. Was that because it was beautiful, or because in another life it had been her home?

She drew a deep breath, focused on her chest and lungs, the weight of air against her stomach, and she listened to the brush of hair on her shoulders as she nodded, felt the press of her heels against her bottom, her bent knees, the line of her shins against the earth itself. Sunlight at the nape of her neck, the cinch of the sash holding her tunic tightly closed.

"I can't be a demon," Nothing said.

The unicorn said, "All right."

Relief melted her backward, until she lay in the grass beside Esrithalan, legs stretched toward the lake, hands under her head. Mountain breeze—the breath of the Fifth Mountain, Nothing thought whimsically—fluttered the alder leaves. They twitched and shivered like little drops of molten gold.

"What does it feel like to be a girl?" the unicorn asked.

Nothing answered without thinking: "Sometimes I feel like a mountain, but other times I feel small and like I'm being watched. Judged. Like I'll never be good enough."

"For what?"

"For anything," she whispered.

"That certainly doesn't sound like something a demon would say."

Anger surged up her spine. "What does it feel like to be a unicorn?" she demanded.

"Like being a unicorn."

Nothing groaned, but the answer deflated her anger. She took another deep breath, her chest lifting, and blew it out in a stream. Like the mountain breeze. Maybe it felt like this to be a mountain: the earth your body, bones of ancient crystals, blood like rivers of magma heating you up. Flowers and stones for skin and your mouth a lake. If she was a mountain, she wasn't a girl. Unless one could be both a girl and a mountain. Like Kirin was both a prince and a maiden. Her sleep-melting mind liked the thought.

The unicorn plopped its head onto her stomach, sighing like a weary dog. Nothing buried a hand in the silky fur at its neck and relaxed further. The air was cool and hazy, and the alder leaves flashed like tiny oval mirrors, catching light in a slow dazzle. The sun made the unicorn's horn into a curve of pure luminescence, a sickle moon.

For a moment Nothing thought she understood what it felt like to be a unicorn.

EIGHTEEN

W HEN NOTHING WOKE, SHE was alone. Annoyed at herself for not asking the unicorn more practical questions—about magic, about finding her way around the mountain—she got up and went to visit Sky.

But in the silent altar room where the warrior slept, with its ceiling of crystal rain, Sky was not alone. A person sat against the base of the altar, youthful and lean. Nothing couldn't tell if they were a boy or a girl, and in a moment of clarity left over from her time with the unicorn she decided it didn't matter. They seemed younger than her, maybe fifteen years old, though in a place like this was it even possible to judge age or gender or more elusive things like humanity? The sorceress looked like a strange young woman, but if the rumors of when she'd arrived at the Fifth Mountain were true, she had to be closer to one hundred years old!

"What are you doing here?" she asked darkly.

The youth opened vivid gray eyes that seemed to fill half their pale, narrow face. Sleek blond-white hair fell to their chin in fine, straight lines, and they wore a gray robe and gray trousers belted with white. They blinked up at her, then drew one knee up against their chest and hugged it to them with oddly long hands. "Guarding him," they said. They were barefoot too and had oddly long feet to match their hands.

"Is he in danger?" Nothing neared the altar, hunting Sky's sleeping face for signs of damage or trouble.

"Not from me," the youth said. "I admire him." As Nothing walked toward Sky's head, they tilted their face to follow her with their gaze. She glanced down at their watery gray eyes. The gray flecks in their irises shifted like tiny ripples. Definitely not human.

"Hmm," Nothing said, and touched Sky's cheek. He was cool, but not cold, and his chest rose and fell as smoothly and slowly as it had yesterday.

"Is he crying? His tears . . ." The youth trailed off wistfully.

Nothing put both hands on Sky protectively. "Selegan River spirit!"

The dragon stood too fast to be seen and stared imploringly at her. "I want him to live."

Nothing and the dragon were of a height, both slender and small, and for the briefest moment Nothing wondered if they were more the same than different. She bit her bottom lip and leaned her hip against the altar. One hand remained resting against Sky's chest. She stared at the dragon. "When you said 'I know you,' were you talking to me or to Sky?"

"You." The dragon frowned prettily. "Don't I know you? You seem familiar."

"Familiar how? Do I look like someone you know?"

"I am unsure," the dragon said. "The potential of the moment has passed—I might have been able to answer had you asked me then."

Nothing sighed in annoyance. Neither spoke for a moment, sizing the other up. Eventually she said, "Do you know where Kirin is?"

"Kirin," the dragon said slowly, then repeated it, the name deliberate and soft on their lips. "The beautiful maiden who is also a prince."

Nothing whispered, "The Beautiful Maiden Who Is Also a Prince," and the rightness of it felt like a name. Both identities true, neither negating the other. Maybe the two together made each other better—made each other more.

"Kirin," the dragon said, "is here in the mountain. I am compelled not to tell you where."

"Of course." Nothing released Sky's hand and sank to the floor, her back to the altar. She cradled her hands in her lap.

The dragon sat beside her. Their shoulder glanced against hers. Both of them stretched out their legs and looked at their four bare feet: two long and silver-white, two stubby and sandy-white.

"Are all dragons like you?" she asked, wiggling her toes. She'd been tempted to ask *What does it feel like to be a dragon?* What a day this was. What a place.

The dragon wiggled their toes too, slower. "Are all Nothings like you?"

Nothing giggled, surprised. "I've never met another Nothing."

"Oh. Well, then, no, and yes. Neither, too."

She laughed a little harder.

"Both no and yes, dragon and human, river and spirit. Dragon spirits are change. That's why we inhabit rivers and crossroads most often. Movement, shifting, fluid. More than both, not either-or: we're the places in between. Potential."

Nothing quieted as they spoke, closing her eyes. Between breaths she felt a pull and tug, to either breathe in or out, suspended there. Between two sides, between ground and air. "I would like to be a dragon."

The dragon lifted a hand into their silky straight hair and pulled out a short, curving feather. They offered it.

As Nothing took it between her fingers, a rainbow gleamed along the row of barbs. "Beautiful," she said, and reached up to pluck a hair from her own head. She offered it in return.

They didn't take it. Nothing, suddenly afraid she'd misstepped—and with a dragon—pulled her hand back and turned her face fully to them.

The dragon's water-eyes were huge. They seemed surprised.

"What?" Nothing demanded, too loudly. Though Sky was under a magical sleep, she feared waking him nonetheless and hushed herself. "What?" she whispered.

"Humans usually take gifts."

"Are dragons not allowed to do the same?"

"A trade is a bargain, not a gift."

"Or just . . . friendship," Nothing said, turning away.

"You are a strange human. Your people usually want something more from me. Power, riddles, never-ending fish."

"I only want Kirin." Nothing offered her hair again, and this time the dragon of the Selegan River took it. She lifted the feather they'd given her from her lap. It felt like a breath of moisture on a summer day. It was perfect, and she loved it as she loved so many things here at the Fifth Mountain.

Maybe it *was* where she belonged. With dragons and uni-corns and sorceresses.

She said, "The sorceress told me I'm her lost demon consort."

Beside her, the dragon went so still it was like a river freezing over in a single snap.

When she looked, she saw they stared down at the line of blackness that was her hair, slicing across their palm. They said, "She has been searching for her demon for a long time."

"Is it possible?"

"How should I know?"

"You're a dragon!"

"I know change and water, river to steam to cloud to snow. I know trickling and flowing. I know raging and vibrant, lustrous storms. But I don't know rebirth and creation." They stood, padded a few paces from her, and quite suddenly instead of a lovely youth, they were their dragon form again, filling the crys-tal chamber with undulating silver-white scales and rainbow feathers and triple tail. The dragon said, "When I shift my shape, I choose who to be, what to be, and make my seeming match my will and core. Inside I am always what I am: potential. Do you know what you are inside? Can you change?"

Nothing stood and held out her hands. She stared at the backs of them, the subtle gleam of sand-pale skin and wrinkled knuckles, the moon-white beds of her nails, and pretty pink shadows. In one hand, the dragon's feather curved away, flutter-ing lightly. She imagined feathers bursting from her skin, then a ripple of pebbled scales growing down toward her wrists.

She did not transform.

She said, "I'm not a dragon. I'm not a demon."

"You know what you are not."

"That's the easy part," she murmured.

"She loved it, you know." The dragon changed again, to their youth form. They stood directly before Nothing, watery eyes on hers.

She tried to respond, but found she did not know how, and touched the dragon's cool cheek.

"That's why she worked so hard to find the right magic to bring it to life again," they said.

Nothing let her hand drift down the dragon's cheek and fall to her side. "Did it love her back?"

The dragon only looked at her, as if to say she was the one to answer that question.

NINETEEN

INSISTENT TIDE CAME TO fetch Nothing for dinner. Finally! Nothing had begun to think the day would drag on and on—not that the Selegan River was poor company, but she needed to see Kirin.

First the old woman dragged Nothing back to her room, where a gown was folded over the makeup chair. Insistent Tide put her fists on her hips, glaring through her wrinkles at Nothing. "Strip," she ordered.

Taking her own turn at grumbling, Nothing obeyed. Insistent Tide thrust a cup of water at her and Nothing drank every drop. The cool water was refreshing, and she shook herself like a dog, rolling her neck and shoulders. She stretched her fingers and reached for the ceiling, then bent in half to touch the floor.

"Finished?" Insistent Tide asked.

Nothing stood and lifted her chin.

The old woman stared. Her long wrinkles shaped her face around her frown. But her dark eyes glittered with amusement. "New underclothes there," she finally said, pointing at some pale silk bits atop the smallest trunk.

Nothing put them on, wiggling her hips a little to appreciate the softness. The thin silk slip tied over her breasts and fell in a narrow shaft nearly to her knees. She smoothed the material against herself, enjoying the sensation. Insistent Tide brought a sleeveless under-robe nearly as thin, but in shell pink, wrapping it around her waist tightly. Over that went a pale-green jacket that left most of her collar bare, hugging her shoulders only a little. Then a set of black and silver wrapping skirts tied at her waist with a bright-green sash embroidered with white lilies. Nothing obliged Insistent Tide tonight by sitting at the makeup desk while the old woman braided and pinned a few pieces of her hair and used a silk-and-horn band to hold it all in place. Then she put coral red on her lips and green around her eyes. Nothing supposed the old woman thought she was being funny, using the same colors as Nothing's outrageous demon face the night before. This time they fit well with the gown.

"Do you have feathers?" Nothing asked, thinking of the dragon's feather. She'd left it with Sky, for he was the one who needed the dragon's friendship most.

Insistent Tide grudgingly supplied a few sleek green primary feathers. She tucked them into Nothing's hair in an off-center crest. "Strange," the old woman said.

"Perfect," Nothing agreed. She wanted to greet Kirin as prettily as she could, as it would be a pleasant surprise for him after so many weeks alone. He did like pretty things. Her chest felt tight with excitement. She'd missed him so much while he was gone on his summer trip with Sky, aching every day in the littlest ways, and then when the imposter returned, fear and uncertainty had overtaken her longing. But now:

she might vibrate herself through the floor with anticipation.

Insistent Tide gave her little black slippers, but as soon as Nothing was in the corridor, she took them off and continued to the geode room barefoot.

Her heart pounded as she entered; she searched every amethyst glimmer and violet shadow for Kirin.

But the geode was empty except for the same low, set table with the same thin golden cushions.

Nothing tapped her fingers against her thighs, wondering how long to wait and what she should do. Certainly not begin eating or drinking. She walked across the clear quartz floor, watching her toes peek out from the hem of her skirts, and imagined walking across the sharp facets of amethyst below instead. At the far edge, she crouched, relishing the slick of silk against her legs, and reached for the nearest spear of amethyst. Her fingers were cool against it! The crystal was warm and humming. And it was no constant hum, but a rhythm like a pulse.

Before she knew it, her own pulse answered, trying to match the slow heartbeat. Nothing closed her eyes, listening. It soothed her, dazed her, like instant meditation.

"Nothing," Kirin said.

She stood and whirled, nearly tripping on her skirts. There he stood: tall and lean, in a long robe of black and red, his trousers loose, hems falling over bare feet. He smiled at her, and Nothing dashed for him, ready to fling herself into his arms.

But she stopped.

Several feet away, she stood still and stared, pulse pounding, stomach rolling. Cold sweat beaded along her spine.

"Nothing?" He frowned. He stepped toward her.

Nothing parted her lips to say his name but couldn't.

He was perfect: vivid brown-and-gold eyes held hers, gently curled lashes blinking hardly at all. His skin was healthy, bright moon-white; his brows lifted elegantly; his hair fell over his shoulders in heavy black layers. He was still rather weedy in his height, not entirely grown into it. There was the familiar cock of his shoulders, and he leaned on one hip. His slightly pink lips tilted as he smiled at her.

His hands were relaxed, elegant and strong looking. It was him. Everything about him was him.

Her hair-bracelet wrapped his left wrist, just over the knob of bone.

And still Nothing could not say a thing. She could not take the final steps.

"Nothing?" asked the sorceress softly.

The word tore her eyes from Kirin to the sorceress.

Power radiated from her luminous face, the round prettiness of her copper cheeks and red lips overwhelmed by those monstrous eyes. Her black-brown-red hair was a mass of coils like tentacles snarled around her head. She wore bold green, blue, and black in lustrous layers, and a single fire-red gemstone hung on a chain over her heart, like a crystalized fist of blood.

She was entirely distracting from Kirin. That shouldn't have been possible.

Nothing forced her attention back to the prince. "Kirin?" she whispered.

"Who else would I be?" He came for her. "Nothing!"

She let him embrace her, flattening her hands on his ribs. He smelled like the mountain, and a sharp tea. His hair brushed her forehead as he curled around her, tightening his hold.

"No," she whispered against the warm spread of his silk-clad chest.

"No? You found me. You did it. I said Nothing would come for me, and you did."

Nothing pushed firmly away. The frown he gave her was only slightly confused, married with a growing irritation. Exactly the right reaction. Kirin would be irritated she wasn't behaving happy or even satisfied to have him again.

Exactly right.

She was still sweating coldly as she backed away and said to the sorceress, "This isn't him. It's another imposter!"

The smile that spread across the sorceress's lips was like an arrow in Nothing's heart.

"How do you know?" the sorceress asked gently.

Kirin crossed his arms over his chest. "You're being ridiculous."

Nothing pursed her lips as her eyes flicked to him again. "I'm sorry, but I know it's not you."

"I am perfect."

"He is perfect," the sorceress echoed.

"I know," Nothing said. "But it's not him."

"Go sit," the sorceress commanded.

Kirin immediately went to the table and flung himself down upon a cushion, leaning his long body back to prop on one elbow. He crossed his ankles and watched them arrogantly.

It hurt Nothing to see. But she knew.

The sorceress approached her like a stalking panther. "How do you know?" she asked again.

"I know him better than anybody." Nothing hugged her stomach as her only defense.

"Explain to me what gave him away."

"So you can make one to fool even me?"

The sorceress reached for Nothing, and Nothing jerked back just as her fingernails grazed her chin.

"I swear," the sorceress said, "I will not make another. If you tell me."

"I . . ." Nothing licked her lips and stared at Kirin. At the fake Kirin. She couldn't point to anything in particular. Each detail, as she thought of it, she realized was right. His smile, his attitude, his pose and the way he plucked a blueberry from a shallow bowl upon the table and popped it into his mouth. Everything was exactly as it should be.

Nothing's eyes pricked with tears. "I just know."

"It's because he's your master," the sorceress murmured in Nothing's ear, hovering just behind her: a cool presence, like a shadow blocking the sun.

"What?" Nothing held herself as still as possible. Eyes on the false Kirin, too aware of the sorceress breathing at the nape of her neck.

"You were my lost demon, Nothing, and when you were reborn, Kirin—your Kirin—somehow made you his. Named you, then bound you with the name he gave you. It's the only explanation for how you know it isn't him, for why you do not know yourself."

Nothing realized she was breathing too quickly. "He wouldn't. He's my friend."

"He might not have meant to if he did not know what you are."

"Only a sorcerer can bind a demon or a great spirit," Nothing said.

The sorceress laughed. "Kirin, more than anyone but his mother, has a sorcerer's potential within him. Not only because he is both a prince and the most beautiful maiden, primed to step into the aether between."

Nothing wanted to argue, but if anyone in the great palace was accidentally a sorcerer, it would be Kirin Dark-Smile. "That shouldn't be enough."

"No. But when you consider the Moon, it might have been."

"The Moon?"

"The great demon of the palace, Nothing. Bound by a powerful amulet to the empress, and to her heir, for generations."

"What?" Nothing whispered, confused. She didn't know what to do.

The sorceress touched her shoulder, gently turning Nothing to face her. "I think in retrospect, tender heart, that it was the only place you could be reborn. Inside another great demon's house. It must have been safe, like an eggshell, to hold you until you were ready. And Kirin Dark-Smile, because he was young, and you were young, and he partially bound to the Moon, already living in a twilight of sorcery, had just enough aether and instinct to give you a true name. Bind you."

Nothing sucked in a surprised breath. "I want my Kirin."

"Because you have to want him."

"No."

"Yes. He named you; he bound you." Something hard tinged the sorceress's words. Frustration, or anger, maybe. "He's powerful because he knows he doesn't fit where he is told he must." The sorceress smiled sadly. "That was my first step along this path too."

"What's your name?" Nothing demanded. "Tell me. If I was your consort, I must have known. Tell me again."

"Not while you are his. I won't let him use you against me."

Frustration clamped Nothing's teeth together. She made fists and squeezed until her bones hurt. "Give me something!" she cried.

The sorceress said, "Kirin helped me with this one."

"Helped you with . . ." Nothing glanced back at the false prince as he arranged blueberries in a line against the edge of the table, then ate them one by one. Lazily, with the affectation of boredom. It hurt her to see it. Under her heart, like a heat in her stomach. "Why would he . . . ?"

"To save The Day the Sky Opened. I bargained, and that is what he gave me for the warrior's life."

"He saved his own life with information about me and saved Sky's by helping you? Why?"

The sorceress shrugged a slender shoulder, her gaze sliding from Kirin to Nothing. When Nothing hadn't been looking, her pupils had shifted from red slits to plain black circles. Nearly human, except no human had a single bone-white eye. "He may be a baby sorcerer, but I am not."

"He gave you the bracelet," Nothing whispered. The one braided of her hair.

"He did. And suggested I try a fox spirit bound to this simulacrum. Last time I chose a crossroads spirit."

"To fool me."

"But, Nothing"—the sorceress lowered her gaze—"you were not fooled."

Nothing sank to the quartz floor. She knelt, staring at the false Kirin, in pain. It was an ache in her center, radiating out with biting fingers, pinching at her guts and heart, and it drove tears up her throat to fill her nose and eyes until her vision wavered with a smoky burn.

What name to give this feeling? Anger, hurt, betrayal?

She didn't know. *Nothing* would be better. To feel nothing, or merely the edges of what other people felt. She was a shadow, a slip of a girl dashing through the walls, climbing into secret chambers folded between rooms and corridors of the seven circles of the palace. Between the world and the world, anchored only to Kirin.

Nobody else had known Kirin was not Kirin. Not then, and certainly they wouldn't know now.

She couldn't explain it.

"I have to see him," she whispered. And she reached for the sorceress to plead.

The sorceress's eyes widened as Nothing touched the back of her hand.

Blackness swallowed her.

Inside the blackness was heat, and a flower. The flower opened and spilled more flowers, oblong, vivid pink and dark purple, falling in crests, into the blackness—no, born of it, falling into—

Nothing opened her eyes to the cutting curve of the amethyst ceiling. She was reclined in the sorceress's lap, held in the pool of her skirts, and the sorceress leaned over her, one arm around her shoulders. The strands of thick tricolored hair fell around Nothing, and both the green and the white eye shone with intensity. "Oh, I do not want to take your heart," she whispered.

"No." Nothing shoved away, awake fast. The sorceress did not try to catch her, and Nothing slid to the hard ground, half rolling onto her side. She breathed quickly, holding herself still, eyes shut, hands flat to the quartz floor. What had happened? Had she fainted when she touched the sorceress? Why? Nothing swallowed. From her position, bowed over the floor, she asked, "What happened?"

"I didn't mean to touch you," the sorceress said.

"You didn't. I touched you."

A rustle of silk taught Nothing the sorceress stood up. "I need it. You. To keep the mountain strong, to keep myself alive. Without the demon, the mountain cannot hold. My power wants yours. I know you. I . . ."

Nothing got to her feet, her back to the sorceress. She looked toward the table: Kirin crouched there like an animal, not like Kirin. On his toes, knees bent, his fingers tented against the floor. She shuddered. He grinned. The fox was obvious in him now. "Take that face away from him," Nothing said, and without glancing to the sorceress, she left.

In the corridor she tore at the bright-green sash and let it flutter behind her, then stepped quickly out of the skirts. She hurried, loosing the feathers from her hair, then untied the pale-green outer jacket, shrugging free. It, too, fluttered behind her: a shed skin, flapping wings.

Nothing ran in only the thin pink under-robe and silk slip, her shoulders bare and cold, her knees bare too. She passed her room, the library, Sky's altar chamber. She passed everything. "Down," she said, and found stairs.

She was not looking for Kirin now—she'd not been able to find him before.

Nothing was looking for herself.

The darkness, the flower, the pain. It was inside her but also here. Inside her mountain.

A string of power, razor sharp. When she thought of it too closely, it bit at her, and her insides seemed to bleed. She kept going.

Down.

The walls changed from granite to sleek obsidian, then layers and facets of huge crystal. There was no light, but she could see.

Nothing stopped. She pressed her hands to a flat face of quartz and pushed. Her hands sank into the crystal and she swept them aside: a door. She'd made a door. Of course she could do such a thing.

It was all hers.

The air froze, cold as death, and she walked through, into deeper darkness tinged with violet. Tinged red in the distance: she followed that.

She followed the string of razors inside her, the bleeding that drew her on. Down. Forward.

The heartbeat crashed into her.

Next, in the massive absence after that single pulse, Nothing understood that the heart the sorceress had used last to shore up the Fifth Mountain's power was nearly dead. Spring's heart, nearly dead. Without the demon come home, the sorceress would hunt again for a new heart. Or take Kirin's.

Down. The violet darkness gave way to red, then to a

shimmering greenish light, as though she were underwater.

The corridor opened into a chamber as huge as the third circle of the palace. Stairs curled around the edges, up and up, and in the center was a platform with more stairs leading toward it and away again. A plinth lifted in the middle of the platform, grown from the mountain.

Nothing walked up a set of stairs toward it, eyes stuck to the dark crystal. Inside, trapped like a dead butterfly, was a heart.

She stopped. To the left, far below, an archway glowed with a warmer kind of light. Firelight.

Making her way for that arch, Nothing felt the huge heartbeat again. It shook her bones and she nearly lost her balance, knees bending. But she stumbled on, caught herself against the arch, and everything righted itself.

Nothing stepped out of the huge chamber and into the firelit corridor. She could hardly think, knowing what lay ahead as she walked. Not as quickly as before, one hand touching the rough wall. It curved sharply and deposited her in a small chamber with glinting streaks of diamond veins and bursts of ruby. Behind a mouth of obsidian bars was Kirin Dark-Smile.

This time, it was him.

Torn and death-pale, he leaned against the wall, legs out before him. His velvety green dress was tattered, the red-black-silver embroidered flowers massive like bleeding wounds. Both his hands lay open to his sides, fingers curled loosely. His lips were drained of color, his cheeks hollow, and smears of blushing blue sank beneath his eyes. He was not beautiful. Streaks of ash smeared the left side of his face. His hair was lank.

But the ropes of white and sea-green pearls around his neck

glinted cleanly in the light of the single oil lamp in the cell with him. Beside it was a tangle of blankets, a bowl less pristine than the one in Nothing's room, and an empty plate.

Nothing crept nearer, as silent as possible, that she might stare for longer.

Her prince breathed shallowly but evenly. Sleeping.

Relief stole her breath, and a crescendo of love grew so loud in her bones she ached with it.

She wanted to brush his hair, kiss him awake, strip the filthy clothing from him and take him to that cold mirror lake to scrub every speck of dirt and ash and tears off his skin. Feed him, hold him, make him warm again.

The string of pain that had led her here thinned and vanished. She felt herself again. Right.

Nothing gasped as she realized it was all true: she was not quite human, and Kirin had bound her to him years ago.

His eyes snapped open, clear and brown as crystalized honey.

She crouched before the stone bars.

"Nothing," he whispered. "You're here."

"I'm here," she said dully.

With a wince and a groan, Kirin pushed off the wall, struggling to his knees. He crawled to her and leaned his shoulder against the bars. "Nothing," he said again. And he reached for her.

She gave him her hand. She couldn't help it.

His fingers were dry, the nails cracked, and she threaded hers with his, pressing until their palms were flat together.

"I knew you would come," he said.

"I'm sure you did."

Kirin frowned at her tone but held her gaze. "Is Sky here? Is he well?"

Nothing lowered their hands. "He was injured when he challenged the Selegan River dragon, but he is here, and alive. She says he's healing."

"The sorceress."

"Yes."

"Can you get me out of here?" Kirin tugged at her hand.

She shuffled closer to the bars. "Maybe."

"Maybe? Have you bargained with her? Or did you find your way here alone?"

Nothing remained quiet, studying him, sure it was him and hating how absolutely certain she was. It was all true.

"Kirin," she whispered, yearning for him to tell her there'd been a mistake.

He nodded.

"I slit the throat of the imposter she sent." Nothing paused at his hiss of surprise. "Then tonight I met another imposter, and I knew that wasn't you either."

He nodded again.

The pain was back, hot as a swallowed ember. "What am I?"

Kirin started to say, *Nothing*. She could see it in the shape of his mouth, in the pull of breath.

But he paused, and instead answered, "Mine."

TWENTY

NOTHING STARED AT HER prince for a long time. He allowed it, silent and still.

Eventually, she pulled her hand free of his. "How long have you known?"

Kirin sighed. "Known? Only since I came here. Guessed? Years."

"You didn't tell me."

"What could I possibly have said? That you'd believe?"

Nothing sat back, hugging her knees to her chest. "You could have tried. 'Nothing, you're a demon. Nothing, I bound you to me. Nothing, I know your real name!'"

"Nothing—"

"No!" She stopped him. "I'd have had to believe you. Because it's you."

"I don't think you're a demon."

Her scowl was enough to make him close his eyes. But he continued. "It's true. Maybe you were, but you're alive, and not possessed. You're not like the great demon of the palace or any other demon I've ever met."

"Maybe just because you bound me when I was a child."

"Demons are never children."

Nothing opened her mouth but found no argument.

"Don't you see? If you were a child, you aren't a demon. You might have been, before, in a different life, but you're new. And that's *amazing*."

She ignored the thread of joy in his voice. The thread of ambition. "I'm still bound. Capable of being bound."

It was Kirin's turn to scowl. On him, so exhausted and pale, it was more of a pinched expression. "Everyone is capable of being bound. By duty or love or blood. I am to be your emperor someday. Wouldn't you be bound regardless?"

"By choice."

"Truly? You think anyone has a choice? Did I? I was born as I am. A prince. I must accept the Moon one day and be emperor. Where is my choice? I can't be who I want to be, not all of me. Stop your self-pity and get me out of here."

She *wanted* to do what he said. She always wanted what Kirin wanted! Clenching her teeth, Nothing stood up and backed away for her own protection. "Sky chose you."

Kirin sucked in a shocked breath. "Sky loves me. That's different."

"Do you deserve him?"

"Nothing!" Kirin stood up, gripping the bars. "I'm sorry! I should have told you."

Her heart ached so badly as she stared at him. Her beautiful maiden who was also her prince. "What's my name?" she whispered.

And he actually hesitated! Nothing made her hands into fists and bared her teeth, but before she could scream at him, he said,

"I could tell you, but *she* might be listening, and I won't give her that power over you. As long as you're mine, she can't force you to do anything."

Nothing's knees wavered. It was all too much. "I want to be my own, not yours or hers."

"You should already know it—you were there when I gave it to you. You should remember."

"You must not want me to remember," she accused. "Or I would."

Kirin shook his head. "It—I don't think it works that way. I can command you directly if I use your full, true name, but the binding . . . I've studied it as best I can. . . . It's not one-way, Nothing. I'm bound to you, too. I want you to be safe and happy and strong. We belong *together*."

"Have you commanded me directly with my name?" Hysteria bit up her throat.

"Once."

"When?"

Kirin did not speak.

"Kirin Dark-Smile, tell me my name," Nothing demanded.

He kept his mouth shut.

"See?" Nothing clenched her fists. "It is not a two-way bond. You're my *master*."

"I'm human," he murmured. "I can't be compelled. Nor can a sorcerer. But I will tell you," he added, hands sliding down the obsidian bars. "If you ask me again. But she might hear it and use it. My binding is . . . amateur. She is a real sorcerer."

Nothing hesitated. "You didn't tell her, not to save your life or to save Sky's. You bargained other things."

Kirin shook his head. "I told her about you to save my life, and I—I helped her make the simulacrum to save Sky's. She didn't want your name. She never asked for it."

"Would you have given it to her?"

"I wouldn't have wanted to."

The truth tucked itself between his words, and Nothing nodded.

"Nothing."

"Kirin."

"I love you, Nothing. You're my best friend."

"Do I love you back?" she whispered. "Or do I just have to?"

The prince flinched. "I've never wanted you to love me because I said so."

She backed away. "You let me believe for years that I'm nothing."

"No, I never treated you like that! I didn't know—"

Nothing left. She ran back down the obsidian tunnel toward the heart chamber.

As she reached it, she slowed, panting. She put a hand over her heart.

"What am I going to do?" she whispered. She was so hot, but melting.

Nothing climbed a set of stairs toward the massive crystal and its trapped heart. The staircase curved over empty air: a ribbon of cut black stone.

She reached the platform. The crystal grew straight, as tall as her chest. It was smoky quartz, perfect gray-brown, and six sided, the tip a hexagonal pyramid. Nothing touched the sharp tip. She traced that finger down the smooth facet. Deep within the crystal, the heart blurred vivid crimson.

Her finger tingled, and she flattened her palm against the facet, welcoming the vibration of power. It slicked up her arm and to her own heart, pulsing into every extremity. Even her tongue tingled, then tasted like lightning and blood. Nothing carefully breathed the burned edge of the cavern air.

The heart pulsed.

Nothing gasped.

She turned and slid down the crystal to sit at its base. It was cold here, but she was warm.

This was the core of the Fifth Mountain. It should have been burning with power. Not cold, not fading. Desperation did not belong.

Anger clenched her jaw, chased by yearning.

It was the yearning that remained when she closed her eyes and leaned her head back against the crystal. She'd believed in being Nothing. The prince's nothing. She'd been content, at least, to exist in his shadows, small and unimportant to the world but intrinsic to him. Nothing would have lived in the palace forever, helping him with her information gathering, a support at his side. Knowing him.

But had she ever even wanted anything for herself?

She couldn't remember a time she'd wanted at all. Not adventure, not a title, not love or family.

"Nothing."

The sorceress.

Nothing opened her eyes.

The Sorceress Who Eats Girls waited on the floor of the cavern, far enough down Nothing would break her neck if she fell. Even in the dim, even from the distance, she could see the dark-green eye and the bone-white eye staring up at her.

"I found him," she said.

"I know. It isn't the only thing you found." The sorceress made no move to climb the stairs. She wore a simple black sleeveless robe that fell past her knees and close-fitting black trousers. That was all, but for the bloodred gem that hung at the hollow of her throat. Her hair was still elaborately knotted and braided, wound like tentacles. But no paint darkened her lips or her eyes. She was almost—almost—normal. Beautifully so, at least, with her round cheeks and long nose and wide, black lashes.

The sorceress folded her hands together before her.

Nothing said, "Spring's heart is dying."

"When you're here, I feel stronger."

"Because I was your demon. I was the great demon of the Fifth Mountain."

The sorceress nodded. "I know it." She touched her chest below the red stone. "Here."

"You don't know me. You can't love me."

"My heart is broken, but you can repair it."

"What spell did you do?" Nothing stood up. "To make life for your demon?"

"I used my own heart, of course."

Nothing gasped, hands flying to her chest. She laced them over the hidden flower-brand.

The sorceress said, "With my heart, my demon had to live. No sorcerer that I know of, in all the stories and lore, in all the books, has done what I did. I split my heart, one half to keep, one half to my demon. Mine struggles to beat, to keep all this"—the sorceress spread her arms—"alive with power. I need help. Other hearts to bolster mine. Until I find the missing half of my heart."

Nothing's pulse shuddered but remained strong. She slid her hands away, let them fall to her sides. How strange, how thrilling, to be told your heart is half of someone else's. A gift from a woman who loved you once. But Nothing felt whole. She said, "I've never had a broken heart."

"It isn't meant to seem broken." The sorceress smiled tenderly. "Neither is mine. We're meant to be together. Beating in rhythm."

That was so close to what Kirin had said! Nothing closed her eyes. "I don't love you."

"I don't love you, either."

Something akin to offense shocked Nothing into looking again. She stared down at the sorceress.

"Yet," the sorceress said. Then, "Will you marry me?"

"Are you joking? After . . ." Nothing scoffed and turned to flatten her hands on the heart-crystal.

"Stay, and I won't have to hunt another maiden's heart. Stay with me."

"Why didn't you ask for my name? He'd have given it to you, for Sky. Then you could make me stay."

"I don't want to be your master," the sorceress called, sounding almost angry. "I want to be your wife."

Nothing parted her lips, as if she could taste the edge of the sorceress's words, the slice of them as they sank into her heart after all. She liked the feeling. She liked the sorceress's plain seduction. But Nothing didn't know what she wanted. She never *had* known. It was the only question that mattered.

She said, "I am going to stay with you for three days. You'll show me everything. Magic. Power. The secrets of the Fifth Mountain. And then I will take Kirin Dark-Smile and The Day the Sky Opened and return them to the empress. You won't stop us from leaving. That is all I have to offer; otherwise steal my name and compel me."

"I accept your bargain," the sorceress said instantly.

TWENTY-ONE

S HE LEFT KIRIN IN the cell.

Nothing returned to her chamber with the red-and-pink door, needing to be alone in the only space that felt almost like hers. Insistent Tide waited. She clucked her tongue as she helped Nothing out of the thin robe and slip, into wool pajamas. It wasn't cold enough to need them, but Nothing found their comfort perfect as she curled in the nest. Insistent Tide blew a gentle breath up at the bat-bone chandelier, and the candles snuffed. "Good night," the old woman said.

It had to be nearly dawn.

She wasn't tired.

Nothing lay there, unsure what to think or feel or do. When her thoughts tilted toward Kirin, she dragged them away before she decided to let him go or forgive him—anything that might please him. Eventually she'd have to do both. But she wasn't ready to give him the satisfaction. She stared at the obsidian walls, tracing flickers of bluish light along their cups and cliffs, along the razor edges and curving planes. Obsidian was volcanic, she knew, and both strong and breakable, sharp and smooth. It made good blades, but they could shatter. She wondered if she could change it if she tried.

How did her power work? She'd have to ask the sorceress.

As she sank deeper and deeper into herself, Nothing stopped fighting the inevitable: she admitted to herself she believed everything. Once she'd been a demon—a great demon—but she'd been reborn a girl in the palace.

Believing it didn't exactly teach her what she should do about it, though.

She still felt small. Maybe not quite nothing, but not strong enough for all this, either.

"Nothing?"

The muffled voice came through the door.

"Come in, Spring," she said.

The girl entered, holding another tray of food. "Good morning."

Nothing grunted a little, indelicately climbing from her bed.

Today Spring was in white and red. Her orchids were peach colored, even tinier than before. They cascaded around the crown of her braid. Little black wisps of hair trailed down her long neck, and Nothing wanted to touch them. Touch her neck.

Then the girl met Nothing's gaze, with eyes brown and honey gold. The same honey color as Kirin's eyes. And a scar where a heart should be.

Nothing gasped. "Sorceress."

Spring's mouth fell open in shock. But not denial.

"You've been lying the whole time," Nothing said. "What was the point?"

"I wanted you to be comfortable," the sorceress said, unchanging. She remained Spring. "How did you know?"

There was such an echo from the night before, when the sorceress asked how Nothing knew the false Kirin was false. Nothing frowned, unwilling to answer that she just knew. It would suggest a closeness to the sorceress she'd not realized. She said, "Your eyes. They're just like Kirin's. It has to be an affectation. I didn't notice before."

The sorceress's shoulders drooped, but her smile was genuine. "I wanted you to be comfortable," she repeated. "Kirin makes you comfortable. Even unconsciously, you like these eyes better."

Nothing shook her head firmly. "Give me your real eyes, Sorceress. What I need is truth."

The sorceress let her honey-brown eyes slowly change: one evergreen, one bone white. Plain black, round pupils.

"Are these your eyes?"

"Now."

"What did they look like when you were born? Before you were a sorceress?"

"One green, the other brown and a little bit of rust red."

"That green?" Nothing focused on the evergreen eye. It was such a solid color, lacking variation but for a slight grayish outer ring. She liked it.

"Nearly," the sorceress whispered.

They stood facing each other, too near. Nothing caught her breath. "Make yourself as much of yourself as you can," she said.

The sorceress's black brows lifted in simultaneous arcs of amusement.

It was on Nothing's tongue to add, *please*, but she resisted.

"It's all real," the sorceress said. "My body. All the shapes and colors. It's all me. You are asking for what I was before, when I was not entirely myself. Because when I was only a girl, I was not entirely myself."

"But you're all yourself now?"

"Missing only a piece of my heart," the sorceress flirted.

Nothing's lashes fluttered before she managed to push down the rush of pleasure. She said, "Then make yourself the you that you prefer."

The sorceress smiled and the moon-pale color of Spring's skin darkened to cool copper, her cheeks rounded out, and her lips thinned. Her nose lengthened. She grew a finger of height. Her hips and breasts and belly swelled so that she was no longer a thin girl, but a willowy and lithe young woman. Her hair stayed braided, but red and brown streaks appeared among the black, and that single bone-white eye remained. It was how she'd appeared to Nothing both nights before, at dinner.

"Here I am," the sorceress said. Her red-and-white robes had lengthened and grown embroidered berries in green and gold. She seemed less innocent, more powerful. Not a maiden with a stolen heart but a woman who'd given hers to a cause. "This is more of how I feel today."

Nothing remained breathless. She felt young and weak, just a slip of a girl without even muscles, much less breasts, and soft skin and layers of hair silky to the eye and—Nothing stopped herself from touching one of the wisps curling against the sorceress's throat.

"Um," Nothing murmured. "Was Spring your name?"

160

"Sudden Spring Frost," the sorceress answered, wry and still amused.

"Um," Nothing said again.

The sorceress laughed brightly—a real laugh, Nothing thought, pleased. Full of surprise and sunlight. But then the laugh shifted, as the sorceress so easily shifted: the laughter became low, dark, full of promises.

Nothing shivered.

Taking pity on her, the sorceress turned to set down the tray of food. She poured tea and offered it.

"Will you eat with me?" Nothing asked, approaching. There were flaky-looking cakes, pears, thin slices of cold beef, and the pepper cheese.

The sorceress acquiesced, and they ate.

Nothing said, "Kirin should be released from the cell. He won't cause trouble for these three days."

"Free him, then," the sorceress answered. Spring. Or Frost: Nothing thought that might be more appropriate. "Your power responds to itself better and better. See if you can."

"I shall." Nothing licked pear juice from her fingers.

"And I will show you my library this afternoon, answer whatever questions you like, and then you'll join me for dinner." The sorceress paused, as if expecting Nothing to reply.

So she asked, "Did you tell the truth when you said you bargained for all their hearts?"

"Yes," answered the sorceress. "They got something in return. But the result was the same: Their hearts were mine, along with the magic of their choices."

Nothing nodded, pressing her fists together in her lap to

control the flare of fear. She had to remember, when she felt drawn to the sorceress, that murder kept this mountain alive. Attempting to sound calm, she said, "Twenty-three hearts in less than twenty years seems . . . inefficient."

"Twenty-three!" the sorceress cried. "Twenty-three, that is . . ." The sorceress's distress translated quickly into amusement. "I have taken only eleven hearts—but I seem to have been blamed for more vanishing girls," she drawled.

"Oh." Nothing swallowed. It shouldn't have made a difference. One murder or twenty-three murders—or eleven.

Laughing softly to herself, the sorceress said, "My heart, I will leave you to your business, to Kirin. But I will find you this afternoon for my turn."

Nothing nodded absently, still reeling.

But after standing alone for a few moments, she marched out of her chamber in her pajamas. She returned directly to the core of the mountain, carefully bypassed the throbbing, dying heart.

In the obsidian room with its thin bars, Kirin sat, glowering. He did not leap to his feet to see her, but lifted his chin and glared.

Nothing stopped before the bars, upset both that *he* was upset and that it bothered her at all.

Kirin did not move, pretending to be comfortable, in command. She knew the look on his face and the catlike grace of his drooping shoulders. One leg stretched out, the other knee was drawn up and his wrist rested against it, hand limp. A pose of lazy contentment.

"Don't you want out of there?" she asked, trying not to love him.

He shrugged.

"I will take you to Sky."

He looked away, the line of his jaw tightening.

"I'm not the one being cruel," she whispered.

Kirin pressed his lips together and slowly stood. He walked on bare feet to the bars. Even in his tattered old dress, he was regal. Her eyes were level with his chin, and she glanced down at the strings of green and white pearls wrapping his neck like garlands.

"I've never been cruel to you," the prince said gently.

"Come out," she said, touching the bars. "Let him out," she said, focusing on the mountain.

The obsidian melted away.

His breath caught, and when she looked at his honey-brown eyes, they were filled with something difficult to read. Surprise and wariness and something else. Excitement?

He stepped out, and before she could move, his arms were around her and he hugged her desperately. His mouth pressed to the crown of her head, his breath hot on her scalp.

Nothing froze a split second, then allowed herself to lean against him. He smelled terrible, but he was warm and tough in all the places she expected, his long arms familiar. Kirin Dark-Smile, finally home. Or she was home: she belonged with him, because that was her nature.

"I don't like this feeling," she whispered.

"I do. I missed you."

"I missed you too, but I don't know if it's real."

"Nothing." His arms tightened. "I was eight years old when I named you, when I bound you, and I didn't know better. I just liked you and *saw* you. Sensed you were different, but I thought it was different like I was different. We were the unexpected—together."

She believed him. Only, a tiny voice wondered if she believed him because she had to. "I'll never know myself so long as I'm bound to you."

He said quietly, but with force, "I want you to be yourself. I want you to feel your own feelings. Believe that. Even if I tell you your name and the sorceress doesn't overhear, it won't free you. You already know it, somewhere inside your memory. If you didn't, how could it command you? There must be another way to break this . . . binding."

Nothing closed her eyes, hoping it was enough. "You stink," she said as she pulled away.

Kirin hesitated. "Should I clean up before—is Sky safe?"

"He can wait another hour," Nothing reassured her prince.

She led him away from the obsidian cell, though the dark tunnel and into the heart chamber. When he slowed down, staring at the curved stairways and the central platform, she took his hand and tugged him on. Kirin followed, though he hummed in slight censure, for he disliked not being the one in charge. It felt good to deny him, just a little.

"Are you wearing pajamas?" he asked, halfway back to her room.

She'd forgotten, but she nodded. In her room she pointed to the trunks. "There's a never-ending, it seems, supply of fine clothing. Choose some, and we'll go up to the mirror lake. For me, too, if you please."

Kirin moved quickly but caught himself up staring at his

164

reflection in several of the mirrors. "Queens of Heaven," he seethed. "I've never looked so terrible."

Nothing laughed outrageously. She clutched her stomach and bent over with glee.

The prince narrowed his eyes at her, staring for a good long moment, before turning sharply. He flung open the largest trunk and began lifting out swaths of silk and sheer linen, embroidered jackets and skirts and slippers in every color. Nothing brought him water when she'd recovered, and he drank, coolly meeting her eyes.

"Let's go," she said, unapologetic.

Kirin grabbed an armful of clothing and eagerly went with her.

They climbed up to the cavernous chapel with its alcoves and god-statues. Kirin flicked his eyes around but wasn't distracted from the promise of sun and a bath. Nothing almost smiled at his single-mindedness as they hurried through the long corridor and out into the cold daylight.

"Beautiful," Kirin said, footsteps slowing but not quite stopping.

The valley was exactly as it had been only yesterday, and Nothing gulped a great breath of fresh air. The sun cut through a cloudless sky to glare off the mirror lake in thousands of painful ripples. Nothing felt the presence of that light slicing through her, and somehow filling her up too. She went after Kirin and reached the bank just as he'd stripped completely and dove into the water.

"Esrithalan?" she called, looking toward the copse of alders. The unicorn did not seem to be there.

She knelt against the damp pebble-sand and brushed a petal of a cluster of purple balsam growing in spindly bunches at the edge of the water.

Out in the lake, Kirin emerged with a yell. He shook his head, flinging hair and water. Nothing smiled, almost deciding not to bathe herself because of the cold. But he lifted an arm and waved at her. "Come on, Nothing!" Then he sank again, treading water.

With a little sigh, she stripped and rushed in, better to get the freezing part over with.

She ducked under the cold waves, scrubbing at her face and hair, spinning to let the water under her arms and behind her knees, to caress her belly and spine and thighs with its icy tentacles.

Kirin found her, his hands hot compared to the water. He grabbed her waist, then her hand, and they swam together, splashing to the center of the mirror lake.

Nothing tilted her face to the sky, staring wide-eyed at the vast blue. It was edged with mountain peaks like teeth, and she imagined this lake the throat of the Fifth Mountain, the valley its lips and tongue. It closed its jaws around her and Kirin, and she held tighter to his hand.

The prince looked up too, wincing at the brightness. "Isn't it remarkable to be here?" he said, breathless with wonder and exercise.

"I belong here," she said.

"Nothing."

She looked at him. Kirin, high cheeks blotchy pink, lips white, eyes wide and somehow just as vast as the sky. His hair hung like black seaweed around his face, drifting against the surface of the water.

"You belong with me," he said.

Nothing thought suddenly of diving deep, dragging him with her until he had to breathe the cold water. She could, she thought. He would die.

The mouth of the mountain was her mouth, and she could swallow him whole.

For a moment she wanted it.

She wanted it like a fire wanted kindling.

But the lake was too cold and her body numbed, like her skin had diffused out into the water, leaving only her blood and muscles and bones, her heart. Her skin became the lake itself.

Kirin pushed closer, frowning as he took her face in his hands. The shock of his touch on her face put her skin back where it belonged.

Nothing gasped and held his wrists. Her legs kicked hard to keep her at the surface, and she felt the swirl of water as Kirin did the same. "Let's dress," she said.

He nodded and let go.

Was that what it meant to believe she'd been a demon? Nothing wondered terribly as she swam. To so suddenly think murder! Drowning. Kill her oldest friend? Who did she love more than Kirin in all the world? Nobody. Her pulse raced and she was grateful to find the sinking shore with her toes and climb out fast.

Kirin was right behind her, a hand between her shoulder blades. He offered her a cloth for drying and wrapped one around himself too. He was quiet, but stared at her, studying her with a very knowing gaze.

They dried and dressed. The prince had brought Nothing a

silky blue tunic, black trousers, and a sash to tie it all together. She finger-combed her hair, digging her bare toes into the spiky grass.

When she looked again, Kirin was buttoning a dark-red robe over his shirt, one with a high collar and full skirts that hung past his knees and rustled like a gown. It hugged his ribs and shoulders, baring his arms. The color made his eyes liquid gold, and he twisted his hair into a knot atop his head, tying it with itself.

"You look cold," Nothing said, noting the pebbled skin of his arms.

"I look beautiful," he replied.

Nothing's mouth twitched, and she let herself smile. She thought, *The Beautiful Maiden Who Is Also a Prince.* "You could be a sorcerer," she said.

Kirin tilted his head in dismissal. "I will be the Emperor with the Moon in His Mouth."

"But you could leave it, learn magic. The sorceress believes it. You're like her, she said."

"How so?" he demanded, flaring with anger.

Nothing glared at him for speaking to her like that. She'd never glared at him before.

The prince smoothed his features. "How so?" he asked more carefully.

"It's what you said about us. You're unexpected. So am I. Not what we seem, and you step fully into that." Nothing twisted her lips. "That's where power waits, she said. Potential. Between edges or dualities."

"Sorcerers are outsiders. I don't want to be forced out of society for my . . . potential," Kirin said. He lifted his chin in an arrogant pose. The sun cast him in vivid contrast: black hair, white skin, red dress. "I want to be what I am *and* belong."

Nothing nodded. "What else do you want?"

"Sky. Queens of Heaven, I want him. And I want you at my side too. I want to go home and put on the trappings of men and women, however I like, and I want people to admire me. I want to be myself, I want to show myself to the entire empire, and I want the Moon. I want a vast family, Nothing, and I want to make the empire flourish."

"They'll say you're not pure if you show them yourself. Take the throne from you."

"After the investiture ritual, they can't. Then I'll be acknowledged by the Moon, and no priest or witch or courtier will be able to strip me of my ambitions."

"The Moon," Nothing whispered, recalling what the sorceress had said, that the Moon was the great demon, and it was bound to the palace and the empress—and her heir. "That's the name of the great demon of the palace."

Kirin studied her for a moment; then he said, "Yes, or part of its name, at least. I won't know its true name until the investiture. But I was told, under great secrecy, that the prosperity of the empire relies upon the bond between the empress and the great demon. Part of the bond is the continuation of the line, and when I was born I was marked for it. The investiture is the next point of the ritual, when I am accepted pure and strong by the Moon."

"You risked more than yourself when you—this summer with Sky." Nothing wasn't sure if she admired his brazen courage or was horrified.

"No," Kirin said firmly. "I have spoken at length with the demon itself, though it rarely answers well, but I know—I know in my heart, Nothing—that what we have come to define as purity is not something that concerns the great demon at all. My secrets are dangerous because of the rules of our people, not the Moon."

She stared at him, believing him. He was radiant in his certainty. That made him easy to follow, to believe in. "I'll get you home, Kirin. In three days, we'll be free."

The prince's luster faded. "I don't want you free of me."

She lowered her gaze to the hem of his dark-red gown. His bare toes sank into the rough grasses. The beds of his toenails were bluish.

He said, "I don't know how to break a binding I don't remember creating. And do you know what else the great demon has told me? That a demon can be mastered, but a great demon must agree."

"You're making excuses. I'm not complicit in this bond. I didn't know—I couldn't have agreed."

Kirin lifted his brows as if to say, *I didn't know, either, so . . .*

Nothing pursed her lips. "We need to get inside. Did you bring slippers?"

He had, and put them on. They dragged the rest of the discarded clothing and their old tatters with them. Kirin wrapped his pearls around his neck again.

"You gave the imposter the bracelet of hair."

Kirin skewed a glance at her. He opened his mouth to say something scathing, no doubt, but paused. Glancing at their feet, he seemed to summon courage, and met her gaze again. "I had to save Sky."

Nothing nodded, hurt but still understanding.

"I had to," Kirin said again. "I don't need to worry about you, but I always worry about him."

"He's strong."

"I wouldn't be, without him," Kirin whispered.

Nothing wrinkled her nose in disbelief.

"Don't tell him, please."

"You should."

The prince grimaced, but didn't disagree. They continued on, and he said, "You weren't born of a mother, were you? So the hair was just between you and me, not a mother you never had."

It hadn't occurred to her. She stopped in the shade of the chapel cavern, surrounded by gods and monsters carved of crystal, obsidian, sparkling granite. They all stared at her, judging.

"It mattered," she said.

"It was a love token, I know that," he insisted. "And it saved Sky. Thank you."

Nothing hooked her finger under the black strands encircling her own wrist and jerked with all her strength. It cut into her skin painfully, but snapped. Nothing let it fall to the floor of the cavern.

TWENTY-TWO

THE DRAGON SLEPT IN its dragon form, twined several times over around the base of the altar. It woke the moment they entered, lifting brow ridges to reveal its spectacular water-gray eyes.

Kirin stopped, lips parted, unafraid but desperate. Nothing realized he was looking past the dragon at Sky.

Had he even noticed the river spirit?

Nothing said, "Selegan, do you remember Kirin Dark-Smile? May he approach?"

But the prince was already crossing the floor. The dragon's scales rippled, and its wings unfolded, drawing in two wide arcs over the altar. It lifted itself upright, claws against the stone, and crouched across Sky. It did not threaten, merely watched Kirin curiously as he halted.

"The prince," the dragon said.

"Hello, Selegan River spirit," Kirin said coolly.

The dragon vanished, replaced in the very instant with the youth, wide-eyed and silver-blond. They tilted their head sideways.

Kirin bowed shallowly, and the dragon returned the gesture. To Nothing it seemed two powerful spirits greeted each other as equals.

"He fought me for you," the dragon said.

"He shouldn't have, but I am glad you both survived."

Nothing walked to the head of the altar and put her hands on either side of Sky's face. He was warm and slept with the same deep peace as before. His face was less sunken, the color better, only a little darkened under his eyes and pale around his mouth. "Wake up!" Nothing commanded.

Sky's eyes flew open and he gasped in pain, wincing as he tried to sit.

"Sky," said Kirin, shocked, and Nothing reached for Sky's shoulder. The warrior slumped back against her hands, one of his arms wrapping his left side.

"Aren't you better?" Nothing demanded.

But Kirin was there, standing beside the altar with a hand barely touching Sky's forearm. The prince breathed carefully, expressionless except the anxiety flaring his nostrils and the hope in his honey eyes.

"Kirin." Sky leaned back onto his elbow, propped there, and with his other arm reached for Kirin. He touched Kirin's mouth, brushing strong fingers tenderly at the prince's bottom lip.

Nothing looked quickly away.

"Is it you?"

Kirin said, "It's me."

The dragon came to Nothing's side. It murmured, "That was chaotically done."

Nothing pursed her lips, annoyed. "I had no instruction."

Then Sky said her name, and she turned back to the altar, bracing herself.

Sky put his hand on her cheek, cupping her face. His brow was low, his brown eyes intense. "Are you well?"

She nodded. His fingers tightened briefly against her, uncoiling her nerves. He was glad to see her; she didn't know why she'd been afraid.

"I'm starving," he said, swinging his legs off the altar. He groaned softly, favoring his left side. His back was bare, as was the rest of him. His muscles rippled as he perched at the edge, blanket draped over his lap. Nothing traced the line of his spine with her eyes, the broadening of his torso and shoulders; blotches of faded greenish yellow marked bruises, but there remained no scabs or remnants of open wounds. Only his old purple scars.

She glanced up and met Kirin's gaze over Sky's shoulder. The prince had been doing the same, cataloging injuries. Nothing said, "There is plenty of food here, and we'll find—or ask for— some clothes."

The dragon piped up. "I can go for such things. I would like to, warrior."

Sky hesitated, then dropped his head in thanks. "You honor me, Selegan River."

"You were a fool," Kirin said sharply. "To attack it."

Sky tapped his fist against Kirin's chest. "I thought . . ." He sighed gruffly and flattened his hand across Kirin's heart. His fingers reached far, being so large, splayed possessively against the deep-red gown. Kirin covered the hand with his own.

"Sky," Kirin said.

"What's happened? How did we get here?"

"You were asleep, healing, for . . . three days?" Nothing said.

"Three days." Sky glowered.

Kirin's whole body suddenly twitched, and he leaned forward to kiss Sky. The jagged movement spoke loudly that he'd been holding himself back the entire time they'd been in the room.

Nothing left in the dragon's wake, hurrying before either could notice and call out. She darted from the chamber and pressed her back to the rough wall of the corridor. Eyes shut, she swallowed the longing that threatened to overwhelm her again. Not for either of them, not for what they had, but for something. Something of her own.

She wondered if the great demon of the Fifth Mountain had wanted anything.

"I'll have to ask the sorceress," she whispered to herself.

"I'm here."

Squeaking her surprise, Nothing flung away from the wall, whirling to face the sorceress.

A private smile graced the sorceress's lips. Nothing glowered, hating to be caught out asking for her.

"Would you like to see my library now?" the sorceress asked innocently. She held out her hand.

Nothing slid hers against the open palm.

TWENTY-THREE

THE SORCERESS'S TOUCH WAS cold and dark, and Nothing closed her eyes. There was a soothing note to the darkness that she enjoyed, like the tension of a delicious promise.

"What does it feel like to you?" the sorceress asked.

Nothing frowned and pulled her hand away.

A sly smile brightened the sorceress's face. She reached slowly toward Nothing, and when Nothing didn't reject it, the sorceress's fingers gently skimmed her jaw.

Darkness flickered and snaked along the edges of Nothing's self, in her peripheral vision but also somehow in other senses. Something in her reached for it, and she told herself it was curiosity. But it was more than that: it was aspiration.

"To me your touch is warm," the sorceress said. "And full of firelight."

"Oh," Nothing whispered, longing. She liked it.

"Do you like it?"

Nothing gasped and pulled away again.

The sorceress nodded and turned to lead Nothing down the corridor.

"Sorceress?"

She paused.

Nothing asked, "Where does my power come from?"

"The aether. That is where all magic comes from."

The sorceress turned to go again, but Nothing said, "I thought demons were cut off from the aether."

"Not great demons," the sorceress called over her shoulder.

Reeling a little, Nothing tried to walk as smoothly as the sorceress, who seemed to glide through the obsidian corridor. The sorceress wore a long, elegant gown in pink and black, her arms hidden in trailing sleeves, and tiny heeled slippers on her feet. She'd left her tricolored hair down but for a few pieces wound with creamy orange orchids. The flowers were exactly the size of her mouth.

Nothing wrinkled her nose and forced herself to think about eleven murdered girls before she thought about kissing the sorceress.

Before too long the sorceress brought her into the library with its vaulted ceiling, narrow wooden shelves, and long tables displaying massive books, skulls, elaborately carved boxes, jewelry, and weapons. More, but Nothing was overwhelmed at cataloging it. She drifted down between two shelves that reached nearly to the toothy, glittering stalactites of the ceiling and touched the spines of many books: some leather bound, some cloth, some bound in metal and scaly skin and possibly worse. Magic books, she thought, though others were thin and marked like accounting books. Some were stamped with the empire's sigils, others text and characters Nothing did not recognize.

"Where did you get all of this?" she asked.

"Here and there, what is mine. But much of it is yours and collected before I ever set foot inside the mountain."

Nothing whirled. "None of this is mine. Your demon is gone, and so, as its wife, it all belongs to you now."

"Yes, it—"

"No." Nothing shook her head and stood her ground as the sorceress stepped close. "No matter what I might have been before, I am no longer that. I was reborn. I was *born*. I was a child and grew up, and I am not your demon consort."

"Your heart, though, is half of mine," the sorceress murmured.

Nothing couldn't dream of how to answer that. She stared, wide-eyed.

The sorceress studied Nothing, standing so near Nothing could see hints of gray and yellow in her bone-white eye, like ancient cracks in old ivory. The green eye had gray in it too, like cemetery stones overgrown by the rain forest. Long-forgotten dead. The sorceress said, "Very well."

Then, politely, she stepped back. "It is a pleasure to meet you, Nothing of the Great Palace—or is it Nothing Dark-Smile?"

Nothing swallowed nerves and nodded firmly. "'Nothing' will suffice."

"Nothing will suffice!" The sorceress laughed three times, *ha ha ha*. Each sound was a deliberate choice.

"It has my entire life."

"Then welcome to my mountain. I am the Sorceress Who Eats Girls."

"Why not Sudden Spring Frost?"

The sorceress let her face fall into a gentler expression. She said, very softly, "That has not been my name in quite some time."

Nothing turned away to hide her feelings, picking a book at random. It was thick, bound with a soft dyed-blue leather. She dragged it out and had to use both arms to hold its weight. The cover was blank, offering no clues as to the insides.

"That is a complete journal of King Lithex of the Hintermarsh, one of the out-kingdoms the empire conquered centuries ago," the sorceress said. "Before the Fifth Mountain died and the empire's boundaries withdrew inside the circle of mountains."

"Heavy to write in." Nothing balanced the corner of the book on the edge of the shelf so she could use one hand to swing open the cover. The front page was yellowing and illustrated with several scepter-like objects.

"Collected works, put together after his death. There are translation notes in most margins, but if you cannot read Feril characters you won't get far. Let me show you the shelves in our tongue and those based in Old Gaulix that you might sound out."

Nothing turned a thick page and touched the lines of Feril characters in columns down the page. She slammed the book closed and hefted it back into place. The sorceress led her to the next row of shelves and said, "Here are histories and biographies of the empire. Many you'll be able to read, though there are a few externally sourced. I find such perspectives relieving sometimes. And next"—she gestured on—"books about places and people outside the mountains, but written for the empire. Those are the shelves with the highest volume of texts you'll be able to read right now, though there are many throughout the library. I don't divide by language in the other sections, for magical studies or philosophy, flora science, and the study of spirits, demons, and living creatures."

With each term the sorceress pointed in a general direction, and Nothing marked what she could, though didn't think in three mere days she'd have much time for reading. "Do you read Feril?" she asked.

"I was learning and have kept up my studies, though they are more tedious than they had been."

Nothing began to ask why but realized: the demon. The demon had been teaching the sorceress languages, history, and anything she'd liked to know. When the demon disappeared, she'd lost more than a consort.

The sorceress had moved on, toward the far wall where something like a hearth was cut into the stone. It gaped empty like an arched mouth, tall as the sorceress and without a grate for wood or any iron stove. She touched a protruding crystal and the hearth began to glow soft yellow, lighting up the smoky quartz coins and jagged crystal teeth inside. "This is where I like to read," she said, glancing back. A single chair waited beside her, low and plushly cushioned, wide enough to curl her legs up with her or to share between two.

Staring at the chair, Nothing imagined falling asleep there, book in her lap, head snug against her own arm. She had a pile of pillows in her abandoned bath in the fifth circle of the palace and two books all her own. One was filled with spirit fables; the other told the tale of a long-dead princess, Heir to the Moon, who went on a quest to each of the then—Five Living Mountains. Kirin had given them both to her and had insisted she could borrow anything from the empress's library. But Nothing usually read only snippets hiding in corners of the library itself, rather than bring books into the damp old bath. Besides, what were books when she could listen to Kirin tell stories, Kirin recite what he'd learned from his own reading, from his tutors?

Would Nothing have liked books better if she hadn't been bound to her prince?

The sorceress was watching her patiently.

"Is knowing my name all it will take?" she asked. "To be free?"

"No, but it is a necessary piece. Your name is merely the key to the bond. You must know it, deep inside you, or it would not bind you together; it could not command you. You must remember the name—the key—in order to unlock yourself. For like a key, it has the power to lock and unlock under the right circumstances. If you are strong enough to fight him." The sorceress spoke as if it did not matter to either of them.

"Why do names even matter?"

"We use names, some words of power, to manipulate the aether. Our voices are the most powerful tool any of us have. What is something if it does not have a name? The stronger the name, the more true it is, the stronger the thing it names. Priests can send ghosts to Heaven with true-name amulets because the amulet focuses the name better than the poor ghost possibly can. Sometimes a name's meaning can change, especially with complicated creatures like humans or demons or sorcerers. Witches bond with their familiars by their names, or master demons with the same." The sorceress licked her lips thoughtfully, making Nothing's pulse pick up, and she said, "A name is the ultimate house—it is where our essence lives."

"That is why demons can be mastered by their names, because they don't have real houses of their own? And ghosts, too?" Nothing guessed. "But spirits choose their own names, and . . . greater demons, too? That is why spirits and great demons must agree to be mastered."

"You let them make you into nothing," the sorceress said gently.

"It protected me more than it hurt me," Nothing said, and when the sorceress's mouth dipped grimly, Nothing realized she'd said it like it was over. That name had protected her in the past, but no more.

"Names can change," the sorceress said gently. "If a person chooses to become something new, to transform. That is a magic we all share."

"If you won't tell me your name, will you tell me what the demon called you?" Nothing asked.

Surprise flashed through the sorceress's eyes, more in her green than in the bone white. Then she pressed her lips together in an amused, flat line. "My demon called me *child* and *impetuous creature* and finally, *sweetheart*."

Nothing laughed a little. *Impetuous creature* made the sorceress seem youthful and wild. But then, the great demon of the Fifth Mountain had been much older than the sorceress. The thought was disconcerting and wonderful. She asked, "What else should I see in your library, Sorceress?"

"What else do you wish to see? Wander, look. When you have a question, ask."

"You have only two and a half more days with me," Nothing said. "Are you certain you wouldn't rather be more direct?"

"This is how magic works: you find it yourself." With that, the sorceress stepped into the quartz mouth and vanished.

Nothing gaped. She huffed in frustration. Then she marched to the nearest shelf—magical studies—and chose a slender volume with tiny glass droplets glued to the spine. She opened it to an elaborate illustration of what appeared to be dancing mushrooms and dawn sprites wearing garlands of flowers. She paged through more paintings of magical plants and creatures. It seemed to be a book of brief stories that mostly was an excuse for beautiful art. Nothing chose another book and then another, standing against the shelf to read bits and pieces she could understand about flower spirits and the behavior of clouds. In the next aisle she read the first chapter of an autobiography of a sorcerer of the Second Living Mountain, long dead—it began with a recounting of the process by which the sorcerer bonded with its great spirit, and Nothing was stunned by how boring it sounded. She carefully did not open a book with an embossed mouth on the cover, filled with razor teeth, and after that moved to the display tables.

There was a jar with preserved eyeballs, and that seemed right for a dead mountain's library. Beside it was a jeweled box holding tiny chipped color flakes that Nothing realized had to be scales from butterfly wings. She found bones, scrolls of leather tied with leather thongs, petrified wood with beautiful red-gold-green rings, crystals growing in the shape of flowers, and more bones, tipped in gold and silver. None of it drew her, though she thought about the butterfly wings and how they'd been harvested, how they'd been pulled into such tiny scales.

Finally, she picked up a comb made of yellowing antler, with tiny characters carved into the tines. She marched to the hearth and, without hesitation, stepped inside.

Nothing found herself instantly standing in a five-sided chamber with glinting crystal walls that slanted up and together into a central point. There was no crystal mouth on this side. No doors at all.

The sorceress crouched against the smooth crystal floor, carving a huge diagram into the crystal with a shining crystal wand.

"You made it," the sorceress said without looking up, her voice strained. "Do avoid stepping on my lines."

Nothing instinctively hopped away, looking down, but there was no line beneath her feet: the nearest began several paces from her bare toes. "What is it?"

"A spell for long sight." The sorceress crab walked on the balls of her feet and one hand, the other trailing the wand with her, slicing through the smoky crystal like it was cheese. Nothing stared at the controlled grace, the slow, precise steps the sorceress took, and her concentration that seemed to vibrate through the air.

When the sorceress reached the edge of her diagram, she blew a low note through pursed lips and linked the line she'd been cutting with another. Nothing felt a tingle, and then it was gone. The air was still.

The sorceress leaned back on her heels, resting her elbows on her knees in perfect balance. She looked up. Sweat gleamed on her forehead and cheeks. Her hair was bound back, clubbed high, and she'd made her black-and-pink gown into a black-and-pink sleeveless tunic and trousers that hugged tight to her body. She was barefoot too.

To Nothing, the sorceress seemed suddenly so mundane, despite being surrounded by crystal walls and a lightly flickering magical diagram. A field worker, weary after a long day harvesting wheat. Just a young woman who could maybe be Nothing's friend.

The sorceress wiped her forehead against the back of her wrist, pushing tendrils of hair off her face.

"It looks like hard work," Nothing murmured.

"It is," the sorceress said. She rose to her feet and leaned gracefully on one hip. "Is that Sary's Comb of Growth?"

Nothing stared in confusion.

"In your hand," the sorceress insisted.

"Oh." Nothing looked at the comb she held, having forgotten it entirely. "I have no idea."

"Does it have runes down the tines?"

"I suppose that is what these are." Nothing pressed the tip of one tine to her palm until it hurt but did not cut. She dragged it across the lines on her palm, leaving a hot trail of pain and a white line against the soft flesh. The line swiftly filled pink. As long as the line hummed, tingling and hot, she focused on it.

"If you tuck it into your hair, your hair will grow swiftly."

"I don't know how." Nothing wasn't truly paying attention, staring instead at her palm and the slowly departing line.

"I do," said the sorceress, directly behind Nothing.

Nothing gasped, shocked the sorceress had moved so silently and fast.

The sorceress lifted an eyebrow, lips cocked in a half-smile, and held out her hand for the comb.

"I . . . I don't need my hair to grow."

"Very well," the sorceress said with a shrug. She sauntered away. "Do you like the pears I've been bringing you for breakfast?"

Taken aback by the change in topic, Nothing simply said, "Yes."

"Good."

Then the sorceress lifted her arms and stretched, eyes closed. She bent her body from side to side, then folded in half to skim her fingers to the crystal floor at her toes. For a moment Nothing thought she'd hop onto her hands and balance like an acrobat, but instead the sorceress stood again and said, "I'm going to finish my diagram."

"Can I help?"

"Hmm. Watch first; then I'll find something."

Nothing knelt, hands flat on her knees, and did as she was told.

The sorceress took her wand from within her tight tunic and moved carefully across the diagram, stepping largely, turning on her toes. Not an acrobat, a dancer.

Nothing wanted to move that way. To be noticed for grace and control, not ignored for tucking into shadows and hugging the edges of a room.

Suddenly the sorceress crouched, brow furrowed, and touched her wand to the floor. It flared and began to slice the crystal floor again, in a curve. Gradually, the sorceress spiraled the line into itself, latched it with a triangle, and moved to a new space where she began a long line to divide the entire diagram into five sections.

As the diagram grew, so did the anticipation vibrating through the air. Nothing was glad for the thin blue tunic and plain trousers Kirin had chosen for her, as they left her arms bare and her feet and did little to muffle her body from the tension of the magic. The tingle was a little bit like gathering storm clouds before it rained, before the lightning struck. It was like the hollow old snag tree, waiting for them off the road, and like the moment after you said someone's name but before they turned to look.

"Here," the sorceress said, glancing up at Nothing. Her white eye was a bright smoky yellow-gray, like the smoky quartz surrounding them.

Nothing picked her way quickly, avoiding the lines of magic, to the sorceress's side. The sorceress's body hummed with energy, and she held out the wand.

"Take it. Hold it however you are most comfortable," she instructed, keeping her voice a very even tone.

Doing so, Nothing held it like a paintbrush, in loose fingers. She did not practice writing or calligraphy but had watched Kirin do it many rainy afternoons. She crouched where the sorceress directed her and tried to calm her breathing.

"I am going to guide your hand. When you are ready, you must will the wand to glow."

Nothing nodded, but the instant the sorceress placed her hand over Nothing's, that same cold darkness encroached upon her sight and body. She shivered.

Instead of releasing her, the sorceress pressed more firmly. "Hold it back or embrace it, or you cannot help."

"Which?" Nothing whispered.

"You choose," the sorceress said angrily, as if she'd said it a hundred times before.

The anger helped, and Nothing ignored the dark curlicues along her vision until they were gone. Then it was only the softness of the sorceress's fingers hovering against her knuckles, her hand at rest against Nothing's wrist. The sorceress's black-lacquered nails seemed to swallow light.

No other part of them touched, but Nothing felt completely in the sorceress's control.

"Now," the sorceress murmured. "Link this line with that, from exactly here to exactly here." She pointed with her other hand.

"A straight line or a curve, or . . . ?"

The sorceress sighed in irritation.

Nothing gritted her teeth. She pushed the tip of the crystal wand against the floor at exactly the correct point and dragged it unthinking to the other line. The wand flared, the floor groaned, but the line sliced into place.

There was a pop inside Nothing's ears, and all the tension and waiting energy faded.

"Good," the sorceress said, soft against Nothing's cheek. Then she added in more of a drawl, "Though it's a deeper line than necessary."

The sorceress stood, and Nothing shivered, blinking at after-images of cold, dark spirals and curling tentacles. She stood too, facing the sorceress, and thrust out the wand. "Thank you."

"You're welcome," the sorceress said mildly.

"What will we do with this long-sight spell?"

"Oh, it isn't finished. Only the diagram." The sorceress walked to the empty wall. "Are you coming?" She glanced over her shoulder at Nothing, then vanished through the solid rock.

As quickly as she could without stepping upon any of the diagram lines, Nothing dashed after.

TWENTY-FOUR

A S SHE WALKED THROUGH the portal after the sorceress, Nothing wondered if she went because she wanted to or because she always followed.

The room she stepped into might've been part of a house. Rich wooden paneling hid the mountain walls, inlaid with carved teak and lattice as if they were windows beyond which one might view the sea. Rugs covered the floor, deep blue and purple with spots of red florals, and the ceiling was banded with thick beams and whitewash. Wooden furniture clustered intimately around a desk and a hearth burning what looked and felt like real fire. Book piles leaned precariously into one another, and pillows were tossed about on both floor and plush sofa. Beside the hearth a real door opened into another room.

Lamps filled the rooms with bright, warm light.

"Sorceress?" Nothing called.

"Through here," the reply came, distant from the other room.

Nothing went into it. An entire wall was mirrors, some human height, some round and small, with floor pillows and bolsters near them, as well as low tables filled with paint pots and powder. There was also a bed on a swaying trestle, and a wide, open wardrobe spilling silks and satins and shining cloth Nothing had no names for.

The sorceress wasn't even in her bedroom.

Nothing paused, feeling like she didn't belong. She heard running water beyond yet another door and peered through at bright tiles, but she refused to walk into a bathing room. Biting her lip, Nothing returned to the sitting room and plopped onto one of the sofas.

What was the point of this? she thought. Was it supposed to be friendliness or seduction or admission to the sorceress's privacy to prove her willingness to reveal secrets?

Maybe the sorceress simply had wanted to bathe away her sweat and work.

Nothing closed her eyes and listened for the heartbeat of the mountain.

She didn't hear it.

"Thirsty?"

Nothing snapped her head around to the sorceress, who leaned her shoulder against the bedroom doorway. Her damp hair fell heavily around her face, making her magical eyes seem huge, her cheeks rounder and prettier. A silky green robe was clenched around her waist with a white and pink cherry-blossom sash, but the collar was an open arrow down between her breasts, revealing the entirety of the bronze-pink scar over her heart. Nothing's own heart clenched at the sight of it.

She wanted to—she wanted—

The sorceress walked barefoot across her plush rugs to a sideboard and lifted a decanter of bright-pink liquid. She poured two small bowls of it and brought them to Nothing, offering one.

"Tea or liquor?" Nothing asked, cupping the bowl with all her fingers.

"A little bit of both." The sorceress sipped at her bowl.

Nothing stared through the pink drink at the shimmering images painted on the inside of the bowl: little gold and blue fish, tiny as grains of wheat. She sipped. The drink was bitter-sweet and complicated, with a tiny burn. She understood how it might be a little bit of both.

The sorceress draped herself upon a low sofa, delicately crossing her ankles. "Tell me what you like to do, Nothing."

"Do?"

"In your old life, at the palace."

"Why?"

"You said you are not my demon, and so I would like to know who you *are*."

"I'm not anybody."

"Nothing," the sorceress murmured.

"Exactly," Nothing said, and drank all the rest of her drink.

"But what do you do?"

"I listen. I—I eat and drink and go where I wish through the walls of the palace. I spend time with Kirin and sometimes my friend Whisper. I trade gossip for what I need, but only if Kirin is not nearby. When he is with me I can have anything I want."

"What sorts of things have you wanted?"

"You know the answer!" Nothing forced herself not to throw the little bowl.

"You wanted what the prince wanted. You wanted to be quiet

192

and unseen, to be his companion without ambition. Never to leave, but only to push or pull what you could to make him happy."

Nothing's voice shook when she said, "I already accept he mastered me, that some part of me was a demon and vulnerable to it. Why are you making me say it again? He was my friend, my prince. Why should it have seemed odd to want to make him happy!"

"Because it infuriates me," the sorceress said coldly. "I would like to put his eyeballs on a platter for it."

"No," Nothing snapped.

"As you wish."

"I was friends with the great demon of the palace," Nothing said, trying to offer the sorceress something.

"Were you?" She looked at her bowl, slowly swirling liquor within it, instead of looking at Nothing.

"I scratched its itches and told it jokes, and sometimes it purred for me and promised to miss me when I left. That is friendship, with a demon."

The sorceress blinked rapidly and her lips parted, but she paused and those lips spread in a real smile. "Would you like me to scratch your itches, Nothing, to win your friendship?"

Nothing felt heat in her cheeks, throbbing from the burning flower over her heart. She certainly needed more liquor for this conversation. "Ah, I . . ."

The sorceress laughed lightly. "I did not get to tease you so, when you were a demon."

"Maybe you shouldn't tease me now, either!" Nothing insisted, trying to scowl. But her answering smile shone through. She dipped her chin, still glancing up at the sorceress.

The delighted expression on the sorceress's lovely copper face faded slowly, in a gentle way like the setting sun. Not closed off, nor cold. But she did not speak.

Nothing wanted to know why. She did want to know this sorceress; she wanted to see the *impetuous creature*.

A gasp caught in her throat. She wanted. Nothing grinned: it was the first thing she'd realized she wanted for no reason that could possibly have to do with Kirin.

The sorceress narrowed her eyes. "What is that smile?"

Nothing laughed. Now the sorceress wanted the same thing from her. It felt *good*. It felt ... powerful. Nothing shook her head slowly. "I should go." Before she lost this feeling. She should go while it reigned in her heart.

Nothing liked how the sorceress seemed to stop breathing for a moment, then drew herself to her feet and pointed imperiously at the wall.

"There is the exit," the sorceress said as a door appeared, carved with flowers painted red and pink. Nothing's door.

"I'll see you at dinner," Nothing said, dashing for her bedroom. She stopped before opening the door and turned to add, "I'm looking forward to it."

Then she laughed again, quite happily.

Only a slight shock began to appear on the sorceress's face before Nothing grasped the many-petaled flower knob and left.

TWENTY-FIVE

N OTHING WENT STRAIGHT INTO her room, turned, closed the door and opened it again. This time it opened into the corridor outside. She headed for the altar room, wondering if Sky and Kirin remained there. It had been hours since she left. But where had they to go, unless the dragon guided them?

The two young men sat together on the floor, backs against the altar that had been Sky's bed. Around them scattered the remains of quite a meal, platters and bowls of crumbs and streaking sauces, and a bottle of wine leaned against Kirin's thigh, trapped between them.

When she barged in, Sky smiled, but Kirin frowned.

"Where did you go?" he demanded, drawing one leg toward him to rest his arm against his knee.

The displeasure in his voice and posture soured her stomach. Nothing stopped and planted her feet wide, fists on her hips to resist him. "I can *go* where I *like*," she said.

"But should you? You abandoned us."

"Kirin," Sky said with obvious censure.

Kirin closed his mouth in a tight line. Even on the floor he looked imperial. Arrogant. A unique flower to be envied in his red jacket and perfect hair.

"If I'd abandoned you, I wouldn't be back," she said, unable to stop herself. Keeping her distance and holding on to irritation seemed the best she could do.

"I should command you to get us out of here *now*," he said. Knocking the wine bottle aside, he rose to his feet. "What I want is to be gone from this place. You can resist my unspoken wants, the drag of our bond, but if I invoke your true name you have to obey."

"You won't," she said as firmly as she could, but wavering. She tilted her chin up to hold his gaze as he came smoothly toward her. "You won't because you'll lose me forever if you do it on purpose."

The prince's arrogant expression melted. He even lowered his eyes. "But you should still get us out of here."

"I made a bargain. We'll be free in two more days."

Sky walked to them with a hesitance born of injury and put his hand on Kirin's shoulder. The bodyguard wore a silver-gray tunic so thin and silky it was like a slip more than a shirt, falling halfway down his thighs over soft-looking black trousers. The tunic stretched against his massive shoulders, not quite large enough.

Kirin turned his head to meet Sky's gaze.

Nothing let her arms relax slightly. She'd only come to see they were well, not to argue. She might as well leave again, before Kirin twisted her up more.

But Sky pushed around Kirin and grasped Nothing's shoulders. He hunched to stare straight at her. "I don't believe you're a demon."

His touch was so warm, so normal, compared to the sorceress.

"Maybe a goblin, though," he added.

Nothing laughed once.

Behind him, Kirin rolled his head dramatically enough to make sure Nothing saw it. Then the prince spun and returned to the altar. He swept up the bottle of wine, lifted it to his lips and tipped back his head to reveal the full, white length of his neck, before bonelessly dropping onto the altar, one hand to his forehead, the other dangling the bottle.

Nothing blinked and Sky hummed, both realizing they'd been caught in the same admiring trap.

Sky slid one hand down Nothing's arm, letting her go with his other. He took her hand, and she wrapped her fingers around two of his. There remained a greenish bruise on the right corner of his jaw.

"It's why I knew and you didn't. Nobody did," Nothing said softly.

The bodyguard's fingers stiffened in her hand, but he knew what she meant. "It doesn't make any sense. You're nothing like a demon. I've met demons."

"She's something new," Kirin said passionately, eyes shut. The vibrant red skirt of his jacket spilled down the altar in a fan. "And . . ."

"And?" Nothing demanded after a long moment.

Kirin turned his head and opened his dark-honey eyes. "And I like that you're mine."

"Kirin," Sky said again.

"No," Nothing said.

"Because you remind me that something new is possible," Kirin said, sitting again in one swinging motion. He put the butt of the wine bottle on the altar and leaned toward her, feet just brushing the floor. "I didn't understand what you are, Nothing, but that's what I liked. That's what I loved. You could be anything. I didn't know it was anything I wanted. I thought you were just . . . you. And I'm not sorry for liking you. I'm not sorry for wanting what we have."

Nothing forgave him. Just like that; she couldn't help it. Or maybe she wanted to. How could she ever know without her name? Without breaking the binding? She went to him, leaving Sky behind, and sank to her knees, pressing her head to the edge of the altar, her shoulder to his leg.

The weight of his hand settled on her head, stroking her hair. His fingers slid into the strands, finding her scalp, and it was her favorite thing in the world. He said softly, "Do you remember the dying orange tree in the Fire Garden? The day we met."

She nodded, scraping her skin on the altar.

"We were all playing, but for you, and I saw you staring at me from behind long leaves."

"Elephant grass," Nothing whispered.

"Yes! You were so small and intense. I stared back. I stared back and I didn't know what you were! A little boy or a little girl, or a spirit or a ghost—I still thought we could have ghosts in the palace then. No matter how I studied you, I didn't know. So I walked nearer and I saw it unfurling in you, the name. The answer. It came from you, so you must know it."

Nothing dragged at her mind, at the Fire Garden, at youthful, beautiful Kirin, at elephant grass and the first time he smiled at her: it wasn't a dark smile, but a brilliant one. Soft, delighted, perfect. He spoke in her memory.

Kirin's hand fisted in her hair, but only enough to tug gently.

She lifted her face. Disappointment drained through her. "Command me to remember," she said.

"You just said if I do it on purpose I'll lose you forever."

Nothing scowled at him.

The prince bit his lip, dragging it against his teeth.

With a little huff, Nothing stood. She left them in the altar chamber, promising to take them to the mirror lake in the morning. Then she returned to her room to dress for dinner.

Insistent Tide awaited her and helped her choose a gown and paint and combed her hair.

For the first time, Nothing gave in to her impulses, instead of fighting expectations or fear or trying to decide what would upset others, and simply pleased herself. She wore a shell-pink underdress with an orange organza robe embroidered with hundreds of tiny butterflies that reminded her of the box of wings in the library. Insistent Tide braided tiny pieces of her hair and secured them with pins shaped like jewel-toned beetles. Nothing asked for dark-red lacquer on her nails and bright pink on her lips and eyelids. Insistent Tide painted sweeping butterfly wings onto her cheeks.

Nothing felt like a swirling swarm of beautiful bugs. She wrinkled her nose in the mirror and forced a laugh. She didn't have to worry. Her friends were safe for now, and even if she didn't know her name, she knew a few things that she wasn't.

Insistent Tide snorted and went back to sleep even as Nothing left for supper.

As she walked, she had to lift the voluminous organza butterfly skirts, feeling her steps more than seeing them. Her feet were bare and her toes painted red to match her fingers. Would the sorceress like it? Nothing hoped so—then realized she was eager to see the sorceress again.

Nothing brushed impatient fingers down her skirts, fluttering the butterflies the way her heart fluttered.

The facets of vivid purple and pale violet amethyst of the dining room complemented Nothing's orange and pink and rainbow bugs, but the dress itself was ridiculous to kneel in. When she settled onto the golden cushion at one end of the set table, the pink skirts settled with her, but layers of butterfly organza crackled and fluffed around her as if she were the center of a soufflé.

Nothing was giggling as she pulled and pressed at different parts of her dress to make the butterflies flutter and swoop, when she noticed the presence of the sorceress.

She froze, catching her breath at being caught in childishness.

But it wasn't judgment or irony or anything condescending on the sorceress's face: it was wonder.

Nothing cleared her throat and the sorceress bowed her head, bending her body in a slight, elegant curtsy. Not as to a child, but to an equal. Nothing froze again.

The sorceress lifted herself and said, "Nothing."

"Sorceress." Nothing smoothed her hands down her diaphanous dress.

The sorceress swept to the table and knelt, tucking her skirts simply around her legs. She wore an old-fashioned wrapped dress in three layers: black, green, and violet, with a wide sash tied in elaborate, stiff loops at her back. Her hair was knotted atop her head, decorated with sprays of orange tiger lilies. White and green pearls very like Kirin's hugged her neck and fell over the collars of her dress. She poured wine, sent a cup floating to Nothing and lifted hers—tonight a cut-crystal swan with its neck curled around itself.

Maybe it was a goose, Nothing thought, taking her cup from the air. She saluted and drank.

"My demon played too," the sorceress said.

"Played?" Nothing took another sip of the light wine, rolling it a bit on her tongue. Honey and cloves and something sharp as pine resin coated her mouth. She liked it.

"With butterflies and color—anything that made it curious. When I walked in, you might never have been gone."

Nothing swallowed at the sorceress's light tone. She was hiding something, Nothing thought, though she could not pinpoint how she knew. "Tell me about your demon?"

The sorceress nodded, but first brushed her hands together gently. Silent, invisible servants lifted trays and stirred sauce, serving a first course of buttery soup to Nothing and the sorceress.

After they'd both tasted, the sorceress asked, "What do you know of demons?"

Nothing set her spoon down. "They are dead spirits. They need a house to make their own, either one that is abandoned, one that never had a resident, or one they can steal. They either want very specific things or not much at all."

"Yes, that is true. But do you know why demons like to be familiars, why they seek sorcerer or witch partners?"

"No."

"Demons are livid with the power they take and can do what they are meant to do—stagnate a pond, hold the walls of a palace together, explode a mountain, or trick crossroads travelers. But they cannot move from their house without the risk of forever death. For plots, for plans, for movement or change, they need a witch to anchor them or a sorcerer to strengthen their house. Even a great demon, who has not lost its connection to aether, does better with a sorcerer."

"Your demon needed you."

"It was mutual." The sorceress smiled nostalgically. "I left my village when I was sixteen because I knew I wanted to be a sorcerer."

"Why?" Nothing leaned forward, ignoring her food.

"I wanted to marry the girl next door, but my mother told me it was foolish. I needed children to take care of me when I was old. She said only sorcerers don't need to worry about family. I said I would be a sorcerer then, and left."

"Just like that!"

"More or less. I went to the Third Mountain, and the Second, but both sorcerers told me the same thing: we cannot make rivals by taking apprentices! Find a spirit to teach you, or a witch. They both suggested I be a witch." The sorceress raised her eyes to the ceiling, then smiled again. "Instead I came to the Fifth Mountain and asked a great demon."

Nothing watched her, waiting, but the sorceress fell quiet. Nothing drank the last of her wine and said, "There must be more to it than that."

The sorceress floated Nothing's cup toward herself and poured another. As the cup returned along a strand of air, the sorceress said, "Naturally. I bargained with a dragon for entry to the mountain, climbed its face until I was nearly dead, my blood smeared against the rocks, and with my final, soft desperation, the demon appeared. *What are you, child?* it asked in an empty voice that touched my equally empty places. I had nothing left, you see, by then. Nothing but my bones and will and a tiny bit of blood. Exactly right to impress a demon when I stood and told it I was a sorcerer and it would submit to me. It laughed but took me inside and gave me the power to heal. It gave me food and lovely clothes, and when I felt stronger, we bargained in truth. Power for power. I had realized, you see, that while a great demon has everything it needs, it may not have everything it *wants*. The demon agreed to help me grow my skills, and I would be its vessel to see beyond the mountain. We traded shards of our shadows, binding to death or destruction." The sorceress paused, sipped, and added, "My demon . . . was a slip of darkness, a shadow that changed on impulse. A slight child, a winged man, a scaled woman, and everything between, or nothing at all but a breeze and a voice. A silver flame dancing in the air. Its eyes, though, when it had them, were like old black pearls. Always. And its touch tender."

"What did you . . . fall in love with?" Nothing whispered, trembling with the need to know.

"Everything. It would sit for hours and watch the reflection of clouds against the mirror lake or hold bumblebees in its cupped palms to laugh at their tickling buzz, trying not to kill them. It crackled like lightning and raged down the mountain in a temper, setting fire to trees and making rabbits scream, withering flowers and scaring the wind still. It teased me. Hid my things, replacing them under cups or in my soup. It combed my hair at night. It hurt me sometimes, too. It taught me to read every language, and held threads of magic in seven hands so I could look inside the patterns. It was infinitely patient. It told me wild and tragic stories it learned when it was alive, when the Fifth Mountain was alive. It curled its fingers around my heart and said my heart was like a core of magma, heating the body of my own mountain house."

A tear spilled over the sorceress's lashes, then dripped raggedly down her cheek.

Nothing touched her mouth and felt her own warm breath against her fingers as the only proof she was breathing at all.

Oh, it was working. The sorceress's story was working: Nothing wanted what she offered. To be everything described. Powerful, mercurial, funny, and patient. Tender and furious.

Who wouldn't want to be such a thing, when such a thing was so loved by a creature like the sorceress?

Especially when what she'd always been was Nothing.

Nothing stood suddenly. "I have to go."

The sorceress looked up at her, otherwise very still. She did not speak, though her eyes glinted. One forest green, one bone white.

Slowly the sorceress rose to her feet and glided toward Nothing. She reached out and brushed her knuckles along Nothing's cheek, leaving trails of cold shadow-silk behind.

Nothing leaned into it, so the sorceress would know she wasn't running away in fear or rejection. It was self-preservation. It was important that Nothing take her time. "Good night, Sorceress," she whispered. "I want to see you in the morning."

The sorceress offered a cool smile of acknowledgment.

Nothing gathered her skirts into her arms, lifting layers almost to her knees, and left, trailing butterflies on the crystal floor behind her.

She ran along the dark corridor and took the first stairway she found. "Up," she said, and again, "Up. Up." She repeated it with every breath, hurrying two steps at a time in places, then slowing to stomp up and up. The stairs dumped her into an intersection of corridors, and she chose with a command: "Up!" and the corridor slanted upward, curving for her exactly as she wished. She reached another staircase, this one steep, and she hooked her skirts over her elbow and half crawled, half climbed.

Absolutely breathless and lost in time, Nothing continued upward. Her muscles burned, and her chest; sweat cooled against her skin. She stepped on her skirt and tore free a string of three cerulean butterflies. They tumbled behind her and landed flat against the dark granite.

Finally Nothing saw a dim glow of silver as the stairs narrowed and steepened until they were more of a ladder than steps. She emerged through a jagged hole, into the stars.

She stood on a shelf against a peak of the Fifth Mountain, formed by black waves of cooled lava. Wind and rain had scoured it into a cupped palm, a tiny valley just her size, and scraggly grasses managed to grow, along with little flowers. Their buds were shut tight against the night.

Nothing collapsed in a heap of pink and orange organza. She hugged her knees and pressed her forehead to them, breathing hard, trying to steady her pulse and calm down.

Wind teased her hair, tickling her neck and shoulders.

She didn't feel powerful.

Nothing leaned her head back. Thin silver clouds floated over the half-moon, glowing with its light, and beyond thousands and thousands of stars spread. She tried to find shapes, but the sky was only shredded silk, a massive pearl, and a million shards of glass.

Beneath the night shine, Nothing felt small. Only a human, with a small heart, small bones, small hopes, and no ambition. She'd never minded before. It had never occurred to her to mind.

And now she wondered. And now she wanted.

She wanted to feel as big as the night sky and as filled with magic. Dark distance, silver light, that night shine—she wanted to know the kinds of purple and midnight blue and sparks of red layered together that made it seem so black between the stars, and she wanted to stare and stare until the stars stopped being silver and turned pink, blue, orange, and gold. She wanted the stars to be butterflies.

Nothing wanted to know what she *could* be. Not what she might have been.

If she was going to return to the palace, she could never resume her shadow role, Kirin's Nothing. She had to be something different, something new.

Two days remained to find out if she was large or small, both, or something else entirely. Two days would not be enough. She needed more time here on the mountain, with the sorceress. She . . . *wanted* to remain with the sorceress . . . and to keep the core of the Fifth Mountain strong.

But she wanted to see Kirin and Sky safely home too, and

witness Kirin made forever the Heir to the Moon. She wanted to speak with the great demon of the palace again, ask it some very pointed questions.

She'd have to find a way to do it all. Everything she wanted.

Nothing curled down on her side, nestled in billowing sheer silk and tiny rainbow insects, against the mountain, and tilted her face to the sky.

TWENTY-SIX

D AWN WOKE NOTHING WITH a gentle caress against her lashes, reddening her dreams. She squeezed herself into a tighter ball and sighed. It was cold on the mountaintop, but she'd nestled into her dress, the loose volcanic gravel, and thin grasses.

She opened her eyes to find a little blue flower nodding at her. It was the size of her smallest fingernail, clustered with a handful of others. Nothing drew a breath to seek a scent: the only perfume in the air was ice.

Her tongue tasted a little sour, and she wondered if demons ever had bad breath.

Probably only if they wanted to. They didn't need to breathe at all.

Slowly she stood and stretched, feeling remarkably rested. Her body was ready for anything, not sore or tired or stiff. She licked her lips and shifted so she could grasp at the rocks edging this natural balcony and peer over.

The Fifth Mountain spread downward in jagged peaks and tumbling boulders and sheer drops. The mirror lake winked at her. She wanted a cold bath. Overhead blue skies rippled with lines of clouds sweeping away from the mountain. The sun was up, a shining full disk, and Nothing wondered if demons could look straight at it without a headache.

Blinking, she went back to the cave entrance and climbed down, letting herself be swallowed again by the shade.

Once she'd made it down the ladder to the stairs, she choose a spot in the wall that seemed shaped the right way and correctly tall: she closed her eyes, reached out, and her hand touched the many-petaled knob.

Inside her bedroom she was alone, and she washed her face, cleaned her mouth, relieved her bladder, and without changing, headed for the mirror lake.

To Nothing's surprise Sky and Kirin were there too, along with the spirit of the Selegan River and what seemed to be a hundred dawn sprites.

The Selegan was shaped like a youth, half-naked and teasing the dawn sprites by lifting handfuls of water and splashing them. The sprites fled, screaming like tiny birds, but swooped around for more, splashing the dragon back by fluttering wet wings at them.

Sky stood farther into the lake, completely naked, and seeming unbothered by the chill of the water. He glistened, scrubbing at his hair, and called to Kirin on the shore.

The prince stood among the alders in trousers and a plain tunic, his hair loose to his waist. Elegant gray-brown alder branches cut across him like prison bars between them. But he glanced toward Nothing and his bright eyes caught hers.

She walked to him, never letting go of his gaze, and Kirin waited.

"I want to know what I can become," she said. "It matters more than what I was."

"Isn't that why you've agreed to stay with the sorceress these two more days?" he asked. "To let her fill your head with magic."

Nothing crossed her arms over her stomach. "Are you so insecure to be nervous at what she may say?"

"*Jealous*, Nothing."

The admission thrilled her.

Kirin pressed his mouth into a line.

"Do you lie to me, Kirin?"

He shrugged lazily. "I've never had to."

Nothing finally broke eye contact. She nodded. "I believe you."

"You have to, don't you?" he snarled softly.

She looked back at his face: his expression was taut, his cheeks pink, and his nostrils flared.

"Don't be so surprised," Kirin said, angry and tight. "I don't like the idea of you loving me because you *have* to any more than you do."

"Then tell me my name so we both know the key to our binding. Then we can break it."

"Not where she can hear."

"I trust her."

"Trust *me*."

Nothing sighed and turned away. Sky was clomping up the beach toward them. He grabbed a thin towel from a boulder and wrapped it around his waist.

The Selegan dove into the lake with nary a ripple, then shot up again with a massive spray of water. Nothing laughed at its expression of joy, wanting to go with it.

Sky said, "Kirin, what's wrong?"

Kirin merely reached for Sky, stroking his fingers down the wet muscles of Sky's arm. The demon-kissed bodyguard let his own expression soften.

It was strange, but good, to see them touching casually. They never did at home. Everything was always careful and tense between them in the palace, to hide their connection. Nothing frowned at them, realizing these days she'd bought herself were also days she'd bought for them. Kirin should not be so sour about it.

Just as she opened her mouth to tell him, rain pattered her head despite the sunlight.

She looked up, and it was the dragon above them, dripping lake water off its spreading wings.

"Nothing!" called the Selegan.

She craned her neck to take in the whole spirit. Its wings did not flap, merely spread in still feathered arcs, yet it floated in the wind, weightless. Hovering over her like a rippling, silver sky.

"Would you like to fly?"

"Yes!" she cried, and held up her arms.

"Without us?" Kirin said.

"Yes!" Nothing said again.

The dragon took her arms and helped her climb against its neck, which fit her exactly as she straddled between ridges of bone, and she suspected it shrank to the right size. Its scales were sun-warm, and feathers tickled her ankles. Her dress had to look like bubbles of diaphanous orange clouds atop it.

Sky lifted a hand in farewell, and Kirin pouted viciously. But his bodyguard threw an arm around his neck and dragged him gasping backward toward the cold mirror lake.

Then Nothing and the Selegan were part of the wind.

They flew fast, darting across the sky, and Nothing shut her eyes against the cold burn. Wind tore at her hair, stripping beetle pins free, tossing them behind her like shed scales. Nothing laughed: it was painful; it was incredible.

Beneath her, the dragon's sinewy neck curved. Nothing bent lower, folding herself against it, and grasped at the ridges. "Where would you like to go?" the dragon rumbled.

"Anywhere! Everywhere," she whispered, and it heard.

Nothing squinted into brilliant light, at silver and green shining below. Sunlight pierced her eyes, reflecting in ripples down the dragon's scales, setting its feathers to rainbow fire. Nothing blinked tears away, pressed her cheek to the dragon, and hugged it with her whole self.

She was a piece of the spirit. Wind and cloud and rippling water. There was so much water in the sky itself! she realized.

The dragon spun them down the mountain, dipping low to skim against its river. A spray of droplets arced against her cheek, raining on her dress, and she laughed.

Then they were climbing again, up and up into the air. They burst across the rolling black-and-green lava field, swept high to crest the canopy of the rain forest, and then the dragon slowed, turning for her.

Nothing sat, balanced, and gazed back at the Fifth Mountain.

It was a furious black slice of stone against the bright sky, majestic and still. Once it must have risen high and sharp in the center, but when it died, when it erupted, the power had blasted the top away, leaving seven ragged peaks in a near-perfect circle. They clawed upward, and Nothing thought of the sorceress saying her demon had held lines of magic sometimes in seven arms.

"Did the volcano kill the great spirit, or did the death of the spirit cause the mountain to erupt?" she asked.

"I do not know, little Nothing," the dragon replied. "I was not friends with the spirit or demon of the Fifth Mountain."

"You are friend to the sorceress."

"Friend is a complicated thing."

Nothing nodded and stroked a hand against the dragon's scales. She paused, touching with a single finger the line of a single scale: it was as wide as her palm, hard and shining white silver. "Are you her familiar?"

"The volcano spilled into my river, cutting me off from the rest of the land. I was stagnating, I was a slow drip of power, a scummy lake, when she came."

"And she freed you in return for service?"

"Yes. And I look, sometimes, for beautiful maidens for her."

A chill shook Nothing. The center of all this beauty remained death. It was her fault, if she'd been the great demon. An echo of her choices before she'd been born killing people now. She swallowed a sliver of grief, though it cut at her insides. "Take me back, please," she said.

The dragon agreed.

Their return flight was more leisurely, and Nothing did not have to close her eyes. The ground passed beneath them, so many colors blurring. She warmed again, slowly, even though it was colder higher on the mountain.

Impetuous creature.

My demon played too.

Sometimes it hurt me.

Nothing tilted her face to the sky so the cold wind could scour away her fledgling love.

The dragon spiraled down to the mirror lake, and Nothing stripped out of the organza dress. She flung it up into the air and it caught a breeze, billowing out.

The cloth drifted lazily, gently, butterflies flitting and spinning, down and down until it touched the lake. It soaked water up, drowning, and melted into the blue depths.

Nothing slid off the dragon's back in only her pink shell underdress, arms and shoulders bare. She wandered along the shore to where Sky sprawled, drying out in the sun. Beyond him, Kirin knelt in the copse of alder trees, speaking intently to Esrithalan the unicorn.

When she passed, Sky opened his eyes and caught her ankle. She paused. He said, "What are you doing?"

Sinking to her knees, she shrugged. "I don't know."

"You're a mess. You look . . . wild."

Nothing touched her tangled hair, finding a single beetle pin. She unlatched it and drew it into her lap. It glinted greenish blue. "Did Kirin tell you everything?"

"I believe so," he rumbled.

Nothing smiled a little. Uncertainty was a constant state with Kirin.

"You have demon in your blood," she murmured, tilting her head to study him. The bluish shade along his wide cheeks and sweeping into his hair. His fading bruises were more purple-green than yellowish, and the tiny hairs along his chest and stomach, along the hem of his trousers, were blue-black. All details she'd noticed before, along with his strength and the eerie blue glint of his eyes in the dark. "The demon-kissed families betrayed a Queen of Heaven once, and this was their punishment."

"That's the story," Sky said softly.

Nothing lay down beside him, tucking her arm under her head to watch his profile. He blinked, then turned his head to look back at her. Eye to eye. She asked, "Do you feel inhuman?"

"When I lift a boulder I do, or when someone reminds me like you're doing now, I feel different." Sky paused, and she waited. He looked back up, at the sky. "I'm not sure feeling different means the same as feeling inhuman. Everyone feels it sometimes, don't they? Even Kirin."

"Especially Kirin," she whispered.

"Besides." His chest rose and fell in a heavy sigh. "It might be a stigma, but punishment? I am strong. I protect the empire and the Heir to the Moon."

"You're beautiful."

Sky's lips curved into a very slight smile. "You're a mess."

"Do you think I'm an impetuous creature?"

"Sometimes. But maybe you're just unexpected."

Nothing sighed too, purposefully mirroring him, then scooted closer in order to lean her temple against his shoulder. He turned his hand and skimmed his knuckles to her bare knee.

The sunlight was thin but warm enough to feel even through the cold breeze and the scent of ice. Nothing closed her eyes and felt it against her lids. She hugged the beetle pin to her chest, over her scar, curled beside Sky. His breathing was soft and even, and she thought he was drifting into sleep.

Water licked at the shore, making tiny splashing sounds, and the alder leaves fluttered prettily.

She wished the sorceress were here too, quiet and resting with them.

Nothing thought of the sorceress lying on the ground in one of her nice dresses, grass in her hair.

A shadow covered Nothing's face, and she opened her eyes to look up at Kirin, who leaned over them with his hands on his hips. "Well, this is something. I should have had myself kidnapped sooner."

Sky grunted. "What for?"

Nothing glanced over. The bodyguard hadn't even opened his eyes.

Kirin grinned, crouching at their heads. "You two getting along." The skirt of his long red jacket brushed Nothing's hair, tickling her. She reached up and touched his chin. When he glanced at her, she touched his lips. Kirin fell still, watching her, shading her from the sun. He was expressionless, his mouth unmoving under her fingers.

Nothing shaped his name with her lips and then pressed at his, sliding her hand away.

The prince caught her hand and brought it back to his mouth. He kissed her palm. Keeping ahold of her, he let his other hand drop to Sky's forehead and slid his hand into Sky's hair. Kirin nodded at Nothing.

She nodded back.

Kirin sat cross-legged. His knees and shins seemed to cup their heads, and he hunched a little, altogether like a jolly hearth god sheltering his altar.

"What were you talking about with Esrithalan?" she asked, eyes drifting closed again.

"We were discussing the Throne of the Moon and what I can do with it."

"Does the unicorn know more about how a great demon was bound to a line of emperors?" Nothing asked.

"It said a god made the palace into an amulet. That's why the consorts and empress can't leave once they're all invested. Why the heir is allowed his summer adventure."

Sky shifted as if to speak, but before he could, a great crack of thunder shook the air and the mountain itself.

Nothing flung herself up.

The sky was blackening with storm clouds in a gruesome swirl.

Dawn sprites screamed and scattered.

The dragon streaked into the air like a pillar of silver, spreading its wings to shield the valley.

A deep voice yelled across the bowl of the storm, loud enough to hurt: *"Sorceress Who Eats Girls, where is the Heir to the Moon?"*

TWENTY-SEVEN

K IRIN AND SKY BOTH stood with Nothing, necks craning to stare up.

"Sorceress, I challenge you! Where is the Heir to the Moon?"

The prince shifted beside her, and she spun to push both hands against his chest. "Quiet," she said.

"But—"

Thunder cracked and lightning filled the air with sickly greenish gleam. It throbbed and flashed, and Nothing tugged at Kirin's hand, dragging him toward the shelter of the alders. Sky put himself in front of Kirin, walking backward to help Nothing corral the prince. Kirin cried out wordless frustration.

"Sorceress Who Eats Girls!" the voice charged again, louder than anything. Nothing winced and covered her ears.

A shriek tore through the sky, high and terrible: for a moment a stripe of blue appeared across the storm, a wound of sunlight, and out of nowhere a giant eagle cut upward.

Its wings were black, tipped in white, and it sliced into the storm, dragging clouds with it. Every scream it made pushed back at the thunder.

The eagle curved, soaring, and screamed again and again.

A silver eagle shot from the northeast, talons bared, and the two crashed together.

Nothing gasped.

The eagles tumbled down, slashing and screaming: wings bent and flapped hard, and feathers tore free.

One broke away, the other chased; then the black-and-white eagle was a massive snake: it snapped fangs at the silver eagle, catching its wing. The snake twisted and wrapped itself around the eagle again and again.

Then it was only a snake, falling, falling toward the mirror lake.

The snake grew feathered wings and caught itself, skimming the surface raggedly, then beat its wings hard, arcing upward again.

Lightning crashed down out of the black clouds and ripped through the winged snake.

It split in two, gore spraying.

Nothing screamed.

The Fifth Mountain trembled and the two halves of the snake were two dragons; they reached for each other and caught together, becoming one dragon with two heads. It struggled into the air again, heading directly for the storm.

"Skybreaker, you will die on the peaks of my mountain," another voice reverberated: the sorceress, sounding as wide and deep as an ocean.

The two-headed dragon spit ice at the clouds, shredding them.

Nothing slipped away from Kirin and Sky, both of whom

stared at the battle. She darted through the alders and slammed her hands against the rocks of the mountain. "Help me get to her," she said. "Help me."

The mountain trembled but did not help.

Above, the clouds gathered into a giant gray-black monster with eyes of lightning.

The sorceress became a beast of wings and claws, a whirlwind that cut and sliced, screaming toward the storm monster's eyes.

Lightning cracked. Sunlight flashed.

"Selegan!" Nothing cried, because the mountain only trembled.

She couldn't see what was happening or where one monster began and the other ended.

But blood sprayed through the wind.

Then it all stopped.

The storm was gone, and the sorceress.

Nothing backed away from the cliffside, staring up and up the mountain. "Where are they?" She tried to climb, but there were no footholds. She could go inside, find the spiral stairs and inner ladder to the tiny high valley.

Someone was yelling her name. Kirin.

She hit both fists against the rocks.

"Here," said cold wind at her back. She whirled: the dragon.

"Take me up to them!" she cried, throwing herself at the Selegan. It grasped her arm and waist in sharp claws. Nothing held on as the ground dropped away from her bare feet.

Lightning flashed, but the storm clouds were thinner, sweeping away in furious winds. Nothing tried to keep her eyes open in the harsh, cold air, but she had to wince away.

She listened: wind, a distant wailing, a crack of thunder, weaker than before. Nothing could not sense the mountain's heart. Already it had been weak, failing. The sorceress had said she needed a new heart or she needed Nothing.

The dragon dropped her, and Nothing caught herself in a crouch against the hard rock.

Wind gusted, shoving the Selegan spirit away. The dragon crashed into the mountain, scrambling to right itself. It growled, wings arcing out; feathers scattered in the wind. Nothing held up a hand to shield her face, staring around. She was on a wide slope of scattered gravel between two jagged peaks, high on the face of the mountain. Near the blasted top.

There: the sorceress, a feathered half monster, dragged herself on long talons, toward Skybreaker in the shape of a bear with horns and scales. He roared and the sorceress screamed. She made an elaborate gesture, and shadows leapt from the mountain, enveloping him.

Nothing climbed toward her.

Skybreaker broke free of the shadows but was stripped to the form of a man. He wore robes, his beard was long and steel gray, and he held a wand the size of a short sword, of vivid purple wood and tipped in silver.

The sorceress charged, beaked mouth open in a shriek.

He cast lightning and it caught her. She shook it off, but her feathers smoked. They vanished and it was only the sorceress standing before the sorcerer, both of them with heaving shoulders, shining with sweat.

"This is the seat of your power and yet you cannot banish me," Skybreaker said.

"I can," the sorceress croaked. Feathers bled down her cheeks, and her mouth was full of razor teeth ruining her words. "Your mountain is far from here."

"Where is your great demon? Where the strength of the Fifth Mountain?"

The sorceress bared her shark's teeth and clapped her hands: wind and shadows poured at the sorcerer again, but he grasped at them with one hand, spooling them around his wand.

Nothing could see the strain in the sorceress. She had no reserves.

"If we'd known you were alone," Skybreaker said, "we'd have come sooner. Where is the Heir to the Moon?"

"I don't have him."

"He has been seen on your mountain—by spirits and Heaven itself. You should not have let him out under the sky, Sorceress."

Nothing slipped on the layers of gravel.

The sorceress glanced over, shock on her face, and swept a hand toward Nothing: shadows rose in a wall separating Nothing from them.

"You need me," Nothing said.

"I don't have any princes here," the sorceress said.

Skybreaker laughed. "When I kill you, I will take your familiars for my own. I will have the prince and the mountain."

"You cannot have me," the sorceress said in her tooth-garbled voice. "There is nothing here. Nothing to be protected. *Nothing*, do you hear me?"

Again the sorcerer laughed, wild and cruel, but Nothing understood: the sorceress wanted her to go, to leave with the Selegan, with Kirin, with everyone. Keep them away from

Skybreaker. The sorceress would hold him here and give them a chance.

She crept along the wall of shadows, freezing and shaking. Icy wind cut at her, and her fingers and toes were numb to the tiny slicing shards of rock.

Skybreaker called lightning again. It was weaker, but even weak lightning can burn.

The sorceress screamed.

Nothing did not think: she found a sharp stone and tucked it against her ribs, running the final space between herself and Skybreaker. He was an old man, but strong and tall, and he pointed at the sorceress with his wand.

She could not lose the sorceress again—she'd just gotten her back!

Nothing leapt at him, bashing the stone against his head.

It hit with a dull *thunk*, and Nothing grabbed his shoulder as they both fell.

They slammed to the ground and rolled down the slope. The sorceress cried her name. Nothing tasted blood. Her shoulder hit the ground; his weight crushed her; they rolled and rolled. She gritted her teeth and let go of Skybreaker, skidding away.

Nothing gasped, spat gravel and blood, and pushed herself up to her hands and knees against the rough mountainside. There lay Skybreaker, groaning, bleeding from his head.

The sorceress ran down to them, setting off a small avalanche of rocks. With a ferocious cry, she grasped at the air itself: in her clawed hands formed a sword of raw shadows and pulsing red light. She stabbed down into Skybreaker's chest.

A low boom sounded, like a single throb of the mountain's

heart. Skybreaker's back arched, blood spurted, and silence fell.

Nothing panted, holding on to her aching ribs, swallowing again and again. Her throat hurt too, and her eyes streamed. Her cheek was sticky.

The sorceress jerked the sword free and flung it into the sky to dissipate. Then she turned frantically and fell to her knees beside Nothing.

Nothing's breath scoured her throat as she stared. Her mouth filled with something huge: panic or fear, she thought.

But a laugh burst out of her!

Nothing grinned around it and reached for the sorceress.

"Nothing." The sorceress grasped her hands. Darkness blotted out Nothing's vision, but she kept laughing, and focused. The sorceress's white eye was streaked with red and black, her green eye luminous. Her skin was sunken to her bones, and feathers sliced across her cheeks, into her hair. Her black nails were talons. She was still half eagle, half monster, half sorceress—too many halves!—but had she ever been more beautiful?

Nothing continued to laugh. She'd helped kill Skybreaker, the intruder! This was *their* mountain. This was right.

"Wild thing," Nothing rasped. "Impetuous creature!"

"Nothing!" the sorceress hissed, her sharp teeth falling from her mouth like pearls.

Nothing pushed forward, trying to catch some of those pearls for her own mouth.

The sorceress stopped her. "Nothing, he's dead."

"Yes!"

"You helped me." The sorceress sounded shocked. "I couldn't have stopped him without you."

"He was going to kill you."

Only plain white teeth filled the sorceress's mouth now, surrounded by red lips. It was too late to catch the pearls. Nothing blinked. She rubbed her eyes.

The sorceress hugged her tightly, and Nothing leaned in, wrapping herself around her sorceress.

They sank into the stone of the mountain together, falling through granite, held by hard fingers of basalt, and the sorceress's arms were around her, the sorceress's breath on her cheek.

Then they were spat out into sunlight again and the sweet-smelling breeze.

"Nothing! Nothing!"

Kirin and Sky called her, and she was surrounded. The sorceress leaned back.

Nothing opened her eyes. She felt . . . clean. Like she'd run hard or danced fast and all her breath and blood was new. Like she'd laughed herself a new heart.

The mirror lake glittered blue beside them, and the sorceress slumped, one hand pressed to the sand at Nothing's knee. She stared at Nothing, and Nothing stared back, sort of smiling, sort of dazed.

"You waited for me," Nothing said, still laughing. Tiny popping giggles bursting into words. "I'm glad you did."

The feathers withdrew into the sorceress's skin, leaving only pink and vivid white burns dappling her jaw and neck, streaking down to vanish beneath the tattered, burned remains of her dress. The sorceress's eyes were massive, her skin almost translucent, bruised.

"What happened?" Kirin demanded.

"Nothing, are you well?" Sky asked, crouching beside her

to put a firm hand to her back. It was cool! Sky was always so much warmer than her! He said, "You're flushed. Are you injured? That's blood on your dress."

Nothing tore her gaze from the sorceress and stared at the splatter wonderingly. She touched a finger to it, liking the color contrast.

"Skybreaker is dead," the sorceress murmured.

"What?" Kirin put one knee on the ground, leaning on the other. "Nothing, what did you do?"

She stared at him, smiling. Her throat felt raw, but good. Or had lava torn up and out of her, spewing into laughter? "He was going to kill the sorceress. And take you."

"Take me back to the palace, maybe. The sorcerers of the Living Mountains are not our enemies!"

"He was attacking my mountain, Kirin."

"Your mountain!"

"Kirin," Sky said in a rumble.

"It is my mountain," said the sorceress firmly. "And now the others will come, because he's dead. His familiar is a great spirit, and they will all know. They know you are here, Kirin Dark-Smile."

"We can defeat them all," Nothing said.

"What is happening to you?" Sky asked, sliding his cool hand up her neck to her nape. He gripped her skull, turning her head to him.

"I am so hot, there's magma inside me," she said, still smiling. Sky would understand!

"What did you do to her?" Kirin demanded of the sorceress.

The sorceress said, "She's remembering. Her heart is remembering."

Nothing laughed. "I don't remember anything. But I like this feeling!" Her laughter forced her eyes closed. She could feel the heat in her cheeks, in her neck and chest, tingling in her fingers! Suddenly the mountain tilted and Nothing gasped, falling back into Sky's arm. "Oh . . ." she moaned softly as her stomach turned over. She was close to something magnificent and massive. It was going to break her.

"It's too much," the sorceress murmured. "Too fast. She's not in control and nobody is."

Keeping her eyes closed was the only way to calm her stomach. She pressed her hands against it, woozy. She swallowed, trying to cool the hot rock in her throat.

"Set us free," Kirin commanded. "Now. Before she hurts herself. We will return to the palace, to the Empress with the Moon in Her Mouth, and all will know I am safe. You will no longer be a target."

"I have two more days with her."

"Is that worth your mountain? It is in danger, Sorceress. You said yourself, they will come."

Nothing pried her eyes open as the sorceress lowered her chin stubbornly. Her green eye burned greener than anything against the vibrant crimson blood of burst capillaries. "I can hold the mountain."

"You're weak and injured," Kirin said.

Nothing touched a burn blister near the sorceress's chin, and the sorceress hissed in shock.

She said, "I will heal. I have the power of the Fifth Mountain still."

"It's weak too, without its demon." Kirin grasped the sorceress's shoulder, digging his fingers in. "Do you want to survive? Can you, against the other Living Mountains and their masters?"

The sorceress looked only at Nothing. "With my demon, I could."

Nothing's eyes closed in a wave of dizziness, and she saw fire, flicking distant and blue, like butterflies. Terrible, beautiful blue-fire butterflies. Everything that was left of a volcano heart, pieced out, fluttering desperately away. She needed to collect them again, cup them in her palms and breathe them back into a conflagration.

"Look at her," Kirin murmured. "Your demon is a barely-seventeen-year-old girl now and doesn't know how to help without killing herself. Is your pride worth her life?"

Silence.

"Nothing," said the prince.

She opened her eyes again, but it seemed to take a hundred years.

Kirin stared at her. He didn't say any more, but Nothing felt the urgency in him, in herself. From the warmth of Sky's embrace, she met the sorceress's gaze. She did not want to speak, but she did. She looked at the sorceress. "You have to let us go."

"I do not."

"I have to go with Kirin," Nothing said slowly, through a hundred days.

The sorceress said, "He doesn't need you to see him safely home."

"I need it. He's mine. I need this, and I need my name . . . ," Nothing said, though this time it took only a hundred hours. The roar of thunder in her ears softened to a hissing. "Let me go. Let the three of us go home."

"You *are* home."

Nothing grinned. It was weak but real. She felt like her skin was solidifying. A hundred heartbeats and she'd be herself again. She was starving. "Not yet. It's not my home yet. But maybe it will be, if I get to choose it. If I get to *choose you*."

The sorceress took a deep breath, and as she released it carefully, the burns on her neck and face faded to pink, then shining scars, and then they were gone. She licked her lips. "Very well. For a price," she said.

Nothing giggled. Always a bargain. "Of course."

For a long moment silence ruled the valley. The sun pressed down, warm in the still afternoon. There were no clouds left whatsoever, only harsh blue sky, jagged black peaks, and strangely still alders. Not even their leaves shook.

Sky squeezed his cool fingers around the base of Nothing's skull.

The sorceress said, "A kiss. You can leave, all three of you, for a kiss."

Kirin scoffed, but Nothing laughed. A springtime laugh, eager as bumblebees dancing against daisies. "Yes!" she cried.

TWENTY-EIGHT

———

THE SORCERESS STOOD AND bent again to take Nothing's hands and pull her to her feet.

Nothing's body ached, not from injury, but as if she had a fever; her heartbeat filled her up, tingling in the tips of her fingers as the sorceress stepped near. She brought their folded hands together, clasped between their hearts.

The sorceress tilted her face down, and Nothing parted her lips with anticipation.

Then she closed her eyes as the sorceress's lips touched hers.

The world was cold and dark, but the kiss pinned Nothing in place.

She was a butterfly embroidered on gauzy silk, bright and fluttering and alive, yet unable to move for the touch of lips to lips.

Nothing breathed in, tasting the air around the sorceress's mouth, and the sorceress kissed more firmly, opening her mouth to taste Nothing, to lick gently against Nothing's bottom lip.

Nothing sighed; the sorceress clutched at her hands, black nails cutting, and she pushed Nothing's mouth open even more.

She tasted a little like blood, and Nothing wondered if she tasted like blood too, because it was smeared on her cheek, because they'd killed the sorcerer of the Third Living Mountain. Together. And Nothing had laughed.

The sorceress let go of Nothing's hands and put hers on Nothing's jaw, tilted her head, and kissed her harder, deliberately stroking at Nothing's lips, at her teeth, and then her tongue.

It did not feel like the sorceress was taking anything. She gave and gave, trying to prove something to Nothing, that they'd known each other for a hundred years, that they used to be married, that their hearts were two pieces of a single heart, that the sorceress would do anything, say anything, to keep Nothing, except actually keep her.

All of it poured into Nothing, and she was holding on to the sorceress too, hands on that slender neck, pulling, tangled in fine hairs, and Nothing whimpered a little bit. There was no need to prove anything—Nothing understood love. It was hot and alive and pulsing. It was a heart. Her teeth sank into the sorceress's lip and she let go immediately, but the sorceress kissed her back, holding her close.

They slowed, their lips and tongues slowed, their breathing slowed, and the pulse that ricocheted between them.

Nothing did not feel tired any longer. She was filled with this kiss, with goodbye and memories of fire. Tendrils of darkness lapped at her mind, trailing along her scalp, until she shivered in pleasure.

The sorceress let her go.

Nothing dragged her eyes open, swaying as if drunk.

The sorceress was whole, and beautiful.

One evergreen eye and one perfect bone-white eye stared back at her, hungry, from that pale copper face, high cheeks and thin, bowed lips. Her black-brown–lava-red hair piled in rolls and curls on her head, dripping with tiny pink and orange orchids. She had on a lavish black and dark-green dress made of silk and feathers and scales and even wisps of smoke.

"Goodbye, Nothing," said the Sorceress Who Eats Girls.

Nothing, barefoot in a ragged pink slip, stumbled back into the waiting arms of Sky and Kirin Dark-Smile.

TWENTY-NINE

———

THE MOMENT THEY WERE alone, Sky leading from a few paces ahead, Kirin took Nothing's shoulders in both hands and drew her to him.

Softly in her ear, he whispered her true name.

Then he said, "Forget your feelings for the sorceress. And then forget what I just said, including your name."

Nothing gave the prince an annoyed little frown. "What are you doing?"

He released her. "I'm glad you're going with us."

"Of course I'm going with you," she said, suddenly a little bit cold. She shrugged him away and dashed after Sky.

THIRTY

T HEY LEFT THE FIFTH Mountain before the sun set, on a slender barge cradled in the gentle, lapping fingers of the Selegan River.

The sorceress had given them clothing and blankets, food, water, and the boat itself, promising the river would see them south fast. They needed only follow the right fork twice, and at the third, some week hence, disembark on the eastern bank. Beyond there, the Selegan poured over waterfalls no ship could survive. But the travelers could join up with the Way of King-Trees and walk the remaining week to the capital city. More than a month's journey shortened by half.

Nothing found herself eager to be back home. She missed the quiet smoke ways and Whisper, and the purr of the great demon of the palace.

Esrithalan offered to visit the Court of the Moon immediately and inform the empress her son was safe and shortly to be returning, thus preventing more sorcerers or even an army from being dispatched to the Fifth Mountain in a rescue attempt. Kirin, smiling his dark smile, thanked the unicorn with an air that Nothing understood to mean the favor was more the result of the prince's conversation with the unicorn than any loyalty to the sorceress.

That was fine: unicorns were avatars of the gods, and nobody's familiar.

To each of the trio, the sorceress gave a gift:

For Sky she offered a sword. He tried to decline, but she smiled with all the humor of the god of ducklings and insisted. "The Selegan tossed yours into the river, I understand, and this is a magical blade, light as a feather and never in need of sharpening."

"Light as a feather will throw off my balance," Sky said plainly.

The sorceress smiled. "You'll learn."

For Kirin she had a strand of black pearls to twine with the green and white pearls he'd worn when she captured him. "Are these spelled?" he asked suspiciously.

"No," the sorceress said. "They were a gift to the spirit of the Fifth Mountain centuries ago, birthed from freshwater oysters in a country so far east even the Selegan could not travel there and back in a year."

He took them and wound them around his wrist and hand. Kirin inclined his head in polite thanks before allowing Sky to help him step off the small dock jutting out from a low cave mouth and onto the bobbing barge.

When Nothing stood alone on the dock, the sorceress held out a small green speckled pear.

Nothing stared at it.

"Here," the sorceress said gently.

Lifting her gaze to the sorceress's face, Nothing frowned. The pear clearly meant something, but Nothing didn't understand.

Strain pinched at the edges of the sorceress's mouth; tiny black feathers rippled along her cheekbones and back into her hairline, as if she did not quite have control of her form. These gifts, including the barge, their clothing, and the food, had been conjured in an instant, when the sorceress was exhausted. It had to be the depleted state of the heart in the mountain's core. Nothing felt a prickle of guilt. But what could she do? She needed to go home with Kirin. Then, after he was safe, find a way to stop the sorceress from killing. "Will you be well?" Nothing asked.

The sorceress hesitated, peering at Nothing as if she could see something beyond the physical world. Then she said, "Go, so that the Selegan can return to me, to find me a new heart for my ailing mountain. Then I will be well enough."

Nothing crossed her arms. She shivered in the mountain breeze. "You can't take more hearts. It's wrong. And you have no excuse that you're looking for your demon any longer."

The sorceress did not move except to blink. The pear gleamed in her outstretched palm. "You cannot say what I can or cannot do. What power have you over me?" The way she said it made Nothing realize the sorceress wanted Nothing to have an answer. To claim power over her.

"None," Nothing murmured. "Whatever we were in my previous incarnation, we are no longer. I don't know what . . . could be. But right now it's only the right thing to do." She tilted her head, staring at the sorceress. Beautiful, strange, with her one green eye and one bone white, and shadow-feathers under her skin. Nothing remembered the volcano of laughter inside herself, and the power she'd felt when she'd helped kill Skybreaker. That was the way to discovering all the colors shaded into the night sky. But it was like a dream. Now that she was leaving.

The sorceress said, "I will die without a heart, and the mountain crack."

"You have a heart," Nothing insisted.

"Only half of one."

Nothing snorted.

Surprise slid across the sorceress's face before she smoothed her expression, but Nothing didn't understand why the sorceress should be surprised. Why should she act like there'd been a connection between them? It had only ever been magic, curiosity, and Kirin.

Nothing said, "Promise me, on that heart. No more murder."

"A half promise on a half heart?"

Nothing frowned, wary. "Promise."

"You have nothing left with which to bargain."

Nothing left, Nothing thought sourly. Only herself. "What if I promise to return?"

"Do you?" The sorceress curled her fingers around the base of the pear, black-lacquered nails delicate against the skin.

"I will try," Nothing said slowly, wishing there were a way to reassure the sorceress, but she couldn't lie about what she didn't feel. Yes, there was more magic for her to experience, and she did love the Fifth Mountain. She'd been cheated of her final two days here, after all. But she had to see Kirin through his investiture ritual.

The sorceress stepped closer and pressed the pear into Nothing's hands. "Then I will try to wait for you, little demon. But do not stay away too long. I do not want to die, and without a heart, I will."

Cradling the pear, Nothing nodded. The sorceress seemed to want more, but Nothing spun away and hopped onto the barge. It rocked heavily in the river, and Nothing threw herself forward to remain on the deck. Water splashed, rippling and winking.

Kirin approached, took her elbow, and lifted a hand in farewell.

Nothing turned, leaning back against his chest where she belonged. Even given everything he'd kept from her, this was where she needed to be: with her prince, whom she loved more than anyone.

Together they watched the sorceress standing upon the dock as the Selegan shimmered in the sunlight, waves as bright silver-white as scales, and the barge pulled away.

She kept watching as the barge picked up speed, as wind tugged at her hair, flicking it across her eyes. She held the pear, staring at the dark pillar of black and green that was the sorceress, until they slipped around a bend in the river and she was gone.

The old lava field surrounded the river here: emerald-green moss and bright grass over the rolling cold lava. Flowers bobbed and bent, and the wind smelled like summertime. Nothing remembered the first moments she'd spent on that lava field, with Sky, and how she'd loved the land immediately. She'd felt like she belonged to the pretty remnants of destruction.

She would miss the Fifth Mountain until she managed to return.

"Nothing," Kirin murmured, and drew her toward the front

of the barge. She tucked the pear into the pocket of the long wool jacket she wore and tightened the sash at her waist.

Sky stood at the prow, one booted foot up on the low rail. It was a long, rectangular barge that sat shallowly against the river, edged with benches that doubled as storage and with a hold under the deck keeping their food and blankets dry. In the center a small pavilion rose, hung with drapes that could be pulled for privacy or against rain, and they had an iron stove squatting like a four-legged spider on the deck. Smoke trickled out of the little holes in the lid.

Nothing took a flat, canvas pillow from beneath the pavilion awning and set it beside the iron stove. She sat cross-legged and watched the smoke slick upward, wavering against the blue sky. The barge swayed gently as it flowed along the back of the Selegan. Kirin joined Sky at the prow. They both wore similar traveling clothing to Nothing: dark trousers, shirts, wrap jackets, and wide sashes. If it rained or grew cold, they had cloaks, and for the arrival at the palace each had a set of very fine silk and a box of paint pots. Nothing should have asked for a game to pass the time. Or anything to keep her hands busy, and her mind.

Especially her mind.

It seemed like she was forgetting something—but she couldn't quite pin down what. Her mind turned itself over, persistent and careful, looking for shadows and clues. But Nothing was probably just asking for trouble, now that they were going home.

She let herself doze, thoughts thinning, as she stared at the smoke and beyond at the banks. The lava field gave way to rain forest on both sides. Then there was no bank at all, only tall, mossy trees and thin red alders, and heavy, curling firs that dipped toward the Selegan. The water rushed over boulders, tearing at the damp mud and roots. It sounded like a song.

The sun arced nearer and nearer to the canopy. Sky knelt and reached over the rail to touch the water. "Selegan," he said. "Selegan, will you rush safely with us all night, or should we find a place to tie down until morning?"

Wings of water lifted to either side of the barge, spraying Nothing with a fine mist; rainbows sparkled in the light. She smiled. The dragon was so beautiful.

Kirin wiped his hands back through his damp hair, scowling slightly.

The Selegan River said, "I can fly easy with you all through the night."

Sky said, "Thank you, dragon."

He opened the panel into the hold and drew out a bag of cheese, handing it off to Nothing, along with oatcakes and dried meat. Then he pulled free a flask of wine.

They melted cheese onto the cakes, setting them against the stove, and shared the picnic as the sun turned the sky violet and pink.

That night Nothing slept curled against Kirin, while the prince leaned into Sky. The stars burned and the moon rose late, waking her with its brightness. Nothing tucked her blanket around herself and pressed her nose to Kirin's back. She listened to the river flow, the cry of frogs and whispering breeze through thick, wet canopy.

She already missed the weird corridors of the mountain, the crystal ceilings and glass-smooth obsidian. She missed the strangeness of the patterns in the Fifth Mountain, though she'd only been there for four days.

Nothing rolled onto her back and dug the pear from the pocket of her wrap jacket. It gleamed with tiny golden freckles in the moonlight. She rubbed it against her cheek, then put her mouth to the smooth skin. It smelled bright and rich. Nothing bit down, tearing a huge chunk free. Juice dripped onto her chin, and she closed her eyes, sinking into the crisp sweetness. It broke over her tongue, perfectly soft between her teeth, and she swallowed.

Darkness consumed her as if she'd fallen suddenly asleep, but when she opened her eyes she stood atop the Fifth Mountain, on a balcony curved out from a brightly lit cavern. The sorceress stood with her, hands on the elegant obsidian rail, gazing out into the night.

Nothing gasped quietly, for it felt real, not a dream.

The sorceress turned, brows up. "Nothing."

Moonlight spilled over her loose tricolored hair. She wore a thin robe wrapped around her, and a long line of her bare skin showed from neck to breast. Including the thin scar over her heart. She was barefoot.

Nothing gaped. She felt the cold wind and smelled the icy evergreen air of the mountain. Behind her warmth billowed out from the cavern.

"You must have taken a large bite," the sorceress said, leaning coolly back against the rail as if the balcony were a throne.

"The pear?" Nothing's voice was hoarse.

"The pear."

"It's magic. I'm really here."

"Part of you."

"How long?"

"Hard to say. But it will work with a smaller slice, enough for you to see me, speak with me. No matter how far from the mountain you travel."

"Why?"

"So you can visit me." The sorceress frowned. "Do you not wish to?"

Instead of answering, Nothing asked, "Is this what we were making with the patterns cut into the floor? The long-sight spell?"

The sorceress slid her hands along the rail and nodded. Draped only in the robe and moonlight, the sorceress appeared human. Just a young woman, not the wife of a demon, not a changeable witch familiar to dragons and unicorns.

Nothing couldn't believe she'd flung herself at Skybreaker for the sorceress.

But she'd been so sure it was the right thing to do. She'd not been sorry at all. She'd laughed! She remembered her glee, the triumphant flavor of her laughter. Is that what it meant to be a demon? Joy in violence?

What if Skybreaker had killed the sorceress? No other girls would be killed for their hearts. The mountain would be free, and so would Nothing be.

It didn't hurt Nothing to imagine such a thing, though she'd thought she was growing to care for the sorceress. Had it merely been proximity and the vibrations of the mountain heart?

"I miss the mountain already," she said, to cover her sudden discomfort.

The sorceress smiled flatly. "I have missed you for so long I hardly notice anymore."

"Not me. It isn't me you've missed," Nothing insisted. "I'm different."

"Yes, you are different. I like it, though." The sorceress shrugged one shoulder. "Come back. Leap off the barge and return to me. Let the prince go home at the side of his heroic lover."

"I can't."

"Why?"

"I want to go back to the palace. I have to. I belong there, with Kirin."

"You *love* him." The sorceress's voice burned.

Nothing stopped breathing for a moment, caught by the vicious word *love*. It seemed as though the sorceress were having this conversation with someone else—someone beloved. Nothing said, "Of course I do. That was never in doubt."

"Isn't it?" The sorceress's eyes cut up, dangerous.

"Do you think my true name could make me love?" Nothing stepped closer, then stepped back again. "When I break his mastery over me, I won't love him anymore?"

The sorceress narrowed her eyes. "I did not think when I found my demon again that it would love someone else."

"I'm sorry."

"I thought you were remembering." The sorceress looked away. Her lithe body turned slowly, gracefully, away from Nothing. She stared out over the balcony, every piece of her tense.

"Oh," Nothing whispered. "I . . . remember the volcano. I remember power. The feel of it. That's not love."

The sorceress was silent.

Nothing clenched her fists, wishing she weren't so cold. Why couldn't the memory of fire and magma warm her again? She said, "Isn't it good? That I can love someone else? If I was a demon and you gave me new life, isn't it good that I have such a capacity for love? I love the red-wash of the palace walls and the rumble of the great demon. I love Whisper and the sound of wind through the smoke ways. I love the Lily Garden. And Kirin, yes, and Sky, too, now. Or maybe I have for a long time but didn't realize it. I fell in love with the lava field and the mirror lake the moment I saw them."

"But not me."

"That doesn't mean . . . I never could." It felt cruel to pretend Nothing could make such a promise. She said, "Every time I think about love, I think of something else that fits within it. Have you truly never loved more than one other thing?"

The sorceress pushed off the rail, stalking toward Nothing. "My one thing filled me up. I was consumed, and that is where power was born. On the edge of devastation, from the desperate urge to be more, to make more."

"That sounds like obsession, not love," Nothing whispered. "It sounds frightening."

"Yes," the sorceress whispered back, dragging the word into a tender hiss. "Frightening, exhilarating."

Nothing's pulse raced, knocking through her blood like thunder. The sorceress's pupils elongated, turning bloodred. Her teeth were jagged shark's teeth, and she reached for Nothing with a hand tipped by curved black talons. She skimmed their points against Nothing's cheek, teasing and sharp. Nothing shivered, flushing because she liked knowing the slightest pressure, any sudden slip, and those talons could flay her skin from her bones. She liked it very much.

"Kirin doesn't do this to you. Your old life, old friends don't. There is *nothing* in the palace of the empress that draws you like I do."

"That's not true," Nothing said, and the words did the trick: the talons sliced into her. Tiny lines of pain flared.

The sorceress whispered, "Don't you want to be loved more than anything else in the world?"

Nothing shivered. Blood slowly slipped down her jaw and onto her neck. The sorceress shifted her hand so that it was the soft pad of a finger that touched Nothing, then drew the finger toward Nothing's mouth.

"When you are far from me, remember what you were and what you long for," the sorceress whispered, leaning nearer.

For a moment Nothing imagined allowing herself to be what the sorceress promised: not a demon, but a lover. A consort to be cherished and touched. She could be a part of something magnificent, and not only a shadow, a word whispered here or there, a bargain of information, a flash of bare feet, but an intrinsic part. The core. A core made in tandem with someone else.

She remembered splattering magma and stone so hot it creaked and cracked. A restless heat, aching to expand, to explode. Her heart was a volcano, waiting. She did want it.

Her eyes flew open.

Nothing was on the barge, splayed on her back, panting up at the stars and hanging moon.

The feeling was gone. Nothing's hand curled around the pear

as if she could hold on to the feeling. She clutched it against her stomach, eyes shut, and calmed slowly down. Her cheek stung, and touching it, Nothing discovered she bled slightly. Only a smear, from the sorceress's talons.

Nothing ached with emptiness. For the first time she felt like she had only half a heart.

But she didn't understand why.

The barge swayed like a cradle, and the wind and frogs were her lullaby. Nothing tucked the pear into her pocket again and sat up. Carefully she crept to the prow and huddled there, staring out into the wind. The moon wavered on every ripple of the river, like a thousand silver-white scales.

THIRTY-ONE

I T WAS BORING ON the barge, especially by the second day. Nothing did not tell her companions about the pear or her visit with the sorceress. She knew it had been real, but she kept it as her secret.

The barge moved faster than the rest of the river as the Selegan pulled them along with its flight. Soon they saw smoke signs trailing up in the distance, from villages in the northern rain forest, and once or twice people fishing from the banks or from small hanging docks were startled as the barge sped past.

The three of them spoke sometimes, reminiscing occasionally about random childhood memories or discussing what might have happened in the weeks they'd been gone. Sky and Nothing told Kirin again everything they knew of the imposter's return, and he told them every dull, slow detail of his captivity, interspersed with a few terrifying encounters with the sorceress before Nothing had freed him.

Nothing did not like speaking of the sorceress.

She asked Kirin about the investiture ritual.

"I have told you most of what I know," he said. "When I was born, I was named as all heirs are named—"

"Kirin for the Moon," Nothing said.

"And called a much better name as I grew up and showed who I am." He grinned. "I am to remain pure, my insides untouched in order to be a perfect vessel for the Moon. And as you both now know, the Moon is part of the name of the great demon of the palace. At my investiture ritual I will be presented to the court and, alone with my mother and the demon, given the demon's full name. I've never been told more details—I've not needed to know them. Probably there is a priest who knows, and I assume my father and the Second Consort, as becoming linked to the demon is the only reason to contain them to the palace. Once I am invested, I cannot leave the palace again."

A shadow flattened his eyes, but Kirin shook it off. "I will be the true Heir to the Moon—you'll both be there to witness it. Once the Moon has accepted me, we can be together, Sky."

Sky pressed his mouth together. "We need a good story to cover up why she took you. Not even your mother and father can know you traveled as a girl. And that I did not tell them."

"Even if they discover it, I will keep you safe," Kirin said, flippant.

Nothing scowled. "You did it for the Moon, Sky. You kept his secrets because you are devoted, because you serve the Heir to the Moon. They can't fault you for keeping him safe."

Kirin studied his bodyguard thoughtfully. "That isn't what he's worried about."

Sky pinned Kirin with a glare. "They could guess what else we've done. It was difficult enough to keep my feelings tucked away before. And difficult enough when I had you for only moments or secret, stolen afternoons. Now that I've had you for so many days, mine constantly, free to be yours, how can I tuck my longing away again? They'll see it in my eyes, hear it in my voice. I am not built for lies. I should not return with you. They will see what I am to you, what I want from you. What I've taken from you, Kirin. It will muddy the inheritance. It—"

The bodyguard cut himself off abruptly, as if so many words tumbling from his mouth were his entire allotment for the next year.

Kirin said gently, but firmly, "You have to endure for only a few weeks, until the stars are right again and the ritual can be arranged and completed, Sky. You can do that. You can hide from my mother and father, from the priests. You must."

"The great demon will see I've ruined your purity."

Kirin stood. He towered over his sitting lover. "Sky," the prince said, voice low, "The Day the Sky Opened." He put his foot on Sky's thigh and nudged roughly. Sky held his ground. Kirin moved behind him, leaning down with his hands on Sky's shoulders. He put his cheek to Sky's cheek. "When you touch me, you make me more myself. I am pure *because* of you, not in spite of you."

Sky's chin fell as if in defeat. His shoulders slumped.

"Do you hear me?" Kirin pushed, hands sliding down over Sky's shoulders onto his chest, and Kirin pressed his whole body against Sky.

"I do," Sky murmured.

"I need you. You make me worthy of the Moon," Kirin said,

and Sky twisted to grab Kirin and was kissing him like he was drowning.

For a moment Nothing stared. She felt . . . hungry. Her mind and heart were missing a piece she'd never known she needed.

The sorceress had kissed her, but not like that. Nothing pressed her hand over her brand, digging her fingers in hard enough to bruise. The sorceress's kiss had been . . . Nothing closed her eyes, trying to remember. It was like a story she'd heard about a kiss. Details, tender caresses, but from a distance.

The missing half of her heart had never felt so heavy.

Nothing left. She went to the prow of the barge, ignoring their noises. She bent over to touch the water. It was cool and crystal clear. She saw tiny fish darting away and round river rocks wavering at the bottom. "Selegan," she whispered. Behind her Sky grunted and one of them moaned breathlessly.

"Selegan," Nothing said more sharply. "I need to swim with you, please."

The river spirit splashed her, and Nothing gasped; then the droplets of water drew out into long feathery fingers. They slid down her neck and arm and twined around her hand, tugging at her. She quickly removed her boots and wrap jacket, then slipped over the rail and lowered herself into the cold water. She clung to the barge, and then a strong scaly neck lifted her bare feet, propping her up in the water. She laughed, throwing out one arm for balance.

With one hand on the barge, she stood, grinning into the spraying wind, as the Selegan drew her along. It was like flying. Water tore at her shirt and trousers, dragging hard. She leaned her head back, eyes closed, and held on.

Then suddenly, Nothing let go.

She fell away, sucked into the river. Currents pulled at her, and she felt scales slip under her palms, claws tangle gently in her hair, then release. She held her breath, feeling only water, like swift-moving blood, roaring around her. She did not swim or fight, but let the river take her.

It lifted her, tossing her into the air.

Nothing laughed breathlessly. She fell beneath the surface with a hard splash. The Selegan embraced her in tails of water, kissing her cheeks with feather fingers and sharp pinches.

She learned the song of splashing and holding her breath, of giant gasps for air, the current in her fingers and combing through her hair. She tasted the river, loved the flow of it against her body.

Eventually, later, she was too tired to balance air and water, and the Selegan lifted her high enough she grasped the rail and dragged herself over it, collapsing on the deck.

She rolled onto her back, panting and drained but happy. Sun prickled her cheeks as it dried her. Her trousers and shirt stuck to her skin as she melted.

"Good swim?" Sky asked.

Nothing opened her eyes to the glare of sunlight. She winced up at him: he leaned on the rail near her in only his trousers. His hair was wet too, flaring blue-black in the wind at the prow. The sun found blue and purple in all the glinting copper of his skin, but his eyes were warm brown and human.

"Yes," she answered, stretching her arms up, arching her back. She felt good.

"I'm cooking!" called Kirin, and Nothing rolled her head to

see the prince kneeling primly beside the iron stove, wrapped in a pretty robe, his hair caught up in a messy topknot. He held a spoon like a wand and smiled very sweetly at her. Then his gaze shifted to Sky and he licked his lips, glancing demurely down.

It was such an affectation, Nothing laughed.

Kirin's expression darkened, and she laughed harder.

"Never mind her," Sky said reassuringly. "I appreciate it."

The prince narrowed his eyes at Nothing, then painted sweetness back onto his face and fluttered his lashes at Sky. "You can eat, then."

Nothing kept her smile on as she stood and stripped off her clothes. Kirin's eyes widened and she just shrugged. She hung the shirt and trousers on the pavilion to dry.

"Demon," Kirin accused as she passed him, walking to the rear of the barge to spread herself out in the sun.

A while later Kirin dropped a robe on her. "Food," he said.

Having been lightly asleep, Nothing rubbed her eyes. Her skin felt hot and maybe slightly burned. She grimaced, practicing wild, scary faces that bared her teeth and widened her eyes into saucers. Then she wrapped herself in the robe and joined Kirin and Sky at the stove.

They lounged on pillows, eating lentils Kirin had cooked with dried meat and peas. The sun dragged down, pulling clouds with it in long orange streaks. At one point Kirin stood and went to the rail to offer lentils to the Selegan. The sight warmed Nothing's heart. Though it had been a long day, it had been a good one, and she wanted to remain on the river forever.

When Kirin rejoined them, his shoulder leaning against Sky's, Nothing said, "Kirin you should make Sky your First Consort."

Sky stilled, and Kirin frowned, carefully not looking at his bodyguard.

Nothing said, "He deserves to be First. What does it matter your heirs would come from a Second Consort? If you can't do it, you should let him go."

"Nothing," Sky said in a warning rumble.

"Make Sky your First," she challenged. "It is a better offer than Second. He deserves it."

"And would you be my Second?" Kirin sneered.

"Kirin, don't." Sky made it a command.

Both Kirin and Nothing stared at him, shocked.

Sky gritted his teeth and leveled Nothing with a brief, meaningful look. Then he faced Kirin. "If you ask, she'll say yes. She always does what you ask."

"We are going to free her," Kirin said, and it was tinged with just enough regret to infuriate Nothing.

She tucked her knees to her chest and planted her chin there.

"Does that matter?" Sky sounded almost tender now. "You never owned my name, and still I do as you wish."

"Because you want to," Kirin argued. "Because I'm right."

"And you're the Heir to the Moon."

Kirin shrugged one shoulder, haughty and cool.

Nothing snorted. "How do we even love you?"

A triumphant smile spread slowly across his wicked mouth. "A heart has many petals."

Sky glowered, but it was shadowed with amusement.

They were helpless for the prince, Nothing knew, and she lay back, hands folded against her chest. She went to sleep listening to her prince and her friend quietly bicker and tease, until Kirin finally whispered, "Would you say yes?" and Sky whispered back, "If you ask."

THIRTY-TWO

NOTHING WAITED THREE MORE days before taking another taste of the pear. Partly because she didn't think to earlier. When she remembered it, she was stunned at her own forgetfulness.

It was just before dawn, before either of the boys woke, before villagers put their small fishing boats out onto the river, and she nibbled at the edge of her previous bite: surprisingly none of the pear had browned or bruised, despite her keeping it in her pocket.

She opened her eyes in the sorceress's bedroom. One entire wall was comprised of mirrors in many shapes and sizes. The sorceress knelt before a rectangular mirror that leaned against the wall. A rainbow of paint pots was arrayed around her. She leaned in and drew a curving feather of bright blue down her cheek with a thin brush.

Nothing did not speak, but met the sorceress's eyes in the mirror.

"Hello," the sorceress said. She flicked her brush against her chin, completing the delicate feather, and set the brush down on a scrap of cloth.

Still Nothing remained quiet. She'd thought, lying awake in the first light over the barge, as the stars diminished, that maybe the sorceress watched the morning arrive too. It had made her feel cold and lonely. So she'd come.

"Nothing," the sorceress said in a light singsong. Coaxing Nothing to speak.

"Do you think I can do magic away from the mountain?" Nothing asked in a rush.

"Yes."

Nothing sat down abruptly. "Just as easy as that?"

"You can speak with spirits and demons, you can hear the aether and see it, can't you? So you can do magic." She picked a new brush and dipped it into a pot of vivid gold. With it, she dotted tiny sparkles along the feather on her cheek, as though it shed glittery sunshine.

"How?"

"Ask a witch. Ask the great demon of the palace. Ask someone who is with you."

"I'm asking you."

"Come home and I'll teach you more."

Nothing scooted closer. "Paint my face?"

The sorceress turned and patted a pillow beside her. Nothing situated herself upon it, facing the sorceress. "Be still," the sorceress said.

Nothing closed her eyes. The first touch of the brush surprised her, and she jerked from the cold paint.

"Nothing," the sorceress chided.

"Sorry," she answered with a grimace before relaxing her expression.

It became soothing: the stroke of paint, the tickle as it dried, the absence and soft *tap-tap* of a brush to the rim of a pot. Nothing tried at first to track the shape of the strokes as they covered her left cheek and curled around her mouth, as they fluttered over her left eyelid and just barely lined her right eye. She breathed slowly and evenly, finding great calm in merely sitting and holding still. It was easy, she realized: just existing in the sorceress's presence. She liked it.

"Do you remember the first dinner we shared?" the sorceress asked. "You arrived with your face painted like a furious green demon, with red eyes and a scowl."

"I was angry. I wanted to be scary." Nothing opened her eyes. "I didn't know how it would make you feel."

The sorceress wore a soft smile. "How did it make me feel?" she asked tenderly.

"Like you were right about me."

"You surprised me, and I am not used to being surprised." The sorceress leaned in. "I liked it. I like you, Nothing. I like what you are now."

"I like you, too, except . . ." Nothing stopped. She licked her lips and tasted paint. As she started to turn to look in the mirror, the sorceress flattened her hand against the frame and it blackened. Nothing scowled for real now. "What?"

"What don't you like?" the sorceress asked.

Nothing had to think about what she'd been saying. Then she answered, "You take hearts."

"Bargain. It is always a bargain."

"That doesn't make it less cruel, less . . ." Nothing fluttered her hands. "Less inhuman."

"Some girls are very willing to give up their hearts, and their lives."

"You take advantage."

The sorceress shrugged. "Sometimes, maybe."

"It doesn't bother you?"

"Why should it?"

Nothing opened her mouth, but she didn't know what to say.

The sorceress reached out and put a finger against Nothing's chest. "Why does it bother you?"

Nothing shook her head. She knew the answer but didn't want to say it.

"Why?"

"Because it's supposed to."

The sorceress's brows lifted in perfect black arcs.

Nothing crossed her arms stubbornly. "It's wrong to hurt other people."

"You helped me kill Skybreaker."

"He attacked you. I was protecting you, and the mountain, and—and Kirin."

"So sometimes hurting another is acceptable."

"Not for selfishness."

"Was it not selfish to save me? You protect Kirin because you care about him. I take hearts to keep myself alive—to save me. And to find my demon, the other half of my heart. Is that a less noble cause?"

"They didn't do anything to deserve it. He did."

"Oh, they were innocent, you mean. Nobody is innocent, tender heart."

Nothing frowned. "If they were, would you care?"

"Not if it meant finding you again. I would destroy a thousand hearts to find you, again and again."

At that, it was difficult for Nothing to breathe.

She was excited by the sorceress's passion—and maybe a little bit afraid. But she wanted more.

The sorceress's bare cheek flushed, and the wing upon her other cheek flashed with speckles of gold. Her eyes bored into Nothing. She said, "I fell in love with a great demon. Why do you expect me to care for the innocent, the noble, the good? There is no such thing: the world is made of shadows and luck, not good or evil, night and day. Humans pretend. They seek contrast and rules. But the forest knows. The mountains know. The sky knows. Those hearts transformed; they became what they were meant to be. They brought a mountain to life."

Nothing leaned away, her breath heaving. "No," she whispered. "Good exists. Evil exists. Maybe—maybe they aren't opposite, not like day and night, but they're real. Good and evil are both shadows."

The sorceress smiled hungrily. "I like that. We're both shadows, too."

"The Fifth Mountain should not consume human hearts. I don't want that. It's wrong."

"But you do want it. You keep coming back to me."

Nothing thrust herself away, shaking her head, dizzy. "I don't know what I want. I don't know what I am—"

And suddenly she opened her eyes to sunlight and Sky's worried face. "Nothing," he said, his hand on her jaw, pressing to wake her. "Nothing."

"I'm—" she tried to say around his strong hand.

He let go. "Your eyes were open, but you weren't . . . aware. And for a . . ."

Nothing shut her eyes, listening to the echo of the sorceress's voice. *You keep coming back to me.*

"You had scales," Sky said. "Silver-green scales on the left side of your face."

Her eyes flew open. She stood up, ran to the rail and lifted the pear. Her pulse throbbed in her skull and she was dizzy.

But she did not throw it away. Her arm slowly fell, and her heaving shoulders drooped. She could not do it. Instead, Nothing tucked the pear back into her pocket.

THIRTY-THREE

NOTHING TOLD KIRIN AND Sky about the pear.

The prince was surprisingly quiet on the subject. He merely said, "A better gift than you'd imagined, then," and started cooking breakfast. Sky, though, studied Nothing with concern.

"What are you doing?" he asked quietly.

"What do you mean?"

"With the sorceress. Is she not your enemy?"

Nothing hugged herself. She didn't know. She felt weird, unbalanced when she thought of the sorceress. Like she just couldn't quite grasp something—but she knew what the shape of it was.

"She is the Sorceress Who Eats Girls. She kidnapped the Heir to the Moon." Sky's voice remained calm, but Nothing heard an urgency hidden within it.

"I know what she is."

Sky was silent. He stared at her, unblinking, hard.

Nothing tightened her hold on herself. "I do," she said weakly.

"Be careful."

"I'm careful."

"Nothing." Sky put his hands on his hips, eyes narrowing as he continued to peer at her. "I do not want you to be hurt. You are a—friend. But Kirin was hurt by her. The empire was. You can't be on her side."

"Her side," Nothing repeated. Something was uncoiling inside her. Night and day, her side, their side.

Sky nodded.

"What do you want, when we are home? Will you be with us? We would like that."

Nothing caught her breath. She held it, tucking her lips into her mouth to make them disappear. She stared at the line of his collarbone and her vision blurred. Not with tears, but with shadows. She remembered wanting. She remembered wanting to know the sorceress, wanting to be hot magic—but she didn't seem to want that anymore. Why?

Sky stepped closer to her. He said, so quietly it was more vibration than words, "You should decide, or Kirin will do what he wants instead."

"What should I do?" Nothing asked before she could stop herself, jerking her chin up to stare back at him. She struggled with her breathing, because her heart threatened to tighten her veins, to make her chest ache in panic. Why did it scare her to think about wanting something? Why was she afraid of what she might choose?

Sky was good. He would tell her the good choice.

"You have to choose what to be." Sky stopped, clenched his jaw, looking incredibly displeased with himself.

Nothing released a shaky sigh.

He said, "Do you want to be Nothing, as if there has been no change between you and Kirin, between you and the world? Or do you to be a hero who rescued the prince from a sorceress and earned a new name? It will be honored. Or . . ." Sky stopped.

Nothing continued. "Or do I want to tell everyone where I come from? Do I want to be a reborn demon, first of my kind?" Shaking off his hand, she stepped the final pace between them. She was so close she could feel the chill of his demon-kissed blood. She had to tilt her chin awkwardly to meet his dark eyes. In the sunlight, they did not gleam demon-blue. "Do you think it's still inside me, Sky? The great demon of the Fifth Mountain? Is it possible? Can I be something so large?"

Sky cupped her face. Holding her gaze without hesitation, he said, "After this summer I can believe anything of you."

"If I was a demon, can I be a girl at all?" None of the options felt right to her. Something was missing. Another choice. Nothing, a new hero's name, or her past. Something neither night nor day, neither her side nor theirs. Her own and between it all. A new name, a shadow name, for the person she could become. A name to make her future.

Kirin appeared beside them. He curled his long fingers around Sky's wrist and pulled that hand away from Nothing's cheek. "I wouldn't complain so much as you if I learned my heart had belonged to a demon once."

The absurdity made Nothing laugh.

Sky put the hand Kirin grasped onto Kirin's face so that the bodyguard held them both. He said, "You're both demons, and I don't know if I can keep you both safe."

"Good thing then that your job is only to keep me safe," Kirin said with a vicious smile.

Nothing jabbed her fingers into his ribs.

"Oof," he said, and bared his teeth at her. "Do you believe you're a demon?" Kirin asked. "You seemed to believe it, when we were at the mountain."

"I did, when we were at the mountain. All the evidence . . ." She shook her head. "I've always heard the aether, and you compelled me as a child with my name. I could do magic in the mountain, and the flower carved into the mountain is just like my brand. The sorceress would know, wouldn't she? How can I not believe it?"

"But do you feel it?" Kirin asked lightly. "A heart has many petals. Maybe there is more than one choice. Maybe you are more than one thing."

Nothing frowned.

Sky's hand on her cheek was cool, and she lowered her chin, letting his fingers slide into her hair a little bit. She said, "When I was there, I think I did feel it, but since we left . . . I'm not sure. Sometimes I feel like my heart is a volcano. But maybe that's what hearts are supposed to feel like."

Kirin pushed away from both of them. He went to the iron stove and knelt to stir sugar into the boiling grains. He said, "Neither of you has ever asked me how I know I'm not . . . a man."

Nothing glanced quickly at Sky, who shook his head at her and went to join Kirin, steps slow with trepidation. "How do you know?" Sky asked.

"I *just know*," Kirin said, hot and immediate. He nailed

Nothing with a glare. "What do *you* know? You decide what you are. You."

"Why don't you tell everyone you're a girl, then?" Nothing cried. "If you're going to act like it's easy, then really act like it."

"Because sometimes I'm *not* a girl," he said. "Sometimes I *am* a man. Sometimes I'm both, or neither. I'm something different, in between. There are plenty of *me*s. Only my body doesn't change. Sometimes I wish it could. Like the sorceress. I wish I could melt between, because I hate that what I am doesn't always fit with what people see. Sometimes that makes me feel . . . distorted. And then some other times I'm perfectly happy with . . . me. And I love what I am."

Sky looked away. His cheeks had darkened. He ran his hands back through his hair.

Nothing understood what Kirin had said. On some fundamental level, she understood. She thought about it, about knowing, and realized that she couldn't trust anything inside herself, any feelings she had or didn't, any understanding of who she was. Not when she didn't even know her name and how she felt about it.

She opened her mouth to ask again, to make him tell her. But she stopped. Sky had reached to tentatively put his fingers against Kirin's jaw and held the prince's gaze as if trying to communicate when he couldn't speak in front of witnesses. Kirin's lips trembled. He was afraid. Her glorious, ambitious prince was *afraid* of how Sky might react to his confession. He was eager; he was determined. He was so many things, all at once.

A Heart Has Many Petals.

The name uncoiled.

Her name. Kirin's name for her. How many times had he said it since they'd left the mountain and she'd not noticed? He'd been telling her for days.

Nothing pushed the heel of her thumb into her chest as the world tilted.

But it wasn't enough. The name was a key, but she had to blast open the door. Nothing had to free herself.

She needed a new name that was all her own. Not what she had been, or was now, or given to her by an accidental sorcerer who was also a prince.

The sorceress had said to her, *This is how magic works: you find it yourself.*

And, *Names can change. That is a magic we all share.*

Whirling, Nothing went to the prow of the barge and gripped the rail. She closed her eyes, ignoring Kirin and Sky as they called after her, ignoring the spray of water, ignoring the brilliant crystal sunlight.

The shadows inside her were growing, warming tendrils of darkness reaching, licking, and eager. So very eager.

She thought of what she longed for.

And Nothing gave herself a new name.

THIRTY-FOUR

N THE DEEPEST CAVERN of the Fifth Mountain, a heart pulsed hard in the prison of smoky quartz, and then the crystal cracked.

The sound echoed sharply throughout the obsidian corridors, skittering along granite floors and pooling around stalactites. The Sorceress Who Eats Girls felt it before she heard it, rather like a flicker of lightning before thunder.

Her own heart had fluttered before, with weakness and skipping, and she thought at first it was only the same such. She paused her reading and slipped the quill between the pages to mark her place before pressing her palm over her chest.

Then the echo reached her library, reverberating through the very stone of the mountain so low, so final, that the sorceress gasped.

She lost control, and sharp feathers sprouted up her cheekbones and down her spine, and her shoulder blades ached with the powerful press of wings. Her finger bones curled and started to crack, but the sorceress breathed again and forced her body to her will.

Standing, she walked at a measured pace, full of dread, through the library hearth and into the heart chamber.

The eerie glow of the mountain had faded quite a lot, but she did not have the energy to spare for a crown of bat-bone light or aether-torch. The sorceress took one of the far spiraling staircases and made her way over an arch and then beneath a perpendicular stair, to the plinth in the center of the cavern.

The smoky quartz had blackened and cracked nearly in half.

That old last heart she'd bargained for sat in a gruesome puddle, congealed and stringy. Dead.

The Sorceress Who Eats Girls did not touch it. She stared, allowing herself a moment to grieve. Not for the girl, or the heart, but for herself. This ending had come faster than she'd expected, and now her choices were two: go find another girl, another heart, and betray her half promise to Nothing, or hold the power of the Fifth Mountain a day, a week, a month if she could, hoping Nothing returned quickly, and in time, before the sorceress was as much a puddle of congealed magic as that dead heart.

She flinched as the heart shuddered, then berated herself for the weakness. To prove she was unaffected, the sorceress grasped the remains of the heart in her hand. It was cold and sticky, only so much spoiled meat.

Lifting it out of its shattered crystal cradle, the sorceress squeezed until globs smeared between her fingers and slithered over her knuckles before plopping to the platform at her feet. One tiny chunk hit the toe of her silk slipper.

The sorceress cast it away with a cry. She flung up her hands and leapt from the platform. Wings unfurled, and she bowed them in wide arcs to slow her descent. She landed on the floor of the cavern in a gentle crouch, black talons gouging the stone.

She strode out, angry enough to go the long way, especially as she should not expend more unnecessary magic traveling through the shadow-ways of the mountain.

She missed the cruel laugh of her demon when she was upset. How it would be amused at her now, judging her for letting it come to this. *How can you despise me for loving you?* she'd demanded once, and it had answered, *Judge me for my weaknesses too, and give me a life of my own to ruin at your side. That is what I want, more than I want to devour the whole world. If that is not love, what is?*

The sorceress closed her eyes and sneered at herself, a high hiss through her razor teeth, because she'd been alone for so long, and then her mountain had been alive again.

Alive with only the energy of that strange, pretty, surprising girl.

How she wanted to shred that pretty skin, reach down that hot throat and awaken the spark of her demon. She would have kissed it to awareness, chewed it into fullness.

"Sorceress!"

It was her.

The sorceress stopped, nearly colliding with Nothing.

No.

She was different. The girl was different, fuller already.

The sorceress's heart began to beat again, and she'd hardly noticed it pause.

But the girl stared up at her, expression wide with . . . It was hard to say.

"What's wrong?" the girl asked. Her voice was thicker, her dark-brown eyes vivid with sparks of fire. Was she slightly taller? More elegant and graceful despite the thin tunic that barely skimmed her knees and her scraggly, tangled black hair. Was the sorceress hallucinating because she was so very exhausted by the weight of the mountain?

No, this was illusion. The girl was on the barge, sailing far from here. This was the magical projection of herself: that was all. The girl had changed her self-knowledge and thus her projection changed.

A shimmer of scales the color of starlight appeared like a sheen of sweat under the young woman's eyes and along her brow.

The sorceress said, "You're you."

A pit opened inside her, filled with fear and love.

The girl smiled broadly, and somehow it was both a dark night smile and brilliant dappled starlight. "I am!" she cried, and then turned in a circle to show off.

A flicker of moon-bright wings spread from her shoulders, moth wings, or butterfly, gone again, and the young woman stepped nearer to the sorceress. "I wanted to show you. I named myself, Sorceress. I am free of Kirin's binding. I feel so massive!" She laughed.

It was another surprise. This young woman, this creature, was constantly catching the sorceress off guard, changing expectations, pushing and pulling. She was exhilarating, and the sorceress tried to smile, but her mouth was a monster's mouth, chitin-hard and full of shark's teeth. With effort, she dragged herself into her woman form, leaving only teeth and eyes like monsters. Sweat broke down her back and under her breasts. It should have been easy. But the mountain's heart was dead.

As the new young woman stared at her, joyous and strange, the sorceress realized what had happened: She'd named herself, and it did break her free. Not only of Kirin, but of everything she had been. The rebirth was complete, finally. That's why the mountain heart had cracked.

"Do you remember?" the sorceress asked in a rough whisper.

The reborn mountain, the girl of the demon heart, grabbed the sorceress's hands, and her eyes sparked again. She squeezed and said, "I remember fire and a joy so sharp it must be ecstasy. That's inside me. Power. I am so large with it."

"Mountain size," the sorceress said.

The young woman laughed. "Sometimes as tiny as a flower—a balsam, I think, with weird petals, but it likes the taste of lava rock."

It sounded like nonsense, and the sorceress wanted to ask for the demon girl's new name. Instead she said, "Be gentle with your body as you learn to be massive, too."

"How can a mountain fit inside this?" She flung out her arms again and spun. "I'm so alive."

"Are you coming home?"

"Not yet. I will, but not yet. I have to see Kirin home, and I have to show the great demon of the palace. I have to see my old friends and make everyone safe. I want to stay for the investiture, to make certain everything is in order. Then I will."

The sorceress held herself still. "Be quick, tender heart," she said with as little inflection as possible.

"Because you miss me?" the brilliant young woman said with an edge. A dare.

"Because I cannot hold the mountain forever. I will hunt again, soon." She would not tell her the heart was already dead, that this rebirth had killed it. The sorceress refused to have her come home to save other girls or out of desperation or a belief that she must.

It would be a choice. This young woman had said it herself when she was Nothing. She would choose to come home, or never do so.

Something like disappointment bled into the young woman's large brown eyes, drawing the sorceress. How the sorceress wanted to kiss her again, to taste the new flavors there. How she wanted to ask her new name.

Instead the sorceress bared her jagged shark's teeth and leaned in. "You'd better be ready when you come back to me. To hold your own against me and with me. I might eat you alive."

The young woman bared her teeth back, but they were only small white human teeth, pretty as pearls. In her eyes, though, the volcano rumbled, and the sorceress felt an answering heat inside her. "I hope you try," the young woman said.

With that, she vanished, pulled back to the barge and her body, pulled away as she always was pulled away.

The sorceress let go a tiny gasp of pain as she listed sideways, sinking against the smooth granite corridor. Her skin ruffled; her bones ached. She was a woman, a monster, both and neither. She gritted her teeth and held on to herself.

But barely.

THIRTY-FIVE

NIGHT SHINE OVER THE Mountain had been her name for only half a day when the sorcerers of the Second and Third Living Mountains came for her.

Something flashed in the east, high in the clouds, like a mirror catching sunlight, and Shine sat up, wandering to the rail of the barge, eyes fixed upon it. The brightness didn't hurt, and that's how she knew it was aether, not real sunlight, which still made her human-enough eyes water if she stared.

The barge suddenly stuttered in its smooth flow, and Shine spun. "Selegan?"

Then she heard a crackling sound and a low groan: ahead of the barge, ice chased toward them.

It clawed and rushed, freezing the river so fast the water moaned.

Sky appeared at her side, and Kirin too, with his hand on her shoulder. "What's happening?" the prince asked.

A ripple of silver scales and choppy waves streaked across their path, and the Selegan burst up, a huge, ferocious dragon lashing its triple tails. It roared at the ice, blasting it back with a wave of itself.

Its wings spread, glinting just like the ice, and Shine saw frost edging the feathers.

She didn't know what to do.

Arrows of ice flung up, burying themselves in the dragon: it bent and screamed, and water splattered down on the trio.

Shine gripped the rail, put her foot up to leap over, but Sky grabbed her around the waist. "Stop," he said.

Kirin leaned over the prow, hands spread, and called, "Release the Selegan River! I am Kirin Dark-Smile and I command you, whoever you are. Release the river, and us."

"Put me down," Shine said, struggling against Sky's iron strength.

He dropped her and unsheathed his sword as light flared around them, warm and sunny.

Shine looked up just in time to see an even more brilliant glow. She flung up an arm to block the radiance: the shape of it echoed behind her eyes. An eagle?

Claws dug into her shoulders, and Shine screamed.

She pressed her fists over her chest, reaching for the volcano inside her, but—

Shine hit a hard surface.

The shock threw her breath away, and she struggled to turn over, choking for air.

It was dark, complete blackness around her, and under her hands and knees was stone. Cold, reverberating stone.

"Kirin," Shine said, tasting damp air—mountain air!

This was not her mountain, though. It felt off, filled with someone else's magic.

Swallowing fear, Shine opened her eyes, searching for aether. Even in darkness there should be strands of it.

Were her eyes even open? There was such complete darkness. She thought she held her hand before her face, and yes, touched her cheek, but saw absolutely *nothing*.

The thought made her panic just a little, which in turn made her laugh.

Then tiny motes of aether appeared, drifting on some eddy through the blackness. She reached for them, and pain screamed through her, white-hot, peeling back her skin, cracking her bones.

Shine screamed—she knew she screamed: it burned in her lungs, and pure cold replaced the pain, freezing her, and she couldn't move, she couldn't blink couldn't think couldn't

—*peace*—

Peace.

Shine drifted in a slow-moving river of darkness, warm, comforting, held up by many small hands. Tender hands, gently caressing her, soothing her as she gasped for breath, slowly calming down.

A hand thrust up through her back and into her body.

Shine arched in surprise, but it didn't hurt; it only ached like nausea drawing up and down her flesh, and she didn't want the hand there, inside her; she didn't want it, so she pushed—

Fire played around her. She was inside a bonfire, itching as the flames charred her hair, from scalp down her spine, along her arms and legs to her toes, but it was all right; she was fire; she knew fire; fire couldn't hurt her—

A whip of pain sliced down her front, splitting her open from chin to groin, and stars spilled out, flaring and arcing: stars leapt up gleefully, shot away as if they could escape! Now they were free! Shine's ribs pulled open like butterfly wings, and there her heart spun in a tight fist of molten rock—

She was sucked down, down, down into an ocean of salt, dragged through clinging weeds, her heels knocked on coral, and she breathed water that tasted like blood, but there were vents in the ocean, too, hot gasping trails of fire from the core of the—core of—

Shine sprawled limp against the rocky floor, exhausted, spent, too weak to open her eyes.

Her lips hurt, dry and cracked, and she breathed harshly. Shallow. Slow.

She was Night Shine Over the Mountain; she knew her name. She was a demon reborn, but her flesh was delicate. More delicate than a mountain's flesh should be.

A dull *thump-thump* echoed in her skull. She thought maybe it was her heartbeat.

Kirin. Sky.

Her eyes shot open.

She closed them instantly, for it was too bright.

Spreading her hands, palms down on the cool rock, she moved them stiltingly. She explored. Her fingertips tingled with tiny licks of aether.

Shine flexed her hands, and flexed something else, too—a spirit muscle, a magic tendon—and pulled that aether into herself. It burned her fingertips, and she gasped.

Immediately she felt a slight reprieve from exhaustion.

This time when she opened her eyes, she could handle the fairly dim bluish aether-glow.

She was in a cavern, surrounded by the thin bars of a stone

cage. The bars grew in a circle around her, arcing up to meet high in the middle.

Shine took a deep breath. She felt better. Her chest hurt, though, like a bruise wrapped her ribs from her heart all the way around.

When she managed to sit up, nausea rolled through her, and she broke out in a cold sweat.

Shine flattened her hands on the cool stone again, and this time pulled hard.

Aether flushed up from the mountain into her arms, brightening her on every level. Her skin felt like it was pulling apart, splitting from the inside, a dumpling with too much filling!

Stop! something growled.

She gasped, then laughed: she was a torch, brilliant in the darkness.

The light faded, leaving her eager and strong.

In the far corner of the empty cavern, a tiger crouched. *I said stop.*

Shine yelped and scrambled to her feet.

The tiger stood. Aether sparked off its body, like little scales constantly shed.

It was a spirit.

"Hello," Shine said, her voice unrecognizably raw. "I am Shine. What's your name?"

The tiger spirit snorted, and its fur rippled back from its head in a long shrug.

"Is this your mountain?" she asked. "Am I . . . ?"

The barge. The ice on the Selegan. The eagle. Now this mountain.

This was one of the Living Mountains. Another sorcerer had her. Which had a great tiger spirit for a familiar?

"Where is your master?" Shine demanded.

Resting, the tiger said into her mind. *You wore them out.*

"Who?"

My sorcerer, A Dance of Stars, and Still Wind.

The sorcerers of the Second and Third Mountains. "Are you the Second Living Mountain?"

I am. But we are here within the First Mountain. What are you?

"A-a girl. I used to be a demon, though."

Patience.

Shine frowned. "No. I have to get back to Kirin. I can't wait. Let me out."

They want to know how you were made.

"They were hurting me," Shine said softly, as she realized it herself. The pain, the cold, the fire—it had been the sorcerers peeling her apart to discover how she worked. She shuddered. "Let me go. You don't want them to keep hurting me."

They can't hurt you.

"They certainly can! They did. And I could die." Shine gripped the stone bars of her cage.

The tiger spirit watched her steadily with wide blue eyes. Its broad face was bluish white, every hair shifting constantly, and it opened its huge mouth in a yawn. Fangs sparked with power. *I am guarding you*, it said, and lay down primly, staring at her.

Shine plopped to the ground again, drawing up her legs to her chest.

She didn't have time to worry. She didn't have time to be

shocked. "Do you know if Kirin is here? Or The Day the Sky Opened?"

The tiger rippled in another shrug. *Only you.*

Shine wrapped her arms around her shins. She put her chin on her knees and stared back at the tiger. The certainty she'd always felt regarding Kirin was gone. Without the binding, she didn't know if he was alive. Shine closed her eyes tightly, refusing to consider his death, or Sky's. Or the poor Selegan River's, who'd been struggling to defend them.

Could she draw enough power from the First Living Mountain to weaken the tiger, break the cage, and escape all at once? When she'd taken just a little bit, her fingers had caught fire. Would more burn her to a crisp? This was the problem with being new: she didn't understand what she could or couldn't do. She'd felt so massive when she'd renamed herself, but the sorceress had told her to be gentle with her body. And when she'd dragged at the aether just now, she'd thought maybe she'd pop like an over cooked dumpling.

But it was worth the risk. She had to escape and find Kirin again. Before these sorcerers killed her. Or worse—and she was certain there could be a worse.

Shine breathed evenly for a few moments.

As she settled herself, she thought about each part of her body, inside and out, noticing temperature and clothing—she was wearing only a thin slip; all her other things were gone—how her bruised flesh pressed to the floor, the touch of her fingers woven together, her wrists against the front of her knees, the rawness in her throat, her fluttering heart, and the heat it pumped.

She thought of stars and the night sky, that vast feeling of infinite strength cupping the Fifth Mountain. She thought of the stars as butterflies and remembered when the sorcerers sliced her open how the stars inside her had popped and swooped and fled just like a scatter of butterflies.

When Shine was ready, she didn't need to press her hands down to the stone. She was inside the mountain, and aether slipped through the air as easily as through stone and flesh.

Shine blew out a long breath, then paused, and when she breathed in again, she pulled on the entire world.

THIRTY-SIX

THE MOUNTAIN SHUDDERED AND gave itself over to Shine.

She cried out in surprise—it was too much! She thrust the power away as fast as it spilled into her: she was a river, like the Selegan, a narrow corridor of rocks forcing vast amounts of water through tighter and faster to make rapids, to make a waterfall.

The power poured in, lighting her on fire! But it passed through, passed everywhere, channeling through her small body with a roar.

Shine opened her eyes just as the bars of her cage shivered and turned to powder, falling around her like snow. She rose off the floor, ascending on eddies of aether, which knotted her spine and heart. Her teeth hurt and her eyeballs, too. She was cooking, a boiling goose, from the vibrations of power!

"Stop!" she croaked, and the word was enough.

The power shut off like a snuffed candle—a candle the size of a mountain.

She fell to the floor of the cave, landing softly.

The tiger was gone, and the cavern was made of crystal—moon quartz—not granite. She'd changed it.

Shine understood that much. She understood fundamentally how rock became fire became crystal or rock again, how stars were made and planets, and—

She swayed.

Suddenly she was very cold, and she looked down at her hands: they were covered in fine lines, cracks.

Far below her the mountain trembled.

Someone else was awake. The sorcerers would come for her.

Shine pushed to her feet and ran.

She hit the crystal wall with her hands and quickly searched for a seam, murmuring to herself, "Door, door, I need a door," until a section of crystal shivered away and she ran through into a corridor.

Aether shimmered along the walls and floor, thin tendrils like tiny vines. They could trace her path. She had to hurry. Out, out, out before this energy faded—she hadn't swallowed it, only channeled it, so maybe it wouldn't last, but she didn't have time to worry.

She found an arched doorway and pushed through carved wooden doors into a large chamber of wood and plaster. Doors opened to either side, and another arched door faced her. She chose right and ran into another hallway with a lower ceiling of carved wood. The air was warm, and the aether clung differently, maybe because this was a building now, not a living mountain. She was in a manor perched on the side of the mountain. "I need an escape," she said. "A door." But buildings probably didn't respond the way mountains did.

Shine paused and touched the wood. It was warm. She heard distant wind. There was a window somewhere ahead, or another door.

How was she going to get back to Kirin?

Frustration made her clench her jaw, and she shivered under an onslaught of nausea. The power had been too much too fast. She didn't know what she was doing.

She had to keep moving or the sorcerers would find her.

They'd probably find her anyway.

Fear snapped at her heels as she took off again. She found a staircase and nearly tumbled down it, catching herself against the wall. This room had pillars carved like trees, holding up a web of rafters. Beautiful water paintings hung between the pillars, and the air smelled like incense.

Shine ran across the reed mats covering the floor and burst into a side room tiled with blue glass. The walls glowed warmly. This had to be an external room, with sunlight filtering in through the blue glass. What if she broke through the wall? But anything could be on the other side, including a cliff, and she certainly couldn't fly.

She turned and went back into the large chamber, choosing a different door.

Her feet felt heavy, and her stomach rolled; she was losing energy. It had been taken wildly and drained away with the same sudden chaos. Her fingernails were cracked and blackened like they'd been thrown in a fire.

Through another short corridor she found a warm bathroom, with long in-ground tubs tiled and filled with steaming water and lily pads.

Shine stopped, looking for drinking water, or spirits. A fountain in the center flowed with clear water, and Shine ducked her head under a stream to take a drink. The water cooled her insides, and she splashed her face.

Then she ran again.

When she found a kitchen, empty, it finally occurred to her how strange it was to have met no people or spirits or anything. Even the sorceress had a few companions. Insistent Tide and Esrithalan and her invisible servants. Had the sorcerers no guards or servants? Where were their familiars?

She was never going to escape. This was no plan at all. The First Mountain was hundreds of miles from where she'd left Kirin. How could she get back to him? She didn't understand her magic and she didn't have her pear!

The realization nearly tripped her, and she gasped. The thin slip had no pockets or ties to carry anything.

When she'd been taken, the pear had been in her tunic. They had it. The sorcerers had it.

If she wanted it back, she'd have to bargain with them.

Maybe the best thing to do would be to sit down right here and wait. Make sure she got a chance to talk to them. To make a deal.

Shine slowed her pace, panting with effort. She touched the walls, trailing her hand through the thin lines of aether but taking none of its power.

The sorcerers were supposed to be allied to the Empress with the Moon in Her Mouth. Surely they'd bargain with a friend of the heir.

When she turned a corner and found herself in another stone

room, she stopped, shocked to be back inside the mountain. But this one was no cavern. It was built of stone blocks. In the center was a cage like her own had been, and inside it lay a person.

Shine darted forward unthinking, but it wasn't Kirin, nor Sky. This person was small and pale like herself or the Selegan's youth form. Their eyes were closed, their breathing shallow and fast. Blood pooled under their head, soaked into the ends of their black hair. Deep cuts bled from their cheek, arms, and legs. A thin gray tunic stuck to their flat chest with blood soaked through from beneath.

Without thinking, she knelt at the bars and grasped them, gently pulling aether out of the stone. The two bars she held shivered, cracked, and disintegrated. Shine touched a few more, drawing carefully on the aether. It hurt, but less if she worked very slowly.

She leaned into the cage and touched the person's neck: their skin was clammy and almost translucent it was so sickly and pale, stretched taut to sharp cheekbones and jaw, a thin nose, and their hair was like ebony silk. Their lips were colorless, and they didn't seem to breathe, but beneath their thin, blue-bruised eyelids, movement darted.

Shine took a deep breath and pushed aether out of herself, shoving it into them.

She closed her eyes and imagined aether-threads sewing up the wounds, filling their stomach and poking their heart into stronger beating.

It hurt her, a little bit, to be so careful, but Shine didn't want to wound them by pushing too hard or too much. She clenched her jaw tightly.

"Thank you" came a whisper.

Shine looked, sitting back in surprise.

The person was whole. They sat up, and with warmth in their cheeks and pink in their lips, they seemed older than before—Kirin's age, around nineteen. Their black hair fell straight and sleek as rain, shimmering with rainbows, and their eyes shifted back and forth from silver to blue like clouds passing quickly over a cold winter sky.

Aether swirled around them, caressing them like they were magic's favorite person.

This was one of the sorcerers. Shine tripped in her hurry to stand, and the sorcerer's smile faded into concern.

"Wait, please," they said. "I will not hurt you, not as those other fools did."

She didn't listen but turned and dashed away.

The door to the stone chamber remained open for her.

"Please, Night Shine, come back," the sorcerer called.

She made it out of the chamber and down the hallway before she stopped. Her chest heaved and she leaned against the wall with one hand, head dipping. Sweat trailed down her temples, and she wiped at it with her wrist. She'd wanted a chance to talk with one of them. She had to be brave now.

Kirin would put on an arrogant smile and return calmly. Sky would—what? Sky wouldn't have gotten himself into this position in the first place. The sorceress would tell Shine to be herself: volatile, cunning, bright.

That, Shine took comfort in. The sorceress would say that Shine could do this and do this well. Volatile, cunning, bright.

Shine returned to find the sorcerer standing in a long gray

dressing gown embroidered with lines of aether and slippers with up-tilted toes. Their hair fell past their shoulders, sliding around their jaw and slender neck, and they smiled in a way that touched their eyes and slowed the shifting of silver and blue.

"How did you know my name?" she asked, trying to sound calm. She didn't remember saying it aloud here, but there might be plenty she didn't remember.

"I can see it, pulling out from you." The sorcerer tilted their head, looking her over from crown to toes. "You should guard the fullness of it better, Night Shine."

"Just Shine," she said.

"Shine." Their smile broadened. "Welcome to the First Living Mountain, Shine. I am The Scale, but you may call me Lutha, as you used to."

Shine's mouth fell open.

The oldest sorcerer in the world.

And they knew her—or had known her before.

"I called you a name before?" she asked, barely getting the words past her teeth.

"We have been friendly for centuries. I knew you when you were a newly great spirit called A Meadow of Fire Balsam, and I knew you when you were a demon called Patience."

"Patience!" Shine laughed in disbelief. What a name for a demon. "That can't be true."

"And yet . . . ," The Scale said, shrugging only one shoulder. "I imagine it was part of a longer name like, The Trouble with Patience, or perhaps *Patience Never Pays.*" They laughed, a bright, amused, friendly laugh, and Shine understood this ancient sorcerer was teasing her.

Shine's knees felt weak, and she slid to the floor, forgetting to be volatile or sly.

Patience. Had the sorceress called her that?

In that moment Shine wanted only to ask, to see the sorceress and ask what the name *Patience* meant. She longed for her cool smile and that summer-green graveyard eye, the haunting, bone-white eye.

Shine's heart skipped, and she felt like she'd forgotten how much she'd enjoyed the sorceress's company until that moment. She missed her.

She licked her lips.

The Scale crouched in front of her, balanced on the balls of their feet, and held out two shallow cups of tea, equally balanced on either of their palms. One cup was delicate ceramic, painted with waves and gilded fish; one was carved of smoky quartz so thinly and perfect it seemed to be made of sunlight.

Shine took the ceramic, and as the sorcerer drank, so did she.

The tea restored her confidence like magic. She blinked and finished every drop.

The Scale tipped theirs back too, then set the quartz cup on the floor and said, "What would you have of me?"

"Um."

They waited, as still as a statue but for the slow-drifting clouds in their eyes. Still crouched in perfect balance.

Shine gathered herself and said, "I need my things back, what I was taken with. And then I need to be returned to Kirin Dark-Smile."

"I will see to it. But that is not what I meant, little star."

"What . . . did you mean?"

The Scale did not answer, but waited.

Shine thought for a moment, of stars spilling from her guts, of patience and fire balsam. She asked, "Can you tell me what I am?"

They smiled again. "You are good. You are compassionate, clever, and loyal."

Shine snorted and repeated their words. "That is not what I meant, old man."

"Am I?"

"Are you what? Old?"

"A man?"

Shame flushed her cheeks, and she felt the echoing heat in her chest. "I'm sorry."

"I forgive you." They put two fingers under her chin, lifting her face. Their touch was neither cold nor hot, but both, like sunlight and a breeze.

"It's a balance scale," Shine said. "Not like armor or a fish."

The Scale nodded. "That's right."

"I'm not one thing, either," she guessed.

They nodded again.

"Not demon or girl or spirit, but many things."

"When you named yourself, you were fully reborn. Did you know that? It rippled in the aether, and that is how they knew to look for you and how to find you."

Shine scowled. "Still Wind and A Dance of Stars."

"They are young too."

"What? They must be centuries old!"

"Babies," The Scale said, somehow both tenderly and annoyed.

It made Shine laugh. But she sobered quickly, thinking of

289

those other sorcerers. "They hurt me. They tried to dissect me."

"They don't understand you."

"You didn't need to hurt me to understand!" Agitated, Shine started to stand again, remembering the pain of cold, the drowning sensation when she'd swallowed that ocean of blood. She shuddered, bile crawling up.

The Scale said, "I did my own experiment, when the others grew weary."

She scoffed.

"You healed me," the sorcerer said.

Of course, Shine thought, furious. She shot to her feet. "It was a trick!" This sorcerer hadn't been injured. They'd staged it, distracted her—delayed her! "Let me go. Give me my things and return me to Kirin. He must be out of his mind."

"He is, but you have some time," The Scale said. "It has already been . . . five days since you were taken."

Gutted, Shine fell back to her knees. She covered her mouth.

"Would you like to see him?"

She nodded, and the sorcerer got smoothly to their feet. They wandered to the stone wall and touched one block. It rippled like water and became a window overlooking a vast valley of evergreen forest. The Scale murmured, and as the words left their lips, they became aether-sigils. Each pinged against the window with the soft ring of a bell, and the window shivered again.

Kirin appeared, and Shine leapt to her feet.

He was surrounded by warriors—imperial warriors in red armor with lacquered white moon chest pieces and demon-face helmets. Warriors of the Last Means. Kirin himself wore a chest piece of red scales, with two wide-bladed swords sheathed at his hips. He was arguing with Sky, whose own sword was strapped to his back over black leather armor. They both had their hair in topknots and wore gauntlets, and Shine saw warhorses and even two cannons in the crowd of warriors. Sky put a hand on Kirin's chest to stop him from striding away, and the prince glared intensely at his bodyguard and covered Sky's hand with his own. Shine saw the tenderness there, in public, damn them both! Then Kirin tore Sky's hand away and stalked off.

"Those idiots," Shine hissed. She could see their relationship as plainly as if it were scrawled in the air with fire.

"He wants to bring the army after you. He will attack the Living Mountains to get you back," The Scale said.

Shine shuddered, shaking her head in refusal. "You did this— you and the others made this mess!"

"I wished to know your nature, Shine," The Scale said kindly. The window faded back into plain gray granite. "A Dance of Stars and Still Wind do not understand that *what* you are has little to do with your bones or magma heart, your old names or old wives or what you used to say or do or be. It has everything to do with what you believe you are. What you believe is right. What you call yourself."

"What it feels like to be me," Shine muttered.

"Unicorns are preoccupied with feelings, but yes, that matters too. Feelings are closer to belief than thoughts."

Shine gasped. "Can you read my mind?"

"Probably, but I did not need to. I know Esrithalan."

Bending over, Shine pressed her forehead to the cool stone floor. It felt good, soothing her hot skin. It felt right. She liked stone, the weight of it, the slow-growing strength of it.

The Scale placed their hand on her back, between her shoulder blades. "You are still a mountain, Shine. You always were a mountain, even when you were only a tiny flower spirit."

"Lutha," she whispered. Not a question, just the flavor of the name.

"My friend."

"What did you learn about me? With your experiment?"

They stroked Shine's back and said, "Think of this: You began your existence as a single flower spirit, and from such a humble, small start gathered spirits to you, became a meadow, a family of flowers strong enough to become a great spirit. Eventually your roots wove into the stones of the mountain itself, and you became even more. You were strong enough that when your mountain erupted, you held on to those deep connections to life and aether, so instead of becoming a demon, you were a great demon, still able to draw upon aether. You were yourself—myriad flowers made of fire and stone and crystal. And consider this, too: I suspect that before you were even a flower, you were fire, born in the depths of that mountain, so eager to push out of the darkness you found a seedling to nurture in the cold black lava. I've known you in many forms, different iterations, but at your core you have been yourself. You still are. I was injured and you sought to help me, though it might've ruined your escape or your prince. Even when you were a demon you were too considerate to overlook a broken bird." Something in the sorcerer's voice tilted toward humor, and Shine lifted her head.

The Scale smiled at her and said, "Your sorceress was a broken bird, and you gave her enough of yourself to make her more than whole—both of you were better for it."

"I don't remember," Shine whispered, wishing more than anything she could recall that moment when she decided to let the sorceress—a sixteen-year-old girl—into her mountain and give her magic.

"Everyone can be bigger than they seem, hold more than their bodies are capable of holding. You have always chosen to grow."

Shine's throat felt tight, her stomach hard with emotions. All the emotions. She squeezed her eyes closed. "How do I learn to be more again?"

"That you haven't forgotten." The Scale chuckled. "But if you need some practical advice: play with small magics before big ones. To take and give in a rhythm. Anything else is too volatile. Grow a seed."

Taking a deep breath, Shine nodded. She held the breath and stared into The Scale's silver-blue eyes. The sorcerer was beautiful in an overwhelmingly perfect way, no distinguishing features to remember when she left this place. "I can do anything," she said. "Be anything."

Their sky eyes widened. "Yes. You can."

Shine licked her lips, thinking. She could stay and blast those sorcerers who'd hurt her; she could return to the Fifth Mountain right away and heal the core, give its power back so the sorceress had no need to take hearts, get to know her old wife; she could wander the entire world and never be hungry or tired. She could discover how near to the moon she could fly. Or float in the clouds, watching stars and lives pass until she understood the patterns of life and death.

But she wanted to go back to Kirin.

And Sky. She wanted to tell them both what had happened to her and see Kirin through his investiture. Safely. That had been the start of this quest: rescuing the prince from the Sorceress Who Eats Girls.

That would be the end of it too.

A smile grew in her chest, warm and sweet, with infinite space to keep growing.

She said, "Send me back, then."

The Scale held out a hand, and her mostly eaten pear appeared in it. They tossed it to her. Then they flicked their eyes again from her crown to her toes, and Shine found herself dressed in trousers and wrapped tunic, with a long vest and leather boots. Everything was shades of blue. She stood, and The Scale said, "My friend the great spirit of the First Mountain will take you," as specks of aether lowered from the ceiling, growing into bird shapes until Shine was surrounded by a flock of silver-rainbow starlings.

"Thank you," she said, bowing, but her eyes were stuck on the spirits—spirit, for it was a single great spirit in many forms.

"You are very welcome, little star," The Scale said, and Shine lost sight of them as she was enveloped in a cocoon of starlings.

THIRTY-SEVEN

———

TRAVELING WITHIN THE EMBRACE of a fluttering, chattering flock of spirit birds tickled Shine—she laughed in delight, eyes closed, giving over to the sensation of pricks and featherlight brushing wings. The magic tingled and popped and rushed like wind around her body, combing through her hair, kissing her lips and palms and the soles of her feet.

She spread her arms like wings of her own and ruffled her fingers in their sparking aether. Her stomach dipped as they dove, and her heart burst with exhilaration when they lifted higher and higher into the sky. Shine couldn't see anything, but she felt it; she knew the speed at which they flew and the distance to the rocks of the earth. She sensed how far to her mountain and that, if she asked, the great starling spirit would take her there, instead.

The pear was a small, hard knot against her waist, tucked into the sash wrapping her tunic. She'd use it as soon as she was able, to tell the sorceress everything. The thought of it filled Shine with warmth.

When the great starling spirit began to slow, Shine asked to see. The fluttering aether-wings parted for her. Dark, rolling rain-forest canopy spread below her, and valleys of wheat and redpop ready for harvest, smoke from nearby villages, and an army.

She was grateful to have had some warning that Kirin and Sky had fallen in with the army, or the sight might've knocked her from the sky.

Hundreds of warriors spread in undulating lines of red and black, camped in a decimated field of redpop. Horses, wagons, cannon everywhere, and steel glinted in the bright afternoon, off halberds and swords and moon-white shields.

There was Kirin, a tiny figure pacing before a round red tent with a layered roof and marked at the fore with two tall poles hung with battered silver circles for the moon. With him were three warriors and Sky—easily recognizable too, for his size and his demon-kissed hair. They spoke beside what seemed to be a map spread across a plank of wood balanced on barrels. A witch sat on a camp stool, the glow of a familiar hunched on his shoulder.

"Set me down away from the army, please," she said to the rainbow starling spirit.

It quickly flew her around to the south, hopefully without anyone in the camp noticing the flock of spirits in the bright sky.

Shine thanked the great spirit when she was on her feet again, offering them a smile since they were not demons and had no use for blood. They took off, spiraling up through the trees, and Shine was alone.

The forest breathed with birdsong and wind and the nearby chaos of the army camp.

Perhaps she should have made a grand entrance, on the wings of the great spirit of the First Living Mountain.

Shine leaned against a narrow hemlock tree, tilting her face to look up at the layers of fanning evergreen branches. It hadn't occurred to her until now that she might've been aided by making a strong first impression on the army. She was so used to being unnoticed, even after learning that she was a mountain inside.

Snorting at herself, she leaned away, patting the furrowed bark, and checked to feel the hard lump of the pear in her belt.

Now that she'd made the choice, she'd see it through.

Shine walked to the edge of the camp, studying the layout and what kinds of people besides Warriors of the Last Means attended. There were plenty. Regular soldiers, drivers and healers and cooks and servants, at least. She walked the entire perimeter before the sun set and decided she didn't need a disguise to slip in; if challenged, Shine only had to say she was from the village down the road looking for her mother who'd come to take wash.

But nobody challenged her. Night had fallen fully, and campfires glowed in regular rows. There was hardly a watch but for a few scouts out in the forest more interested in hunting deer than in finding enemies: this was the heart of the empire, after all. The army witches had set spirit lookouts, but they didn't care about Shine. The one she'd encountered—a lovely long spider stringing spirit webs across the path—seemed to like her just fine. If she'd had time to spare, Shine would've asked how it viewed her, what it thought she was.

She moved through the camp easily, avoiding firelight but trying not to skulk because she did belong here.

Several times Shine overheard conversation as she skirted a gathering of warriors around a fire, but they only discussed weather and songs and people she didn't know, until suddenly she heard the name Kirin, said in a hushed tone, and she froze in the shadow behind a small tent.

"—we just don't know," one warrior was saying.

Another said, "It isn't for us to know."

"But it will hurt all of us if it's true."

"You're asking for trouble," said a new, gruff voice.

"Seems to me that's what the prince is doing. Gallivanting around without priests for spiritual supervision."

"Quiet, Den. You're—"

"He needs to be home so the ritual isn't deferred further. If it can still be done at all. He isn't exactly behaving like—"

"It's loyal, the way he's behaving," the first warrior insisted.

"His loyalty should be to the Moon above all, not to some girl. And Commander Sharp Star couldn't calm him down today, but the demon-kissed could? That—"

"Stop it. We have to trust in the Moon, and in her son."

Shine clenched her jaw and hurried away. Anger made her throat swell, but she knew these warriors were right. There was too much to question for them not to think of it. Kirin had been through too much, and so had the empire. His slightest misstep could spark a wildfire of doubt.

And there he'd been, touching Sky in front of all of them and apparently making outrageous demands on behalf of an orphan.

Thank the Queens of Heaven she'd returned before anybody said anything outright.

Kirin's royal tent was near the center, but more to the west. Shine knew it by the beaten silver moons raised up on polished King-Tree wood poles. And by Sky himself sitting outside the tent at a small fire. He hunched with his elbows on his knees, the sword on his back like a single, mighty demon wing, tightly folded, and his eyes glinted with eerie blue light as he stared into the fire.

Shine went around to the back of the tent, silently exploring the bottom and edges for a way to get in. This had been her original skill: sneaking into places she wasn't supposed to.

The base of the canvas tent was taut, but Shine was able to loosen a stake with slow, even pulls, just enough to peer under and see that it was dark within. Only the glow of fire through the canvas itself cast reddish light.

She flattened herself to the earth and carefully rolled under the canvas, thinking Sky might not forgive himself when he learned Shine had accessed his prince while he sat on guard a dozen feet away.

Shine rolled into something hard and froze, but before she could be too surprised, Kirin had crouched over her and put his hand around her throat, choking her.

Her eyes shot open, and after a single jerk of struggle, Shine forced herself to go limp.

Kirin held a dagger in his other hand, the blade red in the dim fire glow, and she was staring at his face so she saw the swift shock followed by naked relief blow across his expression before he dropped the dagger.

Instead of letting her throat go, he slipped that hand under her head and pulled her up into his arms. He lowered his knees until he straddled her thighs, then hugged her impossibly tight, pressing her face to his bare chest.

Shine put her arms around his ribs and clung to him, shaking as the surge of fear drained away like cold rain.

"Shine," he whispered, and then said her name again, and oh, she loved it: he'd remembered, and it sounded natural between them.

"Hi, Kirin," she whispered back, lips on his skin.

Slowly they both calmed, and Kirin leaned away to look at her face. She pushed his chest gently to get him to back further off. He did, climbing to his feet and helping her, too. The tent was more than tall enough for Kirin to stand throughout most of it.

He held her hand, pulling her toward the sleeping pallet. "Are you all right?"

"Yes, but hungry and thirsty," she answered. They spoke hushed and moved quietly to hide her presence even from Sky just outside. The warrior would likely alert the entire camp if he thought someone was in here with the prince.

Kirin pushed her down onto the pallet, then went to a low table to collect a flagon and a half-eaten loaf of bread. Bringing them, he knelt beside her. "Water and bread, but I have some oat balls and dried cherries."

Shine simply nodded, took the flagon, uncorked it, and poured water directly into her mouth. Her eyes closed of their own accord as she drank her fill. When she handed it back to Kirin, he gave her the bread and a sardonic smile.

Her answering smile was a little sharp, a little bright. "I was kidnapped by the sorcerers of the Living Mountains," she said, then put bread in her mouth so she couldn't keep talking.

It gave Kirin a chance to react: his jaw muscles bunched, and he frowned. Then he got up and picked through the remaining bottles on the table, bringing back wine. He drank some and shared. Shine cradled it in her lap while she picked at the bread, which was delicious and thick with wheat berries.

"I thought you could be dead," he said. "I knew it was a sorcerer. We were—we were going to come after you. The Selegan River returned to the Fifth Mountain to tell your sorceress, but I haven't heard anything from them. The army awaited us at Silverbank, because Esrithalan told my mother where we would make landfall, and she sent a witch-message to Commander Sharp Star at the Silver Rain Fort to escort us home. I wouldn't go home without you, though."

Though he said it with perfect calm, Shine heard the edge, like it was a threat, and she touched his hand, giving him the wine back. "A Dance of Stars and Still Wind hurt me, Kirin. They pulled me into pieces and tore through me, looking for how I was made, for what I am. Because nobody has ever figured out before how to give a demon life again."

Kirin closed his eyes in pain. "I will have their mountains leveled, Shine. Absolutely destroyed."

"No. I will eventually take care of it myself."

"They took you from me—from the Heir to the Moon!" Kirin glared at her. "It cannot stand."

"Then—then when you are invested, discuss it with the great demon of the palace, Kirin. Promise me."

His eyes narrowed, but she saw the glint of them in the creepy red glow. Then he actually bared his teeth at her in a frustrated sneer. "I promise not to take action against the Living Mountains without discussing it with the great demon."

"Good. And . . . The Scale is not my enemy, nor yours. They helped me get back to you. They were . . . They said they knew me when I was a great demon." She winkled her nose. "They said my name was Patience then."

Kirin's expression relaxed. He studied her for a moment, then skimmed his fingers along her jawline. "I can see how you have a core of patience—how else have you slowly, quietly built your miniature empire in the smoke ways?"

"How else have I put up with you so many years?" she teased in a whisper.

"Queens of Heaven," he said, his voice ripening with emotion. "Shine. I . . ." Kirin leaned in and kissed her. It was hard and flat and over quickly, and he put their foreheads together. "I need you."

The words rippled through her, feeding her the way aether did, when she had drained the mountain. And Shine liked it. Oh, she liked it.

"I need you to go back home with me," Kirin continued. "At my side, holding me firm so that I can walk like a man and ignore Sky and play this role I have to play until the investiture ritual. Please. I almost gave myself away while you were gone."

She didn't say, *I know.* She didn't push that in his face. Shine drew a stuttering breath and said, "I am here. I'm going to see you invested, Kirin." She put her hands on his cheeks.

"Good."

Shine opened her eyes. His were closed and too near to focus on. His face was a blur of moon-white skin and black lashes. "What can I do?"

Kirin leaned back, settling his hands on his thighs. "We need a story."

"The Scale brought me back to you because they're allied to the Moon."

"No," he said excitedly. "You escaped on your own, because you're a sorceress too. You're powerful. That's how you recognized the imposter prince and knew I was still imprisoned, and it was how you freed me from the sorceress. You bargained with her and began to learn power. You returned to me because you're loyal to the Moon. That is why you will remain at my side now: a sorceress to guard me against the rest of the world. It will explain so much."

"So would the truth," she grumbled.

"The truth would ruin my purity in the eyes of the world."

Shine scowled because he was right.

Kirin tilted his head so his smile looked like it was spilling off his face. "Let's do this now, surprise everyone. It will work in our favor to have it happen in the dead of night. Make a commotion."

"Kirin? Are you well?"

Sky's muffled question from outside turned both their heads.

"See?" Kirin whispered. He called, "Sky, I am very well! Wake Sharp Star!"

The prince dragged Shine to her feet and grabbed a shirt from the folding stool beside the table. "This was his command tent," he said as he pulled the shirt on. "And I've borrowed more than his bed these three days. I'm sure it's his honor."

That last was said without any bitterness at all, but Shine knew the tension in Kirin's shoulders. "Shall I tie up your hair?"

"No, not for this performance." He grinned at her and flicked all that dark hair over one shoulder. Then he picked up a sword. "Ready?"

"Um," Shine said.

Kirin took her hand again and burst out of the tent with her, shouting elatedly.

THIRTY-EIGHT

S HINE SPENT THE HOURS until dawn standing at Kirin's side with her chin tilted up, eyes wide, speaking as little as possible, and generally trying to look scary.

Kirin told her, later, that she'd managed *strange* well enough, and it served his purposes.

The prince had dragged her from the tent and excitedly declared to the gathering warriors that his friend the sorceress Night Shine—someday, perhaps, to be the sorceress of the Moon itself!—had escaped the clutches of the sorcerers of the Living Mountains with her cleverness and newborn power.

Commander Sharp Star had been a glowering figure, with gray in his topknot and silver charms of rank circling his wrists, but he nodded with relief when Kirin said he would leave in the morning with a slice of the crescent company to hurry south and home before any more trouble overtook him. Sharp Star had met Shine's gaze and clearly been startled by what he found, but he nodded to her and said, "We are all glad to have you safe, sorceress."

It fluttered her stomach to be called such a thing, but she remained silent.

When the army witches tried to touch her, Kirin ordered them away. Shine smiled at their familiars—one had a tiny mouse demon perched on his shoulder, the other a snake spirit wrapping her throat like a necklace. The snake flicked its sparking blue tongue, and the mouse demon shivered so hard it shed flecks of aether.

That made Shine's smile bigger. She wanted to steal them both, talk to them, offer her own patronage.

The only bad moment came when the prince was finished with the crowd and most scattered to obey their new orders for readying a party to depart at dawn with Kirin. Sharp Star had bowed as sharply as his name suggested.

Then Kirin and Shine were left with Sky.

He stared from across the fire, arms folded over his broad chest. His blue-black hair spilled around his shoulders, and his eyes still flickered with bluish flames, though the fire before the royal tent had faded to embers.

"Sky," Shine said, stepping toward him.

Sky flicked his glance to Kirin, and suddenly Shine realized the demon-kissed warrior was furious.

Kirin leaned on one hip, head tilted. "Yes, Sky?" he drawled softly.

Sky uncurled his arms, letting them hang loose at his sides, but his hands remained in fists. He said, very quietly, very pointedly, "Nothing, my prince."

Then he turned and left.

Shine snapped her head around to Kirin. "What did you do?"

The prince shrugged and shoved open the tent flap. He ducked inside, and Shine followed.

"It's how things must be," Kirin said simply. He poured a cup of wine, though dawn approached, and refused to speak more of it.

They departed two hours later, Kirin, Sky, Shine, and twenty-one Warriors of the Last Means, including the witch with the mouse demon.

It was five days to the capital from this far south on the Selegan, less than the sorceress had claimed what felt like ages ago but had been only two weeks. But the horses would eat up distance they couldn't have on foot, and because they rode under the auspices of the army, the roads would be clear for them and inns or crossroads shelters emptied in their favor. Shine had no experience with horses and rode behind Kirin on a tall cream-colored mare with black mane and tail.

The prince wore an army uniform, as he had in the vision The Scale had shown her, and before they mounted, he'd asked Shine to powder his face, line his eyes, and shade in his lips with black. Perfect contrast, a binary lie.

"I can put pearls in your hair," she'd offered, thinking of how pretty it would look around his severe topknot.

"Not too beautiful," he murmured.

She'd knelt and taken the brush from Kirin. He opened the paint pots he'd obtained from who knew where. The powder was easy to smear on, very fine and pearly. She drew black along his lashes, pulling the corners out prettily.

"Are you a boy today?" she'd asked absently, focused on making her lines smooth. His harsh uniform was very masculine.

Kirin had stopped breathing. Her eyes flashed to his. He blinked a few times, swallowed, and Shine waited while he calmed whatever had overtaken him. He said, "No, not really. But I will be the prince anyway."

Sadness pulled her lips into a frown, though Kirin had not let any such emotion bleed into his words. Those he kept cool. Shine suddenly realized how very controlled Kirin always had kept himself. He was cool not by instinct, but necessity.

"Don't look like that," the prince said. As she'd painted only one eye, he was lopsided and silly. But his smile, when he forced it, stretched truthfully. "It surprised me to be asked. But it was good. Thank—thank you."

"I'll ask every day," Shine said ferociously.

"Thank you," he said again. He put his hand on hers, flat on her knee, and pressed.

She nodded and touched his chin to turn his face for easier access to his other eye.

When she was finished, when the red scale armor bulked up his shoulders and chest, he looked strong, bold, and regal.

They left quietly, after Kirin had a word with Commander Sharp Star. As they departed, Kirin lifted his hand in a wave to the whole of the remaining army.

Sunlight pressed hot through the spreading foliage in a final gasp of late summer. The bright-green forest was alive with birdsong and hissing insects. Shine scooted close to Kirin, arms loose around his waist, and pressed her cheek to his back. The rocking of the horse soothed her, though it was so broad she was sure her thighs and bottom would be sore in no time. Kirin sat straight, guiding the horse along behind Sky's with ease. He murmured to the horse sometimes, but otherwise their only lullaby was the wind and birds, the ringing of tack and the clomp of hooves on the dirt road.

As they traveled, Shine looked for spirits and demons, trying to will her eyes to reshape themselves to see aether. She saw spirits often, inhabiting various trees or humming in dens and floating above their animal counterparts as they hid from the noisy passing group.

Seven warriors led their party, then Sky, then Kirin and Shine, with the witch whose name was Immli beside or directly behind them, and the rest of the Warriors of the Last Means arrayed behind or scouting ahead.

The witch attempted to engage Shine twice that first day, but Kirin put him off by answering until the witch's glower grew rebellious. He was ten or fifteen years older than Shine, hardened by the army life instead of soft from living in the palace like the witches she'd known, and she wanted to discuss why he had a mouse demon instead of a more intimidating familiar. But for now Kirin clearly wished her to ignore the witch's entreaties, so she pushed her nose against his spine and obeyed.

Sky rode rigidly and kept his distance. Sometimes Shine peered around Kirin's arm to watch the bodyguard, wishing she'd had a chance to speak with him. When they stopped for a break at midday, Sky moved away, heading into the trees, perfectly avoiding her. Kirin saw her look after him and said, "I'm sure he's walking the perimeter. Doing his job."

"This is almost as obvious as being too close," she whispered.

They ate together, with the captain of the crescent and the witch, and Shine kept her eyes on the mouse demon. It was gray furred, musty looking, with little crystals dried around its milky demon-blue eyes and tiny black claws. Shine entered into a staring contest with it, so intense she lost track of the conversation.

The witch Immli hissed softly at his demon, and the little mouse whipped its tail as it looked at its master. Shine laughed, *"Ha!"* and slapped her knee, only to realize everyone around her was staring at her like she was insane. Most could not see the demon. Her cheeks warmed, but she glowered down at the muddy ground.

Kirin said, "Making friends?"

She said, "I would be a better friend than Immli," lifting her gaze to the witch.

Immli rubbed his hand over his bald, sigil-marked head. "This is Omkin, and you're welcome to try, but we have a strong bargain."

Annoyed she couldn't read any of the sigils, Shine held out her hand, and the mouse hopped onto her palm, its claws pricking her. She brought it near to her face and said, "Hello, Omkin. I'm Shine. Do you get enough to eat?"

"I am always hungry," it said.

"Oh, well then." Shine knelt, her knees sinking into the leaf litter and mud, and flattened her empty hand to the ground. She took a deep breath and pulled at the energy, drawing it through her bones though it burned her a little, and pushed it into the mouse demon.

The demon expanded in a flash, twice as big as before. It squeaked and then bit the meat of her thumb, hard.

Shine dropped it with a squeak of her own, and the demon raced to its witch, taking shelter behind his leather boot. But it peeked around at her, chittering angrily.

Immli reached down to stroke the demon with one finger. But he kept his brown eyes on Shine. "You didn't even draw sigils to pull the aether."

"Maybe that's the difference between a witch and a sorcerer," she said, with a touch of Kirin's haughty tone.

The witch nodded thoughtfully. "Do you have a powerful familiar?"

"I am my own familiar," she answered without thinking, and he narrowed his eyes.

Shine stood and marched away, back to Kirin's horse, where she buried her face in its neck. The horse sidestepped and curved its powerful, elegant neck around, nosing at her belt.

At first Shine thought the horse liked her, but no—it was trying to eat her pear!

Scowling, Shine shoved the horse away with her bloody hand. She spun and leaned her back against it, wondering if she could take energy from the earth and feed it to a living creature like the horse to imbue it with more stamina. But she didn't want to experiment and fail, and maybe hurt the horse. She refused to ask the witch.

She saw Sky return just in time to accept a folded hunk of bread and dry pork before they mounted back up.

Kirin, when he held his hand down for her to pull her up behind him, watched Shine with amusement. She wrapped her arms around his waist, and he covered her hand with his.

That evening, the moment they stopped, Shine slipped down by herself, nearly twisting her ankle, and dashed to Sky.

She thrust her hand under his nose. "That demon bit me, and I need help cleaning it."

Sky clenched his jaw, glanced behind her, and said in a low growl, "That was hours ago. You could already be infected." But he jerked his chin for her to follow him and dug into one of the saddlebags for a scarf and a small glass vial. Then he led her away from the crossroads station, to the nearby creek.

They crouched beside the water, and Shine dipped her hand into the cold stream, murmuring a blessing to the spirit as the ripples stripped away flecks of dried blood. Sky remained silent, and she lifted her eyes to his face, to find him watching her with a soft frown.

She said, "I didn't mean to scare you."

"Kirin was inconsolable," he said, as if to imply that he himself had been fine.

"I would have preferred to tell you myself last night, to have a chance to explain, and—and hug you." Shine looked down, then pulled her hand from the water.

Sky reached for it, but she shook her head. "Watch," she said mischievously. Then she tried the same trick she'd used to heal The Scale, pulling magic from the rocks scattered beside the creek. She imagined the aether threading through the tiny wounds on her hand, knitting them together.

Her skin chilled, except for pinpricks of heat where the injuries were, and she broke into a slight sheen of sweat. But it worked.

"Shine," Sky murmured, clearly impressed. Then he sucked in a shocked breath. "You didn't need my help cleaning it! You—"

Shine winced, then raised her eyebrows hopefully. "I wanted to talk to you."

He huffed, pressing his mouth together to control the affection she could see fighting to get out.

Without waiting another second, Shine flung herself at him, wrapping her arms around his neck. Sky caught her with one strong arm, using the other to balance himself against her momentum.

"You don't have to act like *we* aren't friends," she said in his ear.

He held on to her for a moment, then reluctantly spoke. "I have to be careful. We weren't—when you were missing, Kirin was wild. He felt too helpless, I think. I had to keep him calm, and I think I touched him too often. It was impossible not to, after the—the mountain. There were looks. The witch—not Immli, but the one we left with the army—was suspicious. We're too close to the investiture for me to ruin anything."

Shine kissed his temple. "We both know you won't be the one to ruin him."

"But it won't matter, if they take the investiture away from him."

"I know." She stepped back and put her hands on his shoulders. "I'll do whatever you need me to. I've promised to stay with him until the investiture, and it was his idea to say I'm a sorcerer now, and powerful, and can protect him. Maybe with me between you for the rest of the journey, you don't have to be so distant."

Sky shook his head. "It will help, but better for me to be unconcerned. Unavailable. You should be careful too. He was so worried about you, it would be easy to convince people he was in love with *you* instead. That wouldn't be much better."

"We just have to make it to the ritual. The great demon will accept him."

The bodyguard nodded. He stood slowly, and Shine's hands fell away. He said, "How are you? Have you spoken to your sorceress?"

"No, but I will tonight."

"Why did the sorcerers want you?"

Shine grimaced, skewing her gaze to the gentle rippling creek as it caught the last light that filtered through the trees. In the green and violet shadows, aether-motes appeared, hanging in the still air or sometimes spinning. She wanted to go catch a few, see if they were the seeds of maybe-spirits or could be food for demons, or anything really. But Sky was waiting patiently. She said, "They tried to discover what I was made of, for five days. It was terrible."

"I'm so sorry, Shine. I should've—"

"You couldn't have."

"I hate that," Sky said, dark and wretched.

Shine met his gaze and smiled sadly. She didn't really know how to comfort him from such thoughts.

That night, where she lay curled with her back against Kirin's around the dying campfire, Shine took out the remains of her pear. It was so crisp and clean, despite the abuse it had suffered. She held it over her head, looking at it against the night sky.

Smoke drifted across the stars, and sounds of rustling cloth, the sighs of horses, and low conversation filled the camp. Wind blew and dry seedpods skittered in the breeze, drowning out the song of late-summer frogs.

She was so excited to see the sorceress again. More excited than she thought she should be.

Shine took a very small bite and closed her eyes, but when Shine appeared in the sorceress's bedchamber, the sorceress was asleep.

Her copper cheeks seemed hollowed out, her brow slightly

furrowed, and she curled on her side like a child. Probably if she was sleeping, that meant whatever harm the sorcerers had done to the Selegan was repaired.

Shine wanted to wake the sorceress. She didn't, instead perching on the edge of the bed to stare at the sorceress's black-brown-lava-red hair, braided loosely, at her curved lashes, her strained expression making her look both tired and beautiful.

Had it mattered to Patience the demon that the sorceress had been just a young woman, sixteen and strange, when she left home to find magic? What it had been like, when Shine was a demon?

How had she *felt*? How had the sorceress convinced her to bargain? Had Patience thought that the sorceress would be an easy meal? An interesting diversion? Only to be surprised and drawn to her, to have tricked itself into love? Had she always wanted the attention of *impetuous creatures*?

If only the sorceress would open her eyes so Shine could count the cracks in the bone-white iris and learn, maybe, how to shift her own body's shape. She touched the end of a streak of that rusty lava-red hair, and it occurred to her that maybe—maybe—the color had appeared in the sorceress's hair because her demon had been volcanic.

Before she left, Shine took an orchid from the shallow water bowl and placed it carefully in the sorceress's hand so she would know Shine had come.

THIRTY-NINE

AVING HORSES ADDED A lot of work to making and breaking camps, it turned out.

Kirin himself showed her how to ready their horse's saddle, how to pull off the rug and scrub the horse's sweaty back at the end of the day. They checked its hooves, keeping in close contact with the beast so to never startle it. Shine had to leverage all her weight to get anything accomplished on her own.

And her thighs and bottom were so sore the moment she woke that first morning. By halfway through the day her back ached, especially the small of it. She asked if she could ride sideways, curled up and clinging to Kirin, but he said no, then teased her for being the weakest demon he'd ever met.

The second night, as she sat in front of their campfire, having finished her pan bread and stew, she smiled at the tiny fire spirits and reached for them, to siphon life from the flickering flames. She burned her first two fingers, but it worked.

Kirin, observing, was thrilled and urged her to try drawing power from the wind or passing trees as they rode. She explained about burning her fingers and what The Scale had said about growing a seed, and carefully practiced, pressed to his back, but her efforts drew the witch's attention.

Immli suggested sigils she could use to make charms or coins for such tasks, but without a familiar they likely wouldn't work. Shine said she didn't need sigils or a familiar, determined to prove him wrong, though she caught Sky giving her a *look* and realized maybe she was being too open about her strength and her weaknesses.

That afternoon she dismounted to greet a crossroads spirit in its stone shrine: it was a fox, wily and hilarious. Shine snorted laughter when it answered her obnoxiously, hiding the humor when she translated for her companions and the army, as well as the trio of pilgrims passing by. She informed them the spirit preferred milk to cheese, and resin-gems to gold or silver. Amber was the color of its eyes, and that was why it liked the soft stone. The fox spirit crawled into her lap, but when Sky arrived to collect her, it squeaked and clawed her just hard enough to make tiny drops of blood show on her palms. The pilgrims gasped in awe when invisible claws pricked her skin.

Shine marched to Immli and offered her blood to his mouse demon.

The mouse graciously accepted, flicking its tail into her hand, soaking up her blood.

Immli kept his eyes on Shine while his familiar leaned into his neck. A few tatters of fur thickened with health. The witch said, "Demons draw aether more readily, even small ones."

"Yes." Shine wasn't sure what was the point of him saying so.

"A demon familiar is better for the army than a spirit, unless you can match a great spirit. My Omkin is vital to my battle magic, because it never needs be coaxed to do its job. There is plentiful blood on a battlefield for reward."

Shine shivered, imagining it: death and dying, free-flowing blood. She did not want that, and swallowed, glad to banish the thought. Her fight on the Fifth Mountain had been different. Exhilarating, not sad or gross. As she remembered it, she recalled too how joyful she'd been, ecstatic at having helped the sorceress, unable to stop laughing, and then the kiss. The kiss had—

Immli suddenly reached out and took her bleeding hand. He cupped it in his own, and with a thin wand of lacquered black hair, drew her remaining blood into a sigil.

It flashed blue-silver as it captured aether, and Shine opened her mouth to say her whole name.

But she stopped. She snapped her mouth shut and glared.

Immli nodded slowly. "I knew you were no sorcerer."

Shine bared her teeth and said, "You're strong. I could feed on you for months."

He blinked, and Shine turned away to find Kirin, but made sure not to rush. She felt the witch's eyes on her the whole time, and even the rest of the day as he fell back to ride behind them. Just so he could stare at her, she thought, holding tight to her prince.

She had to be more careful. If the wrong thread of their story pulled, it could all unravel and ruin Kirin's future.

As they neared the capital city, they passed more and more people heading their same direction, all of whom moved off the road for the army to have right of way: itinerant workers traveling south toward later harvests, merchants with ox-driven wagons of goods to sell, pilgrims, tax collectors, and richer folk heading to the city for autumn spirit festivals and family reunions.

Kirin did not hide his presence, sometimes nodding to the crowds arrayed on the road banks, keeping himself neutral, but sometimes flashing that dark smile. Every day Shine powdered and painted his face and helped him wrap his hair into a martial topknot, smooth and tight. She did her best not to engage with anyone, only practicing her aether-sight or pulling gently on a breeze that floated past them. She missed the camaraderie of her trip north with Sky alone, despite how anxious they'd both been about Kirin, and she missed the easy way between the three of them as they slipped down the Selegan River. She missed that dragon too.

Shine hated hiding so much of herself, which was bizarre since she'd been hiding her entire life. The difference, she realized, was that before she'd not thought there was much to her to keep secret. Now she had a secret the size of a mountain.

She wanted to ask Kirin if this was how he'd felt all his life.

It was raining when they arrived at the red gates of the capital city. Not too hard, but enough to wash everything gray and dismal. Shine told Kirin a joke about the Queens of Heaven wishing them back to the Fifth Mountain. The prince smiled darkly and tugged the rim of his cowl closer over his face to protect the makeup. Shine wore no such cloak, preferring the feel of the rain prickling her scalp and dragging her hair against her neck.

She thought of the Selegan River and promised herself to reach the sorceress tonight and ask after them.

The Warriors of the Last Means escorted them beneath the walls and into the city proper, and when Kirin saw people peering through the slats in their shutters and pushing open garden gates to watch, he threw his hood back and let the rain pour over him. It washed the powder away quickly, and Kirin waved with one hand, tending to the black paint slowly slipping down his cheeks with the other.

Shine held on to Kirin, keeping his back warm at least, and looked at the people of the capital without smiling. She was a ferocious sorceress, a bodyguard like Sky, and should make a demon face—she should have painted one on, though it would be melting now too.

"Kirin!" the crowd called, and "The prince!" as more and more gathered, holding up canvas shades and oiled umbrellas painted like flowers. They waved, and Kirin yelled, "How good it is to be home! The sky itself refreshes the city for my return!"

A young woman darted out, offering an umbrella. Kirin ordered the warriors back and let her approach. The rain flattened her brown hair to her forehead, but she smiled happily at Kirin, and he winked when he accepted her gift.

With a flourish, he raised the umbrella—it was violet and blue, dotted with pink and yellow daisy chains—and held it over his head and Shine's. She finally smiled a little bit. The young woman was drawn back by her family, and Kirin rode on. His grip on the umbrella did not waver for the entire ride along the spiraling road to the palace.

They'd spoken briefly last night, heads together at the fire, and Kirin had confessed the return would be the worst part. What if his mother did not believe he was himself? Could Shine convince her? What if the great demon did decide to reject Kirin? Would it not wait for the investiture, but turn on him the moment they crossed the threshold?

Shine had gripped his hand and said, "I will protect you from a measly great demon who never does anything but roll over and complain about itches!"

Kirin had laughed hoarsely, eyes bright with anxiety.

"And," Shine continued, "if the worst happens, you and Sky will go with me to the sorceress and we'll build a cottage next to the mirror lake!"

The prince had avoided her eyes then, and Shine assumed it was because he was embarrassed to long for such a thing, even for only a moment.

Their party arrived at the palace bedraggled. The high lacquered black wall of the seventh circle loomed, capped by red-and-white arrow-shaped spikes, between which warriors stood guard. Rain tapped on the lacquered helmets and leather shoulder pieces.

Shine reached up and brushed the bare skin at the nape of Kirin's neck. It was damp and cold, but he nodded once, slightly. This was the first moment he feared.

They paraded under the long gates, and Shine reached for the tunnel wall to tickle the great demon, but she could not quite touch it. The tunnel led into the wide stone garden. Here the dreary rain had kept courtiers and residents of these lower circles inside. Servants dashed across the gravel to take the horses, leading them to cover near the barracks. Kirin and Shine were surrounded, nearly pulled off the yellow-milk horse.

The moment her foot touched the gravel, a roar erupted from the very walls of the palace.

Every warrior reacted by getting a weapon in their hand, and the horses screamed, tugging to be freed. Immli the witch drew his wand and his mouse demon vanished. Sky grabbed Kirin's shoulders, pulling him into a crouch half beneath Sky, while the bodyguard looked all around for danger.

But Shine knew.

It was the great demon of the palace.

She threw herself toward the red-washed wall, slapping her palms flat. Power stripped across her flesh, and she cried out, sinking to her knees with a scream. It would *not* reject her prince! She would rather destroy it!

"Nothing!" someone yelled—Sky—and then Kirin said, "Shine!" and his hands were on her shoulders. "Night Shine," he commanded in her ear, chest pressed to her back.

"Demon," she said, throat raw.

Kirin pulled at her, but she shook her head, rolling her shoulders through the thick strokes of pain.

The world roared again.

what are You?

The voice drummed hard and low through the courtyard.

It wasn't rejecting Kirin; it was after Shine.

"Great demon of the Palace of Seven Circles," she said, and she leaned forward, though every hot, fiery piece of her demanded she flee. She kissed the wall. "Demon, I was your friend," she murmured. "I am not here to take anything. I . . . Please. I used to tickle your walls with my fast fingers and tripping toes. I promised when I came home that we would fix the patch in your roof that aches when it rains."

Nothing where is Nothing You are not Nothing You are Something.

"Night Shine," she said. "My name is Night Shine. I left and found my old house, great demon. This is my new house. I was Nothing, but now I am full of stars and the rainbow colors in between them. Night Shine."

The pain faded. Shine did not move her raw, hot hands.

Night Shine. Night. Shine.

"Yes."

A cry of alarm from behind her made Kirin move, and she did too.

Turning slowly on fever-aching bones, Shine looked up from her knees at a living shadow. It was spiky, vaguely person-shaped, with rippling wings the size and sharpness of spruce trees. It filled the rock garden, dark and shifting even as it held perfectly still. Then it crouched, leaning toward Shine. Seven eyes whirled blue-black-violet, round as seven moons, and it opened a jagged mouth above those eyes, tasting the air with seven tongues.

Shine tried to take calm breaths, but she tasted it too: lightning-strike, burned hair, very old, overripe blackberries.

"May I stay?" she asked it. "I was your friend and would be again. This was my home, and your prince—this prince who one day will rule this house—is my friend. Do you know him?"

The shadowy figure flicked six of its seven eyes at Kirin, holding her with that one.

stay but do not take, it said in seven voices layered like a chorus of children. *for the dark smile.*

"I will not take from you, or yours," Shine promised. "For Kirin."

The great demon of the palace flicked its tongues and set long arms down, wicked claws digging into the pink gravel.

"You know me," she reminded it.

if I must, I will fight You for Your true name. do not make Me.

"I promise," she said, standing on rickety knees. She held out a hand, palm up.

The demon leaned its large head down and tasted her skin, two tongues curling around her fingers. It breathed hot over her wrist, slithering up to pool in her elbow.

Shine was unafraid, and amazed at herself for it. She smiled.

Then the demon shrieked in her face, *accept*, and blasted apart in shards of black and purple glass that skittered and burst but did not hurt anyone. They clinked to the gravel and shattered anew on boulders, passing harmlessly through flesh.

Shine remained breathless and smiling.

Kirin reached her first. He grinned. "I've never seen it before! Only heard. I don't think anyone has seen our great demon in two generations!"

Sky glared at her.

Shine resisted smarting off to him, but barely. She'd done just fine! And Kirin had passed whatever first test he'd feared when the great demon looked at him and did not reject him.

The captain of the Warriors of the Last Means asked if Kirin was well. His face beneath his helmet was flushed a rich copper, but his expression remained solid. He did not look at Shine.

Well. She was used to being ignored, just not because she *had* power. It felt excellent.

"I am more than well," Kirin said. "My new sorceress and I are welcomed back with quite the fanfare." His words would hopefully plant seeds in the inevitable rumors to angle them his way. Kirin realized he still had the gifted umbrella shoved into his sash and tossed it to one of the palace attendants. He ordered that it be taken to his rooms.

Immli held his tiny demon mouse in his hand, cupped against his stomach for comfort, and watched Shine with too much speculation.

But they were ushered on, and passed through the seventh, sixth, and fifth circles of the palace before Kirin balked. He dug in his heels and demanded a moment to catch his breath and fix his hair before being dragged to his mother.

He was obeyed of course, and he shook off the wet cloak. Shine sat him down on a stool in the curving antechamber to the fourth circle's greeting hall. Sky made quick work of rebinding Kirin's topknot. It was the most he'd touched Kirin in days. They did not have time to powder his face, but Shine touched up the black lines around his eyes and dabbed paint onto his lips again for perfect contrast.

Both Shine and Sky nodded encouragingly at him, and Kirin drew himself to his full height. "I'm ready."

"You look magnificent," Shine said. She still wore the thin wool clothing The Scale had put her in, in so many shades of blue, and her hair now was a mess, but she didn't care.

"Shine, you have little shards of the great demon caught in your hair," Sky said disapprovingly, when he noticed her touching the ragged ends.

Sky had wished to be in full uniform, but the army hadn't had proper demon-kissed bodyguard attire to lend him. He relied instead on a dark-purple wrap shirt from the sorceress that was significantly more luxurious than he preferred and his own black trousers and boots. He had gauntlets on his forearms, sword gloves, and his enchanted sword strapped to his back. Rain dripped off him, as he'd not bothered with a cloak in the first place, but his dark hair had already dried, with wisps messily puffing around his ears and jaw that shone blue when they caught light.

Kirin stared at Sky, and clearly wished to speak something, but they weren't alone.

And suddenly Lord All-in-the-Water was there, filling the doorway to the antechamber with his shoulders.

"Kirin," he said hugely, relief and concern apparent in the set of his jaw and the clench of his fists. The lord commander of all Warriors of the Last Means, he always wore a belt of wide throwing daggers around his waist, cinching his red-and-white robes, and his hair was unfashionably short.

"Lord All-in-the-Water," said Kirin turning easily. He walked to the older man.

"Is it you?" the commander asked warily, lifting a black-and-graying eyebrow.

"I imagine I'll be proving that to my mother, so please don't make me do it multiple times."

The lord commander snorted. His cutting hazel eyes flicked to Sky, held there for a moment too long, then found Shine. Her he studied with open suspicion. "You should have come to me," he said.

Shine realized he meant weeks ago, when she first realized Kirin was an imposter. She did not reply, as she'd never spoken to All-in-the-Water before and had no intention of starting.

"Lead the way," Kirin said, moving to show if Lord-All-in-the-Water did not, Kirin would go on his own.

Kirin followed the lord commander closely, and Shine and Sky fell in together at his wings. Immli came behind them, unfortunately. Shine's pulse quickened as her pace did, and she glanced at Sky from the corner of her eye. He noticed—of course he noticed—but he did not return her looks.

A handful of Warriors of the Last Means came along too, and before them servants scattered, peeking around pillars and from doorways. A few noblemen and -women watched from corridors that spilled into this one, especially as they moved through the third circle of the palace. Shine thought if she were among them, she'd be in the smoke ways, tracing the prince's path unseen and unheard.

They stepped up through the wide, flowing dragon staircase that led into the second circle where the consorts reigned, and in those hallways they had no audience at all. Anyone who could access these rooms would surely be waiting with the empress herself in the first circle.

To Shine's surprise, Lord All-in-the-Water did not take them to the Court of the Seven Circles but veered off toward the empress's evening receiving hall. It was a half-circle room along the western edge of the seventh circle, and the outer wall was composed of open archways leading onto a stone porch over-looking the entire rest of the palace. Rain pattered softly against the roof, draining along hung chains into shallow pools shaped like fish. When the water overflowed, it slid through narrow, gilded channels to the edge of the porch, then poured in arcs from the mouths of spirit statues.

When the sky was clear, the sunset lit the porch and set fire to the gilded pillars and gold-seamed marble walls inside. Lush pillows and benches were casually arranged around the empress's star-shaped chair. Shine had been here for formal occasions, when the setting sun dazzled the air, putting everyone off-kilter and wincing prettily but for the empress, safe with a headdress of shimmering beads or rain-silver shading her face. If they'd been brought here on a sunny day, Shine would have thought something was wrong that the empress wished to set her son on edge. But the rain made it a soft world, comforting and cool, despite the damp breeze.

The empress sat straight-backed upon her chair, hands folded upon her lap. Her face was hidden by a veil of black thread beaded in jet and tiny squares of obsidian that fell down from her forehead to her breast, slipping against the crimson silk of her gown. Black-embroidered peonies darkened the silk like inky shadows, and her nails were lacquered black—just like the sorceress. Shine clenched her hands together, shivering with memory.

Arrayed behind and to either side of the empress were her most trusted attendants, including that pair of palace witches, Aya and Leaf, their heads shaved and painted with sigils Shine still couldn't read, and a single old priest in pink robes. The witches stared at Shine hard, each with a spirit crow upon her shoulder, their misty bodies forming hard and disintegrating and forming up again in a slow cycle. They glared at her with their single aether-blue eyes.

The First Consort Sun-Bright and Second Consort Love-Eyes each waited as well, just as surrounded by attendants, and at the edges of the room Warriors of the Last Means stood rigid and ready.

Kirin strode in with his usual grace, but halted abruptly before his mother, without offering a bow. He stared silently for a long moment, and Shine resisted the urge to step forward and place a hand between his shoulder blades.

Though Shine missed the signal, suddenly the Warriors of the Last Means leapt forward, moving like lightning through the silk-clad attendants, and held spears tipped in steel at Shine, Sky, and Kirin.

FORTY

THEY STOOD IN A circle of teeth. Shine gasped, eyes widening at the nearest spear tip. Beside her Sky twitched but did not grab his own weapon.

Kirin remained still, chin raised.

Lord All-in-the-Water said, "Show us that it is you and not some imposter. All three of you."

With a sigh of weary compliance, Kirin swung a hand up and grasped the end of the spear pointed at his neck. The warrior holding it lowered his eyes before remembering his job in that moment was to challenge the prince, not submit. Kirin gripped the spear and lifted his other hand, pressing his palm to the tip. With a sneer at the pain, he jerked his hand, slashing the soft skin.

The black threads of his mother's veil shivered.

The Second Consort Love-Eyes sucked in a breath: her lovely lips parted, and her green eyes teared. Shine had always found her to be pleasant and willing to allow Shine access to her rooms, and she was sorry to see such obvious distress in the pinking of Love-Eyes' cheeks.

First Consort Sun-Bright, Kirin's father, watched stone-faced as a spirit statue. One of his attendants had a hand on his shoulder as if to offer reassurance.

Kirin released the spear and held out his cupped palm. Slowly, eyes on his mother, he tilted his hand and let bright-red blood dribble down the side, trailing in a vivid line before it dripped once, twice, and a third time onto the lustrous wooden floor.

The empress touched the moon pearl set into the collar of state she always wore in public. Approval.

"Mother," Kirin began, but Lord All-in-the-Water interrupted: "The others too."

Shine wrinkled her nose and said, "May I have a smaller blade?"

The lord commander took a throwing knife from his belt and stepped through the circle of spears to offer her the hilt.

"Thank you," she murmured, and without art sliced open the back of her wrist. She hissed, and held it out, showing the blood.

Sky put his hand before her, and Shine gripped the knife tighter, lifting her eyes to his. She recalled when he'd cut himself before the empress right after she slit the throat of the imposter. Then he'd turned away from the empress; now he did not.

Gritting her teeth, Shine cut into the back of Sky's wrist too, letting the blade clatter to the floor when his blood welled so dark and purple. Then both of them looked to Kirin, and they all looked at his mother.

"Everyone out," said the Empress with the Moon in Her Mouth. Shine had heard the empress's voice only a handful of times in her life. It was both rich and gentle.

First Consort Sun-Bright moved nearer to his wife and said

to the room, "Tell the palace the Heir to the Moon has returned to us, whole and wholly himself."

Some left quickly, others reluctantly. The pair of witches were the last to go, staring at Shine over their shoulders. She widened her eyes, hoping they could see sparks of fire in her pupils.

A departing attendant offered Shine a bandage with which to wrap her wrist and hand. She wished she could steal some power and heal herself. But she'd promised the great demon, and besides, it might be dangerous to display her power to everyone still watching so carefully.

Soon it was only herself, Sky, Kirin, Lord All-in-the-Water, the two consorts, and the empress.

And the witch Immli, who had knelt beside the exit, head lowered and hands clasped, asking silent permission to remain.

No one made him go, to Shine's irritation.

The empress stood, and all but Kirin knelt as she approached him. She lifted her hands to remove the combs holding the black-rain veil against her looping, thick braids. Second Consort Love-Eyes moved to her wife's side to gather the combs and veil.

Shine looked down fast, before she saw the empress's revealed expression.

"Kirin," the empress whispered, and then Shine heard the motion of silk, and the two embraced. "My son," the empress added. "Oh, my son."

"Mother," he said, calm. Too calm.

"We'll send for your mother too," First Consort Sun-Bright said to Sky. "She came to the palace two weeks after you left. Terrified out of her mind."

Sky's jaw clenched, and he bowed his head sharply.

"Nothing," said Lord All-in-the-Water, but Kirin interrupted him:

"No, that is not her name." The prince drew himself up, leaving his hand lightly on his mother's wrist. "This is Night Shine, and she is a hero."

From the edge of the chamber, Immli said harshly, "She is a monster and should be put in demon chains."

Shine whirled on him, furious. Her fingers curled into claws, but Kirin said, "You overstep, witch."

"Kirin," said the First Consort.

"Father, we owe Shine my life, and the sanctity of the Moon. Everyone else in this room would have attempted the investiture ritual with an imposter and likely lost all the support of the great demon. That the situation is not so dire has everything to do with Shine."

Shine willed herself calmer as she listened to the prince defend her, but she couldn't stop glaring at Immli.

Sun-Bright said, "I understand that, my son, but we would like to hear what the witch has to say."

Immli bowed deep enough from his kneeling position to brush his forehead to the ground. When he leaned up, he put his hands respectfully on his knees. Omkin was nowhere to be seen, but Shine knew the demon was nearby.

The empress returned to her chair, and the Second Consort replaced her veil.

Then the witch was given permission to speak. He said, "Empress, my lord and lady, my prince, Night Shine herself is some kind of great demon—she is no sorceress. I have witnessed her drain aether like a demon, and at night fall into such a deep trance there is no telling what she might have been doing, away from her body. She is susceptible to a witch's naming magic, though too strong for me to make her my familiar. Unless she can prove she is no threat, how can we not take precautions, or risk her befouling the prince, who must remain pure?"

Though Shine hated to put her back to the witch, she turned to look at the empress and her consorts. She held her fists against her sides, breathing a little too hard, and tried to seem non-threatening. If only she still were Nothing—she should have waited to rename herself until she'd gotten Kirin home and safe. This was her fault.

Everyone stared at her.

Kirin said, "Shine is not dangerous to me."

"But to others?" Lord All-in-the-Water said sharply.

"The great demon of the palace has allowed me to be here," Shine said softly. "The Moon itself."

The empress's mouth flattened, and the First Consort glanced across his wife to catch the gaze of the Second Consort.

Second Consort Love-Eyes nodded to her partner consort and then turned back to Shine. She asked gently, "Shine, can you explain away this witch's concerns, then? Tell us what you have become?"

Shine looked to Kirin, who gave her one of his single-shoulder shrugs, performing a greater degree of nonchalance than he likely felt. "I can tell you some, but I do not entirely understand what I am now. No one does." She licked her lips, slid a glare at Immli, and said, "I am the reason Kirin was taken by the Sorceress Who Eats Girls."

Love-Eyes gasped, but nobody else reacted visibly.

"Long ago, the sorceress created a powerful spell to help the great demon of the Fifth Mountain be reborn to life, and it worked—only not exactly as she intended. The demon was born again, here in the palace, because the palace is a safe place for a great demon." Shine paused meaningfully.

The empress nodded. She understood why.

Shine continued. "I didn't know. Nobody did. But the sorceress has been looking for me. That is why she killed girls."

"Kirin is not a girl," First Consort Sun-Bright said in a warning voice.

"He was bait," Shine said quickly. "To lure me. The sorceress realized where I must be, so she took Kirin and replaced him, knowing I would come because of what I had been. And it worked. The Day the Sky Opened and I went, and when I faced her, she agreed to let Kirin go. It was that easy—because she got what she wanted. Me."

Kirin sighed, as if a little bored, and his father shook his head in disapproval. But the empress spoke quietly, her veil shivering. The First Consort relayed her thoughts. "You are here, though. Not with the sorceress."

"Kirin needs me. Whatever I was, or—or am—I was Kirin's first. My loyalty is here."

The prince shifted toward her and put his hand on her shoulder. He held his gaze on his mother. "Shine is powerful, and new, and we are lucky to have her. I trust her, Mother. If you trust me, you must trust her."

A movement behind them reminded everyone Immli remained.

"Yes?" the Second Consort said, as sweet as always. Perhaps it was her mask, just as Kirin's arrogance was his.

"At least, Glorious Moon," said the witch, "let us be cautious with the reborn demon. She killed Skybreaker."

Shine's eyes widened, and she sucked in a breath to argue, but Kirin squeezed her shoulder, saying, "Skybreaker attacked us, Immli. Shine protected me—would you have had her do anything different?"

But Shine saw the doubt in the Second Consort's bowing lips and found no encouragement in the First Consort's hard expression.

Immli bowed again. "My prince, I apologize, I—I only report the whispers of the aether, the gossip of spirits and demons, because it is what we all hear, we witches with our familiars. And what we hear is that your *sorcerer* Shine is dangerous. She herself claims she does not know everything that she is, and so might be volatile. How can even she predict what she might do? Let us put sigils on her to bind her power while she remains here."

Kirin frowned, but the First Consort said, "Will you submit to such a thing, Night Shine?"

Shine did not want to, but she nodded. *Gossip,* she thought. *What other rumors might spirits spread about Kirin?* She had no choice but to obey.

"Then go with this witch," Kirin's father said, "and see it done. Sky, you will make your full report now to Lord All-in-the-Water, and you, my son, will remain with us."

Sky bowed deeply, barely glancing at Shine and Kirin before departing with the lord commander.

Kirin squeezed Shine's shoulder and let his hand fall. "Come find me in the morning."

She nodded, then bowed to the empress before reluctantly going at Immli's side.

The two paired witches, Leaf and Aya, waited just outside with their crow familiars, and Immli told them they were to fit Shine with binding sigils.

Shine kept her jaw clenched shut as they led her to the fourth circle of the palace, to a bathroom she'd never seen before, as it had no smoke ways in its walls and a thin glass roof smeared with gray rainwater. The chamber glowed with violet twilight: it had a deep central pool and four shallower and crescent shaped, each a different composition and temperature. The women witches bathed Shine in warm saltwater to cleanse influence and aether-marks from her skin while Immli fetched a priest. They gave her salt to put on her tongue until it dissolved and burned spruce incense, murmuring quiet blessings. Their crows flew back and forth across the chamber, drawing aether-winds into simple patterns of balance and cleansing. They chattered at each other, and Shine could hear them but did not think Leaf and Aya could. It made her smile meanly.

When Shine was clean, they wound her hair into a simple knot, dressed her in a plain gray tunic as long as her calves, and painted sigils on her palms, the soles of her feet, and beneath her ears.

They laid her down on a thin mat and called in Sovan the dawn priest and Immli. The army witch was still dusty and wearing his uniform, but Sovan had on the same sickly pink robe and egg-blue sash as always, his long white hair bound in blue ribbons and his beard dyed harsh black. His copper skin had age spots, but his eyes were wrinkled in a friendly way. "I remember you," he said.

"You look like all the dawn priests look," Shine answered.

He laughed, and one of the witches did. Aya, Shine thought. Leaf pressed her palm to Shine's forehead and said, "Hush while we cast our spell."

Immli lowered his mouse demon to the tiles of the floor, and the two crow spirits snapped playfully at it.

Shine closed her eyes. She listened to the cackle of the crow spirits and the rush of aether surrounding her. It wasn't like wind, because it was too rhythmic, but nor was it like the heart-beat of the Fifth Mountain. More like a river. Outside the palace, fingers of the Selegan rushed toward the sea, two cupping the capital city gently. All much too distant be heard from here, even echoing through the aether.

The rhythm was soft and extremely slow.

It was the great demon of the palace, breathing.

"Why does a demon breathe?" she asked.

Nobody answered, and she slitted open her eyes. The witches and Sovan the priest stared at her with variations of surprise and suspicion.

"They don't," said Aya.

"I can hear the great demon," Shine insisted.

"Then it is affectation," said Sovan.

Immli stared at Shine with narrow hazel eyes. "You can hear it? What does it sound like?"

Shine wrinkled her nose. "A long, quiet snore."

"Hello, great demon," Leaf said respectfully.

Her twinned witch, Aya, repeated the greeting, but the dawn priest did not.

Shine closed her eyes again and relaxed into the demon's aether-breath, letting her own breath slow, though she was much too alive and small to match its pace. To her, it seemed the rhythmic breath was like rushing blood as the great demon slowly took and returned power from the living of the palace, rooting itself in a loop, deep in the earth. Give and take and give and take, just like The Scale had said.

Would the great demon teach her that skill?

She felt the brush of the witches' fingers sometimes, and a murmured blessing or prayer. And the scratch of quill on paper.

Then a silky net tightened around her, and Shine cried out. It hurt!

She struggled, trapped, and gritted her teeth to call on her fire. Cold tendrils flickered in her mind, and she reached for her heartbeat, for the pulse of volcanic violence. It answered in a gasping rage, flaring out to her fingertips and toes, and she opened her mouth.

Shine sat up, energized, alive with new power—not only from the fire inside, but from the silky net. She'd drained it, swallowed the sparkling aether it had been.

She stared at the witches and the priest, but before they spoke, the aether tightened around them all, as if the air itself thickened into honey. The crow spirits screamed, and the witches clutched their heads. The dawn priest sank to his knees.

And the great demon rumbled,

Night Shine, You have taken from Me.

"No," she said, throwing out her hands against the stuck air.

"Great demon, they surprised me. I did not think the binding would hurt. I apologize. It will not happen again!"

tricky witches are too weak to bind You, it said, unconcerned. *do not fear them and do not break Your promise to Me.*

"I apologize, great demon. I won't fear them again."

Then it was gone, its weight releasing like a popped bubble. Shine glared at the rest. "You should have warned me."

"We didn't know it would hurt," Immli said maliciously.

"But what are you?" Sovan croaked—the priest was clearly shaken.

Shine went to him and helped him up. He was like an old grandpa, a kindly one who made her think of the unkind Insistent Tide. She said, "I'm something new."

"A spirit enfleshed? I have heard of that," said Aya the witch.

"A *demon* enfleshed," answered her twin. She approached Shine and put both hands on her face. "Does the prince know your true name? Does anyone?"

Shine did not let herself be intimidated. She allowed the memory of the volcano inside her to grow hot again but was careful not to take anything from the hands pressed to her cheeks. "I know my name. That is enough."

FORTY-ONE

O NCE THE WITCHES' BINDING net had been cast again, more gently this time, Shine redressed in her blue clothing from The Scale and fled. She felt slightly diminished but wondered if it was her imagination. The net was intended to keep her under some control, to stop her from unleashing waves of power or shaking down the palace, she supposed. She could break it. But if she did, the great demon of the palace would be waiting to squish her.

An attendant led Shine to a guest chamber in the third circle, saying it was to honor her as the prince had requested. But as soon as she was left alone, Shine crawled into the smoke ways and returned to the old bathing rooms where she'd slept all her life.

Removing the pear from her sash, she set it on an old stool like an altar. The fruit meat shone white as the moon, glimmering with juice, and the skin was as golden green and speckled as always. Shine could step on it and the magic would keep it whole and fresh.

She stripped and dug through the piles of old clothing she'd gathered the past few years. Untouched for nearly two months, it all smelled slightly musty, thanks to the damp air, but she pulled on loose pants and a thin tunic, finger-combed her hair, and went to the wall. Pressing both hands to it, she said, "Great demon, will you teach me to take and give and take and give?"

I am weary little demon hush You tire Me and I cannot take more without consequence.

Shine supposed it had been a long day for the great demon. So she said, "Good night," and went to the pear. Suddenly it occurred to her the magic might not work while she had this binding net marked on her body.

She leaned against the wall, stomach fluttering, and wondered if she should ask the great demon. She had to see the sorceress! It had been days and days.

Her heart pounded, churning with heat.

Might as well find out.

Shine took a bite.

She opened her eyes in the Fifth Mountain's library.

She grinned in silent relief, nearly falling as her knees weakened. Of course a spell made by the Sorceress Who Eats Girls could penetrate a measly net made by palace witches.

Dim blue and orange lights wavered gently from both the wide crystal hearth and globes hanging free in the air between the cluttered shelves. It seemed poor reading light to Shine, but then, the sorceress's eyes were unnatural.

The sorceress sat at one of the long tables, elbows on the worn wood, with a large book open before her and a trim quill in hand. She frowned as she marked a notation in the margin. Her tricolored hair was pulled into two high knots, and she wore a sleeveless wrap tunic similar to what she'd had on when she'd cut the diagram into the crystal floor with Shine.

For a moment Shine didn't move or make a sound, watching hungrily. It was strangely pleasant to observe the sorceress when she thought she was alone. Something so mundane and easy about her obvious concentration, the frustration in the line between her eyebrows. Shine wanted to know what she was working on, but she also wanted to keep staring. Both filled her with anticipation, like she was about to jump off a cliff!

The sorceress turned the page aggressively. "What?" she snapped, lifting her gaze to Shine. Pinched annoyance faded into a more guarded interest as the sorceress realized who was spying on her.

Shine said, "I didn't mean to interrupt."

The sorceress leaned back in her chair, rather lordly. "I gave you the pear for a reason. Interrupt away." Shadows shifted on her face, making her seem exhausted.

Shine darted forward. "Are you ill?"

"I'm fine. I'm holding the weight of an entire mountain as the heart slowly dies. I will have to hunt if you don't return to me."

"You can't."

"Then I will die."

"I will return soon," Shine swore breathlessly.

The sorceress did not move but to curl her fingers around the arms of her chair. Her black-lacquered nails glinted bluish. Her chest rose and fell, her eyes held easily to Shine. Green and white. Life and death.

As Shine stared, tiny cracks appeared in the ivory-white iris, like it was too dry and splitting with drought. A muscle shifted in the sorceress's jaw, and the eye faded to its pure solid white, with pretty flecks of gray.

Distressed, Shine put her hands on the edge of the table. "How is the Selegan?"

"Quite well. They were distressed when the sorcerers took you. Those idiots were messy, and harsh." The sorceress paused, briefly lowering her eyes. "I was worried, but The Scale told me you would survive."

Shine swallowed. "I did." She wanted to ask about Patience and about being a meadow of flowers, but she was nervous. She should remember the sorceress now—if they'd been married, if they'd had a strong bargain. Why couldn't she? To distract herself, she glanced down at the book. Tiny lines of writing scrawled in columns she couldn't read. "What are you studying?"

"Power."

It was said slowly, with such a drawl Shine shivered. She glanced up at the sorceress again, and the sorceress said, "Have you reached the palace?"

"Yes! I came to tell you." Shine smiled. "Just today. The great demon of the palace is unsure of me, but—"

The sorceress sat forward quickly. "What did it say?"

"It knew immediately I was no longer Nothing. Because I freed myself." Shine laughed and it licked up her throat like pretty blue-white flames, like stars to spill through her teeth.

The sorceress stood and stalked around the table, intent upon Shine, and Shine kept laughing, but it shifted breathy as the sorceress neared. Shine turned to put her bottom against the table and let the sorceress pin her there, not touching, with only the force of her presence. Oh, Shine liked it.

"What should I call you?" the sorceress asked quietly, but not softly. A ripple of dark feathers appeared along her cheeks like a cresting fish with black scales, then vanished below the surface again. Shine reached to touch the tip of her finger there, intrigued, but the sorceress caught her wrist in a hard grip.

Shine pulled on her hand until she could slip it down to hold the sorceress's hand and draw both to her chest. She pressed the sorceress's palm to herself, feeling the cold skin through the tunic she wore. "Night Shine."

The sorceress closed her eyes, and it was her turn to shiver. "Night Shine," she said, and it was a tug of power, a breath of air on open flame.

Shine gasped. "It's not the whole name. I've not told that to anyone. You can't bind me with it."

"I told you," the sorceress said, pressing closer. "I do not want to be your master."

Shine nodded; she couldn't do anything else. Her heart pounded, and her skin was rippling too, like its own feathers desperately tried to burst free. It felt so good and right. But Shine would have scales, not feathers: bright silver-black scales that shimmered like the sorceress's nail lacquer and like the black between the stars. She wanted to learn to shift her shape, to help her scales emerge, but could not speak it with the sorceress so near.

The sorceress drew a deep breath, her eyes taking in every detail of Shine's face and hair and eyes, then drifted down her neck, and Shine was thrilled at the possibility the sorceress could see the thrum of her pulse. A smile like a little butterfly trembled across Shine's lips.

She tilted her head to reveal the hollow under the corner of her jaw, then gasped as the sorceress pressed a kiss to her pulse point. Shine was melting into lava again; she could hear the clinking of scales tumbling in a breeze, like chimes. Her knees tickled weakly, and she sighed.

The sorceress whispered against her skin, "Will you marry me, Night Shine?"

Shine pushed away. "I can't! Stop." She moved to the other end of the table, and the sorceress did not follow. For a few long moments Shine settled herself, but her insides were too hot and she missed the touch.

"I must have a heart."

"I know. Just wait a little bit longer. I will come back, I promise." With effort, Shine looked back at the sorceress. "How long can you wait?"

"I do not know."

Shine said, "Promise. I will come back; only wait."

"Very well," the sorceress whispered. "Come what may."

The words gave Shine what she'd asked for, but something in them frightened her. She stepped back to the sorceress and leaned up to kiss her lightly on the lips.

She woke immediately in the abandoned bathroom, shocked and hot and gasping.

FORTY-TWO

I T WAS SURPRISINGLY DIFFICULT to get everyone to use her new name.

The empress held a formal court two days after their return, during which Kirin was reintegrated into the palace circles and guests from the city, The Day the Sky Opened was awarded a cuff for valor, and Night Shine was announced. Kirin and Second Consort Love-Eyes had crafted her introduction together, and it was lovely, embellished, with the slightest hint of threat. She had been Nothing but was reborn Night Shine, still the friend of the prince, and now hero of the empire.

Shine hated it. She hadn't changed as much as she'd expected, either. The attention was like sand caught in her slippers, rubbing her raw and impossible to shake free. Especially with the witches' net itching against her skin. It made the small hairs all over her body stand up sometimes, and she had to wiggle to make it stop. Wiggle! That was hardly intimidating.

They'd put her in vibrant red and cold pale green for the court, which was an excellent contrast, powdered her cheeks and painted her lips and eyes black like Kirin's, *and* darkened her hair uniformly black. She fit beside the prince in his imperial black and white as never before. Because she was tense, she drank too much of the wine and lost herself a little bit, fumbling through the lords and ladies, witches, priests, warriors, and richer city families, baring her teeth and struggling not to get too hot. She fluctuated hot-hot and cold-cold, in a pattern of waves she couldn't balance. Especially not without annoying the great demon of the palace.

A few courtiers tried to touch her!

Sky stayed far away from her and Kirin both, rigid at the side of the room, his cuff clenching his wrist like a manacle.

Finally two peacock-painted serving girls pulled Shine aside. One fanned her with the sleeve of her robe while the other fed her fluffy bread and promised it would help with the wine. Their round copper cheeks were painted in rainbow wings that seemed to flap gently when they blinked or smiled, and Shine told them they were perfect butterflies—and she'd worn a magical dress once made of butterflies and sunrise silk, so she should know!

The girls helped Shine slip out behind a pillar, where Whisper awaited, hands folded and wearing a demure tailor's robe, sleeveless but embroidered with the skill of her career. "I thought you would sneak away, Nothing," she said, then winced. "I'm sorry. Night Shine."

"Shine is enough," Shine whispered, throwing her arms around Whisper.

"Shine," Whisper repeated. "Shine, Shine, Shine. I like it."

They clasped hands and dashed down the corridor, hurrying to avoid anyone in the first circle who might drag them back to the court. Whisper knew where to get a stack of tiny, rose-shaped dumplings filled with hot cherry preserves and bowls of spiked cream. Shine tugged her through a smoke way, and they emerged with dusty hems into the Lily Garden of the fifth circle. Its central pond glinted under a half-moon, and Shine rushed to say hello to the little dragon-lily spirit.

It hid from her beneath the spreading, heart-shaped lily pad and refused to come out, flicking its tongue angrily when she claimed to be its old friend.

With a frustrated growl, Shine plopped down against the edge of the pond between tall, furling-lily pots. Whisper joined her, more delicately, and they shared their feast. Whisper had heard the official story and a few unsanctioned bits of gossip, but she asked, "What do you think is the most important thing, Shine?"

Shine licked cherry gore from the corner of her mouth and said in a rush, "I think I will fall in love with the Sorceress Who Eats Girls!"

"What!" Whisper hissed, her version of a shriek.

"I know." Shine laughed and looked up at the starry sky, streaked with glowing thin clouds and that happy, delight-ful moon. "She wants me, and I have to return to her, so that together we can teach the Fifth Mountain to live without stolen hearts. I miss her—I miss . . . something. . . ." Shine trailed off, feeling dreamy.

Whisper shook her head in wonder, eyes wide. "Tell me everything about her."

And Shine did tell her quite a bit, but not *everything*. As she spoke, she pinched off pieces of cherry pastry and coaxed the dragon-lily spirit over. It blinked its blister-pink eyes at her suspiciously, but finally took a rolled-up ball of dough.

Shine promised to come back every day with treats for it.

The next day she met with the pair of witches again, to renew the binding net. Shine bared her teeth at them and refused to answer their invasive questions, but at least Immli had returned to his Silver Rain crescent, taking Lord All-in-the-Water with him. This surprised Shine, as the lord commander should have been in the palace for Kirin's investiture.

The ritual would be in ten nights, when the moon was full.

Shine's days, in the meantime, were spent with Kirin, attending meetings, luncheons, tea services, and occasionally a nightcap. At his side, Shine mostly remained silent as Kirin discussed their adventures, only sometimes offering a more vivid description of a part of the Fifth Mountain. It was a performance, to show as many important people as possible that they mattered enough for a private explanation. That Prince Kirin Dark-Smile was home, and more than worthy of the Moon. He was mature, worldly, clever, and beautiful—everything a people could hope for in a future emperor. And, of course, pure.

Kirin thanked her, when they were alone, for being willing to play the game. And he confided to her that his father suspected more had happened during the summer, that Kirin was hiding secrets. They could not slip in the slightest, even around his family. Especially around his family.

But it was her pleasure to behave like a dangerous pet on the prince's leash, she said, distracting the court from the weirder questions of the summer and gaps in the prince's story. She liked the game, liked knowing it *was* a game.

It made her smiles dark, Kirin said, and he liked that.

Between them they developed a signal: if Kirin wore a single red earring, he felt like a man today; two, he was shifting in and out of man uncomfortably; three he felt good in between; four, he was a woman; five, he hated his body. If there were six or more earrings curling up his ear, he was wild. Depending, Shine secretly called him Kirin Bright Smile and Kirin Full of Potential, Neither Kirin, the Prince Who Is Also a Maiden, Kirin Consumed, and Kirin the Wild. He was always Kirin, somehow.

Shine had never felt more a part of him, and free to enjoy it. That was the consequence of choice, she thought, even if her old self hadn't realized choice was missing.

The prince was the only person never to mistakenly call her by her old name.

That is, other than Sky, who did not have the opportunity, because Shine rarely saw him. When she did, he was firmly on duty guarding Kirin's back and made no time to chat.

The great demon, it turned out, was unwilling to teach her its way of giving and taking and giving and taking. *You are annoying enough*, it said.

And the dragon-lily spirit never warmed to her, though she brought it pieces of her breakfast every day. She told it a story that once upon a time a tiny flower spirit had learned to make a family of flowers until it became a great spirit, and then when its volcano died, it became a great demon, eventually being reborn in a tiny garden guarded by a mighty, curious dragon lily. So maybe there was an impressive future ahead of it.

The dragon-lily spirit dived into the pond, then peeked only its eyes up to stare at her with extreme suspicion.

Day and night, Shine thought of the sorceress. If someone flashed past in a vivid emerald necklace or wearing ivory combs, Shine saw her evergreen eye and her bone-white eye. She lay in her abandoned bathroom, wrapped in soft new blankets, and whispered stories of her day as if she related them to the sorceress. Sometimes the great demon was listening, and Shine rolled over, pressed a hand to the wall, and told it what she'd learned about reborn hearts and demons falling in love. She played games with it, childish games she invented, and remembered her sorceress saying, *My demon played too.*

She knew the sorceress needed her, but Shine had to stay just a little bit longer. It would all work out. They would all be fine. Her, the sorceress, Kirin, and Sky.

The sorceress would make it, she'd promised.

She saw the sorceress again at the end of her first week in the palace, in a room Shine had never found when she was at the mountain herself. Blue crystals glowed along the ceiling of the cavern, lighting up rows of flowers growing in boxes. The flowers were strangely shaped, made of feathers or scales, scarlet maple leaves, slithering tongues, and worst of all, tiny blinking eyes. The air smelled sweet and sour, oddly pleasant. The sorceress tended a long box of drooping daisies with petals the color of salmon meat and tiny stamen singing a sad song. With delicate silver scissors, the sorceress trimmed red from the edges of the petals.

"What is it?" Shine asked.

The sorceress did not lose her concentration. "Fellwort, and it makes a tincture to keep me awake."

"You look like you need sleep." Shine disliked the heavy

darkness under the sorceress's eyes, which made them seem huger, more monstrous. The monstrousness didn't bother her: it was the unintentional nature of it. As if the sorceress couldn't help appearing exhausted.

The sorceress hissed suddenly as she trimmed too much from a pink petal. She set the scissors down, and Shine saw a faint trembling in her hands.

"Sorceress," Shine said, ducking under the row of flower boxes. She stood with stinky dirt on her knees but took the sorceress's hands in her own. "Rest."

"I am fine, Night Shine." The sorceress regarded Shine coolly, and her eyes again seemed bright, awake.

Shine tried out a smile, and the sorceress returned it slightly.

She asked after the rest of the garden, and the sorceress walked her along the rows, pointing out natural flowers and magically sourced, adding details about their care and uses. Shine slipped her hand into the sorceress's, and the sorceress stroked her thumb down Shine's but did not speak of it.

The bluish crystal light cast even, shallow shadows, and Shine listened for the heartbeat of the Fifth Mountain. She could not hear it, perhaps because this was a long-distance spell. She stopped and said, "Kirin needs me."

"So do I," the sorceress said.

But she seemed all right, and strong, and Shine said, "I'll be here soon."

"Good," the sorceress said, and Shine disliked even more than the shadows under her eyes how light and uncaring the sorceress's tone was. As if there was no trust, as if the sorceress did not believe Shine would return.

"I promise," Shine said, even as she woke up again in the palace.

Every day Shine was given new clothing to make her beautiful, and her hair re-dyed black, her face powdered as pale as Kirin's. She learned to like the taste of lip paint, which was good because she did not learn how to avoid eating it off or stop smearing it on the rim of her glass. Whisper was allowed to dress her, and it was considered an honor. She never tried to put Shine in anything stiff with hidden architecture, for Whisper understood without asking that Shine wouldn't tolerate bindings or corsets or shoulder wings or starched layers like rose petals.

Her only real frustration was the restricting net. She couldn't even practice siphoning enough power to fill a cup of tea! But Shine knew after the investiture ritual she'd tear through the sigils and join the sorceress. There on the Fifth Mountain she would gain skills and eventually thread power from the wind to fuel her transformations, or heal great injuries, or maybe move the course of a river. She had her entire life to learn. Maybe she would live for hundreds of years!

When Shine imagined her future, it cycled like seasons: winter with the sorceress, summer with Kirin, sometimes changing it up, staying or going for longer, and even traveling to the farther corners of the empire, or making herself into a shark and swimming across the sea. She was a demon reborn; she could do it! She would bless the empire, and Kirin, and make sure he was happy and healthy, and his eventual First Consort, and Second, and children. Shine could see the future of the empire itself spool out if she tried.

She would have the sorceress with her for it.

That felt right. The missing thing inside her could be filled up by the sorceress. Somehow. Like a puzzle box, Shine would simply have to keep reworking herself until they fit.

Once the Selegan River spirit had told her dragons were possibility and potential, and Shine finally understood what that felt like. In her was the potential of all the world.

Two nights before the full moon and the investiture ritual, Shine held the pear in her hand.

It was almost gone.

One good bite or two small ones. She considered waiting but wanted the sorceress to know when to expect her. So Shine carefully bit into the pear, enjoying the flavor as always, and once the taste had vanished down her gullet, she opened her eyes into the library of the Fifth Mountain again. She said immediately, "The pear is nearly finished, so I may not have much time. I'll leave the palace in three days. Expect me in a little less than a month. I can travel more quickly than a human girl now."

The sorceress looked up from her work, tired, but she smiled, and her evergreen eye and her bone-white eye both gleamed. Little spiking feathers darkened her cheeks, and her teeth were sharp. "That pleases me, Night Shine. Will you marry me when you arrive?"

Shine laughed and said, "Probably not yet! But you will have every day to change my mind."

When Shine woke up, she carefully wrapped the final small bite of pear in a cloth of fuchsia silk and kept it with her always. Just in case.

FORTY-THREE

——————

THE MORNING BEFORE KIRIN'S investiture ritual, Shine was awakened from a dream of the mirror lake and the sorceress by a sound at the boarded-over, rusty, unused door of the abandoned bathhouse. She thought at first that the great demon was laughing in a hollow-walls sort of way.

But the noise stopped and then started again, in a distinctly knocking-for-entry pattern.

Shine sat up, rubbed her hands down her face, and walked around piles of broken tiles and the laundry line tied between pillars on which she'd hung her new clothes. She put her hand on the dusty old door and called, "Hello?"

Sky's muffled voice answered, "Night Shine."

For a moment she didn't answer, she was so surprised.

"Shine?" Sky called again, soft and urgent.

"Yes, Sky. I'm here. The door—how did you know?" Did everyone in the palace know she was slipping out of her guest chambers to sneak here to sleep every night?

"Can I come in?"

Shine slid her hand down the old wood. "I can't open it. Is everything all right?"

"Are you?"

Why would he be worried about her now? she wondered, irritated. She wanted to send him away, because he'd pretended for weeks they'd never been friends. But she wanted to know why more. "Go to the Lily Garden. I'll meet you there."

"Now, Shine."

Shine didn't answer but took care of her morning ablutions and dressed in a tunic and trousers and thin slippers good for climbing the smoke ways. She tucked the final bite of the pear into her sleeve, climbed into the ceiling, and quickly headed toward the Lily Garden.

The Day the Sky Opened already waited. He stood stiffly in the pale sunlight, at the edge of the heavy shadow cast by the garden wall. His blue-black hair ruffled in a slight wind, and his hands clasped together behind his back, holding something small.

Nerves fluttered Shine's stomach as she stepped out under the trellis of sunset lilies. Their vivid orange and pink flowers were furled closed for a few more hours. Her slippers crushed slightly on the thin gravel, and when she stepped on weeds, she smelled sweet perfume.

Sky turned at her footsteps. His whole handsome face was furrowed and frowning.

"What?" she asked, slowing her pace. "What is it?"

"How are you?"

"Fine, Sky. Why do you care suddenly?"

He went still, then sighed. "I care about you. That has

never stopped, Shine. Even if you can't believe it after today."

Shine scowled, suddenly very hot. The binding net itched, and she angrily scratched at her forearm. She marched to the pond and stared at the messy array of dragon lilies.

"I wanted to give you this. I found it and thought . . ." He offered the thing he'd been holding, his movements stilted. Where was his warrior grace?

"You're scaring me," she said.

Sky's frown, if anything, deepened.

Shine reached him and took the ivory ball he offered. It was warm from his hands, carved with vines and flowers and tiny elephants. Dark white and yellowing, like the sorceress's eye when she was tired. The nerves in Shine's stomach sharpened. "Sky."

"I found it in the city, and I thought it might remind you of . . . her."

"Sky." Shine looked up, clenching her fingers tightly around the ball. "I am going to the Fifth Mountain after Kirin's ritual tomorrow night. I am going to learn magic from her. I don't need to remember anything."

The bodyguard stared down at her, his expression slowly falling out of hard concern into raw surprise.

"Sky!" She threw the ball and heard it crack against the garden wall, then pushed both hands on his chest, shoving with all her might. "Sky, tell me!"

He did not budge but gripped her wrists. "I thought you knew. I thought he would have . . ."

Shine's heart heaved, and sweat broke across her face and down her chest, her back, everywhere. Like she was melting into tiny streams of lava. She had to grit her teeth to control the binding, the need to drag at the bodyguard's life. "Sky."

"I'm sorry." He started to say her old name, but stopped. "I thought you knew. I would have made him tell you."

"Tell me what?" she whispered.

"The morning we left the army, when we went south, Kirin sent the entire Silver Rain crescent to the Fifth Mountain. They have twelve witches with them, and—and he told them to bargain with the other Living Mountains—the two who took you—to join them. They attack the mountain today. This afternoon. The empress approved of his plan when he told her. Said it showed strong initiative."

Shaking her head, she jerked away from Sky. "No. He wouldn't. He wouldn't!"

Sky simply looked at her, because obviously Kirin would do exactly that.

And keep it from her.

And pretend everything was fine. Pretend he loved her.

Shine ran, tripping on the uneven gravel and star-lily vines.

She burst into the fifth circle corridor, startling two passing servants, who widened their peacock-painted eyes. Disregarding them, she slammed her palms against the wall. "Moon, where is the prince? Tell me where Kirin is."

The demon rolled over, or sighed, and the wall shuddered under her hands. Dust drifted down onto her hair.

with his father in the second circle, the demon murmured.

Shine ran, up through the palace, using the wide corridors and dashing across courtyards instead of sneaking, ignoring upset servants and shocked lords and ladies, until she reached the second circle. She stopped, chest heaving, and jerked open a lattice to crawl into the wall. She tore off her slippers and dropped them. This was the only way into the private residence of the First Consort without fighting her way past Warriors of the Last Means or secretaries or who knows!

Thin smoke pricked her eyes as she climbed into the rafters of the second circle, careful and silent. Her whole body felt tightly wound. A harp string vibrating too high to be heard.

The sounds of the palace tried to soothe her: they were so normal. Soft chatter, softer footfalls, sometimes the clack of armor or a burst of laughter. The trickle of water as she crossed behind the half roof of the Second Consort's fish garden. She smelled bread and sweet breakfast meats. Thin chocolate smells, and then she popped open an old smoke shutter and reached through into the dim rafters of Sun-Bright's room.

Kirin's voice drifted up. "... you'll see."

First Consort Sun-Bright's voice answered after a slight pause. "Everyone will, Kirin. If it comes down to it. Everyone will see."

"That's what it takes to prove I'm better for—everything I've done."

"Perhaps, son."

"They're only rumors," Kirin insisted.

Shine crouched against a narrow ceiling beam, separated from the prince and consort by a thin decorative lattice hung with lights. Maybe Kirin would say something to exonerate himself of Sky's accusation. Oh, she hoped so.

"Rumors are an important thread in the weave of the empire," the First Consort said.

"Do you trust me?" Kirin asked lightly, and Shine almost

snorted. Her heart thumped faster and faster. Kirin always had more than one plan. She'd forgotten—or stopped thinking it could hurt her.

Sun-Bright said, "I know you, and that is both reassuring and decidedly not."

"Father."

"You will succeed—that I trust—though between now and the moment of triumph I will suffer through extreme heart-burn."

Shine bit her lip. Maybe Sky was wrong. Maybe Kirin had not set the army after the sorceress. Surely he would be more concerned now, busier, or checking in with army witches who could communicate through their aether-ways and spirit familiars.

"Drink less tea until the ritual," Kirin teased. The prince sounded amused. He sounded relaxed. Like he'd already won.

A commotion below had Shine spreading her stomach flat against the beam. At the door, someone knocked. Then a voice she didn't know said, "The prince's man is here, and says it's urgent."

"Sky?" Kirin asked.

At the affirmative, Kirin told them to show him in.

First Consort Sun-Bright said, "Trouble? We shouldn't have news from the army witches until later."

Shine clenched her jaw and pressed her forehead to the ceiling beam, hard enough to make her entire skull hurt. It was true.

"I don't know what it could be," Kirin answered.

The door slid open and Sky said, tightly, "My lord consort, my prince."

"Warrior," Sun-Bright acknowledged. They were shadowy blobs below her, cut into pieces by the lattice.

"Is she here?" Sky said.

"Shine?" Kirin sounded sharp. "Why?"

Sky hesitated, then with careful control said, "I told her about the army. I assumed you had done so yourself."

Sun-Bright said, a frown clear in his tone, "She didn't know?"

Ice blossomed inside Shine. No lava, no rageful volcano, just ice crystals growing over her bones like frost kissed to a glass window.

Kirin said, "She would have tried to stop it."

At least he did not try to excuse himself. Betrayal was so cold.

"Kirin, that was a mistake," Sky said, too familiar with the prince.

"Prince," the consort corrected Sky, and then asked his son, "Will this be a problem for us? Will she act foolishly?"

"Where is she?" Kirin asked.

Shine wrapped her hand around a branch of the decorative lattice and tore it up with all her strength. Through the hole she heard cries of alarm, and her name, because Kirin knew. He always knew.

Carefully, she dropped herself through the ceiling and landed in a crouch. "I'm right here," she spat. She shook her hair to dislodge dust or musty muck. "You liar," she said, straightening up to face Kirin.

"Shine," he said, reaching for her.

"Stop. Don't touch me. Tell me what you did." She jutted out her chin, trying not to shiver.

Sky said, "Shine, just listen and calm down."

"Kirin!" she cried, anguished.

He let his hands fall to his sides. He was beautiful and elegant in a lush red-and-pink robe, tied with black and embroidered with thorns in the same. Three red earrings said he was having a good day, happily between prince and maiden. It curdled Shine's stomach. He didn't deserve any good days. Especially not today. "It will be quick," Kirin said. "The sorceress is weak."

"Because I came home with you!" she said wildly. "Because I left her! And I begged her not to take another heart and she agreed to wait for me—so I could be here with you! How could you do this? She was—"

"A killer!" Kirin looked at her with angry pity. "She is a killer, and dangerous, and must be removed from the field."

"You only say that because she knows what you are," Shine hissed.

The prince snapped his mouth closed. His honey eyes narrowed. "I say that because she is a murderer and kidnapped me. She nearly took everything from me—and has already taken you. You would forgive her so easily? You aren't supposed to care this much about her."

"Not supposed to care? I . . ." The look in Kirin's eyes flipped Shine from icy darkness into horrible, scorching sunlight. "What did you do?" she demanded.

He said, coolly, "I commanded you to stop caring for her. By your name."

"No," she breathed out her shock.

Sky said, *"Kirin,"* with outright horror.

But Shine stared through her prince. She remembered feeling diminished. As if the farther she traveled from the Fifth

363

Mountain, the less she became. Until she gave herself a new name. The half-a-heart feeling, the strangeness of longing for the sorceress but not understanding why. The . . . exhilaration she couldn't explain.

Kirin still did not try to defend himself. He probably did not think he required defending. Cool and sure as a god.

Sun-Bright crossed his arms. He was tall, like his son, and lean, with honey-brown eyes, but his skin darker, face more square, his lips less pretty. He said, "Night Shine, if you are a loyal servant of the Moon, sit down and end this fit before I call my warriors."

Shine ignored the First Consort and said softly to the prince, "You were supposed to trust me. Like I trusted you."

Kirin flinched.

"I'll never forgive you," she added, because he deserved it. Her ears filled with the song of rushing blood.

Sky said, "Warn her."

Shine's hands flew to her sleeve, and she dug out the final bite of pear. Backing away, she glared at Kirin. "Don't stop me," and she put the whole thing in her mouth, chewed once, and swallowed it down.

FORTY-FOUR

SHINE OPENED HER EYES at the mirror lake.

It was perfect. Clear blue skies, a ruffling cold wind, and the lake a wide drop of heaven glittering like diamonds. The alders bent as if they said hello to Shine.

The sorceress lay in crushed purple flowers, near the shore, one hand flung out and her fingers trailing in the water. Sun sprites slept in her hair, like gently breathing combs.

"Sorceress?" Shine ran for her, grass slapping her ankles. The sorceress didn't move. Her monstrous-perfect eyes were closed, her lips parted a little bit, revealing a sliver of blackness inside.

"She's dying," said Insistent Tide. The old woman crouched beside the first alder, wrapped in several wool blankets. Her gray hair was loose and flowed around her like a storm cloud.

"No," Shine said. "She can't be. She promised she'd be well until I came back. She could hold it together."

Insistent Tide shrugged. "If you say so."

Shine fell to her knees at the sorceress's shoulder. "Sorceress," she cried. "Wake up!" She touched her cheek, then hit her chest. The dawn sprites squeaked and fled in a flurry of light. Shine leaned over and kissed the sorceress's dry lips. She pressed down, kissed again and again, taking the sorceress's face in both hands. She breathed, sucking air from the sorceress's mouth. She tasted like pine resin, a sharp, wicked flavor. Almost like poison.

"The heart died weeks ago," said Insistent Tide. "Days after you left. She's been holding it alone."

Horror tingled under Shine's skin, hot and cold and hot, and she felt like her ears needed to pop. "Sorceress."

"Night Shine?" the sorceress whispered. Her lashes fluttered. When she opened her eyes, they were only slits: one terrible sickly green like rot, one gray-white and fuzzed like bread mold.

"You have to wake up," Shine said. "They're coming. You have to hold on. The army is coming, and sorcerers, too. Please!"

The sorceress lifted her hand and skimmed her black nails against Shine's cheek. "I can't. I can't even change myself."

Some of her hair had fallen out, settling in curls around her skull, a nest of lava-red and black snakes. Her lips were cracking. She was smaller, older, skinny to the bone.

"Where are your feathers?" Shine begged. "Your shark's teeth and your vicious heart?"

"I love you," the sorceress said. "What you are now."

Shine's tears plopped onto the sorceress's forehead, dissipating like smoke. They weren't quite real. This was a spell. The pear didn't make real tears.

"Strong, surprising," the sorceress added.

"I have more surprises," Shine said fiercely, and grabbed the sorceress by the shoulders.

She shoved life into her, though she'd taken it first from

nowhere. Shine pushed power, this life, her own life, into the sorceress.

The sorceress's eyes flashed open. "Shine!" she cried. Her back bowed and she scrabbled at Shine's arms.

"Get up, secure the mountain, and *wait for me!*" Shine cried. She clenched her jaw and hissed at the effort of pouring life into the sorceress.

She felt the pear stop a split second before she opened her eyes in the First Consort's chamber.

Kirin stared at her, haggard, held back from her by his father's arms. They were sprawled on the floor, as if blown away from her. Warriors poured in, weapons drawn, and Sky grabbed Shine's face.

"You're back," the demon-kissed warrior said. "You were gone, and Kirin was holding you, and he just started . . ." Sky shook his head.

Shine sucked in a huge breath. He'd been touching her, and she'd been siphoning life for the sorceress. The binding net was gone, and she felt so *good*.

Before she could speak, the great demon of the palace hissed loud enough for everyone to hear.

You shall not harm My things!

"I have to go," Shine said, struggling to her feet. She used Sky, who helped her.

First Consort Sun-Bright snapped, "Stop her."

The palace rumbled with the demon's displeasure, and Shine tried to think of something to do to fix everything. Her mind spiraled with thoughts and images and her blood was a loud roar still. She could take power and escape, maybe just enough from the great demon to get ahead of it. And . . . and what? She let go of Sky, stepped away to distance herself for whatever she was about to do. At least seven warriors were inside with them, weapons ready, and the demon thickened the air, making it difficult to breathe.

Its head appeared, with seven bluish moon-eyes and a mouth with seven tongues: it hovered above Kirin.

Shine took a breath. She had to try.

I will annihilate You.

But Kirin said, "No, wait, Great Moon."

All eyes snapped to him.

The prince swallowed. "Let her go."

Nobody moved. Sun-Bright said, "Kirin."

Kirin sat up. He stared only at Shine. His look was intense, his mouth bent crookedly but could not be called a smile.

Shine glared back, feeling the rage of her volcanic heart boiling up, turning her skin translucent, her blood lightning white.

"Let her go, I said." Kirin held her gaze. "She is not my prisoner, and never has been. It is her choice—your choice."

The First Consort did not argue again, and Shine did not wait for another chance.

She barely glanced at Sky, whose frown was so anxious, it had no place on his strong, demon-kissed face.

Shine ran, out into the corridor, shoving past warriors and courtiers. She heard a surprised squeak maybe from Second Consort Love-Eyes, and low in her skull, thrumming like a force more than a voice, the great demon growled and growled.

She was not welcome here. Good—she needed to leave. But there was no fast way.

The army was there, at the Fifth Mountain, now. And those cruel sorcerers! Even if Shine had fed the sorceress enough power to get up, to close any doors, there was no way that without a heart the sorceress could hold the army off for the days or weeks it would take Shine to arrive. She didn't know how to sprout wings! Would The Scale help her?

She couldn't ask them: she didn't know how.

Shine pushed out onto a balcony and turned around, climbing the outside of the second circle wall. The corner was blocks of heavy dark stone, and there she found the grips she needed. She dragged up onto the next level: the first circle of the palace was all red-washed, but there were spirit statues and rain catchers she could use.

This was the first time she had climbed the outside of the palace instead of its guts and bones.

Sunlight glinted off the jeweled eyes of the spirit shrines. Their open mouths gaped, dry without rain. The air smelled cool and sunny, with none of the city scents, none of the palace. Her own breath was as loud as the wind.

Night Shine strained, pulling hard up and up, all the way to the peak of the highest slant roof of the first circle. Five spirit statues crowned it: eagle, bear, dolphin, lion, bat-winged demon. She knew their names, but she ignored them. Wind hit her, pulling at her hair and tunic, but she clung tight. Her fingers ached, scraped raw, and her toes, too. But she was strong.

She grabbed the horn of the demon statue and swung behind it, standing in its minimal shelter. It was shorter than her, but broader. Folded wings pointed up and cast shadows back upon her. This one faced northwest. That was the way to the Fifth Mountain.

If Shine threw herself off the roof, if she died, she would be fully a demon again.

It was that simple.

She swallowed terror. There was no other way. A demon needed its house, and without her body, she could snap home to the mountain. Inhabit it again, give the sorceress all her might, and together they could drive off the army. Together they could drive off anything.

She'd died before. She'd been many things. It was all right to change again. That's all death was. She hoped.

Shine stared out over the layers of the palace and the city beyond. It was beautiful. A mountain, too, but not her mountain. Red-and-white walls and roofs, curving roads, movement of people and wagons like tiny fish in a huge garden pond. Beyond it, the Way of King-Trees drove north and to the east went the Sunrise Crown Road. Dark-green rain forest pressed down in narrow scoops, set between rolling golden fields and the scarlet fields of redpop. Dots of villages. Smoke drifting up. And the horizon was all rain forest.

Threads of blue light pulled down from the northwest, running toward the city and around it on the west, as the tiny fingers of the once-wide Selegan River reached for the ocean, miles of flat delta, and terraced fields to the south. So close she could imagine the bright line of that horizon was the broad gleam of deep water.

Did demons love beauty?

Did demons love?

Night Shine took a deep breath.

This was the only way. She climbed onto the demon statue's

back, gripping its wings. Her toes scraped on its tail. Her heart beat hard, but this was the fastest way, the surest.

She clenched her teeth and closed her eyes. Sunlight turned the black of her lids red, and she heard voices in the wind.

Shine stopped. She didn't want to die. She didn't want to be a demon again, alone, without a house. Without life.

But how could she love the sorceress and be unwilling to make this sacrifice?

Pressing her forehead to the rough marble, she held tight to the demon statue's horns and thought: The sorceress had gone through so much to give her demon consort life. If she died, it had all been for nothing.

She laughed at the thought. For nothing.

She wasn't nothing anymore.

When Night Shine opened her sticky eyes, the Selegan River caught her as it flashed brilliant silver in the sunlight.

"Selegan," she said, and touched the tears smearing her cheeks.

FORTY-FIVE

I T TOOK AN HOUR to reach the river.

Too long.

Shine slid and climbed down through the innards of the palace as quickly as possible, but distance was distance, and the great demon refused to go still and make it easier. She fell twice, bruising her knees and her shoulder. She sliced open her palm on a loose nail and bit back a mean sneer at the territorial demon.

Once outside, she ran, but she didn't know the fastest way through the city to the docks. She'd always taken meandering paths, dashing across walls and roofs. Shine tried to keep her course west, but the city was not laid out with straight lines and she kept curving north and north, having to switch back or find the sharpest left. The smell of fish and dank wood grew, and she followed it through a neighborhood of leaning taverns and past a market of fresh fish and mollusks and perishable goods from up and down river. She heard the river birds crying and the rough chant of sailors and burst out of an alley onto a narrow dock, nearly spilling off into the water.

Shine pressed her back to the wall. Her toes ached from the gravel roads and were caked with mud. She was a mess, a ragged doll. Below her several barges bobbed where they were tied to private piers, and south where the river deepened again were the ocean ships with their red sails tied down like cocoons. Shine peered over the edge of the dock. The tide was low, the water brackish here, between freshwater river and salty marsh. She didn't know if the Selegan was strong enough to hear her.

But she had to try.

Scooping off the edge, she dug her toes into the rough, wet wooden pillar supporting the dock. She climbed slowly down, until she could see the muddy bottom of the river, several feet below the brownish water.

She pushed off, slamming into the river.

Shine turned and swam north, kicking hard. In the center of the river, she treaded water and tasted it. Not too salty. Muddy, churned. Unpleasant. Not like the clear, silver upriver water she'd flown through last month with the dragon.

"Selegan," she said. She ducked underwater and called its name again, a muffled, bubbly sound. *Selegan.*

Then she dove forward, swimming as hard as she could. North, toward brighter water.

She rose for breath, careful to note where boats floated, careful to avoid them. But she didn't care if she was seen and ignored a few startled cries. Let them think she was a spirit or a demon.

Her fingers numbed with the cold, but she clawed at the water. She could hear her heart loud in her ears, pulsing out and out from her body as if it could ring through the river.

Selegan, she cried.

When she emerged to breathe, she yelled with her voice, "Selegan River, please! I need you."

She treaded water in a thread of silvery current, where dark-gilled fish stared at her from just beneath the surface and there were no barges or fishing boats. Shine took a few deep breaths. Then she pulled on the life of the river.

It sucked into her in a gasp of power, and Shine trembled, losing her rhythm for a moment. She sank down and hung there, suspended between life and dark depth. She opened her eyes, though they stung, and gently kicked, spreading her arms to hold herself in the deep. *Selegan, I need you*, she called. *I can save your friend. I can save her. Let me save her!*

She closed her eyes, feeling like the whole river was her tears.

If the dragon did not answer, she could still die here, mouth full of the river. Die and let her demon heart fly up the water road directly to the Fifth Mountain.

Shine's body ached, and her chest burned. She had to breathe. She parted her lips and let the water slip inside. She thrashed and coughed, gulping, and human instinct shoved her up to the surface.

Scales touched her toes, pushing up, and Shine burst out of the river into the air.

She breathed, she choked, and tears poured down her cheeks along with snot and thin bile from her heaving stomach.

She collapsed onto coiling hard dragon flesh.

"Night Shine!" the Selegan River spirit hissed, shocked.

Shine wrapped her arms around its neck, white bone ridges shoving into her shoulder and chest. She hurt everywhere, but she held on. Her fingers dug into the feather beard. "Take me . . . Selegan, take me home. I will save her. As fast—as fast as you can."

"Hold on, Night Shine," the dragon said, and with a shudder of power it unfurled its wings and shot into the sky.

———

FORTY-SIX

THE DRAGON FLEW HARD and fast as wind. Shine clung to it with body and will, gritting her teeth and imagining herself smoke and fire. They tore through the sky, leaving tatters of themselves behind, little smoke butterflies and falling leaves and feathers of flame.

Her heart pulsed hard and she focused on it because she couldn't see through the shredding wind or hear the dragon. There was only blood and air and desperation.

Shine did not let herself think the sorceress had already died, had failed, that she hadn't stood up with Shine's gift of power to secure the mountain against the army.

On and on they flew, into colder, wetter air, into lacerating clouds.

Tears turned to ice on her lashes, then ripped away, rimming her eyes with red.

The dragon slowed and Shine clenched around it, panicked that it was too soon; they couldn't be there yet.

She pushed up and looked: ahead was the dark outline of the Fifth Mountain miles and miles away, below the rain-forest canopy so vivid green it was black in the late sunlight, shimmering in wind, an ocean of emerald, jade, obsidian leaves. The Selegan slipped like a vein of opal through it all.

"I smell them," the dragon called to her, its voice rumbling through its scales.

They sank lower, pushing north on a gust of wind.

The rain forest broke open to expose the lava field and the vast meadow. Covered in soldiers.

Clusters of men and women lined up in lacquered red and brown armor, painted with gleaming teeth, their helmets crested with feathers and horns. Warhorses and wardogs stomped, snorted, and howled, lifting their long faces and baring teeth at the dragon as it drifted high overhead. Shine stared down at hundreds of soldiers. Too many—so many! They were putting together catapults and archer platforms near the front, where the mountain started. Forward scouts already climbed, hunting for doorways or passes.

Shine's gaze was drawn to one sorcerer just before he thrust a staff into the ground and released a wailing ball of fire directly at them.

She thumped the dragon's neck and it curved away and higher, pumping its wings to take her to the peaks, to the mirror lake.

"I hear her calling me," the dragon said, tilting sharply so Shine yelped and fisted her hands in its feathers.

It wiggled like a snake, up and down, keeping close to the peaks, then it dove down toward a jut of mountain. The balcony outside the sorceress's rooms.

Shine tumbled off as the dragon transformed beneath her, so they both landed on their human feet.

"Sorceress!" Shine cried.

The cave mouth leading inside shifted wider and Shine saw lights glowing inside, a diagram cut into the stone floor and the sorceress crouched, cutting with her wand. Flares of black feathers arced off her back almost like wings, and her hair was a black-brown-red mass of hair and feathers and tangling claws. Her legs were bent wrong, too many joints and talons dug from her toes into the ground. She had so many teeth, and when her head snapped toward them, the bone-white eye burned like a star.

She was perfect.

Shine stopped at the edge of the diagram. "Sorceress, what can we do?"

"I am holding it," she answered roughly, tongue and lips working hard around the sharp teeth, blurring the words. "Not enough power."

"Is my heart enough?" Shine asked. She knelt and stared intently at the sorceress. She wanted to dig her hands into the other woman.

The sorceress paused. A ridge of feathers along her cheeks flared. "Together. Maybe."

"I am the Fifth Mountain. I can wake it up. We can."

"Maybe," the sorceress said again.

"Will you marry me?" Night Shine asked. "Will that . . . ? Will you?"

The sorceress darted in one powerful leap across the diagram and landed before Shine, knocking her over even as she threw her arms around her. "Let me in," she whispered.

Shine kissed her.

Teeth sliced her lips and she tasted blood. Salty, hot, sweet blood, and behind it a burst of power. Shine wrapped her arms around the sorceress's head and her legs around her waist. "Take me to the heart of the mountain," she said against the sorceress's mouth.

They fell into the stone, sliding through cold rock, liquid rock, glittering granite, and embracing fingers of crystal.

Shine held tight, and when they hit the floor of the massive cavern chamber with all its stairs and the broken crystal, she couldn't breathe for the sudden whoosh of pain.

The sorceress rolled off her, and Shine sat up.

Around them, the mountain was layers of rock and ash and eager, pulsing crystal. Shine rolled onto her stomach and spread her arms against the stone floor as if she could hug the whole mountain.

She whispered, "I'm home."

"Roll over," the sorceress said, kneeling beside her.

Shine did, onto her back. She looked up at the sorceress's mismatched eyes, one alive with emeralds, leaf green, the other a moon, a star, night shine. Her bloody lips, her shark's teeth, her wide copper cheeks flourishing with feathers. "You're beautiful," Shine said.

"Do you trust me?" the sorceress asked, sliding one leg across Shine's hip to kneel over her.

Shine licked her lips and said, "Night Shine Over the Mountain."

Her full, true name. New and gleaming. Unused. A secret shared.

The sorceress gasped and it turned into a laugh. A bright

379

laugh, a dangerous smile. Perfect. She put the tip of her wand to Shine's chest. It was cold and sharp. "Night Shine Over the Mountain, your heart is ours, and mine ours. What is my name?"

Shine said, immediately, "Shadows Between Hearts."

"Shadows," the sorceress whispered, tasting it for the first time. It was new; it had always been there. Waiting.

"Shine," Shine whispered back.

Then the sorceress stabbed her crystal wand into Shine, who screamed. It pierced her chest and heart, driving down through bone, flesh, skin, tunic, and into the stone below.

Night Shine flared to life, her blood thick, viscous magma rolling inside her, just as it rolled in the chamber-heart of the Fifth Mountain.

The chamber was old and buried deep, had been left alone, sleeping, for almost two hundred years. Since it had killed her, consumed her, turned her into the demon of the Fifth Mountain.

Made her fire.

Shine curled her fingers and tugged, screaming as she dug her hands into the molten rock, as she drew the magma up and up the throat of the mountain, screaming as she blew steam out of overgrown vents, screaming, screaming, screaming as the Fifth Mountain rumbled from tip through foundation and out, out, out into the jagged foothills.

The mountain bucked, and blood pooled beneath Shine. The Selegan River rushed away, churning with heat, and splashed up at its shores, a sparkling wet warning to the army. Get out. *GET OUT.*

Smoke shot up, steam and ash, as the mountain burped its poison, darkening the sky.

Shine felt every creased valley and peak, every streak of crystal and finger of magma reaching up, up, up to find a mouth. She felt the mirror lake boil and pebbles tripping down the slope into the alder grove. She felt the panic of the army far below, their pounding steps, the wheels and hooves as they fled.

She screamed at the sorcerers, showing them what kind of stars were inside her guts now.

As she dragged the mountain to fiery passion, she felt the cool shadow of her wife using the anchored power to push harder at the invading sorcerers. A barrier of light and ice-knives thrust up and out, laughing as it chased them.

Together the mountain and her wife were fire and shadows, just like the stars and the black night sky.

FORTY-SEVEN

YOUR HOUSE IS THE mountain now
    its bones are your bones. your heart is its heart. all that
    power and life part of you
draw on it
the heat of the earth the fire heart the molten blood
draw on it
make your little soft body hard again, healed and whole again.
the mountain's house is your body, too
and both of you
mine

FORTY-EIGHT

THE SORCERESS WAS WHISPERING to her.

Shine swallowed a weird, tangy flavor and cracked open her eyes to radiant sunset streaks of red-orange cutting between thick black clouds still puffing up, up, up from the volcano.

She sprawled surrounded by grass and sparkling pebbles in the bowl of the mountain, easily sensing her exact place. The mirror lake was just past her feet, and bright dawn sprites peeked up nervously from the shore. The Selegan River spirit coiled far at the foot of the mountain, silver-happy and relieved. The mountain groaned and burped smoke, but the anger she'd awakened rested again. Like a snoring giant, they'd reminded the army of their potential.

The sorceress stretched beside her, one arm around her waist, the other pillowing her head as she whispered into Shine's ear. Her words danced along Shine's jaw, tickled her cheek and lips, and she smiled a little bit.

the mountain's house is your body, too

She was whole. Strong. Crystal bones and slow-flowing

magma in her arteries. Muscles of long, sinewy quartz, skin of hot ash and fertile earth growing tiny grasslike hairs. The mountain was pink flesh, sand-pale skin, freckled, and laughing.

No, wait, Shine was flesh and bone and skin, smiles and teeth and feathers. The mountain was stone and crystal freckles. No—

It didn't matter. Both were both. She felt so good.

And extremely exhausted.

"Shine," said the sorceress, and Shine tilted her head to meet the sorceress's eyes. Evergreen and bone white, perfectly bisected by red-slit dragon pupils. "Shine," she said again. She skimmed her hand up Shine's stomach and breast and neck, to cup her jaw. She scraped her sharp lacquered nails at the soft skin. "I love you."

"Shadows, I'm too young to be married," Shine whispered.

The sorceress bared her teeth and rolled away, up to her feet with easy grace, and wandered toward the copse of aspen trees. But she glanced over her shoulder and smiled.

Shine laughed happily and got up to chase her.

SHINE AND SHADOWS

A T THE FOOT OF the Fifth Mountain, where the spring that birthed the great Selegan grew wide enough to be called a river, a demon-kissed young man knelt to dip his hands into the clear blue water.

He was a warrior and had traveled over a month to reach this place, from the distant capital city in the south, up through the King-Tree forest and rising rain forest, alone and serious-minded, but for the occasional little forest spirits who trailed along in his footsteps. When he arrived at this rolling, emerald lava field, he'd stopped and remembered his old friend and the wondrous smile that had filled her face with such joy and awe the first time she'd set foot here.

A breeze ruffled pink and purple balsam on the opposite side of the river; here the bank was black sand, and the warrior sighed softly. He'd almost died here once.

"Hello, Selegan River," he said, widening his fingers to allow the water to play around his fingers. "Do you remember me? Last year I arrived with desperation and vengeance, but this summer I come with respect in my heart."

The surface of the river flickered silver-white under the sun, and a tiny flip like a fish's tail splashed water up at the warrior.

He smiled and wiped at the water.

Then the Selegan River spirit leapt up, snapping out its wings. It grinned as water streamed through its curved teeth and lashed its tails in greeting. The demon-kissed warrior held out his hand again, and the dragon licked it, wiggling happily, and fell again into the water with a massive splash.

The young man laughed, though he was soaked and dripping.

Behind him, he heard a low rumbling, like distant rockfall. He stood, turning, in time to see a hill of grass-covered lava tremble, heave, and then open like a mossy stone mouth.

A young woman climbed out, and behind her, the earth knit itself back together.

She stared at him blankly for a moment, seeming like nothing more than a goblin or a strange meadow spirit in scraps of a tattered gray silk dress that might've been woven of spiderwebs or clouds. Her hair was longer, but still chopped in uneven layers, the ends lifting out as if they'd been charged by lightning. Her skin was suntanned and her cheeks too pink, with freckles and a small pink mouth. Her eyes were round and dark now as obsidian caverns.

She wasn't wearing any shoes.

The demon-kissed warrior smiled. "Shine."

In answer, she smiled back: wide and wild. "Hello, Sky!"

Shine danced eagerly toward him, her bare toes pressing down the thick grass that popped upright immediately.

He held out a hand for her, but she ignored it, jumping up into his arms.

Sky staggered. She was as heavy as if her bones were made of quartz. He grunted and reframed his stance to stay upright, holding her tightly because now he knew she wouldn't break.

"It is good to see you," she said in his ear.

But Sky stared past her: bright, white summer air darkened into shades of gray and black as if a raven blotted out the sun. The shadows coalesced slowly, elegantly, drawing out of light itself, until a beautiful lady stood with them in a complicated black-and-pink gown, edged in mint green and embroidered with scarlet peonies. She smiled too, showing sharp teeth; one of her eyes was summer green, as green as this fertile lava field, while the other was as white as ivory.

Shine let go of him, hopping down, and she said, "How are you?"

Sky nodded to the sorceress and said to Shine softly, "He asked me."

The young woman gasped and held her breath. Sky could see tiny shards of light in her big black eyes; they turned slowly, like stars. "First?" she whispered.

"Yes."

"And what did you say?"

"That I will answer when I return to him."

Shine looked over her shoulder at the sorceress, who lifted one of her elegant eyebrows and drifted gracefully toward the Selegan River. Then Shine touched Sky's chest. "What can I do for you? Invite you here instead? You are welcome here, with

Shadows and I, if you would rather. Here you can be anything."

"If I say yes to him, I can't return here. I could never visit you." Sky took her hand off his chest and held it. "And since his investiture ritual, he has been confined to the palace forever."

"That is the destiny he wanted," she said sharply. But her eyelashes fluttered, and again she glanced at the sorceress. "I have not forgiven him."

The warm breeze blew, bending the flowers and bright-green grass. It smelled sweet, and a little bit charred, like a fire burned just past the next rise. At the river, the sorceress knelt, her skirts spreading in perfect arcs against the gleaming black sand.

Shine licked her lips. She put her hand over her own heart.

Sky said, "Would you make a bargain with me, Night Shine of the Fifth Mountain?"

She wrinkled her nose. "Maybe."

"Try to forgive him. For me, and yourself. And the whole empire."

"What would you trade for my efforts?"

"What do you want?"

Suddenly, the sorceress was behind him. He stood trapped between Shadows and Shine, growing cold as ice even under the afternoon sun, and the sorceress said softly, "We like hearts."

But Shine laughed, as if it had been a brilliant joke. She laughed and shook her head, gleefully saying, "Sky, we are so full of our own hearts; she is teasing you."

The warrior shivered, stepping out from between them.

Shine said abruptly, "Say yes to him. Become his First Consort. That's what I want."

"Good," he said, relieved. "And you'll try, and because every-thing you try you eventually manage to do, someday you will forgive him and come to us."

Sneering a little at the complimentary trap, Shine crossed her arms. Little sparks of shadows puffed away from her body, as if she shook off magic when she shook off her mood. They curled like wisps of fog. She nodded. "It might take until you have children and they're grown tall as him."

Sky said, "All right," because he thought, as he looked at her, that it was already done. She'd done it the moment he asked. Sky couldn't help the slow smile that spread over his mouth.

She saw it and narrowed her eyes. "You'll stay for a few days on my mountain and tell me everything."

"Then the Selegan will take you home," said the sorceress. "As fast or as slowly as you like."

Sky nodded, looking forward to the mirror lake and the strange mountain, to being entertained by Night Shine and the Sorceress of Shadows. He wanted to hear what they'd become together, what they'd discovered. He wanted to fall asleep with her head on his shoulder.

But Shine stepped close to him. She lifted her chin to stare up at his eyes. "And when you return to Kirin Dark-Smile, you will give him this message from me."

"Yes," Sky said, waiting.

Shine put her hands on his face and leaned up on her bare toes; she kissed him.

Surprised, Sky caught her at the waist and kissed her back, gently.

"You will say," she whispered, barely pulling away, "that it is a kiss from the great demon of the Fifth Mountain and a promise to the entire empire. Kiss him, from me, in front of whomever you like, or nobody at all. Your choice. That is my message."

He put his forehead against hers, smiling at the choice, and then he kissed her again, soft and warm, because it would be better to give Kirin two kisses than one.

ACKNOWLEDGMENTS

Though I've been thinking about Shine and her story since 2012, I didn't decide it was The Time to write it until late September 2018. At a mere two years, from proposal to first draft to copyedits to hardcover, *Night Shine*'s journey has been the shortest and smoothest (so far) of any of my books. Maybe because I drafted it partly in a desperate fugue state, but probably because of the amazing team supporting me and the book, both in my personal life and professional life.

I'd like to thank everyone at McElderry Books for the gorgeous design, detailed copy work, proofing, and art and all the marketing that put this book into readers' hands. Especially thanks to the editors, Karen Wojtyla, Nicole Fiorica, and Ruta Rimas. You all not only let me write the weird things I want, but encourage me, then press me to make it better.

Thank you, Laura Rennert, my agent. It's officially been over a decade since we began working together, with countless short stories, nine published novels—and more to come. Here's to a couple more decades together.

As always, my family is my glorious, gallows-humor salvation, even when I don't tell them what I'm working on and therefore when the cover goes live I get a series of surprised texts because nobody knew I had another book coming out so soon. My bad. I promise this one is a lot shorter than the last one, and nobody's parents die.

I want to thank my readers: the ones who've stuck with me and the ones just discovering me. First of all, I have an amazing backlist—check it out—and second of all, when something I write shows you the world, that's how I know I belong, too. Thank you for reading, for telling me you're reading, and especially for telling me when it matters to you.

Thank you, Natalie, for letting me be your villain love interest(s).